Tim Glencross

Tim Glencross studied modern languages at
Cambridge University. He worked as a Shadow
Minister's researcher and speechwriter before
qualifying as a lawyer. He lives in London.

Praise for *Barbarians*

'An engaging and impressive debut . . . Glencross
feels like a writer to watch' Andrew Holgate,
Sunday Times

'This is a clever, amusing and well written debut
novel by someone who has great fun at the expense
of the so-called elite classes' *Daily Mail*

'A dazzling debut' *The Times*

'Hurrah for the novel as entertainment' *Guardian*

'Entertaining, with a rich array of snobs and
halfwits' *Independent*

'Glencross is a ripping writer, perfectly weaving
his discrete storylines one into the other, creating
believable ambitions and outcomes, and pacing
events with aplomb. We'll definitely be looking
out for his next effort' *Herald*

Barbarians

Tim Glencross

JOHN MURRAY

First published in Great Britain in 2014 by John Murray (Publishers)
An Hachette UK Company

First published in paperback in 2015

1

A CIP catalogue record for this title is available from the
British Library

Paperback ISBN 978-1-444-78851-8
Ebook ISBN 978-1-444-78853-2

Typeset in Sabon MT by Hewer Text UK Ltd, Edinburgh
Printed and bound by Clays Ltd, St Ives plc

John Murray policy is to use papers that are natural, renewable and
recyclable products and made from wood grown in sustainable forests.
The logging and manufacturing processes are expected to conform
to the environmental regulations of the country of origin.

John Murray (Publishers)
338 Euston Road
London NW1 3BH

www.johnmurray.co.uk

To R.L.G.

Part I

Part I

I

Art, ruined

'Ah – it's the beautiful young things.'

Buzzy sways, partly from the G and T she has just gulped down, and for a moment sublime even in its awkwardness presses against Marcel as the two of them (not a couple, alas) sidestep Sherard Howe, their host. Puffing on a cigar, the latter resembles an ageing Tweedledum, with his hoisted trousers, spindly legs and cannonball middle. But his real tragedy, Buzzy cannot help thinking, is his jowls. Without the avalanche of flesh beneath the line of his lower lip, he would be – and probably once was – a handsome man, given his surprisingly delicate mouth and quick grey eyes of a hunter. Reflexively, Buzzy brushes her own jawline: in mild panic she imagines she can feel the beginnings of a soft mound beneath her chin. She must drink less; either that or join a gym, as everyone else suddenly seems to be doing. Though if the chin situation ever becomes as out of control as Sherard's, there is always suicide.

As if they are not expecting to discover a house full of strangers, Buzzy and Marcel stop in the hallway and look uncertainly back at Sherard. With a smile that might be pitying or might be amused, he squeezes past them, almost burning a trail across Buzzy's forehead with his cigar in the process. From ahead comes his commanding boom, 'Keep straight, follow me.' They pass roomfuls of guests keeping up a relentless chatter and wafting flutes of champagne. Howe custom is to serve Dom Ruinart for the first hour, Afua once explained; after that everyone (or almost everyone) has to make do with the 'R' de.

3

Buzzy wonders if they are being discreetly led as far from the epicentre of the party as possible, a suspicion that is confirmed when they end up in the kitchen.

'I'm sure I saw Henry and Afua in here – they were helping Daphne.' Sherard's basso causes the army of caterers to look up in unison from preparing the trays of drinks and hors d'oeuvres. Buzzy smiles at a harried waitress, a recent graduate of around her age, who squeezes past to replenish her ranks of stuffed squid. Sherard takes a lordly puff on his cigar, oblivious to the fact that he is in everyone's way, before abruptly swivelling and returning to the throng.

It's not clear if he intended Buzzy and Marcel to follow, but follow they do. Sherard looks mildly annoyed, having squeezed the arm of the culture secretary and exchanged kisses with Juliet Stevenson ('My dear, I demand another Chekhov'), introduced Tariq Ali to Mehdi Hasan and instructed a drinks waiter to avoid the ageing Young British Artist drunkenly denouncing Sir Nicholas Serota, to find the two of them still by his side. Buzzy is conscious of him taking them in, properly now. Not for the first time, she wishes she possessed Marcel's ease, his foreigner's ability simply to stand there, a hint of a smile at his mouth. Perhaps sensing this, Sherard's darting gaze passes over Marcel and settles on her. She feels under suspicion for her suburban upbringing, which smacks of Toryness, however submerged, and for her uncertain position in relation to Sherard's son (Afua, two years his senior, is Henry's sort of sister; Marcel is Afua's boyfriend. Buzzy is Henry's vague non-girlfriend girlfriend).

'Now don't tell me your name . . .'

She tells him it's Elizabeth. When he looks confused, she says he might know her as Buzzy, the silly childhood name she is trying and mostly failing to shed.

'Buzzy, yes. Henry tells me you've been in South America.'

'Yes – Argentina. I got back about a week ago.'

'Did you, ah.' Sherard sucks on his cigar twice in quick succession, his wandering eye obscured under cover of a thick cloud of smoke – or so he seems to think.

Summoning her courage, Buzzy says, 'Now I'm on the dreaded job-hunt. But with arts and the media, which is what I'm *really* interested in, openings are so difficult to come by . . .'

Sherard frowns, and she waits heart-in-mouth for the response (*Time Out* is looking for a film reviewer? *Dazed & Confused* a features writer? Martin Amis an amanuensis?). 'I was in Rio a couple of months ago.'

Confused, she replies, 'Oh, as in Brazil?'

'Well not as in the Rio Grande, my dear.' Buzzy gives a startled smile: she is unused to being patronised. 'I was there for the *MoMA in Rio* show. I collect a little, as you can see.' He gestures towards the walls, which are covered, aside from one very small portrait – an oily nude that looks as if it might be a Lucian Freud – with abstract-ish pieces from the nineties: one of Gary Hume's life-size Door Paintings; a Tracey Emin monoprint entitled *Fucking Margate*; a framed splash of yellow by Sandra Blow. 'Discovered a wonderful young photographer – Romero Ferreira?' This seems directed at Marcel in particular, as though it were just the sort of thing a Belgian might know.

Marcel times his response artfully, leaving enough of a pause to imply that he is acquainted with several emerging Rio artists, but alas Romero Ferreira is not one of them.

'Well he's about to be very hot in New York. Actually he's here this evening, you must meet him.'

'That might be interesting,' Buzzy says airily, in the manner, she hopes, of one anticipating many claims on her time besides hot Brazilians. The other two look at her as though her continued presence were something unexpected, and she feels blood rushing to her cheeks.

Sherard asks Marcel how he finds working for Devereux, the head of the department he has just joined at Sullivan and Ball. 'I was at school with him, you know. Rather a bully back then.' Buzzy listens while Marcel talks enthusiastically about his boss, in marked contrast with his demeanour in the pub earlier, where he sipped the gin and tonic bought with her dwindling funds, nodding politely but not really listening to her prattle about

Genoese immigrants and the birth of the tango. Before disappearing, Sherard introduces Marcel to Sir Ronnie Goldstein, a Labour Party donor who does something with a hedge fund (owns it perhaps?) and who wants to discuss the US government rescue of Fannie Mae and Freddie Mac. Two years ago, before she went away and he started his job at the law firm, Marcel might have confided to Buzzy what he thought of this topic via the merest twitch of an eyebrow, the bushy blackness of which she now finds herself admiring.

On the other side of the room she spies Afua, talking to a youngish man in faded jeans and a T-shirt that says THE GOOD GUYS DON'T SHINE AT MIDNIGHT; early thirties perhaps, nicely tanned but goggle-eyed. Afua smiles and beckons her over. It is a compassionate act – she has evidently seen Buzzy's discomfort and is offering her an escape route – that Buzzy resents since, unknown to Afua, they are engaged in permanent social competition. Buzzy is not winning.

'Can I get anyone a glass of champagne?' she asks.

Sir Ronnie, to whom Buzzy seems to be invisible, wafts a half-filled flute towards Marcel, and says, 'Of course the *real* story is the US Treasury buying mortgage-backed securities . . .'

Buzzy drifts off in search of champagne, not in the direction of Afua. She can't quite bear how amazing she looks in that black dress with the red shawl draped around her shoulders, like Gauguin's *Sorcerer of Hiva Oa*. She narrowly avoids a head-butting from a blonde radio presenter who throws her head back in mirth as someone says 'he thought it was *Peter* he was talking to!' What should she respond, if someone asks her what it is that she does? Is it acceptable to describe herself as a writer when she has only written four poems? It feels like an unconvincing line, particularly when there in the corner is Ian McEwan, looking at his feet while Lord Bragg gesticulates grandly next to him (of course neither of *them* has been left without champagne). She'll have to play the outsider, the spirit of Youth.

At last! A bearer of champagne ahead, with a single remaining glass on her tray. The sight of the gleaming bubbles causes the back of her throat to itch. Her stride becomes more determined, her *excuse me*s faintly impatient instead of apologetic. Three more steps and she is there ... But then as if divining Buzzy's presence, a generous form resting slightly apart from a group of drinkers turns round and blocks her path to the waitress, who slips away.

'Hello Henry, this is quite a gathering.'

'Buzzy, it's l-lovely to see you. Welcome back.' He kisses her, wetly, on each cheek.

Surprisingly touched, she replies, 'Thanks. It's nice, you know, to see you too.'

'How was Buenos Aires?'

'Oh fine, fine. My school was in a neighbourhood called Hurlingham, so they were already fairly civilised.'

He nods gravely, as if genuinely reassured by this news. She realises this is all she wants to say of her last two years, even before he points and says, 'Look, there's Afua. Doesn't she look fabulous in that dress?'

'Too fabulous.'

'We should rescue her. She's been stuck with that chap for ages – some Brazilian artist my father knows. I think he's interested in her.'

'Aren't we all?' Buzzy says, mischievously, before hurrying on: 'But first you must tell me, how are *you*, Henry Bean? What have you been up to?'

'Me?' he asks, colouring slightly. 'Nothing really. I started the Bar Vocational Course – law school, you know – but it wasn't . . . So I'm just sort of thinking at the moment. My father wants me to work for a friend of his in the government, a junior minister, except I don't know if politics is really, you know . . .' Henry takes a large gulp of his champagne, which Buzzy notes out of envy and because he is not normally an enthusiastic drinker. Poor flapping Henry, so used to ceding the limelight to his beautiful half-black semi-sister.

As though Buzzy's attention is too much for him, he says, 'Really we should rescue Afua from the Latin fellow. Is Marcel here?'

'We arrived together, so he must be here somewhere. I'll join you – I'm dying to catch up with Afua – but first I'd quite like to find a drink.'

'Oh, there's someone with champagne now.' Henry looks past her shoulder and Buzzy twists her body round with undignified urgency. She's dismayed when she sees the waiter is doing top-ups with a bottle of 'R' de, so she's missed the Dom already.

'I'll need a glass first. Unless, do you think he'd object if I relieved him of the bottle?'

Henry looks a little startled by the suggestion, but he seldom gets her jokes. Buzzy watches him diffidently make his way across the room. Before he can reach Afua and the Brazilian artist, however, Marcel is there, his arm discreetly placed around Afua's waist.

Not quite a Romeo, Buzzy thinks of the now retreating artist, to distract herself from a familiar spasm of jealousy. She turns away, almost spilling Asian crab cakes over the wife of a *Times Literary Supplement* editor, a barrel-shaped woman who falls into a desperate lament about the stupidity of her children, which she wouldn't mind but it's so *expensive*, what with the cost of good private tutors. At first, Buzzy wonders if the woman is under the mistaken impression that they know each other, before deciding she is simply tired and drunk and beyond caring who is listening.

'. . . and then to cap it all off,' she is saying, 'we lost Will for the whole summer because some Russian oligarch wanted an Oxford graduate to discuss world politics with. Can you imagine? He whisked him off to Ibiza in a private plane!'

'Come with me.' A Gallic voice, so soft in her ear that at first Buzzy is not sure she has not imagined it. With a quick apologetic shrug she abandons the editor's wife, who looks oddly crushed, but what does Buzzy know about being fat, or middle-aged? In the presence of Marcel, she cannot be expected to care.

Weaving their way through the crowd, Buzzy tries to tell him that she is without a drink and is not sure what she will do if she doesn't find one soon. He seems not to have heard her as he heads for the French windows and terrace beyond. They pass Sherard, in conference with a craggy-faced man who looks like Samuel Beckett – or perhaps she only thinks that because of the literary milieu. Either way, she feels a momentary sense of pride to be among these worldly guests.

Buzzy can't tell how far exactly the garden extends beyond the torch-lit terrace, just that it's significantly larger than her parents' in Orpington. Marcel says there is a pond at the bottom and asks if she would like to have a look, though on arriving there's not much to see except a tarry pool smelling vaguely of fish pellets. He lights a joint and passes it to Buzzy. The smoke passes into her lungs as a smooth, almost imperceptible, heat: it's pure skunk, she realises, no tobacco has been used. This will shortly be bad news for her ability to hold a conversation, but right now, as Marcel asks *ça va bien?* and the air turns green and dances, everything does indeed feel fine.

The moment is ruined by someone called Gijs, who joins them by the pond and announces in short order that he works for an art hedge fund, has an uncanny ability to locate drugs at parties, and is an Arsenal fan. 'Anyone know the score this afternoon, by the way?'

Marcel tells him that they beat Blackburn Rovers 4–0, with Adebayor scoring a hat-trick. Buzzy is surprised: she has never known him to take an interest in football. Of the figure-of-eight-shaped pond, Gijs smirkingly tells them the previous owners were 'fairies' and Sherard had the phallus section removed when he bought the house.

'You must come across a lot of "fairies" in your line of work,' she replies, getting the stress wrong so the embarrassing silence seems to belong to her remark, not his. Gijs shows no sign of going anywhere, and Buzzy is about to give up and leave – if she delays greeting Afua any longer she will cause serious offence – when Marcel asks, 'Did you say you wanted a drink? *Tiens*, I have this for you.' He holds out a 33 cl bottle of beer, the label indiscernible in the darkness. Since Buzzy is now trembling from insecurity and genuinely in need of liquid, she takes the beer gratefully. 'Thanks. Where did you get this?'

Marcel shrugs. 'I found it. But wait, let me take the lid.'

Retrieving the bottle, he puts it to his mouth. She glimpses an incisor as he bites down on the metal bottle top, which falls to the ground with a soft hiss.

'Nice trick.' The light from Gijs' BlackBerry makes his cheeks glow. 'Bollocks! Chelski nailed Man Shitty 3–1.'

Sherard is scowling at Buzzy when she re-enters the sitting room. Really, it's too much: why invite her, or at least permit Henry and Afua to do so, if he is going to treat her so rudely? Is it her fault her father works in a furniture shop? Surely not everyone can be a dialectical materialist.

She raises her bottle to Sherard, thinking how funny it is that 'progressives' cannot handle the sight of a girl drinking beer. The noise of surrounding conversations hits her in waves – as expected, she is now very stoned. She makes a beeline for Afua, who has not moved from her spot by the wall but is receiving a procession of gentlemen callers, the latest a reedy American fashion writer. Henry is not far away, listening intently to the story of someone's recent charity climb of Mount Kilimanjaro.

'There you are! Douglas, this is Buzzy,' says Afua, firmly grasping her arm, from which Buzzy understands her friend is a little tipsy. This is confirmed when Afua strokes her hair and says, 'We're twins, can't you tell?'

Douglas stares at them both in dull panic, unsure if this is a private joke or some sort of test. 'Oh, why's that?'

'Well, *obviously*, we have the same hair. Look,' – she flicks playfully at Buzzy's locks – 'frizzy.' Except Afua's black hair is straightened, so that with her caramel skin and angular features she might at first glance pass for Andalusian or Cherokee.

'I prefer to think of it as curly.'

'Slumming it in South America hasn't cured you of your vanity, I see,' Afua teases. 'I take it you're enjoying the party, since you've been ignoring me so long?'

'It's fine. I just hope the crab cakes aren't poisoned or there'll be nothing in the *Guardian* for a few days.' Douglas looks mildly offended, but Buzzy is too filled with righteous anger at Sherard to mind. 'Love the house though. I didn't realise the *Liberal Review* was so profitable. I thought I read somewhere it was haemorrhaging readers.'

'Darling, so naive. Sherard doesn't have the magazine to make money.'

'Oh my God,' Douglas says, 'I read – is this true? – that Sherard commissioned Chris Ofili to produce a brick of elephant dung inscribed with some colourful insult – literally, it was written in red glitter paint – and sent it to that guy who writes for the *Independent*. Bruce Henderson, I want to say?'

'The inscription was *Eat this, you shit*. And he actually sent it to Simon—'

Afua has abruptly stopped speaking. She is staring at Buzzy with a curious fixity. Despite her slender frame, she has an aura that is resolute, if not intimidating. 'Where did you get that bottle?'

It's only then Buzzy notices that although the label on the neck of her beer says *Beck's*, the main sticker underneath is not the usual logo, but an arrangement of coloured dots. Very much, in fact, like the one famously associated with Damien Hirst. Her immediate thought is that this is typical of Sherard Howe; he can't just have an ordinary *Beck's*, it has to be some ridiculous personalised—

She watches Marcel return through the French windows. Daphne, Sherard's famous wife, is placing a hand on each of his shoulders before kissing him. As he dutifully offers a cheek, Buzzy meets his gaze. Worry that she might be hallucinating the entire scene is replaced by a thrilling fear that she might not be.

'I found it on the mantelpiece.'

'Okaay, it's just that Sherard usually keeps that bottle hidden away. He bought it at an auction. It's a special edition – Damien Hirst, obviously.'

'How much did it cost?'

'A few hundred pounds, I suppose.'

Douglas gasps. From the corner of her eye, Buzzy is aware of Sherard making rapid progress in her direction.

'Perhaps you should leave, darling,' says Afua, in a voice quite unflecked by panic.

2

Hearts aren't gentlemen

In the kitchen, Daphne is standing by the radio, clasping her tea in both hands as if in prayer to the god of *Desert Island Discs*. Sherard is reading the *Observer* comment pages. He holds aloft a slab of toast, from which fat drops of butter are falling unnoticed onto an editorial on the use of waterboarding at Guantánamo Bay.

On entering, Henry offers his parents a genial and general hullo, which his father ignores. His mother presents a cheek, rather distractedly, but makes Henry leap back by shouting, 'My God, you lying cow!' After a moment of confusion he realises the intended addressee is Germaine Greer, her fellow Antipodean, whose voice is filling the room.

In *The Third Sex*, Daphne advocated a female political discourse competing within the capitalist hierarchy. A dissenting letter was written to the *London Review of Books*, and the odd invitation to dine at the Howes' went unanswered, though the book was well received in other quarters. It didn't come to wider public attention until Professor Greer made a few semi-jocular comments at a literary festival – 'triangulating Blairite bollocks' is one phrase Henry recalls – which were then widely disseminated, including in publications not known for their interest in feminist theory – 'Me-Howe, It's Germ Warfare!' is a headline similarly etched in his mind.

The photograph of his mother used by broadsheets and tabloids alike was an old one, taken in the sixties, of her on a Mallorca beach in a bikini. Her mouth seemed somehow larger then, and the deep pouches under her eyes were missing. According to

Sherard, she resembled Jean Seberg, with her gamine haircut and boyish chest: Daphne herself found this ridiculous and often said so.

Now, a decade after *The Third Sex*, Daphne has a new polemic coming out. With *The Prodigal Sister*, his mother has repudiated, so far as Henry can gather, the central (and centrist) thesis of her previous work, and sought to return feminism to its radical origins. It's fair to say he is dreading the inevitable hoopla. He pours himself a lukewarm coffee from the pot Marta has left on the Aga. The smell of it, mingling with the faint trace of lemons rising from the floor, is a little nauseating – Henry is hungover for once.

In the background the soothing Scottish radio presenter, whose name Henry can't remember, is prompting her guest to describe a recent collaboration with the artist Stella Vine. 'Gosh,' Henry says, 'you'd never know there was a party here last night. What time did the caterers finish clearing up?'

Sherard looks up from his paper and regards Henry with blood-shot eyes. Often his remarks seem to have this effect on his father: unfocused reflection, prompted by but essentially ignoring the comment itself, as a painting of a sunset might inspire a more general critique of watercolour. 'Talking of jobs – darling I really cannot stand to listen to that terrible woman, *please* switch it off – should we have a discussion concerning your own prospects, Henry?'

Germaine Greer abruptly shuts up. Henry thinks he might be sick, which could in the circumstances have a certain eloquence, except he is loath to make more work for Marta. He looks to his mother but it is clear that she is in no mood to offer a reprieve. Instead she draws out a chair, which scrapes as she sits down with a convening air.

In the end he is rescued by Afua, who enters the kitchen, despite the autumnal nip outside, in shorts and a grey T-shirt bearing the words 'Cambridge University Hockey' and the corporate logo of Ernst & Young. There is a wine-red flush in her cheeks from exercise and the base of her neck glistens with sweat, as does her forehead, against which a few stray strands of hair are coiled. She greets them with her usual half-ironic smile, as if acknowledging some intimate and possibly embarrassing (though not for Afua) secret, and pours herself a glass of tap water, which she drinks down in efficient, rhythmical gulps. The rest of the family looks on, despite themselves a little rapt.

'How are we all feeling today?' The choice of pronoun is ironic, since she is plainly in better shape than everyone else. And such a magisterial voice! So languid yet imperious! Buzzy, whose turn of phrase is vastly superior to Henry's own, once noted that words seemed to arrange themselves out of Afua's thoughts, like well-trained pageboys, so as to save her the trouble.

'Sherard says he feels like John Hurt in *Alien*, though you'll see he's bravely managed half a loaf of bread.'

'That is because, my dear, I was so invigorated by your account of the film as an allegory for the psychotic male super-ego.'

Still standing – Afua often gives the impression she is late for another appointment, and almost equally often is – she asks Henry if he enjoyed the party. He starts to mumble, unsure himself what he is saying, until Daphne cuts him off. 'The boy was drunk, I'm delighted to say.'

'Naughty Hen.'

'Yes, talking of which, I do think it is disappointing when my guests *imbibe* my artwork. Was the silly girl indulging in some sort of reactionary protest? On second thoughts, I'm not interested. Only refrain – both of you – from inviting her here again.'

Henry expects Afua to put up a spirited defence of Buzzy's actions, and it is a terrible blow when she seems to accept Sherard's injunction almost straightaway. He himself only offers the weakest of protests, which are immediately waved off by his father, now apparently bored of the subject. It's true that Henry doesn't know precisely what Buzzy is accused of doing, only that it involved the Damien Hirst beer bottle and a hasty exit. Asking for more details would probably only harden his father's displeasure, though a more cowardly reason for Henry's reticence is that he avoids mentioning her name for fear of revealing his feelings.

To change the subject, Henry asks, 'What about you, Afua – have you been running this morning? Is Marcel still here?'

Afua feigns a graceful forehand. 'Tennis. We got up early and played at Highbury Fields, and then he went home.'

Marcel rarely stays the night at Canonbury Lane, and if he does, often leaves early the next morning. For such a sexually liberated household, in some quarters, the relations between Afua and Marcel are an oddly sensitive issue. Henry is dimly aware that as with most things his father might be at the centre of this. In any event, the result is that the couple spend most of their time at Marcel's Barbican bachelor pad.

'Who won?' Daphne wants to know.

'We got to six-all and played a tiebreak, which I won, but he let me see him let me, if you know what I mean. Somehow that seems less gentlemanly than just beating me.'

Daphne purses her lips, torn between distaste for Marcel's lack of sportsmanship and for sport in general, to say nothing of the patriarchal fantasy of the 'gentleman'. 'Have some coffee, love. I think Henry has just finished the pot but he'll make some more.'

'Actually I'm meeting Grace for coffee at the Tinderbox; I'm probably late already.' She doesn't make any movement, but stays leaning against the Aga, a hand resting on her hip. It's difficult not to admire her smooth limbs. 'Did I interrupt something?'

'Only Henry's employment, or lack thereof,' says Sherard, suppressing a belch.

'Oh God, I need to think about that.'

Henry is grateful to discover that 'that' refers to her own career plans. Since coming down from Cambridge in 2004, two years ahead of Henry, she's written a political blog on the *Liberal Review* website underneath an angled headshot ('I don't know what's meant to be more haunting,' Buzzy once commented, 'her cheekbones or all the injustice she writes about'). It's a modest success. Traffic to her posts is routinely among the highest of the magazine's online content, and Afua was recently asked to attend a round-table discussion at Labour HQ on the rise of new media, where Party strategists were impressed by her contributions.

He can't help wondering if Afua's doubts about journalism – she is saying to Daphne, 'I just feel the need to be more, what's the word? *Engagée*.' – emanate at least in part from a recent Hackwatch column in *Private Eye*. If so, he certainly wouldn't blame her. Attention was snidely drawn to the fact that the 'sultry *LR* blogger Afua Nelson just happens to live under the same roof as the proprietor of, whaddayaknow, the *LR*!' The article went on to describe a 'series' of embarrassing inaccuracies and crude misrepresentations of Tory policy in her blog posts, culminating in the revelation that Afua's greatest scoop to date, a *Today* presenter making an expletive-laden comment about the prime minister, was in fact from a conversation overheard at one of Sherard Howe's dinner parties. The latter was not sorry to fall out with his guest over the incident; he had always suspected him of being a closet right-winger; just as he seemed rather pleased with the *Private Eye* hatchet job, assuring Afua that he would have fired her had she lasted much longer without being targeted by the Gnome.

'My dear, no one doubts you are engaging. But one always needs a plan.'

'Well then,' Daphne says, 'let's think. Charities, NGOs, that sort of thing? How about Liberty? You know I could always call Shami.'

Afua smiles benevolently at Daphne. 'Not lobbying, please. I want to *do* something.' She sighs. 'It's hard to explain.'

'I think Afua is saying she wants to be the woman in the arena. You know, "whose face is marred by dust and sweat and blood".' Henry looks to the others. 'Theodore Roosevelt, wasn't it?'

Daphne clucks at Henry. 'Trust a Republican not to spare us the macho bullshit.'

'Well,' Sherard sighs, rubbing his eyes like an awakening Buddha, 'Merton needs a bag-carrier, but I wondered about Henry for that.'

Silence descends on the kitchen. Henry feels his stomach muscles tighten: he dreads the thought of becoming a special adviser, especially to Alec Merton, a fortyish and fearless Treasury minister, very much on the up.

'Alec Merton? That could be sort of interesting. I mean, isn't he supposed to be leader-in-waiting, or at least leader-in-waiting-after-next?' Then she shrugs and says, 'But Henry should do it. He'd make a great SpAd.'

'The thing is,' Henry replies, 'I'm not sure that I would. I'm not sure I'd be any use *at all*, to be honest. Whereas Afua is much more clued-up about Westminster and, well, it might be just the arena she's looking for.'

'She would be great with the press.' Daphne runs a hand through her wiry fringe. It sounds like she is making a concession, though her cadence, despite the softening of her New Zealand accent, still naturally inclines upwards. In the end, it's agreed that Sherard will propose Afua for the position of Merton's aide, and the 'Henry problem' goes unresolved. Afua announces she must go and shower before meeting her friend. Before she leaves, she squeezes Henry on the shoulder and reminds him people have dropped out of law school to do great things, citing Henry James. 'Don't forget Flaubert,' Daphne adds with a wink. 'Not bad for an autodidact, hey?'

For his part, Henry offers a wretched smile: he is grateful for the support, and to have escaped the Merton job, but he is left with the impression that, from the rest of his family's point of view, the only justification for the course on which he has set himself is the accomplishment of something magnificent – especially after his father says, in a tone that is not entirely jocular, 'Well, Henry, I should get writing if I were you.' Whereas the truth of it is that Henry has abandoned the bar because he feels unable to master private speaking, let alone the public variety. But anyway, he's not interested in greatness or posterity. Or at least not for himself: all of his ambition is reserved, in secret, for the recent recipient of one of Sherard's fatwas.

3

Every savage can dance

Buzzy can only intermittently glimpse Marcel at the next table. Next to her on one side is Henry, wearing a slightly stunned expression. On the other is Panos who, given the firm's conservative reputation, is surprisingly camp – though somehow it makes sense that he should have been placed with her, the great and omniscient Sullivan and Ball having divined she is unlucky in love and made its arrangements accordingly. (No doubt Afua is next to a demi-god.) When he leans in close and mentions that he is going to Heaven later if she'd like to join him, she replies rather primly that she's never heard of it, and feels guilty when he straightens up and says coldly, 'Oh I see' – especially since she's been there twice and thoroughly enjoyed herself.

'I mean,' she protests, 'I'm sure it would be fun. But I really ought to stay with my friends.'

'Of course you must,' he replies with a dismissive wave. His stubby fingers are covered with thick black hairs and Buzzy feels a sudden conviction that so is his back. Thinking of the sculpted torsos in Heaven she wonders how many Dionysian encounters he has enjoyed there: probably lots, which is depressing.

'Who are you with, anyway?' It's clear that in the course of asking the question Panos's expectations have transferred from unconsciously to consciously limited.

Buzzy explains that she was at university with Marcel Moreau.

'I didn't realise you were at the Other Place. When you referred to "uni" earlier, I assumed you meant one of the new ones. No matter: *what* scrumptious skeletons may we find in our Belgian friend's closet? You will tell me everything, you know. People always do.'

She surveys her salmon mousse with despair. Henry is providing a faltering account of his employment situation to a blonde girl on his left, who every now and again casts her eyes around her surroundings – the ballroom of a Mayfair hotel, peopled with several hundred corporate lawyers and their guests – with a martyred expression. He is saying something about applying for a job as a private tutor. This surprises and slightly annoys Buzzy: it was *her* idea, one she has been meaning to follow up ever since her conversation with the wife of the *TLS* editor. When she'd called Afua the day after the Howe party, Buzzy heard herself switching a little too quickly from apologising for her hurried exit after the incident with the Hirst bottle to recounting the story of the oligarch lavishing money on an Oxford graduate in exchange for the latter's (surely limited) insights into world politics. Perhaps the anecdote prompted Afua to suggest to Henry that he look into this tutoring business.

In the end, Buzzy doesn't have to tell Panos 'everything' because Marcel rises and comes over to her table. Crouched down beside her, he leans against her chair for support.

'Are you having fun?' she asks. 'Henry says it feels like we're dining on a grand steamship.' She's hoping for some hint from Marcel that *of course* he isn't enjoying himself, and has come to share his horror at the atmosphere of stuffy self-congratulation.

'Oh God. The *Titanic* maybe,' Panos says, dispensing with any pretence of not listening in.

The interjection is so loud that Buzzy can't ignore it. Briefly she considers plunging her fork into his thigh. 'Marcel, you know Panos?'

'Yes, of course,' responds Marcel gravely. Removing his hand from the back of her chair, he holds it out for Panos to shake. The latter does not at first react, and she is aware of him absorbing the perfection of it, supressing no doubt the urge to trace his own stubby digit across the beautiful blue vein that runs from above his watch (Chopard) to the base of his wedding finger (ringless, thank God). Eventually Panos reaches out and holds the Belgian's fingers, as if weighing them.

'Do you know, I don't believe we have met.' It's not clear to Buzzy if he is refuting Marcel's suggestion that they have already been introduced, or pretending to for the thrill of feigning indifference. She's only certain that because of him she will never find out the reason why Marcel came over to speak to her. 'You must be from the September intake. What group are you?'

Marcel replies with the initials 'PQSD'.

'So we are a mergers and acquisitions man. And who is our superviser – not Jonathan Rove, is it? He of the roving eye,' he adds, rolling the 'r' and winking at Buzzy.

'No, Philip Devereux.'

'*Le grand seigneur*; I saw that he was on your table. Rather you than me, old boy.'

He sits back in his chair with the look of someone who has gorged himself. Marcel takes advantage of this to ask Buzzy to join his and Afua's table after the senior partner's speech, and, with a brief nod to Panos, slips away.

Buzzy takes a deep gulp of her wine and discreetly scans the room. There is Afua in a blood-red head-wrap, resting a hand to her cheek. She is listening to a tall, broad-shouldered man who reminds her of an Argentine ex-president, with his impressive mane of suspiciously un-greying chestnut hair swept in wings over his ears. He looks suspiciously tanned, too, for someone who must spend all hours inside the offices of Sullivan and Ball. It dawns on Buzzy that this man must be the famous Philip Devereux, who being Marcel's boss is of great interest to her. (She couldn't care less that, if Panos is to be believed, he is the highest-paid transaction lawyer in the City.)

Buzzy watches Philip unfurl his wrist elegantly but manfully as he makes some point or other to Afua. Abruptly he throws his head back and lets out a thunderous laugh. She tries to picture him in his office, studying cases and statutes, but he doesn't seem the reading type. Not for the first time, Buzzy is jealous of her friend and yet relieved not to be in her place. No doubt Afua is as unfazed by this middle-aged alpha male as she is by Sherard or, for that matter, any of the overlords she now deals with as special adviser to the financial secretary to the Treasury. The title doesn't sound *that* important – an aide to a secretary – though in multiple discreet ways Buzzy has been given to understand that it definitely is. For example, Afua's emails since she started the new job are getting shorter and shorter: one of the last ones, in response to a suggestion to meet for lunch at the weekend, was simply 'Y'. When they did meet up, Afua was an hour and a half late, which was extravagant even by her standards. The conversation that ensued was full of references to Treasury 'asset protection schemes' and 'emergency recapitalisations' and other phrases at which Buzzy felt she needed to nod gravely.

What's galling is not that Afua now talks endlessly about herself as if she were saving the world, but that it sort of *is* what she is doing, at least according to the prime minister. How can Buzzy object in these circumstances if her time in South America is passing into history without comment? She might as well have spent it, like her gap year, waitressing at Orpington Pizza Express. It reminds Buzzy of her last two years at Cambridge, when Afua would come up from London to visit Marcel and never ask her about her boyfriend situation. On the one hand, it was tactful; on the other, Buzzy resented the presumption, however rational and evidence-based, that she would have nothing of interest to report.

But it would not be true to say that Afua takes no interest in her life, now or then. She is starting to dread the moment during the telephone calls that are getting later and later at night, and often interrupted at the start by muffled directions to Canonbury Lane, when Afua asks her what she has done that day, or how her job search is going. Or, worst of all, how she is finding being back in Orpington with her parents (Afua's own arrangements, still living rent-free with her guardians at twenty-five years old, are somehow not the same thing at all).

'Why did you say that – about Philip Devereux? Is he a brute?'

'On the contrary; they say he's terribly suave.'

Sensing Panos doesn't intend to remark any further on the subject, but wishing to deny him the pleasure of confirming as much, she asks him what sort of law he practises.

'Antitrust,' he replies. Then, seeing her expression, 'I could explain, but we might both expire from boredom.'

The senior partner's speech, delivered over coffee, refers only in passing to the financial situation that started off as a crunch but that is increasingly, Buzzy has dimly noted, referred to as a crisis. After thanking the retiring partners and current staff, and after a quick canter through the year's *pro bono* highlights – including a recent charity cycle ride in Namibia with lots of in-jokes about the participants that Buzzy laughed along with anyway – he sits down to relieved applause. The band strikes up with 'Beyond the Sea' and the senior partner, still a little flushed from his speech, leads out his sturdy and rather fierce-eyed wife to start the dancing.

Feeling alone and undesirably sober from the coffee (Henry has been whisked off to the dance floor by his blonde, and Panos has gone in search of port), Buzzy decides to accept Marcel's invitation. She weaves through the bodies between their tables, only realising what a terrible mistake she has made when it's far too late. Afua is on her feet, chatting with Philip Devereux and now arching her eyebrows at Buzzy. There's no sign of Marcel.

'Here's someone who'll dance with you,' Afua says. She takes Buzzy lightly by the wrist. 'There's a panic at the Treasury and I have to call Alec – come and find me in twenty minutes.' Then she is gone, leaving Buzzy frowning at the floor.

'Philip Devereux.' The statement of his name, offered in lieu of a handshake, suggests a firmly rooted self.

'Elizabeth Price,' she mumbles. 'But some people call me Buzzy.'

'Well, Elizabeth, I think your friend has rather put you on the spot. You know, I won't be offended if you don't want to dance with me.' This is not the escape route it appears – it's clear that beneath the wry delivery he fully expects her to accompany him.

'It's only that I'm useless – you have no idea.'

'Oh, I shouldn't worry. Just follow me.'

The band is now playing 'Fly Me to the Moon'. At least the dance floor is filling quickly, mostly with older couples. Is it a show of machismo from the partners, she wonders, to demonstrate they aren't afraid of making fools of themselves when the occasion demands? One youthful face catches her eye: Henry, sending his limbs in desperate search of the beat, while the poor blonde is yanked to and fro as if tussling with a bear.

Philip Devereux is holding her against his stately frame, moving her from side to side with decisive steps. After a few moments pass without obvious humiliation she decides that, if she permits herself to breathe, she might just make it to the end of the song. Except now he is talking! Surely it's unreasonable to expect her to keep up with his mind as well? At first his words simply reverberate inside her head, and she is astonished when she hears herself reply that she is a writer.

'Oh – would I have read you?'

'No. At least, I shouldn't think so,' she adds quickly. In vain she tries to think of a remark that might make him toss his head back with amusement.

'The Victorians knew how to write,' he says with great naturalness, despite the pause that has gone before. '*Middlemarch* – a wonderful book. I was always terrified of ending up like Casaubon, less than my ambition.'

So she was wrong – he is a reader after all! A real one, too; not the arid sort who admires Eliot the chronicler of country life, as though the provinces of nineteenth-century England and the human heart were of equal interest. Intrigued, but not quite ready to abandon her initial impression, she asks if that means he has completed the *Key to All Contracts*.

'Ha! Well no.' (She is looking at her legs, which are still shaking a little.) 'One has juniors for that sort of thing.'

'At least now I know why Marcel no longer seems to sleep.'

Philip raises an eyebrow but otherwise ignores the reference to his trainee. 'Perhaps what I need is a Dorothea.'

Buzzy is suddenly aware that they are being discreetly observed by other guests of the Grosvenor. It occurs to her that she doesn't even know if this man is married: is she becoming a scandalous woman, like Countess Olenska? As it turns out, the attention of the room is diverted by a yelp from the other side of the dance floor.

'That's unfortunate,' observes Philip, who continues dancing. 'It seems someone has injured Mrs Lyle-Smith.'

'Oh no, really?' Buzzy tries to catch sight of the victim among the gathering melee. 'Does she seem all right?'

'*She'll* be fine, I expect.'

The matronly woman clutching her calf, Buzzy now sees, is the wife of the senior partner. The perpetrator is hovering nearby, trying to appear attentive and invisible at the same time.

'Poor Henry,' she sighs.

'Know him, do you? Hopefully he wasn't planning an extended career at Sullivan and Ball.'

'No, he doesn't work for you,' corrects Buzzy. 'He's a guest, like me. Actually, I think you know his father – Sherard Howe?'

'*That's* Howe's boy, is it? How marvellous. He was my fag for a while at school. I gather he has disparate passions these days – modern art, I mean, and the Labour Party.' These are uttered with a faint air of distaste, as if unserious and yet not a laughing matter either. 'I shouldn't think he remembers me very fondly.'

'I doubt his thoughts of me are overwhelmingly fond either, to be honest.'

'Oh?'

'He had a party at his house in Islington recently. The long and short of it is that I ended up drinking a very valuable bottle of lager belonging to him.'

'Belgian or something, was it?'

'Sort of. Actually, it was more like a piece of art.'

It wouldn't comfort Sherard, she imagines, to know that Philip's laugh eases some of the tension created by his son's faux pas. 'Elizabeth,' he announces, 'you have made my evening.'

'It's not that I'm *proud* of it,' she adds guiltily. 'The Howes can be very' – somehow 'kind' is not the right word – 'generous people. For example, when Afua had problems at home Sherard and his wife took her in. They treat her like their daughter.'

The music has stopped and Philip, smoothing his hair back (it really is very thick for a man of at least fifty), doesn't seem to be listening. She notices a signet ring on his little finger. 'Stately' – yes, she thinks excitedly, that is exactly the word for him, in a floating sense of present and antique, material and grand. That her excitement is relative goes without saying: for Buzzy, the universe is measured by unconscious reference to the young man who appears from nowhere and, with a stiff smile at his boss, says that if she is not too busy he was wondering if Buzzy would care to join him outside for a cigarette.

'I think not,' says Philip, 'it's such a sad little habit. Besides, the lady must dance – she's learning fast, you know.' The band starts playing Elvis Presley's 'All Shook Up'; somebody whoops drunkenly. 'Oh rock'n'roll, marvellous. Now, are you ready?'

4

Ones to watch

Daily Telegraph, *15 November 2008*

It isn't often, one presumes, that a denizen of the Cleethorpes Working Men's Club receives a telephone call from the office of the French finance minister; still less that he replies as confidently in la langue de Molière as does the MP for Great Grimsby, Alec Merton, when the *Daily Telegraph* met him for a pint of the local bitter.

'It's been frantic,' confesses the 42-year-old former banker. If capitalism's near collapse has meant a few sleepless nights for the financial secretary to the Treasury, it is clear that Merton is relishing every moment of his job.

After the chancellor announced details of the bank rescue packages last month, the City minister, as Merton is informally known in Whitehall, was everywhere on the airwaves, reassuring jittery markets – and voters – of the government's plan. He dismisses the suggestion that few of his colleagues are permitted a similar media presence. 'It's the usual Westminster nonsense. You'll be saying I'm the leader-in-waiting next, and that really will be the end of my career.'

Alec Francis Merton was educated at Langley, a grammar school in Berkshire. His father was an accountant; his mother an art teacher. He studied – of course – politics, philosophy and economics at Oxford, narrowly missing a first because he was 'too busy singing'. A keen chorister, he met his wife, Rebecca, when she was the organ scholar at Oriel.

The couple have four children: twins Andrew and William, 12, Samuel, 7, and 6-month-old Alison. They are clearly delighted by the arrival of their baby daughter: 'My wife wouldn't say it but the prospect of a fourth boy was slightly terrifying.'

After a year at Yale, where Merton studied 'something to do with continuous time optimal control theory – it was very dull', he returned to London to work for Standard Chartered. He entered Parliament a decade later, joining the government as a junior transport minister in the same year (2005).

Privately wealthy, Merton made a sum 'in the millions' during his City career. He is highly valued by Downing Street for the same reason he is treated with a certain scepticism by some backbenchers: it's harder to argue Labour is nationalising Britain's biggest banks for ideological reasons when the City minister hails from the Square Mile.

'First of all, this is emphatically not nationalisation, it is temporary public ownership.' This remark rather proves the point. 'Look,' he counters, 'when I was a banker, I steered well clear of the sort of investment activities that have got us into the current mess. But does it hurt that I have experience of dealing with these people, that I speak their language? I would say not.'

It is hard to disagree with his argument – Merton has a knack of presenting opinions as inescapable truths – but there is also a sense that the world of Oxford and Yale and high finance belongs more to *Great Gatsby* than Great Grimsby. His aide, Afua Nelson, laughs and says they should steal the line for one of Merton's speeches. Alas, she adds, his twin obsessions of Gillingham Football Club and *Strictly Come Dancing* are 'definitely not very Scott Fitzgerald'.

Ms Nelson, who attended a comprehensive school in Islington and whom Merton describes later as 'indispensable', is the adopted daughter of Daphne Depree, the feminist writer, and her husband Sherard Howe, the publisher and *Liberal Review* proprietor. There is almost a diplomatic incident when the *Daily Telegraph* asks a shade too loudly what Ms Depree would make of her drinking bitter in such an old-fashioned male venue.

'Oh, she would hate it,' the young adviser confirms. 'Daphne only ever drinks Guinness.'

The room erupts. Like her boss, it seems, Ms Nelson is not one to waste a crisis.

5

The boy

'Are you sure you don't want some water?'

Henry, whose mouth is uncomfortably dry, gazes at the bottle of Evian in front of him. 'No, thank you, I'm fine.'

He has forgotten to check whether Ramadan has finished. It definitely began quite recently, because his mother wrote a piece in the *Independent* praising its message of social solidarity while regretting the fetishisation of physical contact. Although he *thought* the article was published over a month ago, Henry cannot help suspecting that his cultural sensitivities are being tested (the PA has after all now asked the question twice, and neither she nor Riyad is drinking anything).

'As I was saying,' Riyad resumes, 'the boy was studying in Lugano but it didn't work out. He's a great kid, very sociable – *too* sociable if anything. Do you like parties, going out?'

'Not excessively, if I'm honest.'

The youngish PA, Louise, scribbles something on a pad. 'What *do* you enjoy doing in your spare time, Henry?'

'Well,' he begins, feeling his cheeks burn, 'I like country churches. I visited a wonderful one in Tudeley, near Tonbridge, not long ago. Perhaps you know it, it has a beautiful set of, ah, Chagall stained-glass windows. Actually I might have a drop of water, if you don't mind.'

'Of course.' Louise's accent has a transatlantic note, like Riyad's chinos and polo shirt. Like, indeed, the small Mayfair office itself, which has the glossy and anonymous feel of a chain hotel.

'So history, can we say, and art: these are interests?'

'Yes, I suppose so.'

'And literature, theatre, opera?'

'I like them. I couldn't say—'

Louise interrupts, 'What about soccer?'

'Not at all, I'm afraid.'

'The boy is a big Chelsea fan. *Very* big,' says Riyad, with a conclusive air. 'But I was telling you about his situation.'

Riyad's manner of referring simply to the 'boy' – in case, Henry presumes, he is deemed unsuitable for the job – lends the tale, of the rake who falls in with the wrong crowd in Switzerland and is banished to London to study engineering at Imperial, a *Bildungsroman* quality.

'Ah, I'm afraid there must have been some sort of mix-up by the agency. I know nothing about engineering – absolutely nothing,' Henry adds, feeling the need for emphasis. 'My degree is in law, you see, and my A Levels were all arts subjects.'

Riyad brushes this off. 'That's fine: the boy's academic tutors will come with him to London. What we're looking for is a lifestyle mentor; a young man to supervise him and introduce him to English culture.'

'A sort of chaperone, you mean?'

Louise laughs. 'That's an old-fashioned way of putting it. We see it more as a professional friendship – someone who will be, you know—'

'—a civilising influence.'

Henry is blushing again. What would *Private Eye* say about the son of Sherard Howe, founder of the *Liberal Review*'s Edward W. Said journalism prize, 'civilising' an Arab for a living? His parents are sufficiently unimpressed as it is. His father wondered, witheringly, why he would not want to teach children who really needed his help; while his mother poured herself a large glass of white wine and said, 'Oh Christ, it's not like he's fucking Eichmann,' which Henry felt was a wounding analogy, even in the negative. Only Afua, whose idea it was initially, was wholeheartedly supportive, suggesting it was totally fair that Henry take a job like this 'while he gets back on his feet'.

Afua is right, he believes. Increasingly Henry thinks he has experienced something like a crisis of self in the last few months, albeit of an unremarked and unremarkable kind. Abandoning law school was a symptom of this; the decision taken so precipitously, and after he had studied so hard for his undergraduate degree. (Henry is too embarrassed to confess to anyone that he would have got a first had he not messed up his tort exam by writing one more essay than was required.)

Since then he hasn't really *done* much, apart from attending the Sullivan and Ball Christmas party – which was hardly pursuing an interest, at least of the mentionable kind – and making the outing to All Saints' Church, where again his chief motive was seeing Buzzy, this time in Orpington on his way home.

What he has found himself doing, especially recently, is spending long and secretive stretches lying in the bath. Early afternoons are his favourite time, when he has the house to himself. Only once has he been caught, by Marta, who normally works mornings for the Howes but started late that Wednesday because of a doctor's appointment. As he emerged from the bathroom, steam still rising from his mottled upper body, he discovered her plugging the hoover into a socket safely distant from the one used for the second-floor landing shelf's centrepiece, a portable DNA refrigeration unit containing – or comprising, Henry is not exactly sure – Per Berg's *Self-Portrait*. 'Hullo Marta,' he said in his habitual over-friendly manner, at the same moment as the hoover whirred into action.

Before he leaves, Riyad asks Henry – without any embarrassment or explanation as to why he knows, for example, of their association with the Labour Friends of Palestine – if he shares his parents' views on the Middle East. 'It's not that I *disagree* with them; it's just I try to steer clear of politics.' He isn't sure if Riyad and Louise are chuckling at or with him when he concludes, 'I suppose I'm the black sheep of the family, in that sense.'

At half past six that evening, he is lying on his bed, staring at an old film poster in which the smoke rising from Jack Nicholson's cigarette merges stylishly with Faye Dunaway's hair. Outside,

Canonbury Lane is quiet apart from the homecoming of a man whose heels clip the pavement grandly. Only Henry and his mother are in: Afua is still at the Treasury and his father is at the Groucho Club. Daphne is in her study on the floor below, writing an article. When his mobile rang a few moments ago, he was wondering if he might suggest warming up the lasagne Marta left: having little appetite, his mother often forgets to eat if the Howes are not expecting guests.

It was Claire from Oxbridge Tutorial, sounding as usual slightly harried. '*Fabulous* news, they want to offer you the job.'

Henry asked if she was quite sure. He felt the interview had not been an unmitigated success, and he knew that the agency had put forward a number of candidates. From the sample of profiles he'd viewed on the website, the other tutors all seemed terribly attractive and confident, managing to convey enthusiasm for teaching while hinting at noble or exotic other lives in which they set up charities or trained at RADA or sailed the Atlantic.

She confirmed, after checking, that Henry Howe was the successful candidate. They both agreed the salary of £1,000 a week, in return for nine hours' 'mentoring', was not inconsiderable. Henry's duties would comprise such things as attending cultural activities of his choosing with the boy; devising a list of key works of English literature and supervising the boy's reading of these; diary management to ensure the boy's timely arrival at family engagements in London or at the correct airport for those outside the UK; and monitoring the boy's maintenance of his core studies preparatory to starting his engineering degree in September 2009. Compliance with these duties, Claire speedily intoned (he had the impression she was reading from a prepared document, a draft contract perhaps), was to be demonstrated by means of an email update sent twice weekly to Louise Ryder. The engagement was for twelve months, with a performance review at the end of the third month and a bonus payable on improvement to the boy's comportment measured by—

At that point Henry cut in. In his surprise, he'd almost forgotten that he was essentially unenthusiastic about the position. The notion that *he* of all people might be paid to provide lifestyle coaching to a troubled (troublesome?) young man was deeply morally questionable.

'I'm sorry Louise – ah – Claire, can I interrupt you? It all sounds tremendous, at least *in abstracto*.' He hadn't intended to sound pompous, and shut his eyes. 'What I mean is: I don't think I'm the right person for this role. I'm so sorry to inconvenience everyone . . .'

'Are you sure? Because really all you have to do is keep the boy out of trouble. Take him to private views of the latest exhibitions; opening nights at the theatre – whatever you want, the family can arrange and obviously pay for. And you haven't even heard the best part yet.'

'I haven't?'

'They're offering you *rent-free* accommodation in a mews house in South Kensington, near where the boy lives. Trust me, it's a nice area.'

'It sounds very generous, all of it,' Henry replied. 'But I'm afraid it doesn't change my answer.'

6

Independent moves

Sherard, who is oblivious to the jaded splendour of the Bar Marsella (he has seen it all before), lights his cigar with quick hard sucks, conscious of the match warming his fingertips. On the next table a glass is on fire. The girl is just young enough to be forgiven for ordering one of the establishment's famous absinthes, he decides, if not for making such a fuss about it.

He holds the cigar between his thumb and forefinger, one of the Romeo y Julieta Belicosos he orders from Fox of St James's: a hardened turd which might one day kill him. Not that he will stop smoking – that would be seen as a significant if ambiguous gesture ('Sherard has quit, you know'), and certainly he would not like the many irritating people his smoking irritates to think he was doing it for them.

On the subject of hardened turds, he is still puzzling over his recently renewed relations with Devereux, the indirect reason for being in Barcelona. The idea, first set out on partner-headed paper, is for Sherard to arrange for a small exhibition of contemporary art on the theme of 'turmoil', to be shown at Sullivan and Ball's London office. There would be a drinks reception and a carefully selected private view, with a proportion of any works acquired donated to Centrepoint, the homeless charity.

In their following brief exchanges, Devereux at least had the decency not to try and strike a sentimental note, nor pretend to have any interest in art. That Sullivan and Ball, with their impeccable list of blue-chip clients and famous aversion to self-publicity, would wish to organise this event now, while their rivals are busy firing employees and slashing corporate entertainment budgets, is an act of thuggish good taste that Sherard cannot help but admire.

Yet for Devereux to contact his former fag for what looks suspiciously like a favour breaks an unwritten code of their hideous alma mater. (The fact that the mentions in *Apollo* and *Art Review* will not be unhelpful to Sherard is immaterial.) He is pleased in a way, since it confirms his judgement in mistrusting him for the last three or four decades, and not (or not just) for locking Sherard in his own trunk and kicking it down the Wellington House stairs. That at least had a ring of authenticity to it, unlike his now ungrey hair and mahogany tan. Not for the first time, he wonders if anyone has properly looked into Devereux's claim to be related to the Viscounts Hereford; then again, if this exhibition secures Sherard the Turner Prize chairmanship, the other man can be related to the Virgin Mary for all he cares.

The only slight concern is the amount of time he has to assemble the exhibition. When Devereux proposed holding it in February next year, Sherard, despite reservations, agreed immediately; he knew enough of Sullivan and Ball to know that, in the field of mergers and acquisitions, the firm prided itself on working to impossibly abbreviated timetables, and shuddered at the thought of Devereux's derision if he caused a fuss over a mere display of art. But he is confident the challenge is not insurmountable. 'Turmoil' is a broad category, after all, and he only needs perhaps fifteen or twenty pieces. So long as two or three of these are from genuinely celebrated artists – the sort even City types might have heard of – he can assemble the rest from a combination of private galleries who owe him a favour and lesser pieces from his own collection. It's not very different to topping up the Dom with the 'R' de.

He takes a large, head-clearing gulp of lager and checks his watch. The bar is busy even on a Wednesday afternoon but Sherard, hidden in clouds of cigar smoke, feels pleasantly shielded from the foreign chatter around him. That's what he enjoys about smoking: its cloak-like aspect. Carles's gallery is also in El Raval, not far away, and they had agreed Sherard would be there at three o'clock, in ten minutes' time. He decides he will be late. Another Estrella, perhaps even an absinthe, may be required to endure Carles's gruesome euro-English, any trace of a Catalan accent almost entirely washed away by a Columbia PhD.

Wind whips along the narrow streets of the Ciutat Vella when he leaves the bar after the second beer. It has an abandoned feel compared with the summer months, when the shutters of the flats above are flung open and there is a Havanese atmosphere of salsa music and neighbourly screaming. The gallery, which with its frosted windows might be mistaken for one of the neighbourhood sex shops, is not far from the Museu d'Art Contemporani and the Plaça dels Angels.

'Hey Sher-*rard*!' Thick plastic frames perch on Carles's shaved crown, the same shocking red as the lolly he is sucking, putting Sherard in mind (who knows, possibly intentionally) of Sue Lyon in *Lolita*. 'How was your journey?' There is a trace of accusation in his nervous laugh, and he plants an unwelcome strawberry kiss on Sherard's cheek.

'Tolerable. All hangovers considered.'

Carles ignores him, telling a bafflingly long story about a recent flight he took to Miami where his luggage ended up in Bangkok. 'Never fly American Airlines, that's all I'm saying,' he concludes with a sweep of his slobbery lolly.

Sherard glances ostentatiously at his watch. 'Now I don't have much time . . .'

'No, are you serious? I thought we were going to have dinner later, at least.'

'Out of the question. I already have plans.'

Carles sulkily drops the lolly in a bin. But having established a clear time limit to proceedings, and taken some wind out of the gallery owner's sails, Sherard finds his own mood improving. 'Now what have you got for me, anything good?'

That evening, at L'Imprevist, he is in a distinctly positive frame of mind by the time the second bottle of red arrives. Esther is of a glamorously indeterminate age, though if one were to place a gun to Sherard's head he might say late thirties. It had been a successful afternoon with Carles and he is enjoying arousing her professional jealousy by describing the works he has chosen for the Sullivan and Ball exhibition.

'. . . The Rodoreda piece is a veil or screen of diaphanous dollar notes, with three mannequins behind melded in the pose of *The Three Graces*. Except if you look closely through the veil, the Graces are trying to strangle one another. It's called *Final Curtain*, I think. What else? Ah yes, *Cow in a Tornado*, a film installation by Aoyama Aoyamaai. It's rather beautiful actually.'

'Fabulous,' says Esther, a touch automatically. 'But I hope there's some space left in your exhibition, because I thought we could drive to Sitges tomorrow. There are some artists you must meet, if you haven't already. Sherard Howe knows everyone,' she adds, giving him the unusual impression of hearing a dramatic aside about himself.

'Who are they?' he asks, with wine-induced patience.

'I didn't say – am I tipsy already? Let's see: Joan Ferrer, Ignacio Villarroel, Sandra Charolet . . .'

'Not familiar.'

'Fantastic, so I can take you to the *finca* where they live and work. It's actually just outside Sitges. They can show us around their studios and then we can all have a long lunch, maybe an *escudella*. Sound good?'

'What? Ah yes, indeed.'

He stares idly at their plates, finding that he has lost interest in the subject of art. A smear of prune sauce is all that remains of his grilled duck, while Esther's falafels are barely touched. 'Mind if I smoke?'

'Not at all.' She smiles unconvincingly. There is a satisfying (because it has nagged at him all evening, and he has at last put his finger on it) resemblance to Gwyneth Paltrow.

'Tell me, what is happening in Spanish politics these days? Presumably things are better now the awful Aznar has gone?'

The mention of the former prime minister's name causes the neighbouring couple to look up from their soups, and Esther to colour.

37

'This is not a good moment for Espain. In the last years we have been building houses like crazy — that's really the word, it's been *una locura*, a form of craziness. You know, there is something like a million unsold new homes in this country? Now it's all collapsing.'

'Not the new homes, surely?' he asks, thinking of Spanish builders.

'The construction business, I mean.'

'Ah,' is all he can manage while lighting his cigar. 'Still, I suppose that means you won't have so many Brits moving here, vomiting in your town fountains.'

She places her hand over his. 'Sherard! Don't speak like this of your countrymen.'

'Why not? They're utterly foul, mostly.'

'The English are gentlemen,' Esther insists, deliciously scandalised.

'Oh God, the English are worst of all. I'm afraid they are barbarians, especially the gentlemen.'

Still smiling, and perhaps not quite wanting him to stop, she asks, 'What about your family? I am sure *they* are not barbarians.' When he only grunts, she adds, 'How is your wife?'

'Daphne is in America giving a lecture. When I last spoke to her an exchange of views with a radio jock had gone viral, whatever that means. In any case, I'm not sure I've heard her happier. More wine?'

'Only a little — really, that's enough. And the children?'

Sherard is unable to recall how much he's told Esther about his 'children', a choice of word which might suggest either sensitivity towards or ignorance of the Afua situation. When he tells her that Afua is an adviser at the Treasury, and doing very well, with some talk of the Party finding her a safe seat at the next election, she seems surprised, but he can't be certain at which part.

'And your son . . . Henry? What is he doing now?'

'Who knows . . . Not the law, he abandoned that.' He puffs frowningly on his cigar in a way that might express paternal concern. She is not wearing a ring, but something (a new

38

brittleness in her manner, his own lack of interest, the fact he should know already) inclines him against asking about her own personal life.

'You're so lucky to have kids.'

'Oh, of course, in a way . . .'

The sip of her water is alarmingly preparatory, and Sherard summons the waiter with a little nod. 'Yes, can we have the bill?' Parenthetically he asks his companion, 'You weren't after pudding or anything, were you?' and she raises her perfect eyebrows, startled perhaps at the idea of more food. 'Also a quick brandy while you're at it. Any sort will do.'

'I suppose it's just my age. I'm thirty-five, you see.'

'You don't look it.'

Stroking her blonde highlights she tells him she adores her job but sometimes questions how meaningful it is. Sherard, who is less than pleased to discover her admiration of his place in the art world is qualified, finds even her confessing little laugh objection-able, a way of disguising her bad manners as some sort of joke. One must acknowledge, though, her looks – except he decides that they actually work against her at this stage, emphasising as they do the improbability of her singledom.

Afterwards, Sherard walks her to her car, a new-style Beetle parked nearby at a slight angle to the pavement. Esther offers to give him a lift back to his hotel; he declines on the ground that where he is staying, the Barceló Raval, is only a few streets away and he could do with a stroll. They agree she will pick him up at ten o'clock tomorrow morning. 'Don't go too far south by mistake,' is her parting warning. 'This area is not the best at night.'

Yet when Sherard reaches the Barceló Raval, alive and glowing under its sleek metal skin, he walks on, numb now to the cold, enjoying the light, childish feeling that accompanies night-walking in a foreign city. He crosses Sant Pau into the Barri Xinès, meaning Chinatown, quite perversely since there were never any Chinese here. What *is* the bloody story behind the name? He knew it once.

At first it all seems more salubrious than he remembers. There are of course a few drug dealers around – Moorish like their wares, he might once have said, though one would not know from the perfunctory English *no thank you*s he offers now. Perhaps red light districts are fading from civilization, like rural post offices; or there was a police raid earlier; or everyone's off at adult education. He passes an enshadowed tramp crouching in a doorway: they make an intense form of eye contact before Sherard realises the other is defecating. It is enough to make him wonder if he ought not to be doing something more uplifting himself.

He is almost as far as the old docks at Drassanes and ready to turn around, when he notices a lady loitering on the other side of the street. She is wearing a beautiful rabbitskin coat whose lower third has been inexpertly removed in order not to obstruct the view of her slender legs. She hails him with a throaty '*Venga, guapo!*' which he recognises as Castilian, most likely of the South American variety, from the speaker's dusky complexion. She is crossing the street, calling and waving an unlit cigarette at him.

With only an inadequate flip-open set of matches they stand there for a good half-minute, in silence apart from the occasional *bugger* from Sherard as another prematurely expires. Finally one flares and he manages to shield it long enough for the lady to dip her fag in the flame, exposing the contours of her jawline and tell-tale bulge of her throat. '*Gracias, mi amor.*' She gives him an amused once-over before exhaling a long stream of smoke and night air. '*Hace frío.* Cold. You wanna come back to my flat, warm up a little?'

'I could always try.' For once Sherard is rather amused himself. 'I'm not promising anything.'

7
The intruder (1)

When she looks up to find a strange boy standing at the threshold of her bedroom, Buzzy is lying on the bed, re-reading *Middlemarch*. She is enjoying it more now there is no tutorial with Dr Drayson looming, and some of the hazier aspects of the story the first time round, such as the precise connection between Mr Bulstrode and the Vincys, are cleared up; though in her heart of hearts she is disappointed not to recognise Marcel in Lydgate or Ladislaw or even Fred Vincy, and as a result finds George Eliot's canvas deficient in a way Dr Drayson does not.

If Marcel is conspicuous by his absence, surveying her own fortunes Buzzy feels she has been transformed from an abject Dorothea into a smug Celia. First and most obviously, there is the change in her geographical circumstances, having escaped the Orpington semi of her father, a self-described 'furniture man' (not the sort of ornamental title she would have hoped for), and her mother, a housewife who once a week visits a family, the Latimers, to do some cleaning and ironing. She's done this for so many years that Buzzy knows, via Mrs Latimer via her mother, more or less everything about the sons, their sporting triumphs and girlfriends and the oldest's mysterious African illness. The Latimers even gave Buzzy a silver bracelet for her twenty-first birthday, except – embarrassed her mother is apparently the last indigenous English cleaning lady – she heard herself tell people it was a gift from her grandmother.

Her snobbishness towards her parents is something she's deeply ashamed of; an ungrateful response to their working hard and sending her to a grammar school and generally giving her the opportunity to acquaint herself with people and books from far outside their experience. She understands, without having a firm idea of how to counter it, the dangerous egotism in being twenty-four and knowing more about the world than your mother and father. This is already clear from the impossible criteria by which she'll measure her success: to learn to observe everything; to acquire the highest sensibility; to become, in short, exceptionally civilised.

At least now, thanks to Henry, Buzzy has something she craved – time and space in which to write. A house of her own! (She has no money, of course, but there's her miraculously capacious overdraft, and one of her student-era credit cards still seems to be working. The combination of these and not needing to worry about monthly rent means the job search can wait.) It's over a fortnight since she moved in and she still can't quite believe her luck. She takes herself for wanders around the neighbourhood, savouring the cool hush of the pavements with their regular pools of Range Rover shadow. The most immediate landmark from Buzzy's modest (for the area, she supposes – but completely *perfect* for her) two-bedroom mews house is the Vietnamese embassy, a white stucco-fronted villa with mounted security cameras and a communist flag, whose presence in Kensington feels as unlikely as her own. Sometimes she strolls towards Gloucester Road, at others past Wódka and the Buttercup cake shop (which she has tried and failed to stay out of) as far as High Street Kensington, before eventually doubling back and collapsing with a cup of tea in the comfy and only slightly chintzy front room.

Buzzy's other cause for happiness was the taxi ride back to Canonbury Lane after the Mayfair party, the eyelid movie of which she hasn't tired of rewatching. It was Afua who insisted on discussing her dance with Philip Devereux. 'I knew something had happened when you didn't come and find me,' she remarked. Pressed on what they talked about, Buzzy replied, 'Nothing of great importance – *Middlemarch*, at one point,' and gazed mysteriously out of the cab window.

'Well I'm excited, even if you're not,' declared Afua. 'A partner at Sullivan and Ball, that's quite something.'

'Compared to my usual nothing, you mean?'

In the darkness, Buzzy was conscious of Afua's elegant little frown. 'When are you going to see him again?'

'Never, most likely! It was just a silly dance, and I only did it because *you* made me.'

'It was at least three dances, and I saw him give you his business card at the end. You'll back me up, won't you darling? Tell her your boss is smitten.' Marcel was staring out of the window; now he startled Buzzy by looking at her with coldness, even fury. 'You should be careful.' He gripped the door rail of the black cab tightly and it occurred to Buzzy he'd probably had a lot to drink.

Afua squeezed her hand. 'Don't listen to him, he's just jealous.'

'Are you sure it's all right for me to stay at yours?' Buzzy asked, relieved it was too dark in the taxi for anyone to see her blush.

'Oh, definitely,' said Henry.

'You can relax,' Afua added. 'Sherard's in Barcelona.'

And yet Buzzy has to be careful, as a shift in perspective can easily transform Celia back into Dorothea. Wonderful as her new South Ken address is, it's a shame to have to keep it a secret. Neither the owners of the property nor her parents are strictly speaking aware of her residence. Buzzy told the latter she was moving in with her friend Abi, who lives in a converted warehouse off Kingsland Road, which has made her mother worry incessantly about the safety of night buses in Hackney.

She is also wary about the Henry situation, for all that she's grateful to him for rescuing her from suburbia and for his now regular visits after teaching sessions with his mentee. He won't laugh off the arrangement with the house as youthful cheek, and so neither can she, and however much she resolves to be a perfect house-sitter, or reminds herself of the Saudi family's apparently vast wealth, there remains a lurking guilt.

Henry's constant consideration for others – explaining both his generosity in giving Buzzy the use of the property and his terror at the impropriety of having done so – is mostly very endearing, like his belief, easily mistaken for dullness, that it would be too self-absorbed of him ever to talk about something that actually interested him. And if just occasionally he can come across as a little saintly, perhaps there will be less of that from now on. Somehow it would be typical of Henry if, by accepting his offer and entering into his debt, it was *she* who was deflowering *him*.

As for Philip Devereux, it's true that he gave her his card, saying she should call him about some George Eliot letters recently acquired by the British Library which, being a patron, he could arrange for her to look at privately. The offer left her both flattered and confused. Why did he leave it like that? He must have known she couldn't call him, even if she wanted to – and as to that, she's unsure of her own mind. He *is* handsome, and being with him *was* a thrill. But how much of that thrill was retrospective, in light of Marcel's reaction in the taxi? And if Afua thought there was the vaguest chance he was really jealous of her and Philip, would she have joked about it?

'You must be looking for Henry.'

The boy (what is he, nineteen, twenty years old?) is the first to avert his gaze. Buzzy is conscious that since *she* is the real intruder it should be the other way round, but finds herself – perhaps it is his baseball cap and black jeans, his shady adolescent slouch – assuming an attitude of cool understanding of his bursting in on her, and is surprised at the ease with which she inhabits the role.

'Is he, like, around?'

Buzzy is on her feet now. The boy is half turned from her, facing the door frame. He is tall, she thinks, for an Arab; in profile his long nose, with its cavernous, rather distinguished nostrils, points upwards at the tip.

'He was here but he dashed off to check on his father,' she lies. 'Apparently the poor man's got a terrible diarrhoea bug.' Then, brightly, 'Shall I call him?'

The boy shakes his head.

'I'm Buzzy, by the way.'

44

'Oh,' he says, as if faintly interested she would think he was interested. 'Abdul.' He was stopping by to check what time he and Henry were leaving for Stratford-upon-Avon this afternoon (she reassures him the trip is not cancelled), and had let himself in. From there the conversation doesn't soar. He hasn't heard of Antony and Cleopatra, either the historical figures or the play they are going to see. Switzerland was 'boring'. He notices she is holding *Middlemarch*, which, it transpires, Henry has suggested as Abdul's first set text. Asked what else is on this reading list, he replies, '*Vanity Fair*?' And after a laboured pause, 'There's another, it has a question for a title?'

'Not *Can You Forgive Her?*'

'Ya, I think that's it.'

Trying to be helpful, Buzzy suggests he talk to Henry about starting off with something shorter and more immediately engaging, like *A Clockwork Orange* or a Roald Dahl short story. Abdul nods without giving the impression of straining to remember her recommendations. She sits down again on Henry's bed, suddenly tired of his loitering presence in her room. Too late Buzzy realises the pose is over-suggestive, and is annoyed with herself, since she feels a silly urge to impress this spoiled rich boy with her superior worldliness. In the end she gets rid of him in the conventional English manner, by asking him if he would like some tea.

The intruder (2)

Tired from New York, from the flight, from the harrumphing surliness of her taxi driver (but why should she hear about his brother-in-law's pub?), Daphne is looking forward to climbing into bed and watching *Newsnight* with a bottle of white – New Zealand, of course, she is strangely loyal on that point. For once, she may even have the whole house to herself. Sherard is in Barcelona – no, Paris – finding works for his show, and Afua normally stays at the Barbican with her boyfriend on Friday nights. As for Henry, he emailed to say he was taking his Arab student to Stratford-upon-Avon. He didn't mention what they were going to see – not *Othello*, if the boy has any sense, but that's not a question she feels like dwelling on right now.

The hallway light is on, but this is usual practice: they don't like to advertise when the house is empty. The tidiness of the kitchen, on the other hand, lends weight to the theory that she is alone. 'Hello *hello*?' she calls with a measure of uncertainty lacking when she stood before the packed NYU lecture hall and began, 'Thank you, Camille – now *there's* three words you don't hear very often . . .' Marta has left a risotto in the fridge, which Daphne takes out and briefly picks at with a fork before deciding she isn't hungry. She puts it back, leaving behind a few globules of rice that have fallen onto the counter.

On her way to the wine cellar, she pauses instinctively by the neat pile of unread *Guardian*s at one corner of the kitchen table. She casts an expert eye over today's edition. The news of the $800 billion US government bailout is already familiar from the *New York Times* on the plane, so having scanned the masthead she has a quick fillet of the comment pages and G2. There is nothing in there from any of her more serious rivals, though in the letters section someone with a name she doesn't recognise has written something on the United Nations Day for the Eradication of Violence Against Women. It turns out this was on Tuesday. She makes a mental note to bring up the subject with her so-called publicist, Annalisa, next time she sees her, especially if the shock-jock set-to wasn't picked up by the UK press. It's all very well joking that BBC producers have her number taped to the studio wall next to emergency services, but Daphne has heard the line about 'refreshing the comment pages' from more than one print editor recently. With her reputation staked on the new book, due out next month, it's little wonder she needs that bottle of Mountford Estate.

It is when she is downstairs in the basement, noticing how dusty it is and how neglectful Marta has been, that she hears, or thinks she hears, a noise on the first floor landing, and for a vivid and almost nostalgic instant she recollects the cheap slasher flicks her brother Rod used to watch, curtains drawn against the Christchurch sun.

Georgian houses groan with age sometimes. Nevertheless, she treads a little more softly on her way back up the cellar stairs, trying to remember which lights she switched on while walking through the house earlier. The kitchen looks identical to how it did thirty seconds ago, but the gleaming surfaces and bulging red Aga have a newly inscrutable, if not inhospitable, feel to them, as though some sort of retribution were being exacted for their being so unloved. Then upstairs she definitely hears a door close. She eases the largest knife from the rack by the sink, the shaking blade so enormous it renders the situation vaguely comical.

More creaking, this time from her own feet moving over the hallway floorboards towards the bottom of the stairs. She remembers Afua never actually confirmed that she'd be with Marcel tonight; it was just an assumption that hardened into a fact in Daphne's mind because it was what she wanted. Even so, she doesn't call out Afua's name before starting up the stairs, or turn on any more lights, or lower her knife.

47

The first floor landing appears to be dark, but as Daphne nears the top of the stairs she finds that light is in fact leaking from a bedroom. It's Afua's, she realises, feeling more foolish than relieved, and very slightly annoyed with the girl for not giving any forewarning of her presence or coming downstairs to say hello.

'Is that you, love?' she calls. 'I didn't know you'd be—'

Afua's empty room is so neat and organised! Books are not strewn everywhere but tidily shelved, starting with Althusser and ending with Weber (it was Daphne who suggested she study Archaeology and Anthropology). Yesterday's clothes do not lie in a heap on the floor. Her shoes are in a row declining from leather boots to summer flip-flops that bear, Daphne notes with a flicker of disapproval, the red Prada stripe on the heel strap.

Out on the landing again: 'Love?' The original sound was that of a door shutting, whereas she found Afua's bedroom door half open. At the other end of the landing, beneath the bathroom door, there is a sliver of light. This is puzzling, because Afua has her own en suite, which Daphne checked and found empty. She can't in fact recall Afua using the main bathroom at any time in the last nine years. She notices how light she feels, and how much her heart wants to stay pumping.

She creeps towards the bar of light. At the last minute she abandons the softly-softly approach, rapping the door with the handle of her knife and shouting '*Who the fuck is in there?*' There is a shuffling inside the bathroom, the light-strip broken in places. A few seconds' silence and to her relief the loo flushes: it seems an unlikely act of propriety from a violent thief. Unless they are insane, it occurs to her as the door opens.

It is Marcel. He is wearing a suit and tie, and his face has recently been splashed with water. He looks at the drooping knife with dispassionate concern – even with slight regret, it occurs to Daphne, that finally something interesting was about to happen.

'*Christ* you gave me a scare.' The relaxed slumber in front of Paxman is now a remote fantasy; she is so wired she will be lucky if she gets any sleep at all tonight. 'C'mon, let's go down stairs and have an enormous drink.'

He's been staying here with Afua the last few days. He didn't realise Daphne was getting back tonight and is terribly sorry to have frightened her like that. Afua is running late, but they are going for dinner at the Albion if Daphne would like to join them.

They take their glasses of wine and the bottle to the ballroom, as the family jokingly calls it: a gallery with French windows and few places to sit, so that visitors find themselves obliged to admire the artwork. She realises they haven't entertained any guests in here since the party back in September, then wonders if you can call Marcel a guest. She decides she can.

Daphne slumps into the small sofa and, in the absence of any nearby chairs, Marcel perches at the other end, his ankles elegantly crossed. He wants to know about her trip. Where in Greenwich Village was she staying? Did she know that Willem de Kooning lived nearby? How was the symposium? She is surprised to find he is familiar with the anti-feminist reading of *Sexual Personae*. He read an article somewhere, is his offhand explanation. 'Speaking of books, when is yours coming out? Afua and I are impatient to read it.'

Ignoring the question, she asks him to put on some music, 'something soothing'. Marcel crouches, frowning, by the glass case housing the Bang & Olufsen and Sherard's smallish CD collection; just as Daphne is about to tell him to Jesus forget it, he finally makes a choice. He refills their wine glasses and for a while they sit listening to the piece's caressing opening.

Ambitious little fucker, she thinks, her tiredness returning from the wine. She has never fully understood why Afua chose this prissy boy, who never stays the night when there are others in the house and whose milky skin is always hidden from view. Even now, the top button of his shirt remains determinedly done-up underneath his tie. She finds this an obscure insult, the assumption that she'd like to steal a peek and his pleasure in denying her.

'The *Moonlight Sonata*,' Daphne says, rather pleased, at least until she notices Marcel's faint smile, and realises her need to identify such a well-known piece of music is embarrassingly common.

49

'Beethoven dedicated it to his pupil, a teenage girl with whom he was apparently in love.'

Is the blandness of his delivery a little too consummate? It occurs to Daphne that ever since opening the bathroom door, from his reaction to the knife to his unlikely interest in feminist theory to now his choice of music, Marcel has been privately mocking her. Perhaps it's just her irascible mood, making her imagine things. 'I wouldn't mind if he was, you know.'

'Pardon?'

'In love with his pupil. Henry, I mean.'

'I see. But I don't think he is.'

Daphne watches him take a sip, not token but not greedy either, of his wine. 'What were you doing in the bathroom just now?'

Marcel responds with a little smile intended, she surmises, to show he is mildly amused and appalled. He retrieves his mobile phone from his suit pocket; it's a message from Afua to say she is five minutes away. A solicitous crease appears on his forehead. 'I worry that she works too hard.'

'She says you work pretty hard yourself,' Daphne replies. 'Or is it not the same if you're a man? But you're right: she's giving a lot to Merton and this job; it's the sort of chance that comes along and you just have to grab it and keep holding on. Afua knows that.'

When Afua comes in, poised but shiny-eyed from battling Tory-supporting journalists, Daphne suggests she be rewarded immediately with some wine. They all drift through to the kitchen. Accepting the glass but not taking a sip, statuesque with fingers coiled through Marcel's hair (he is sitting on a chair, legs crossed, but might as well be lying at her feet), she describes how the Treasury has been dealing with the fall-out from the pre-budget report and, specifically, the announced increase in the top rate of income tax for high earners, the first of its kind since the nineteen seventies. The media instantly declared the death of New Labour, causing panic in Number Ten (the reaction in Number Eleven, she adds wryly, was more sanguine). Merton was sent out onto the airwaves to assure the electorate, with Afua briefing the same behind the scenes, that the rise was a direct response to a global crisis, quintessentially New Labour in its pragmatism. 'He was so imperturbable! You should have seen Andrew Neil when Alec asked him if a traditional left-wing administration would be announcing a tax exemption on foreign dividends.'

'If Andrew thinks this government has any left-wing tendencies, traditional or otherwise,' says Daphne, 'he's more of a moron than I thought.'

The speed and lightness (those perfect teeth!) of Afua's smile reminds Daphne that she has carelessly breached a family principle. On political or ideological (including artistic, in the case of Sherard) matters, they tend not to criticise each other out of recognition that, occasional nuances aside, they are all pitched against the forces of conservatism.

'Do you know,' asks Afua, 'who Max Hastings compared the chancellor to in today's *Mail*?'

'No, but I *really* don't give a fuck what that man has to say . . .'

'A "Stalinist commissar"! It's easy to argue we're not socialist enough, Daph. But you have to remember the relentless *context*, what we are up against every day.'

Daphne has a feeling, the thrilling element of which instantly fades, of behaving ill-advisedly. 'I know how the British media works, my darling: I've been part of it for longer than you've been alive. And I don't object to this government not being socialist. I know it never claimed to be that. It's the fact that it's not even social democrat.'

The other two are watching her, more curious than hostile. *What are they doing in my house?* she wonders. Sleepy solitude, watching TV in bed, was all she'd wanted for this evening.

'It's just you were in favour of it at one time, weren't you? The idea of combining economic efficiency with social justice.'

Daphne realises in a moment of cruel epiphany that this is how everyone will receive *The Prodigal Sister*. They won't see her retraction of the third-way feminism she's famous for espousing as nuanced or novel, a rare example of Keynesian humility, as

51

encouraged by the book's epigraph ('When the facts change, I change my mind. What do you do, madam?'). They will see it – of course they will: what on *earth* was she thinking, she who claims to understand the British media so well? – for what it very possibly is: a ridiculous volte-face, for which she will be lovingly and eternally derided. *Michael Foot's 1983 election manifesto was famously called 'the longest suicide note in history'. At 520 pages, Daphne Depree's latest work* . . .

Perhaps she could call Cathy, her agent, right now, and cancel everything. But that would also be career suicide, albeit of a less spectacular kind. Besides it's probably too late. The book's release date is scheduled for early in the new year, less than eight weeks away. Review copies are already in circulation; the publisher's advance already spent. There is to be a whirlwind of interviews and literary festivals and book tours in the UK, Europe, North America, Australia and New Zealand . . . Of course she won't be doing them. She is finished. Angrily she wants to know why no one warned her, when she announced the project, that it was an awful idea? All right, not the idiot publicist, but Cathy, Sherard, Afua – Henry even? Would she have listened if they did? Did they, in fact?

'Yeah, look I didn't mean to criticise you, love. I'm just jet-lagged and grouchy.'

'Of course you're exhausted, we completely understand,' says Afua, who comes and slides an arm round her, allowing Daphne to rest her head on her shoulder. 'What's that doing out?'

She looks up and discovers Afua observing the enormous knife lying on the empty surface, near the stray bits of risotto. In the relentless context, it looks rather foolish. Before she has a chance to respond, Marcel says, 'That was me. I had difficulty with the wine bottle; a piece of the cork got stuck.'

'Oh,' says Afua, turning to him in surprise. 'Darling, you should have told me.'

He offers to open a new bottle. 'Shouldn't you two be at the Albion, having dinner?' Daphne objects. 'Don't hang around on my account. I intend to go straight to sleep.'

'But you can't – I haven't asked about your lecture yet! Anyway, we're so late for dinner it hardly matters any more. Does it, darling?'

For her sake as much as his – Daphne really is exhausted now – she gives an abridged account of the NYU symposium. She is surprised at one point to catch the usually tiresomely courteous Marcel let out a small but unmistakable yawn. The little shit, she is sure, is letting her see that he covered for her with the knife and saved her from appearing foolish in front of Afua only because right now, watching her grasp how easily he has outplayed her this evening, is the more satisfying humiliation. What's more, he's done all this for no greater purpose than to try to relieve his boredom.

Later, at the front door, she shivers as she waves them off: Sherard will murder her but she's given them the keys to his Figaro. As they pull away Afua winds down the window. 'Sweet dreams, my darling! Oh by the way, your brother Rod left a message. I think he said he might bring the family over for Christmas. Sounds fun!'

9

The complete works of Elizabeth Price

Untitled (Mysterious Entity) (2003)

Like some half-caste lust of confused origin,
Fruit of the cypress tree next to the grave by the sea,
Like the rabid progeny of vagrant and Penelope,
Untethered, vile, consumed from within,

Comes still the night, starry-eyed and love-struck,
Cursed and kicked and out of luck.

A, B, C (2004)

Pythagoras is lost – yes – I can see clearly now,
Infinity separates A from C.
The line, drawn, stands proud and erect,
Love and structure, love as structure.

Under the microscope, discontinuous points.
A. Sea. Of. Silence. Separates.

A Kiss Before . . . (2005)

Lips pass over leaving
wheat stubble fire raging.
The wounded image
screams
and dies, admitting nothing.

Historia de una gotita (2007)

Relámpago violento caribeño
ilumina puerco que pasa:

suave testigo espectral
de vertiginosa nada.

Cielo en llamas se refleja
en sola gotita de rón.

¿Doloroso paraíso, dulce instante,
real maravilloso, a dónde fuiste?

Story of a droplet

Violent Caribbean lightning
illuminates passing pig:

gentle spectral witness
of vertiginous nothing.

Burning sky reflected
in single droplet of rum.

Dolorous paradise, sweet moment,
marvellous real, where did you go?)

IO

Soho

The commuters scurry across Charing Cross concourse to catch their departing trains. Charlie Wynter is waiting where he said he would be, by the Platform 6 barriers, earlier than arranged (Buzzy knows because she is one minute early herself) but looking nevertheless a little uncertain, as if nagged by a feeling that he really ought to be getting on a train since that's what everyone else is doing.

Buzzy is back from Kent after a day of unsuccessful bonding with her mother. They went to Bluewater, which was a terrible idea. For different reasons they both hate shopping malls: Buzzy finds them depressingly devoid of anything she wants, while her mother is assailed by potential purchases everywhere she looks (the Christmas shopping has been dealt with, as usual, in the previous January sales).

Realising that she was going to be early, Buzzy got off at Waterloo East to complete the journey on foot via Foyles, where she passed a happy twenty minutes making a mental note of all the books she would buy when she had some money, and secretly measuring her taste against that of her fellow browsers. She's relatively pleased with her plan, which involves going to Terroirs for some wine and maybe a few cheese-based hors d'oeuvres. The good thing about this venue is there's no option of a drawn-out, expensive meal, but neither will Charlie (whose text-message suggestions to meet up she has been fending off since returning from Argentina) feel he's been fobbed off with just a drink.

What she hasn't anticipated, after kissing him on each cheek and realising, while thinking what a bitch she was as she spoke the words, that it really *was* quite nice to see him, is discovering that the stranger next to him is his girlfriend, Fiona Bodham-Whettam, whom he's brought along because he thought it was 'time the two of you met'. Although Buzzy gives the girl credit for being notably larger than her, she can also tell Fiona is the sort of person who if you told her with an air of modest finality you were a poet, would immediately ask what sort of poetry you wrote. As well as the crafty absence of prior warning on Charlie's part, Buzzy objects to his suggestion that she and Fiona 'must' meet each other. This surely implies an exaggerated level of intimacy, given their relations only ever amounted to the odd coffee after lectures. And if the hint of some sort of romantic past with Charlie were not intended, there is the even more insulting suggestion that Fiona is on display to *her*, as if Buzzy were some sort of spinsterish aunt whose approval was being sought.

If Charlie, who is a strange mix of cold Aryan looks and puppy-ish neediness, really wants to know what she thinks of Fiona, perhaps she ought to take him aside after he says 'We could do that . . .' about the Terroirs plan and grins guiltily at Fiona, who it transpires can't stand the food there. Anyone who objects that much to a plate of *saucisson sec* and *bleu d'Auvergne* must be unhinged on some level. Instead, Fiona suggests an Italian restaurant a little further down the Strand that Buzzy has walked past many times and on each occasion marvelled at the effort it went to to accentuate its awfulness.

Because of the roar of the traffic, it's difficult for the three of them to keep up a conversation as they walk to the restaurant. Feeling unpromisingly sulky, Buzzy drifts far enough from the couple to exclude herself from their self-conscious chatter. It's pretty clear that right now they're feeling as though they've said everything they want to say to each other, possibly for the rest of their lives, but this isn't going to be allowed to diminish the essential smugness they feel in her presence. She sees that her role will be to elicit from them, as if it mattered to her in the least, how long they've been seeing each other and what their holiday plans are and generally to provide them with maximum opportunities to deploy the first person plural, so that by the end of the conversation, feeling a recharged sense of unity and sentimental from the alcohol, they can reflect on their good fortune, especially when you look at poor Buzzy.

Working herself up with such thoughts into an increasingly black mood, she finds her face tensing into a grin as soon as she enters the trattoria, as if to compensate for the décor and to emphasise that she doesn't look down on the other people who eat here. At least they're given a table by the window. Buzzy sits under a painting of Vesuvius that seems to have been painted by a child and watches more fortunate people stroll into the Savoy.

The waiter brings them menus; his skin is so dark he must be Sicilian or perhaps Corsican. He asks in a tone of fathomless indifference if they would like anything to drink. 'Shall we try a bottle of wine?' suggests Charlie, and Buzzy is relieved when Fiona readily agrees. 'You choose,' she commands, which prompts a flustered, 'Oh, ah . . .' from Charlie, who studies the wine menu in panic until the waiter rescues him by saying, 'Is nice the *vino da tavola*.' 'Great, let's have that then,' he gushes as he snaps shut the leather-bound menu, and then flushes when the waiter gives him a now-I've-seen-it-all look and asks if *signore* prefers the bianco or the rosso. 'What do we think, perhaps the red? Yes, the red, please.'

Buzzy pretends to scan the menu with intent, further delaying the moment when she will have to talk. She is conscious of Charlie panting next to her. She offers him a bread stick, wondering if he might not prefer her to throw it. Finally he cannot bear it any more. 'Well this is nice.'

'Isn't it? How's the accountancy going?'

'Great thanks, yes. Well a bit dull, and quite stressful, but I don't want to moan.'

'Is Charlie moaning already?' Fiona asks without looking up from the *primi piatti* page. 'Is anyone having a starter?' The question is addressed with steely nonchalance to Buzzy, who was hoping they might go straight to the main course. Shortening the meal by fifteen minutes, she now realises, will mean the lifelong hatred of Charlie's girlfriend.

'Actually, I was thinking of skipping it.' There is a short and terrifying silence. 'But if you guys are keen, I'm sure I could . . .'

Charlie is nodding vigorously. 'We could, couldn't we? I mean, why not?'

The waiter returns with the wine and Buzzy waits out the ritual of the tasting like a passing cramp. They give their orders. Fiona requests the *bruschetta*, which Buzzy also wants, though whereas in other circumstances she would have gone along with the latter's incorrect pronunciation, a riled competitive spirit forces her to pronounce it *brus'ketta*. She speaks quietly, half hoping that Fiona will not hear the 'k' sound, but contorting his features the waiter asks her to repeat herself.

After the ordering is finished, Charlie, who is oblivious to the fact that war has been declared, asks Buzzy about Argentina. His blue eyes are so guileless that her voice is absurdly choked at first, and this allows Fiona to interject that she too has lived in Argentina, working for the *Buenos Aires Herald* during the year-abroad component of her modern languages degree at St Andrews. Very soon, Buzzy is hearing all about the inadequacy of her journalism course in Cardiff last year and the stress of her present job as a sub-editor for a well-known diary column. Buzzy dutifully asks which newspaper, and smiles tolerantly on hearing it's the *Daily Mail*, but the minor triumph is lost under a gathering dread that this real writer, or at least someone who is paid to think about words, might at some point ask what she does herself.

The problem with her life, Buzzy decides, is that its recent triumphs – the Kensington address, the flirtation with Philip Devereux, finally loving *Middlemarch* – are only visible from a certain perspective. The conventional onlooker sees only the desolate landscape of the (illusory) Hackney flatshare and lack of job or steady boyfriend. This would not be such a problem if most of the people she knew were not fairly conventional, and if she didn't in the end care a great deal what most people thought of her. In that sense, she admires Marcel's and Afua's disregard for anyone who does not amuse them or further their ambitions. Bores aren't actively shunned, of course; they stay away by some sort of subconscious agreement and, if they don't, Buzzy's friends will be slyly charming unless it turns out being rude is more diverting. They pursue what is appealing, and Buzzy pursues them, and she can't therefore complain – part of her actually relishes it – when they do things like forget her birthday or embarrass her with beer bottles. The exception is that they tolerate Henry, or at least Afua does.

'So tell me,' Buzzy says, 'what are the two of you planning for Christmas?'

By the time Buzzy has finally said goodbye to Charlie and Fiona (she lied and said she had a party to go to), her Celia self has slid so far from reach that any reason to be cheerful is not immediately accessible. For a start, it's eight thirty p.m. on a Saturday evening and she is alone. The thought of going back to the mews house with nothing but her book for company is depressing, as is the fact that she doesn't want to meet up with anyone, not even Marcel, though she can afford to believe this because it's so hypothetical, that he might be free at this stage of a weekend and that if he were he might call her.

Detached from the atmosphere of successfully proceeding intoxication, she wanders back down the Strand and considers what to do with herself. Might the National Gallery still be open, she wonders? She is sure someone was telling her about a late-night opening they'd been to recently – Henry, was it? From nowhere, the idea has become overwhelmingly attractive: she *must* do it, despite her traditional belief that wordless art forms are only serious to the extent that they are taken seriously by great writers, even when they do not, like the sort of thing Sherard Howe collects, actually advertise their lack of seriousness. Her particular craving is to find Seurat's *Une Baignade, Asnières*. The colloquial English title of *The Bathers* is much better, she feels, since the bovine solitude of the figures themselves feels the only thing capable of giving her comfort just now.

It's clear on entering Trafalgar Square that the National Gallery is shut. She walks right up to the front steps anyway, feeling the victim of an elaborate hoax that includes the redemptive possibilities of painting. 'At least I tried,' she is tempted to say as she passes a pair of community support officers wide-eyed before the heady communing of tourists and beggars and winged suburban youths. She crosses the road towards St Martin-in-the-Fields and the Chandos, where a pint of own-brand lager is enormously cheap for such a central location.

Inside the pub the air has a sweet, pre-thunderstorm smell. Even if she manages to fight her way to the bar and get served, the seats round the perimeter are taken and the middle has been cleared to resemble a makeshift mosh-pit. It's a challenge to drink a pint gracefully at the best of times, and she doubts even Afua could pull it off while being jostled by shaven-headed louts. She makes a swift exit, convinced that despite the deafening noise levels the entire establishment is fascinated by this decision and what earlier failures must have led up to this point.

Buzzy finds herself continuing up St Martin's Lane. On the radio recently, she heard researchers describe how decisions are taken by unconscious brain activity before the mind is even aware of making itself up. Always out of the loop, she reflects self-pityingly. She passes the English National Opera, where something called *Riders to the Sea* is playing. She is trying to see who wrote it when she hears a soft hovering voice say, 'Hey, er Buzzy?'

Turning in the direction of the sound, half thinking she must have imagined it, she is confronted by Henry's pupil. He is standing on the entrance step of the ENO, smoking a white-filter cigarette. A fabulously fitted leather jacket adds an illusion of tone to his upper body (it seems particularly cruel that teenage boys should not even *want* to be that skinny); underneath it the collar of his pink dress shirt has been popped but at least the baseball cap is gone, exposing a jumble of recently-washed curls. A rolled-up programme is stuffed into the pocket of his dark jeans.

'Oh, hello, Abdul.' To distract from her annoying blush she asks, 'Are you with Henry? Is it the interval or something?'

Abdul nods sombrely, despite the absence of other operagoers milling around. He seems to be registering her presence more deeply than on the last occasion, and his brown eyes no longer slide automatically to the ground when she looks at him.

'How is it, any good?'

'It's about a man who wants to sell some horses,' says Abdul, in a manner that suggests this is not considered very noteworthy in his part of the world. 'Are you going somewhere?'

'People usually are,' she replies, and laughs to dispel the cheap sarcasm. Now he has started she doesn't want to put him off the business of asking questions. Her instinct is to repeat that she has a friend's party to go to, but she decides this recent habit of lying about aspects of her life is increasingly impractical and she needs to draw a line somewhere. (Earlier she told Fiona she was helping Alain de Botton research another book on Proust, and can picture her even now debunking this claim via a simple Google search.) 'Though as it happens, I'm not actually going anywhere in particular. Well, towards Soho I suppose, for a drink.'

'Isn't that in New York?'

'I think there's a SoHo there too.' Buzzy represses her belief that it can't be much more authentic than the Eiffel Tower in Las Vegas. Together with not telling the truth, she must stop being snobbish about things she knows nothing about. 'Hasn't Henry shown you *anything* of London?'

'Only the cultural bits,' Abdul says, with evident regret.

'But Soho is *full* of culture; I barely know where to begin!'

'Perhaps,' he ventures, with a hint of immodest reticence, like the demureness that is simply an expectation you will ask him about himself, 'you could show me? If it's nearby, and you're going there anyway?'

'Um . . .' Buzzy remembers she is quite desperate to have a drink, and also not to have to walk into another packed bar alone. While it's true Abdul is not a conversational maestro, at least he's not going to tell her he's dating a producer on the *Culture Show* or that he's just had a short story accepted by *Granta*. 'Perhaps I *could* point one or two things out en route to the mojito you're going to buy me.' (She's also remembered she has no money.) 'But what about your opera – won't Henry be very annoyed with us?'

Abdul shrugs, as much as to say one might as well wonder whether pets have souls. 'We can always text him to let him know where we are.'

The tour of Soho is by mutual consent an abbreviated one. Buzzy's calves are aching from padding up and down Bluewater earlier in the day. What's more, her knee-length navy overcoat was chosen specifically because it was not unflatteringly padded, which means it's hopeless at keeping her warm. Nevertheless, walking up from Cambridge Circus she shows him Greek Street, valiantly pointing out that Becky Sharp, the heroine of *Vanity Fair*, lived with her father in one of the garrets. Going on his reaction she decides not to bother with Hazlitt's and they cut straight through to Dean Street, where she recounts how, during the war, Charles de Gaulle wrote or gave an important speech at the French House. She is bogged down in an increasingly dubious history of Vichy France when on Wardour Street they pass the Floridita, a Cuban restaurant on the site of the old Marquee Club, and she breaks off to mention that Pink Floyd and the Rolling Stones played there in the sixties. 'I've heard of them,' Abdul says, at which point Buzzy smiles tightly and suggests perhaps they have earned themselves a drink.

The bar that she picks at random is in fact more of a club, the entrance a downward-slanting neon walkway. The bouncers half-heartedly query Abdul's age as they size up his expensive leather jacket and the probable funds at his disposal. The interior is so classically seedy that she is transported back to Odyssey and other teenage haunts – all smoke and mirrors and disco lights that cut through the empty dance floor as if searching for survivors. Where it's a little busier, at the bar area, girls in sequined dresses dart like quicksilver. Though the guys with elaborate tinted fins are missing, her past nevertheless floods into the present. The feeling is less one of transcendent liberation than limited amusement that she's engaged in Proustian field research after all.

They find an empty table with two stools and Abdul volunteers to get the drinks; Buzzy has mixed feelings about the fact that he sounds as keen at the prospect as her. The mojitos he returns with taste like sweetened swamp water, but there is definitely rum in there, and Buzzy can feel it fortifying (at last!) her interest in the exterior world.

Partly in response to the snogging couple at the next table, she finds herself studying Abdul. He seems determined to appear nonchalant despite the vigorous slurping going on and she wonders how far he would be capable of keeping this up. Actually they may find out if they stay around long enough: already Soho seems to be asserting itself, the drunkenness of the passing and mainly provincial trade giving way to a deeper, more imaginative insalubriousness.

'Why did you leave Switzerland?'

'My aunt wanted me to.'

'What did your parents say?'

'It's my aunt who decides.'

'Where does she live?'

'Different places. In Dubai now, I think.'

'And she disapproved of your lifestyle in Switzerland?'

'Ya, I guess.'

'Why – what did you do?'

Abdul shrugs. 'Shall I get two more of these?'

Buzzy feigns surprise at her almost finished drink. 'That went down quickly.' Ignoring any thoughts of aunts, she adds in the same breath, 'Sure, why not?'

He leaves his leather jacket on the stool and saunters off to the bar, which has suddenly become very busy, lazily untucking his pink shirt as he goes. Buzzy has hardly been left alone for two seconds when she hears an approving voice in her ear: 'I see what you mean.'

'Panos!'

'If anyone should be surprised, my dear, it's me.'

'No, I'm just having one of those days when I keep bumping into people,' she says, inwardly wincing at being discovered in a Soho bar after having claimed to be ignorant of Heaven.

Fortunately Panos is distracted. 'Does he speak English?'

'Yes, of course he does.'

'You don't know how lucky you are. If it's not that it's drugs or – does he steal from you?'

'If anything it's the other way round.'

Panos, looking as much as ever like Rubens' swollen Bacchus, regards her with new respect. 'You'll introduce me, of course.'

'If you like. But I have to say I really don't think he's available in that way.'

Panos smiles as if listening to the opening sally in a complex negotiation. 'I've heard that before. Now tell me, you greedy girl, what has happened since your intriguing encounter with PQSD?'

'Who?'

'Devereux, of course!'

Buzzy rolls her eyes delightedly. 'I *wish* people would stop going on about that.'

'There has been much discussion, as you can imagine, about this *Turmoil* exhibition. Everyone thought he was above that conceptual rubbish. Mind you, it is rather bold; one has to give him that. Did you put him up to it, my dear? Or perhaps it was the *charmant* Marçel? I gather his girlfriend is somehow part of the Howe clan.'

'I couldn't possibly tell you.' Buzzy has no idea what he is talking about, but feels a lurching seasickness at this suggestion of Marcel existing outside of her presence.

'Here comes our boy; perhaps I should find a stool. I always think it's best to identify one's prey before one gets too drunk. It's tiresomely complex to find someone who is exceedingly handsome and not *too* stupid or insolent. Sometimes the effort is almost, well . . .'

'Like looking for a needle in a gaystack?'

'Indeed,' he observes sharply. Inexpert vulgarity is not to be encouraged, she sees.

'Everyone is very friendly here,' Abdul remarks when he gets back. Buzzy looks over towards the bar area: the barmen, who must model for fitness magazines during their time off, have removed their shirts.

'Far too friendly, some of them,' says Panos with an avuncular smile. 'I should watch out if I were you.'

'Abdul, this is Panos.' She wonders if she is going to have to witness another hand-groping episode from Panos, but Abdul is too busy draining his second mojito and looking round the room.

'Do you come here often?' Panos shouts over the music, which has been turned up a notch. Abdul ignores the question. On the dance floor a group of girls are surrounding an athletic-looking black guy on a podium, screaming at him while he heaves himself up the pole like a fireman who has forgotten something, his clothes perhaps. The girls scream even louder and he obliges with a dazzling ultra-violet smile.

Buzzy, torn between incredulity and admiration at Panos's self-confidence, explains that Abdul has only recently arrived in London.

'I see – AND WHERE DID YOU COME FROM?'

'Lugano,' answers Abdul.

'Oh Lugano, I know it well. Wonderful place. I said, WONDERFUL PLACE.'

'Do you like dancing?' Abdul asks Buzzy shyly.

'Not really – I'm pretty awful at it.' Had Buzzy been chatting to a man she wanted to impress, she would have been annoyed at Panos's ungentlemanly failure to contradict her. 'In places like this, I normally end up kissing some random guy to spare myself the indignity.'

'YES, I STAYED AT THE *VITA NUOVA*.'

'Sounds better than the *Inferno*, anyway.'

'I like it,' declares Abdul. Looking relieved to have got this off his chest, he attacks his drink.

'OH YOU KNOW IT, DO YOU? WORTH EVERY PENNY ONE FEELS.'

'I think he was talking about dancing,' Buzzy tells Panos, who is turning an improbable shade of puce.

'What's he talking about?'

'He wants to know if you've heard of some hotel called the *Vita Nuova*.'

'Of course I have,' says Abdul. 'My family owns it.'

Realising the game is up, agony jostles with ecstasy on Panos's features, or would do if there were not ample room for both. He needs a drink, he announces, no longer shouting.

Abdul is suddenly interested. 'We're having mojitos.'

'I don't think he'll be back,' says Buzzy when they are alone again.

Abdul receives the news philosophically. 'Do you know a new club called La Collezione?'

'Afraid not. Where is it?'

'Mayfair somewhere, I think. Some of my brothers are having a New Year's Eve party there.'

'When you say some of your brothers, how many do you have?'

'Lots; I can't remember exactly.'

Buzzy is starting to wonder if Abdul is not slightly drunk.

'Anyway, you can come.'

'Thanks. I mean I've got a few options already,' she lies, 'but I'll think about it.'

'Ya, cool. Bring friends if you want.'

Would Marcel and Afua find this an interesting prospect? She hasn't heard either of them mention anything about New Year's Eve. It's possible they have been too busy to make any plans yet; either that or she is being excluded from them, a possibility that would require several more mojitos to confront.

'Is Henry your boyfriend?' Abdul asks, definitely slurring.

'Of course he isn't, what a silly – oh my God, Henry!' She grabs her phone from her bag: no reception. She has completely forgotten to text to let him know Abdul is in her custody.

I I

Festive cheer

'Everyone is doing it,' Afua is saying, with the confidence, Henry feels, of one who will never have to do it herself. 'It's nothing to be ashamed of.'

They – Afua, Buzzy and Henry – are sitting in Starbucks on Upper Street. Henry has joined the girls, fighting his way through the maze of Christmas shoppers and jutting chair legs. At one point he almost tripped and spilled cappuccino over the lap of a shattered young dad; the latter watched this happen without flinching, content, it seemed, that there was nothing Henry could do to lower his day any further.

Henry sets his coffee down as far as possible from Afua's MacBook, and parks his Borders and HMV bags by his feet.

'Sorry,' he says, vaguely wondering if what he meant was 'hello'.

Afua blows Henry a kiss without looking up from her laptop. 'Hi, darling, we're having a look on Guardian Soulmates. I was just saying to Buzzy: practically all the fast-streamers at the Treasury met their partners here, and don't at all mind people knowing.'

'They might have had reservations about logging on in the middle of an incredibly busy coffee place.' Buzzy smiles conspiratorially at Henry and blood rushes to his face, rattling his windpipe on its way past.

'This one's good-looking,' Afua says. '*And* he loves literature.' She angles the screen to give Buzzy a better view.

'You're right, he is handsome,' Buzzy concedes, 'but not enough to make me want to finish *Gravity's Rainbow*. I told you, there's always a catch.'

'There's always a catch if you're always determined to find one. Hen, what do you think?'

Henry does not dare answer this truthfully, that he feels a complex mixture of relief and emptiness on watching Buzzy reject potential suitors. 'I suppose you could agree to disagree on Pynchon; there might be other books you both enjoyed.'

Buzzy sighs. 'I'm just disillusioned.'

'How can you be disillusioned before you've given it a try?'

'I've seen enough profiles to know that there's always a disappointing detail that exposes the fantasy. Look, at least this guy is considerate enough to include it in his name: Des Demona. Is that meant to be funny? The lack of effort is just . . . I saw one earlier where the guy described his favourite pastime as "whining and dining", with an "*h*".'

Afua closes the MacBook. 'It's a stupid typo. Who cares?'

'And don't get me started,' Buzzy continues, 'on the men who think you'll go weak at the knees at their preachy little aphorisms. You know: "Some day your whole life will flash before your eyes. Make sure it's worth watching."'

'That does sound tiresome. How are you, Henry?' Afua irreproachably asks. He sees that she is displeased by Buzzy's refusal to be helped.

'Fine, thanks,' he replies, neglecting to mention the odd twitching that has started up in his right index finger. It's probably anxiety-based, and his fear of others realising how anxious he always feels is partly what makes him so anxious.

Afua squeezes his leg. 'Did you get your Christmas shopping done?'

'Yes. I struggled a little with what to buy Jake, but I think I got there in the end.' To Buzzy, he explains, 'Jake is my eight-year-old cousin.'

'Afua mentioned your New Zealand relatives were staying. What did you buy him?'

'A Jenga set. I was quite fond of mine when I was younger.'

'Oh, I used to love Jenga! Who did you play with?'

'Myself, mostly.'

69

'I think it's a lovely present, Hen,' Afua says.

'What did you get Jake?' Buzzy asks her.

'Some computer game Marcel chose. It looks disgustingly violent; I'm sure he'll hate it.'

'Not at all,' Henry reassures her, though he wonders if on some level Afua knows full well how much Jake is going to love her present. 'He seems extremely attached to his little PlayStation.' He has come to view Jake's electronic toy as emblematic of his complete failure to connect with his cousin. He once heard his father observe that the problem with children is that they've rarely had dinner with Chomsky, and without apportioning any blame to Jake he would admit to understanding the sentiment. What on earth is there to say? For his part, Jake seems to have a Sherard-like contempt for Henry's inability to string two passes together on *FIFA 2009*.

'On the subject of our guests, I suppose it'll be lunch fairly soon and Granny P does hate to be kept waiting.'

'Doesn't Henry want to finish his coffee?' Buzzy asks, taken aback by Afua's uncharacteristic regard for the time.

'It's all right, I forgot that I don't actually like the way they make it here. But thanks.'

When they're outside, Afua and Henry wish Buzzy a happy Christmas, and Afua asks to be remembered to her parents.

'They're always asking after you,' Buzzy assures her as they hug.

'How sweet of them! You must get them up to town in the new year. We'll have lunch or something.'

'They'd love that – thanks, Afua.'

Henry says he hopes Buzzy hasn't come all the way up to Angel just to see them. He can't be sure that Sherard has forgotten his ban, so doesn't dare invite her back to Canonbury Lane. He's relieved when it turns out she plans to drop by some friends who live off Essex Road.

'Very mysterious,' Afua remarks, plunging Henry into instant despair: it hadn't occurred to him that these friends might include a romantic interest. 'Speaking of secrets, when am I going to see your Kensington pad?'

'On New Year's Eve, if you come to Abdul's party. We can hardly let poor Hen go by himself . . .'

Henry is not at all sure that *Abdul* should be going to this party, let alone him, let alone his friends. Yet, witnessing Buzzy's enthusiasm, he represses both the minor suspicion that he should tell Louise Ryder about the party and the major one that he wrongly accepted the job in the first place and then wrongly offered the mews house to Buzzy. In his pocket, his finger twitches like a fish suffocating in air.

'I told you,' Afua says, just a fraction impatiently, 'I'll speak to Marcel when he's back from Brussels. Of *course* I'd much rather be with you guys. But we *have* kind of said yes to this dinner party.'

'We could always just stay in, the four of us?' Henry offers weakly.

'And play Jenga?' laughs Afua.

They take a taxi to Canonbury Lane. Henry dislikes wasting the money but he knows if he objects Afua will insist on paying.

'Is that the turkey for tomorrow?' For a moment Henry is genuinely not sure if the enormous plucked bird on the kitchen table is real or part of the *Turmoil* exhibition, various pieces for which are scattered about the house.

Sherard gives him and then the turkey a distracted frown, as though weighing up which was more likely to say something sensible. 'If he starts another sentence with "back home" . . .'

Daphne groans. Among other things (the forthcoming publication of *The Prodigal Sister*; the arrival of Granny P this morning), managing her difficult brother and Sherard's contempt for him seems to be taking its toll on her energy levels.

'It's just that you're opposite personalities,' Afua says from by the Aga. 'Gorgeous carrots, Marta. They taste of honey.'

Marta, on her knees checking the joint of lamb, thanks her curtly.

'I don't disagree,' Sherard says. 'For example, my phrase of choice would be "home back".'

'Two more days and then they're gone. Really I wish you'd be more of a man about it.'

'Are feminists allowed to say that sort of thing?'

'Gee, I dunno, I better check the rule book.' Henry has noticed Daphne's accent has become more obviously Kiwi since her brother and his family arrived, but (*plus ça change*) isn't sure what role irony has in this. 'You might give Rod more credit for liking Paris,' Daphne continues. 'You're always going on about what a philistine he is.'

'Oh, I do give him credit. I don't believe for a second he actually admires that Haussmann Disneyland. How could he? I mean, it's not *actually* Disneyland, is it? But at least by pretending he's showing more imagination in his efforts to irritate me.'

'I don't know why you imagine no one has anything better to do than irritate you. Rod is a pain in the arse; some people just are – your mother, for example. There's no sinister plot behind it. He's also my brother and it's bloody Christmas tomorrow.'

'I'm certainly not ruling out the possibility of bloodshed.'

Afua suggests one thing they definitely ought to rule out is hiding in the kitchen all day, and anyway she loves hearing about life in New Zealand. Henry wonders if Sherard is going to ask why in that case she has been so absent since their guests' arrival a couple of days ago, but he is too busy drinking a stiff gin and tonic (he has mixed it himself) and instructing Marta to bring the drinks tray through in exactly five minutes. 'How do you say "five minutes" in Polish?'

'*Pięć minut.*'

'A pinched minute, even better.'

When they troop into the ballroom Janet is again blinking nervously (she can't get over her luck at getting at all Rod's money, according to Daphne) and Rod says, 'Her Majesty was looking for you lot; she's not happy.' Not for the first time since his relatives arrived, Henry wishes he was wrapped in warm waters, the door of the second-floor bathroom firmly bolted. It's a fantasy he has surrendered any hope of actually realising, since good manners suggest he confine himself to quick showers until he no longer has to share his bathroom with the Deprees and Granny P.

With Abdul temporarily in Jeddah, he has lost his excuse to escape to Kensington. He wishes he could explain to Buzzy, who frequently says how guilty she feels about his constant journeying up and down the Piccadilly Line, that it's become a great solitary pleasure, like bathing. He loves to be buried in the belly of the city: sometimes, inevitably, he thinks of Buzzy, reliving their previous encounter or absorbing the happiness of knowing he'll soon be in her presence again; at other times he thinks of nothing at all or reads the books that he will later discuss with Abdul (so far the discussions mainly take the form of Henry relaying the plot). He is 500 pages into *Vanity Fair* and finds it slightly disappointing after *Middlemarch*, having struggled to warm to Becky Sharp ever since she threw Miss Jemima's dictionary out of her carriage window. Not that Henry deludes himself that he is free to take moral positions any more.

He grips his right hand with his left to conceal the twitching finger.

'Henry,' his mother says, 'could you go and find Granny P and tell her we're having drinks before lunch?'

'Tell her to bring the drinks down while you're at it!' Rod's abrupt and rather frightening laugh causes his face to stretch dramatically, like a hound on a chase.

Granny P is not in her room. Absurdly, he even checks under the bed, though this is the least Granny P-ish place she could possibly be in. Eventually – he checks here last because it's normally out of bounds – he finds her in Sherard's study.

'There you are. Have those ghastly people gone yet? I was telling them about Nancy's darling pug – Molly, you know – and they kept insisting that she should eat it! Why else would one keep one, they asked me. Wait a minute, you're not Sherard – you're Henry.'

Although her diction is as precisely enunciated as ever, it's apparent to Henry that his grandmother is intoxicated. Moreover, this has been achieved by helping herself to her son's prized bottle of Balvenie.

73

'I think it's a misunderstanding Granny, because they're from New Zealand. When you say "pug" they hear "pig".'

'Well, they ought to bloody control themselves.'

It seems sensible not to persist with this topic, so he relays his mother's message about pre-lunch drinks in the sitting room.

'I don't see why I should come trotting along because you have emerged from your hiding places. By the way,' she adds, 'someone knocked on the front door earlier, looking for Sherard.'

'Did they say who they were, Granny?'

'I don't remember the name. He claimed he was a writer.'

'What did you tell him?'

'That I very much doubted it. I have only met one writer in my life – Mr Powell – and my husband owned a publishing house. But what about you, Henry? I gather you have abandoned the law. What is *your* occupation now?'

Bracing himself, he explains that he is a private tutor to a Middle Eastern pupil.

'I see,' she says, making it clear from her tone that she does not. 'I thought Sherard found you something to do in government.'

'Oh, Afua took the adviser job. Did no one tell you? She's doing frightfully well at it.'

'What is frightful,' she says, after a glacial silence, 'is the egotism of your parents. They never gave a thought to what that awful comprehensive was going to do to you. Sherard loves to recount the horrors of boarding school, but we sent him because we cared to make a man of him. There's a difference.'

Henry wishes he was allowed to take possession of his own failures, so he could bury them with as much dignity as possible. 'I'm not conquering the world,' he says with rare conviction, 'but I never wanted to. If anyone's to blame, it's me.'

Granny P, the real barrister manqué of the two of them, will use this admission against his parents as evidence of his stunted self-esteem; all Henry can hope for is that she won't do so over lunch.

'I mean, Afua went to the same school as me, and look at her.'

'I rather think there are enough people doing that. I'll take your arm,' she says, preparing to rise from Sherard's armchair.

He helps his grandmother, discreetly retrieving her half-finished Balvenie and placing it on a copy of the *Liberal Review* on the desk. Underneath the glass, an unnaturally golden Bernard-Henri Lévy reminds him of the leonine solicitor Buzzy danced with at the ball.

'Do you ever wish you could start all over again, Granny?'

'Certainly not,' she says, as if he were offering.

Sherard's habit of offering his fitness obsessive brother-in-law a drink each time he refills his own is starting, Henry senses, to get under Rod's skin. With the lamb not yet served and Sherard brandishing a second bottle of Domaine de Chevalier Rouge, he counters that in New Zealand alcohol is considered 'kind of a lower-class problem – especially for the Maoris, poor buggers. Not that we're so conscious of class back home.'

'Marx aside, I suppose the only virtue of class consciousness is that one tries to avoid mentioning it,' Sherard replies. He fills Granny P's glass almost to the brim again, prompting Henry to wonder if he ought to alert his father that she wasn't entirely sober to begin with. In the end it's Daphne, whose sidelining of Marx in *The Third Sex* is a sensitive subject, who gives her husband a warning look.

'Don't pay any attention to Sherard,' she says. 'He's snobbish about snobs and any non-snob who hasn't had to transcend their snobbery like he has.'

'Now which ones are the Maoris?' asks Granny P, evidently considering this the lesser conversational abyss.

'What's a snob?' Jake asks, aping the last speaker's incuriousness. He has abandoned his roast lunch in favour of *Prince of Persia*.

Henry is relieved when this dangerous question goes unanswered. 'The Maoris are the indigenous people of New Zealand, Granny.'

'Because it's the Mayans who invented chocolate.' Granny P nods after speaking, forgiving herself this momentary didacticism.

'The *Maoris* probably have a few sorrows to drown,' Afua remarks, 'given their land was taken from them in exchange for measles.' The sharpness of the observation is softened by her delivery, which sounds as if she is charmed by something, even if what that is isn't immediately apparent.

'I wouldn't feel too bad for them. For a start your boy is wrong, they're not the indigenous people of New Zealand. *They're* no longer around because the Maoris ate them. Second, at school those guys were real nasty bullies' – Rod holds his hands up in a don't-shoot-the-messenger gesture – 'sorry to say, but it's true.'

'I don't remember you getting bullied much in school, Rod,' Daphne says, perhaps prompted by the sight of his large ex-builder's palms.

'All right – the blokes I got into fights with.'

In the last decade Rod has made the transition from construction worker to property developer and as a result, contrary to expectations not least of his first wife Lynne, has become rich. His frustration that Daphne and Sherard and Sherard's mother should feel, respectively, hostility and disapproval and pity towards self-made millionaires is to Henry understandable. It may be especially galling in the case of Sherard, who sold most of the share he inherited in Howe & Steen in the early eighties for what Henry imagines was a fairly significant sum. Sherard has kept the family seat on the board and a minority interest in the company, but it will not be passed on to Henry, to the latter's and probably everyone's relief.

Janet is laughing hysterically. Henry assumes this is because someone told a joke while his thoughts were wandering. In puzzlement he surveys the surprised faces around the dining table: even Jake has provided a rare sighting of the lower half of his head.

'I'm sorry . . .'

The fit, or whatever it was, seems to be petering out. Her mouth puckers and relaxes in a settling rhythm before emitting a final shriek which makes Henry jump.

'I'm so sorry,' she repeats. 'It's really not funny, but no one ever told me the Maoris came along and, you know, just like that, ate – the – locals.'

The last words are timed with the contractions of her stomach, which Janet, now bent double, hugs with both arms.

'I suppose that is quite humorous, up to a point,' says Sherard during a pause.

'Are you sure it wasn't their chocolate they were eating?'

'No, Granny, you told us it was the Mayans who had the chocolate.'

'For God's sake, stop blathering and give her some water,' Daphne snaps.

Henry obliges, wondering if Janet herself knows if she is now laughing or sobbing.

'It must be the jet-lag,' Rod says. 'She doesn't laugh at anything normally, do you love? Certainly nothing *I* say.'

'Perhaps she should have a lie-down.' Spoken by Afua, the words have an immediate quieting effect. They also have an invincible logic, and it's swiftly agreed that a short nap might be the best course of action. Janet slinks out of the dining room, avoiding eye contact with everyone. No one remarks on it when Jake gets up and follows her out.

'I'm sure she meant to thank you, my dear. The lamb is nearly as good as what they give us at Sunnyview,' says Granny P, seizing the opportunity to insult a fellow guest and her hostess simultaneously.

'Yeah, not bad, Daph. Was it New Zealand?' Rod asks with an air of deferring judgement.

'Yes – I expect so. And how *is* Sunnyview, Granny P?'

'Hellish, thank you for asking.'

It is fairly common, Henry understands, for there to be a difficult adjustment period when elderly people move into a residential home. In this case it seems to have been the other way round, with Sunnyview telephoning Sherard roughly once a day during the first fortnight to complain about Granny P. She has been accused of bullying fellow residents; smoking in the residents' dining room; assaulting a carer; refusing to take her medication; and excessive drinking. Noting that she has not at any stage demanded to leave, Sherard has concluded that she is having the time of her life and no longer returns Sunnyview's calls. When Henry mentioned to Buzzy that Granny P was apparently romantically linked to a resident called George, she gave him a funny look. 'To summarise,' she said, 'spiteful eighty-year-old with alcohol problem bags herself boyfriend. Are you *trying* to make me cry?'

Sherard asks Marta, who has come in to collect everyone's plates, what they can expect for pudding.

'Cantuccini.'

The word is laden with defiance, as if she will not stand for public accusations, what with four extra guests in the house and a turkey looming large in the kitchen.

'Don't forget the vin santo; we'll need six glasses. Also I think we'll take it in the ballroom.'

Afua's BlackBerry is vibrating on the table. 'Sorry, I've got to get this.'

'Of course, love,' says Daphne.

Outside the dining room, the throaty tinkle of Afua's laugh can be heard as she heads for the stairs. Somehow Henry knows she will not be back. He cannot help stealing a glance at his watch (not yet half past two), and wishing he were somewhere else.

12

The Member for Great Grimsby

Alec Merton wakes as usual around five a.m. It's Boxing Day, so for once he doesn't need to spring out of bed. On her side, Rebecca is grinding her teeth, a habit whose power to annoy has waned so much that he almost misses it on the Mondays to Thursdays he's away from the constituency home.

Alison will be up sometime in the next hour, wanting a feed. He grins at the memory of Sherard Howe telling him the problem with other people's children is they've rarely had dinner with Chomsky. Imagine if he'd said that to the *Daily Telegraph* hack! (Or something equivalent, anyway; he's not a Chomsky man himself.) As it was, his aide, Afua, lightly wondered if in future he should avoid using the word 'terrifying' in the context of his kids. This was followed by a condescending little smile when he replied that many parents would be apprehensive at the prospect of a fourth boy, which was of course the adjective he should have used. He sulked a bit after that, pretending to make progress with his red box while Afua chatted to the driver. As much as anything, it was his absurd resentment of being left out of the conversation which made him abandon the pretence of reading through his papers and ask her in a friendly, almost pleading tone what it was he was supposed to be voting on that evening.

Certainly, no one could accuse Sherard of squandering the freedom denied ministers of the Crown to speak and act as he pleased. A man like that of course has his enemies. But he's only ever been supportive of Alec, and without asking for anything in return, apart from suggesting that he hire Afua. Even that has been helpful, on balance.

79

Then again, balance is part of the problem. Afua's manner of crossing his private office, the subtle motion of her hips as if, frankly, she were carrying water on her head, provokes an unprecedented surging of his blood. He is not quite sure what to do about it; he can hardly go to his GP and complain of an ancestral urging to combine his genes with a woman other than his wife. Actually he probably could clear some space in his diary to do that, and Dr Herd would probably prescribe him something rather fun; only the banking system is teetering on the verge of catastrophe and, as City minister, he's supposed to be doing something about it.

He's in the middle of a fantasy involving Afua and a conference hotel room when his mobile telephone starts ringing. Grabbing it from the bedside table, he hurries away from his wife and baby daughter, neither of whom is pleased to have been startled awake. The withheld number and early hour alert him to the possibility that it might be the prime minister. When he presses the answer button and announces his name, he's uncomfortably aware of standing on a chilly landing briefed only in the sense of wearing underpants.

'Pinter's dead then.' The voice is laconic and northern. It's also chewing on something.

'Oh, it's only you Keith, thank fuck. I thought it might be the Supreme Being for a minute there.'

'You thought God was calling you.'

'No, not Gus O'Donnell; it's far too early for a civil servant. I mean the PM. Anyway, who's dead?'

'Some playwright or other. Hated Tony it seems.' It's clear Keith's usual disdain for members of the arts world is partially mitigated on this occasion. 'But that's for the culture secretary to worry about,' he continues, still munching on what Alec is now sure is a bacon bap. 'He's next on my list. As far as you're concerned, a think-tank is saying the economy will shrink 2.9 per cent next year. For some reason this wasn't on the grid. Gordon's hopping, obviously, and we need you to do the media.'

'Oh perfect,' Alec says, 'what am I looking at?'

'We'll see how it plays, but assume *Today* then News 24 and Sky, maybe *World at One* for lunch. You'll probably be done by the afternoon, especially if they go big guns on the luvvie bloke. You in Grimsby?'

'No, Putney, so that's easier at least.' Ignoring Keith's sardonic silence he asks, 'Does my SpAd know about this?'

'I think someone's calling her now.'

'Jesus. Let's hope Humphrys had an extremely boozy Christmas.'

'Some chance.'

Alec hopes his heavy sigh, mostly for Rebecca's benefit, doesn't stretch credulity. He never normally makes a fuss about media duties, whatever time he's called or however little notice he's given. His work ethic and numerical understanding of the world are among the reasons for his harmonious relations with Number Ten, the main one being he hasn't screwed up yet. Alec is well aware that he has enjoyed a charmed political career to date. The Brownites tolerate him because he's their man in the Treasury, with access to the increasingly unreliable chancellor's inner thoughts. The Blairites forgive him for keeping his distance because he's Home Counties and telegenic, not to mention rich (Tony himself never took it personally, of course). His future leadership rivals won't touch him, at least not yet, because they recognise that if they don't want a financial crisis to become an electoral one they need to establish their narrative – tsunami from abroad, Labour leads global response – in the public consciousness immediately. Alec knows they know he is the best placed to do that, with his rational manner and commercial *savoir faire* that even the Tory papers treat with a measure of deference.

After he leaves Keith to ruin the culture secretary's Boxing Day, he returns to the bedroom where his wife is groggily breastfeeding Alison. 'I need a quick shower. There's a car coming to take me to White City in twenty minutes.'

'Why this time?'

81

'I must inform the nation,' he answers while rummaging for a fresh pair of pants, 'that the economy will definitely grow in 2009 in spite of all serious research and evidence and for that matter common sense suggesting otherwise.'

'Yer pick yer topics,' she says in an unconvincing Scottish accent. This is a private joke. When they had the Browns to dinner recently their son William, inspired by a radio programme he'd heard with his mother, solemnly informed the prime minister he was penning a novel about the life of Spinoza.

'When will you be finished? Don't forget your parents are coming for lunch, and you know they always arrive early.'

'Lunch is off the menu, I'm afraid.'

'You mean you're leaving me all by myself? What the hell are we going to talk about?'

'I don't know darling, anything.'

'The boys will be so disappointed. Why is it always you who has to push the boulder up the mountain?'

'Modesty forbids me from answering that.' He kisses her on the forehead, which is clammy and smells of baby. 'I'll be back as soon as I can. Now I better dash in that shower.'

'. . . and poor old Alec here has been wheeled on – I've been listening to him all morning, actually – to claim something that simply defies all common sense.'

'The shadow chancellor feels sorry for you, Alec Merton.'

Alec laughs good-naturedly, as if he hasn't noticed the smug BBC anchor is implying, with the unnecessary translation, that he has learning difficulties.

'Look, my friend George is trying to suggest that I'm only saying the economy will grow next year because that's the chancellor's view. You know, I would advise him to waste less time reading the political tea leaves and more time thinking about why since the start of this global crisis he's made the *wrong* call to oppose taking Northern Rock into temporary ownership; the *wrong* call to oppose the recapitalisations of RBS and Lloyds—'

'I'm sorry, I know it's the season of goodwill, but the financial secretary knows that's absolute nonsense. The key point here, just before you interrupt me . . .'

Outside Millbank Studios the shadow chancellor is in conference with his gilded young entourage, whose glares Alec has no difficulty ignoring. 'God that presenter is hopeless. What does he get paid, do you think?'

'It's an interesting question; if you decide to raise it with the culture secretary you can count on my full support.'

'George, I'm starting to think you might be my guardian angel. Though just at the moment the man in question is too busy pretending he ever got through a Pinter play without falling asleep.'

By his side, Afua has a method of exerting her presence that resists description. As far as Alec can detect, nothing actually happens except a flexing of her willpower. Osborne notes it too. 'How are you, Afua? I do miss your *Liberal Review* blog.'

'I'm surprised to hear that,' she replies coolly, 'I don't recall saying anything nice about your colleagues.'

Alec has a feeling the shadow chancellor's boyish guffaw is at his own punch line, which he has decided he doesn't trust Afua enough to say out loud. 'Let's hope we've seen the last of each other for today, Alec.' With that he turns back to his CCHQ apparatchiks, who have probably never received a compliment like Afua just has and appear more seething than ever.

Millbank is unusually free of traffic. Afua is about to call for a car but Alec claims he could do with some fresh air, despite the threat of rain. He suggests they walk the short distance to Westminster. It's an intentionally vague plan; he's been released of his media duties and is wondering how to make the most of the situation. He's pleased to note that Afua doesn't seem especially keen to rejoin the Howes – she has discreetly and rather charmingly hinted that Daphne's brother is over for a rare visit that she doesn't want to intrude on – and there's an adolescent uncertainty in the air as they approach the Palace of Westminster. Or at least there would be, if she wasn't on the phone to a friendly *Mirror* hack, asking if he'd seen or heard Alec today having to firefight Number Ten's mess. He's a little angry at her for telling the reporter about the grid cock-up – what if it got back to Downing Street that the leak had come from them? – and betraying the private conversation with Osborne by reporting, not entirely accurately, that he'd let slip the Tories' intention to slash BBC funding. But his irritation is hard to differentiate from his stirring excitement, and besides, one has to admire the girl's sharp political instinct.

He checks his own phone: two text messages from his wife. The first reads 'TWINS IN RAGE W/ SAM FOR BREAKING WII. S SAID F WORD B4 GRANNY AND GRANDAD. OTHERWISE STRUGGLING 4 CONVO. WHEN U BACK?' The second is more succinct: 'HELP'.

When Afua has finally finished with the *Mirror* man, Alec announces that after the morning they've just endured he's earned himself a drink. 'Feel like joining me?' he adds casually, hoping it sounds like an afterthought.

'Is this the Christmas party we never had?'

He scans Afua's face for clues to her intended meaning. Is she (ever the helpful aide) developing his pretext? Or is she chiding him for his employerly bad manners – or simply digesting his offer, considering its implications, buying herself time? Beyond mild mockery, her expression is indecipherable. He hopes his laugh is not too imploring: 'Precisely!'

The problem with his suggestion, which he knows will set the terms of trade between them – or rather everything not to do with trade – is that there is really nowhere to go for a drink in Westminster. Yet he feels that, to keep things sufficiently casual and to avoid the risk of her changing her mind and returning home or, worse, meeting her boyfriend, they shouldn't wander far from the immediate surroundings. As quickly as this occurs to him, a resolution presents itself. Why not go back to his office in Portcullis House? It's much more private than the Treasury, where who knows what press officers or ministers might be lurking, and he keeps a small drinks tray there for when he has to hang around for late-night votes. By the standards of the current front bench he's considered fairly clubbable, if not immune to the occasional faux pas, such as when he got Simon Cowell confused with Simon Callow, the narrator of his *Aeneid* audiobook. Football, on the other hand, has proved easy, being essentially a matter of league statistics that he can absorb without effort and, more interestingly, of patterns and probabilities. Having a successful fantasy league team buys him a degree of slack (though no more than that) from parts of the backbenches when he gives an interview to the *Spectator* or is spotted at the Cinnamon Club lunching with Lord Saatchi.

'The Red Lion might be open . . .'

As expected, Afua raises a quizzical eyebrow. He can't imagine her in a pub outside the Islington gastro variety, and perhaps not even then.

'. . . or we could go back to my office at PCH? I keep a stash of drinks for when the occasion demands.'

'I hope you're not talking about whisky.'

'There's also gin and vodka. I might even have some tonic.'

'All right then,' she replies with a brightness that's somehow both stiff and shrivelling.

The guard inside the entrance to Portcullis House is black and Alec is surprised when he barely glances at Afua as he waves them through the security detectors. By contrast, the guard at the main desk eyes them both suspiciously even after they identify themselves, the blank appraisal of his green MP's pass in itself an unjustified humiliation, when Alec's name has appeared in the national papers almost every other day over the last few months and he spends his whole life traipsing from *Question Time* to *The Politics Show* to *This Week*. He needs to get himself on Andrew Marr's sofa, that's the sort of thing more normal people watch.

'Just nipping up to fetch some papers,' he explains, with the sort of grovelling faux bonhomie that his working-class colleagues would never feel the need to display. On the plus side, this casual dissimulation, which Afua allows to stand (the reception area is silent and his voice is naturally strong; there's no chance she didn't hear it), contains an arousing hint of complicity. By the time they are up in his office he feels his confidence starting to return.

'What'll it be, gin or vodka or both?'

'Vodka, I think. With plenty of tonic,' she adds, just as he's wondering how much he can ration the latter without drawing attention to the fact. He's unsure what to choose for himself: he doesn't think he's quite able to match Afua's choice, which only someone who takes the most fleeting pleasure in alcohol would go for; but nor does he want whisky on his breath if Afua wouldn't approve of it. He decides on a G and T.

'Nice view,' she says, a little subdued on account of the drizzle and darkening sky.

'I forgot you haven't been up here before. These corner offices are hard to come by: it's good to know all the after-dinner speeches in the chief whip's constituency weren't a complete waste of time.'

'Time is something you must be acutely aware of in this office.'

They both glance up at the face of Big Ben. It hangs outside the window like a stage moon, adding unhelpfully to the stilted atmosphere.

'It's bloody irritating actually, that constant gonging.'

Alec slumps into a chair (standard issue House of Commons green), loosening his tie (claret red, of the kind favoured by the PM) a little showily. Afua hasn't finished wandering around the room. She stops in front of the solitary framed print, Monet's foggy depiction of the Houses of Parliament, and sucks her cheek in a fraction. He spies the expression and laughs. 'I haven't had much time to think about the décor. Just don't tell Sherard.'

'I better not, or he might rescind your invitation to the *Turmoil* private view.'

'Is this the great Sullivans exhibition he's planning? I should put in an appearance, though I can't quite make out why Sherard is mixed up with them.'

'How do you mean?'

'I was going to say they are famously arrogant bastards' – their sly exchange of looks registers in Alec's loins – 'but in an old-school-tie sort of way. It's funny: people – well, most of my constituents – imagine that that's what the City is like in general. But it's not really, not these days. The Sullivan and Ball chaps are sort of the last of the Mohicans.'

'Sherard went to school with Philip Devereux, so that's the connection. Though I think Sherard finds him as repulsive as he does the concept of an old boys' network. He's also my boyfriend's boss – Philip, I mean.'

'Good luck to him,' he says, taking a long sip of his gin and tonic. 'I did hear somewhere that Devereux was a monster, though I met him once and he seemed pleasant enough. Obviously there's an ego. He's supposed to have designed that enormously complex defence merger last year.'

'A dual-listed structure, the first of its kind,' she recites, 'I've heard a lot about it.'

Alec is heartened by this hint of ennui at her boyfriend's conversation, even if he has only discovered it by being equally dull. He wonders, if he had her now, against the closed door, if the first thrust would be heightened beyond reach for having imagined it so intensely in advance. Would he even be able to wait long enough to get her knickers down (if she wears them: it's impossible to tell, though not for want of trying, through her black suit trousers) or would he have to draw them with two fingers across the soft coffee mounds of her buttocks? Perhaps he wouldn't even have the patience for that, and would try to push brutishly through the fabric of her underwear. He feels an urgent need to hear her gasp as he did so.

At last she decides to sit, cruelly choosing a spot on the sofa as far as possible from him. She leans back and rests her head against her palm. Wearing what looks, with its silk lapels, a little like a man's dinner jacket over her black blouse, she resembles a survivor of a marvellous party.

'I thought I did all right today,' he says casually, though in fact he's slightly stung she hasn't yet commented on his performance.

She laughs. 'Are you fishing for compliments? You were fine. Except for that last interview; you were too friendly with Osborne.'

'Perhaps. But he was right – the idea that the economy will grow next year is risible. Getting very cross with George Osborne might impress the backbenchers, or Number Ten for that matter, but I have a reputation to consider.'

Afua smiles and he notices – it's surprising he hasn't done so before – how she uses it to show her anger. 'It's a mistake to treat him as your equal – or friend, even. If you're right and the country is in for a prolonged recession or some sort of depression, then voters have to believe they can't trust the Tories on the economy. This isn't about some silly class vendetta.'

'Thank you for explaining all that. In return, could I ask that in future, if you're going to brief journalists about my private conversations you let me know first? From now on, let's agree in advance what you say off the record, in my name.'

'Of course,' she replies with affected tolerance – he knows this because of what she says next. 'Alec, you talk about your reputation. Whose support will you need after Gordon? It won't be the *Daily Telegraph*. Think about it, you're the City minister and the Square Mile – the people who nearly brought the country to its knees – they all love you. How is that going to look in six months' or two years' time? I've realised, maybe too late, that Number Ten doesn't wish you well, certainly not in any future leadership contest. Every time you go on the air at their bidding you're helping them destroy you. Your only chance is to fight back.'

Alec brings the gin and tonic to his lips too quickly, and some bubbly mixture escapes down his chin. He carefully wipes it away.

'It's funny,' she continues in a different tone, as if they were having a congenial but meaningless chat, 'Henry is reading *Vanity Fair* at the moment. He says there's a character called George Osborne, who's conceited and bad with money.'

'So there is. I wonder how I forgot that – because there's no mileage in quoting Thackeray, probably.'

'It's true, you'd never live it down.'

'Who's Henry, by the way?'

'Sherard and Daphne's son, and possibly the sweetest man in the world. Have you not met him?'

'Yes, I think I possibly have.'

Rebecca calls his mobile and Afua, knowing who it must be, waits for him to answer it with an indifference he realises is genuine. Patiently, he listens to his wife complain that his parents have still not left. When she says she would rather put her head in the oven than endure another silent round of tea, he tells her he's on his way home.

After he's hung up, Afua says, 'I've been asked if I want to put myself forward for the approved candidates list.'

'I'll support you, of course.'

'Thank you. There's a reference form to sign, but we can talk about that later.'

He sighs. 'You're a bit young, aren't you?'

'I'll be twenty-seven by the next election,' she replies, as though that rebutted his argument. 'Assuming Gordon goes for May 2010, that is.'

'Have you thought about seats?'

For a second, Afua almost looks embarrassed. 'It seems Islington South might become available. The Party would want an all-women shortlist.'

'Islington, I see. Well, you'd win it, of course.'

Is this what she accepted the drink for? To inform him that her career was headed for early success as surely as his was headed for early failure? (Because Afua, with her looks and brains and back-story – whatever it is exactly, he's curious enough about it to assume it'd be impolite to ask – will win the seat, even if the Party wasn't behind her; even if Sherard and Daphne didn't know the chair of the local association.) To think that an hour ago he was casually admiring her political instincts.

'It seems you were wrong,' he says, as they prepare to leave.

Afua, at the door, smoothing down her coat, looks politely puzzled. 'I'm sorry?'

'About realising Number Ten is out to destroy me. You weren't too late after all.'

13

New Year's Eve

'Are they even coming at all?'

Henry looks away, hurt, and Buzzy regrets snapping at him. It's not his fault if Marcel is still at his dinner party, having promised (or at least implied) that he and Afua would join them by eleven p.m., over half an hour ago. She takes a sip of her eye-stingingly strong martini and scans the VIP room for the millionth time since they arrived and were implausibly ushered into it. Her disgust at what she sees is more at the room's Marcellessness than its kitschness. *Muy fashion* they'd call it in Buenos Aires, approvingly she suspects, not that she isn't interested in the framed Anita Ekberg dress or the handsome Mediterranean bearing an Armani gift bag, to whom she smiled and said 'You're not Greek, by any chance?', earning her a cold stare – but then, as poor Panos might say, it's a bit much to expect them to know Virgil as well.

There's no sign of Abdul, which makes Buzzy worry that there are several divisions of very important person at La Collezione, each with its own room. What if Marcel is somewhere upstairs, politely declining an offer of a film role from Bernardo Bertolucci?

'It's funny,' she says, resolving to make more of an effort, having earlier batted away Henry's questions about her uneventful Christmas, 'all these preppie rugby shirts made in China so that Russians and Arabs can look like East Coast WASPs pretending to be English.' She doesn't mind showing off in front of Henry.

'It *is* funny, isn't it?' Henry agrees, his enthusiasm taking her by surprise. 'Though I suppose no more than when, in the same shirts, the English gentry try to look like the American upper class trying to look like the English middle class.'

'Do you think there are any other English people here, apart from us?'

Henry appears pensive for a moment. 'It's hard to say. The DJ, perhaps.'

They look over at the skinny bald man in his booth, expertly mixing Depeche Mode's 'It's No Good' into the Prodigy's 'No Good (Start the Dance)', unmindful of the fact that everyone's doing their best to shout over it.

'At least he's being paid. So are you, sort of. What am *I* doing here?' she whines. 'Sorry Hen, I'm being a bitch. I'll get us some more drinks and when I'm back I'll be positive and fun, I promise.'

Henry offers to take charge of the round again but she declines, not wanting to be left on her own and knowing he'll take for ever to get the attention of the bar staff. She heads first to the loos, pushing her way through the crowd, all the while conscious of the men sizing her up with grim indulgence. Reviewing herself in the lavatory mirror, she decides she hates her black dress, the slimming effect of which doesn't extend to her arms. These are not fat but nor are they exactly toned, which amounts to the same thing in a place like this. Her skin, the kind that burns at the first hint of sun, now looks greyish. She's preparing to loathe the drabness of her dark ginger curls when she's disturbed by the two girls in the cubicle behind, whose Slavic exchanges are replaced by violent giggles. Desperate not to meet two histrionic seven-foot blondes, she scurries out before the bolt can slide across and release them.

At the bar, which is busy, a black guy in a white Ralph Lauren shirt appears next to her and demands a bottle of something the name of which she doesn't catch. His accent is gently but indistinctly African. Buzzy is surprised when instead of pointing out that he's in the middle of a complicated cocktail order and in any case she was next, the barman goes off in search of ice buckets.

'You want some champagne?' he asks, noticing her indignant expression.

The barman returns with the buckets and unceremoniously pops one of the bottles. 'One more glass,' the black guy tells him.

'Actually two, please,' she corrects.

'You like Ace of Spades?'

Buzzy, who is noticing how tightly his skin stretches over his sternum, replies that she's never tried it. He pours out two glasses and hands her both.

'It's quite yeasty,' she muses.

'Is ve-ry expensive!' he says in a singsong voice.

'Oh, well in that case I'm sure it's nice,' she replies ironically, but also half meaning it.

'You want to join us? If you want, I can introduce you to my cousin.'

She follows his eyes in the direction of a bejewelled young man of roughly her age. He is lounging on a cream leather banquette, listening to an anecdote from someone in his mostly white group with a guarded smile.

'I don't think so,' she replies, thinking of Henry. 'I'm with someone. But thank you for the champagne.'

'As you want.' He launches off with a bucket in each hand like a boy at the beach.

She finds Henry flanked by Doris and Sigrid, two familiar-sounding Estonian girls. 'Apparently there is a famous Chelsea player here tonight,' he shouts cheerily, though his eyes bulge like a cow awaiting a bolt through the temple.

'A hundred thousand pounds every week,' Sigrid recites.

'It's disgusting.'

'I know!' Doris agrees. 'Frank Lampard has two times this, and never comes to party.'

Buzzy looks across at the African footballer on his banquette. Could it work? She's pretty sure she detects a certain coiled intelligence: he could teach her about football, perhaps that is interesting after all; in return she could read him *The Portrait of a Lady* in the bath. Maybe they would understand each other perfectly. 'It must seem unlikely, our little communion,' she imagines telling Mariella Frostrup on *Book of the Week*, 'but then what do bodies in space know of souls in time . . .?'

'Hey it's fuckin' midnight!' someone shouts as the DJ slides Mylo's 'Drop the Pressure' into Prince's '1999'. Henry wishes her

Happy New Year. He sounds like he really means it, which Buzzy initially ascribes to feeling sentimental from the martinis and champagne, but then realises that's only why she noticed. Overwhelmed by his goodness, by his unearned faith in *her* goodness, she kisses him on the lips. As she does so she wonders vaingloriously if, like Isabel Archer, she is not affronting her destiny by avoiding a passionless marriage to someone like Henry.

An unmistakable voice behind her causes her to break off from Henry. Her feet almost lift from the ground as she spins round to face Marcel, who has come after all.

'*Je croyais que tu m'avais abandonné.*'

'You do know that it's Spanish I speak?' She has immediately lapsed into her habit of denouncing a pleasure in case he abandons it first. As if she wouldn't make it her business to understand him! 'Anyway, why would you think that? *I've* been here all evening.'

'This is Conrad,' Marcel says. 'He was at the dinner party.'

Conrad stares at her in a wild-eyed manner. The absence of Afua is a tricky subject: mentioning her to Marcel is painful and Buzzy instinctively wants to nurture the fantasy that she's not here. But not asking after her friend will only make it more awkward when Afua emerges from the cloakroom or wherever she is. Besides, if she doesn't say anything then Henry will, and she doesn't want to hold that against him.

She discovers that Afua really hasn't come, preferring to stay at the dinner party. What's more, there's been a disagreement.

'Oh dear, what about?'

'Conrad has certain habits she doesn't approve of.'

'I suppose she's against them, now she's in government. It's probably understandable.'

Buzzy watches Marcel beautifully grind his jaw, knowing Afua wouldn't approve of her ecstasy either. There are drops of sweat at his temples that she would quite like to lick off.

Conrad, who's been jabbering at Henry and the Estonians, interrupts by throwing an arm around Marcel and saying, 'Let's go downstairs.'

'I don't know if there's much to see,' Buzzy says.

'There's a club on the basement floor; we've been down there for ages.'

'I don't know . . .' she begins, feeling the sting of Conrad's words and hoping even now that Marcel might say he's staying with her.

'Don't be boring, Doris and Boris are coming.'

'Sigrid!' says Sigrid.

'*Tu viens?*'

'I don't mind staying up here . . .' Henry offers.

'No,' she sighs, 'let's all get disgustingly sweaty and not have a conversation for four hours.'

Everything about the basement club is vile. Buzzy accepts a pill from Conrad and obeys his emphatic advice to swallow the whole thing, even though the previous times she's done E she's started with half, and knows the initial rush will be frightening. Doris and Sigrid are pretending to want to say something to Marcel while taking it in turns to put their tongues in his ear. Henry has gone off to find water for everyone.

'Mates of yours, are they?' asks Conrad.

'I've never met them before,' she replies, slightly surprised by the question. 'They're Estonian, didn't they tell you?'

'Odd,' he says, 'I didn't think they took girls.'

'*Estonian* I said.'

'You as well? I'm a Wykehamist so don't judge.'

'I don't understand. What's a Wykehamist?'

'See, you're starting already. For fuck's sake, let's get mashed and forget all that.'

They dance in silence for a while, though Buzzy is aware of Conrad's terrible urge to speak. It's a relief when Henry returns with bottles of water.

'Thanks, Hen. This hasn't been much of an evening for you.'

He assures her he is having a wonderful time.

'I don't see how you can be,' she says, a little impatiently. 'You hate noisy clubs, you hate getting drunk, and you hate the idea of us taking drugs.' She doesn't catch his answer the first time because of the pounding house music.

'I said hate is rather a strong word,' he says, trying to sound jovial.

'You don't always have to pretend to be happy, Hen – you don't have to be so *worthy* all the time!' She feels a tingling in her brain, and takes Henry's hand. 'What I mean is you're my friend; I wouldn't like you any less if sometimes you admitted you were fed up with everything, including me.'

'I will!' He smiles faintly. 'Or anyway, I'll try. You know, I have such strongly amicable feelings for you too, Buzzy. No, that's not it!' he says, sounding quite angry for a moment. 'What I mean to say is that, is that—'

'God, Hen – this pill is strong!'

She hugs him enthusiastically, then she is embracing Doris and Sigrid; Conrad next, not caring that his T-shirt is soaked through or that for some reason he addresses her as 'professor'.

'Let's go and find Marcel!' she yells at Henry. They start working their way through the crowd of dancers. Buzzy keeps seeing Marcel's face flicker across those of strangers. Some guy gives her a familiar wave, and she wonders if he too is looking at her and seeing someone else.

'How are you feeling now?' Henry asks anxiously.

This is clear. 'Like happiness is water and my head – my *brain* is the Trevi Fountain.'

They bump into Abdul. It's definitely him because Henry is shaking his hand, obviously relieved that his pupil's eyes aren't dilated and he isn't slurring. Buzzy finds that she is holding on to Abdul's hairless forearm; a spurt of serotonin has required her to steady herself. She is aware of him addressing her but is distracted by momentary nausea.

'Happy New Year!' she shouts, removing her hand. Abdul's friends are staring and she tells them what an amazing time she is having. This makes her mouth very dry, so she takes a long drink from her bottle of water.

'Aren't fountains beautiful?' she asks the nearest friend.

'They're not bad. The ones at my home, anyway.'

'Is that in Kensington?'

'No, Jeddah.'

'I would *love* to go to Jeddah.'

'You are very welcome to visit.'

'I certainly will!'

Conversation is so easy, she reflects; it's a mystery why she spends so much of her time avoiding it. A glimpse of Marcel – the real one, she is sure – darts through a gap ahead of her and she follows; there's no time to explain to Henry, she'll have to catch up with him later. She keeps her eyes trained on the back of Marcel's head, bumping into people and spilling water as she goes; at one point she almost trips over someone's handbag. At the threshold of what must be another dance floor or bar area, he looks back as the lights become stroboscopic and it's as if he's become lost in a flapping of wings. By the time they change back he's gone.

It's a bar. Buzzy finds him sitting alone in a booth, drinking lager. She slides in beside him, the way she used to in the lecture theatre. The first time she sat next to him, or almost did, was a Monday towards the end of the Michaelmas term. Arriving unusually late she took the nearest empty space, beside a beautiful brunette in pearl earrings and a pink dress shirt rolled to the elbows. On the other side of the brunette was Marcel.

Buzzy had seen him the previous Saturday night at a masked ball at Corpus Christi. He'd looked extremely handsome in white tie and narrow black leather mask, unlike the burlesque creations most of the other boys were wearing. He had the same ability as Afua at parties never to move from the same spot but instead receive a steady stream of visitors. Though there was nothing awkward about his demeanour – indeed he seemed particularly interested in whatever the other person was saying – she constantly felt he was on the verge of leaving, having not arrived, she was certain, with any one group.

Buzzy herself spent the entire time talking to Emma and Christine, a natural scientist and geographer with whom she had little in common beyond the fact that they were also single and had gone to state schools. As usual at these social events, it wasn't especially late when her friends started talking about all the studying they had to do in the morning and the cold walk back to Clare. Reluctantly, Buzzy left with them, certain she was missing out but not drunk enough to mingle with the handful of students she recognised from lectures.

So it was a shock when, as they waited for Professor Blom-Cowles to start reciting one of the *Lyrical Ballads*, Marcel leaned across the brunette, who was in mid-sentence, and asked, 'Did you enjoy the ball?'

Buzzy had the strange impression that he wanted her to pretend they knew each other, so held back from introducing herself. 'Yes, thanks. Well, sort of. I hardly knew anyone there, so . . .'

'What a shame, it was so much fun. Maybe next time introduce yourself to a few people.'

'This is Venetia,' Marcel said.

'Hi, I'm Buzzy,' she replied, to a look of piercing enmity. It was clear the other girl wanted her to busy herself with the lecture hand-out and not disturb them further, but Buzzy said, 'You must have felt at home at a masked ball – with your name, I mean.'

Venetia produced a brilliant smile. 'What a *very* odd thing to say!'

'I thought it was quite funny,' Marcel said, approvingly she felt. He was appraising Buzzy with an intensity she felt sure she'd never until now experienced.

'I haven't seen you before. In these lectures, I mean.'

'This is my first time.'

'He studies *law*,' Venetia smirked.

'Oh . . . So, what are you doing here?'

'It was Romantic poetry or Roman inheritance law. I'm considering making a habit of choosing this.'

The first Romantics lecture of the Lent term, Marcel was there again, and the space next to him was empty. Buzzy was grateful that he didn't make a fuss when she sat next to him, just smiled politely as if they were resuming an old habit. It was later, through him, that she met Afua, and then Henry.

Now, she asks, 'How are you feeling?' It's quieter here, though she can still feel the bass throbbing under her feet.

'Fine, and you?'

'Sort of amazingly happy, I suppose,' she says airily, as if, like Marcel, she finds a state of ineffable joy rather tiresome. 'How was Christmas in Brussels?'

'It was agreeable, thank you.'

'I'm glad. I thought maybe you weren't looking forward to it.'

He shrugs and Buzzy tries not to dwell on the contrast between the desultory conversation – since she returned from Argentina there is an awkwardness between them that they've yet to get past – and its ecstatic reception in her brain. By the time he says 'Everyone has reasons to hate their father,' she has forgotten what they were talking about.

'*I* don't. The absolute worst thing you could say about mine,' she says, already feeling terribly guilty, 'is that he's a little provincial.'

He laughs. 'That is the worst you could say.'

'Don't say that.'

'Why not?'

'It gives me an idea of what you must think of me.'

'Not at all – you are the most interesting person I know!'

'I'm sure you tell that to all your friends.'

'How could I, when I don't have any others?'

'You have Afua.'

'Afua is not my friend. *Elle est ma copine.*'

'Oh, I didn't realise they were incompatible.'

Marcel smiles, as though satisfied with her ignorance. The silence grows and he seems to deliberate something. Buzzy waits, unable to breathe. Eventually he finishes his drink and suggests they go and find Henry, who is probably looking for them.

14

New Year's Day

Sitting up in bed, Sherard wears a grotesque expression. 'My dear, what *did* you do to the coffee? It tastes as if someone's left one of my cigars in the pot.'

Next to him, Daphne takes a sip. It's undoubtedly revolting, as it always is when she has to make it herself. 'I haven't the faintest idea what you mean.'

Since the departure, thank God, of Rod and his frightful wife and child, she has noticed the odd phrase of hers mimic Sherard's dry public school idiom. Didn't Lacan consider language the foundation of patriarchy? She must have read his *Écrits* (in English) a quarter of a century ago, during her Great Reading Phase, so much of which seems now to be slipping from her memory. She makes a mental note to look it up later. Right now, what she could really do with is a massage, having woken up with an agonisingly stiff neck, the final stage of a migraine that began last night with lightning flashes at the edges of her vision, followed by a thunderous headache that came on shortly before Jonathan Freedland turned to her and said, 'But isn't there a chance *Israel* will split in two. . .?' It would probably be a mistake to invite Sherard to put his hands around her neck, even if such a sensual task were not beyond him. Perhaps she'll ask Afua for a quick rub with those graceful fingers of hers.

It's stress, of course – the fucking book, the month of publication having arrived as it threatened to. There are still moments, often around dawn as dry-eyed exhaustion merges with a fleeting optimism, when she can recall the conviction she felt while writing *The Prodigal Sister*: that it was to be a searing account of the ideological betrayals of the Clinton–Blair era, in which her own *mea culpa* – as the 'high-priestess of third-way feminism', in the insulting media phrase – would be seen as powerfully original and authentic. Then, as at last night's party, some ill-wishing acquaintance will ask her what it's about and Daphne is momentarily struck dumb by the foolishness of what she has produced, essentially a 500-page attack on the 400-page work that made her name. She may be quite literally her own worst critic, but others are sure to follow suit. If Daphne was, in her own words, 'muddled, misguided and naive' to declare new feminism more interested in Madeleine Albright than Marx, why should her returning to the socialist fold be seen as any more lucid or wise?

Divining her thoughts, or possibly just exacting revenge for the coffee, Sherard says, 'There was a lot of talk about your new book last night. I said you've invented an entirely new type of polemic: the *je m'accuse*. Everyone was most intrigued.'

'Ha bloody ha,' she says flatly, pretending to be absorbed by the *Prospect* article in her lap, on loft insulation and climate change.

'Well, *je m'amuse*.'

She looks over at his fat, overflowing face, his grey eyes enlivened by mockery; an act which costs her a searing pain at the base of her neck. 'There's something very odd about you this morning,' she says, closing the magazine. 'Don't tell me you're not hungover?'

'Of course I'm hungover,' he says. 'It's New Year's Day.'

But Sherard has been unusually perky lately. This is partly from seeing off Rod and Granny P but mainly because *Turmoil*, opening in early February, is coming together quite impressively. Ever since Tracey Emin agreed to contribute a work, a neon installation consisting of the phrase 'Turmoil . . . (love is)' in blue lettering, he has known, she can tell, that the exhibition is going to be something interesting for interesting people to talk about, starting with himself. Mistakenly finding herself in his vicinity last night, she heard him booming at Tyler Brûlé: 'Well, you'll come to the private view, of course. I expect Merton, the City minister, will want to say a few words about the crisis and so forth. Do you know him? Ah, Jay, I was just saying to Tyler . . .'

Evidently he is going to be unbearable, and Daphne already regrets sharing her anxieties about *The Prodigal Sister* with him. He dismissed these as pre-publication nerves, to her irritation, though knowing she would have felt even worse if he'd concurred that it was probably true she had needlessly shat all over her reputation.

It's not as if she didn't have to contend with the odd hostile response to *The Third Sex*, most notoriously from Germaine Greer, though secretly she had been rather flattered to discover women with PhDs and professorships taking her work seriously enough to want to attack it, especially as she'd felt shielded by more positive pieces (including, it must be said, in the *Liberal Review*). In public, she'd had no difficulty laughing off these criticisms, some of which were in any case faintly comical, such as the pugnacious letter in the *LRB* from an address, a Jesuit university in Battle Creek, Michigan, which Sherard refused to believe was real. This time Daphne senses it is *her* who is going to be the joke, and she wonders if Sherard is not going to enjoy her humiliation slightly, especially if followed by his triumphant exhibition.

Afua pops her head round the door – Daphne realises she must have left it slightly ajar after carrying the coffee tray up from the kitchen. Lately the girl has been experimenting with a pair of black framed spectacles: they undoubtedly accentuate her cheekbones, as if that were required.

'Hiii, you guys.'

'Ah, it's Afua,' says Sherard with brisk satisfaction, as though spotting an Old Master.

'Happy New Year, love. How was your dinner party?'

'Oh, it was fine – fun,' she corrects, with a slight wry smile from having, for once, made a minor slip.

Instead of leaving them to it – Daphne is not a prude but she is, after all, in bed with her husband – Afua reclines against the door frame. Evidently some sympathetic follow-up is required. 'Bunch of awful hooray Henrys, were they?'

'Oh, they weren't that bad, mostly,' Afua replies, mildly chastising. 'Besides it was good to meet some of Marcel's friends, or colleagues anyway.'

'Speaking of Henrys,' Sherard says, 'has anyone seen the boy?'

Afua shakes her head. 'Actually, that's what I wanted to ask *you*. Marcel left the dinner party to join Hen at a club in Mayfair, but neither of them is answering their phone this morning. I just checked Henry's bedroom and he's not back yet.'

'We are talking about Henry *Howe*?'

'Well now,' Daphne says, her amusement tinged with odd relief at the news of her son's unlikely carousing. 'I'm sure they'll surface soon enough.'

'Can we offer you some coffee, my dear?' asks Sherard, who appears entirely unembarrassed chatting to Afua in his red Liberty silk pyjamas. 'I should warn you it's quite foul.'

'Thanks, but I should really get on with things . . .'

'Not working today, surely?' asks Sherard, sternly admiring.

'Not so far as I know. But if I *do* have the day off, I should work on my shortlist application. And that's just the start, really: assuming I'm successful' – she avoids his knowing smirk – 'there are all those practical issues to consider. Do I need an agent; campaign leaflets; a team of canvassers . . .?'

'Absolutely not. Apart from anything, you'll look like the official Party candidate—'

'Which you are,' Daphne cannot resist pointing out.

'—which is not sensible in Islington. No, better to do as little as possible to advertise the selection meeting. I meant to say, Frank tells me the meeting is pencilled in for the first weekend of February. The NEC wanted it even earlier apparently.'

'Christ, they're really going to rush this through, aren't they? Ruth hasn't even announced she's giving the seat up yet.'

'Hmm,' says Afua, biting her lip. 'Early February is actually not perfect for me. One of those weekends I'm supposed to be in Brussels, for Marcel's father's wedding.'

'Well, I'm afraid you'll have to tell *monsieur le ministre* that your attendance will be *totalement impossible*,' Sherard says in his negligible French accent (Daphne, who does not have the benefit of her husband's education, always tries to get the

102

pronunciation right). 'Unless, that is, you want to give the unions time to get their act together . . .'

'Would that be such a bad thing?' asks Daphne.

A cold, curious stare from Sherard. 'My dear . . .'

'Only I've just written a book arguing that the labour movement and feminism need to reunite.' She sighs. '*Of course* I want Afua to win. But it's not thrilling to see the Party use an all-women shortlist to thwart the prospect of a trade union candidate.' To Afua, she says, 'You understand that, don't you, love?'

'I'm not sure I do, really. You seem to be suggesting it's somehow my fault if the unions can't find a woman they want to back.'

The flash of anger at this sarcasm, delivered so casually to Daphne in her own bedroom, cuts through her headache. This is followed by a calm dislike for the girl whom people frequently refer to, without Daphne bothering to correct them, as her adopted daughter. How stupid to convince herself that Afua's habitual elegant archness towards her – towards the whole family – was essentially a form of modesty, a way of acknowledging her outsider status and all the more charming for her otherwise extroverted nature. Sometimes disdain is just disdain, to paraphrase an old enemy.

With equal calm, she suppresses these thoughts. There is nothing to be done about the situation – it wouldn't be any use confiding in Sherard, whose approval of Afua is notable not by its degree so much as its simple existence. For him the question of the young girl's merit has been settled beyond doubt now that her political career is looking promising. He wouldn't thank Daphne for reopening it; would no doubt accuse her of petty jealousy. Besides, it is not only Sherard: *everyone* approves of Afua and of the way the Howes have supported her over the years, since she first became known to Daphne and her husband as Henry's protecting angel at school. (And what inspired Afua to look out for the timid rich boy two years her junior? Was it altruism pure and simple, or did she weigh up the benefits of allying herself with the Howes of Canonbury Lane?) Regardless, it wouldn't be well looked-on for Daphne to fall out with the girl.

Downstairs, the front door can be heard to open and clatter shut. Afua steps into the hallway: 'We're up here, Hen!'

'The errant son returns,' Sherard says to Daphne. 'I do hope Marta keeps a stash of fatted calves somewhere.'

They listen to Henry's heavy tread on the staircase; when he finally enters his parents' bedroom, he looks sheepish.

'Hullo everyone. Happy New Year to all.'

'Henry, you're slurring. Where have you been?'

'Yes, Hen,' Afua says, 'where *have* you been?'

Henry apologises; he has been at the Chelsea and Westminster Hospital since the early hours of the morning. Backtracking further, he explains that after the club he'd gone back to Abdul's flat in Kensington with Marcel and a few others. It turned out one of the party (Henry refers to him vaguely as someone they met at the club) had taken Ecstasy, after which he introduced himself more than once as a world expert on apes.

'*Apes*, you say?'

'Yes, he was convinced he'd just come from some sort of ape symposium.'

Sherard brushes something from his cheek. 'Are you sure he wasn't being figurative?'

'No, I don't think so. Still, I hope calling an ambulance wasn't an overreaction on my part. Conrad, the chap in question, was very upset about having his stomach pumped; they had to sedate him in the end. Fortunately he's fine now, just a little sore.'

'Well, an unfortunate tale,' Sherard says. 'I wonder if your aunt from New Zealand would enjoy it. Still, Henry, letting an over-dosing stranger into your pupil's home is an unimpressive start to the year. I don't know if Henry James got up to that sort of thing, perhaps he did, but it doesn't feel as though your life is in the ascendant since giving up the law.'

A miserable-looking Henry starts to reply, but Sherard cuts him off.

'No, I don't want to hear it,' he says, throwing off the duvet to reveal his silk-clad legs – it's always a surprise to Daphne to note how skinny they are. 'Now, I think I shall have a bath. For some quite inexplicable reason there's never any hot water in the evenings these days.'

15

Dorothea

In the end, she decides to call him. The email that began as a breezy few paragraphs has shrunk as the afternoon wore on, as each time her cursor hovered over the 'send' button she would read over the message and make a minor change or two, and this process was repeated until it became a full-blown editing frenzy in which sentences were moved around, gutted, rewritten and in many cases cast aside. The jagged lines she ends up with (far worse than her initial draft, which she didn't save) are mysteriously abrupt and informal, slightly resembling the sort of fashionable modern verse which, in the hypothetical scenario of her actually writing any poetry, she would certainly avoid. They scream, 'Reject me!'

The official explanation for getting in touch – the one she will give Afua – is that he promised to arrange a private viewing of some original George Eliot letters at the British Library, and it would be rude to ignore such a generous offer. (Having proved herself lacking in that area, Buzzy really does see the point of studying the Eliot correspondence.) If pushed, she would admit that a couple of hours in the company of Philip Devereux might not be so terrible. There are, however, certain things that she would not under any circumstances mention to Afua or anyone else. That, for example, less than two months ago she considered doing this beneath her dignity; or that even though Devereux has become a somewhat blurry figure in her imagination, and even though she never actually gave him her details, she is a little hurt that he has made no effort to contact her since their dance.

Underneath this is the fact that Buzzy has started to feel depressed about her existence in South Kensington, whose oppressive quiet now gives her a lump in the throat. She even half-heartedly raised the subject of moving out with Henry, who was against the idea, arguing it was vital she had a proper setting in which to write (he was too tactful to say away from her benignly meddling parents) without worrying about having to pay rent. The impression seems to have formed in Henry's mind that Buzzy is working on something quietly significant. Her failure to correct him on this stems mostly from the guilty knowledge that, in taking advantage of his Saudi employers by letting Buzzy stay at the mews house in his stead, Henry is sacrificing a large part of his self-respect. Even more disgracefully, she enjoys the hushed tone he adopts when referring to what he seems to imagine is a growing and transcendental pile of pages.

For all Henry's optimistic assurances, even if she were still happy there she knows she couldn't stay in the house much longer. For one thing, sooner or later – however hard she tries to remember to keep her possessions stashed in her suitcase, and make herself scarce before the cleaner's weekly visit – the penny is going to drop with Abdul. Only his narcotised state prevented this happening when they returned from the club on New Year's Eve: in her rush to meet Henry on time at the start of the evening, she had left her things scattered everywhere.

She has decided to give herself another month – assuming she is not caught out before then – as a resident of South Ken, and to use this time to apply herself to writing in a way that she has failed to do since moving in, or indeed ever. If at the end of this period her laptop screen is still blank, she will confront reality, even if that means finding an office job and moving back in with her parents, at least until she can afford to start renting somewhere. And if she *has* started a project that looks vaguely promising – well, she'll have to think of a different plan.

After the club on New Year's Eve, Buzzy found Marcel in her bedroom doing coke with Abdul. He'd gone up there ostensibly to find some speakers for his iPod, with the Saudi trailing after him. Before entering she paused for a moment outside the closed bedroom door and listened to the sound of Abdul's laugh on the other side. 'We were just talking about you,' he said, when she walked in without knocking. They were sitting in mirrored positions on the bed, facing slightly towards each other with ankles crossed. Between them was a copy of *Cosmopolitan* (the shame!) with a coiled banknote on top. Marcel gave Buzzy a clenched stare, unhappy she presumed at the unannounced entrance, but Abdul seemed pleasantly surprised by the effect of his words because he added, 'Don't worry, it was nothing bad,' and closed his eyes and grinned.

'Henry's worried about Conrad,' she announced, aiming to strike an appropriately grave note, one that didn't entirely kill the mood.

'That dude's crazy.'

'His soul is mad,' said Marcel, drily quoting the Conrad of *Heart of Darkness*.

'Seriously, he's not going to die or anything is he?'

'He's fine, just tripping a little. It's sweet the way you worry about everybody.'

Abdul said, with sly excitement, 'Don't you want to know what we were saying before you came in?'

Buzzy managed a shrug.

'Marcel saw you kiss Henry!'

She was about to dismiss this as a silly New Year's celebration. 'Why did I hear you laughing, in that case?'

'Oh, it was just something Marcel was saying – about Henry,' he added, with an evident sense of gallantry. The boys smoked in silence for a while. Abdul's fidgety gaze often came to rest on her; yet she was conscious it was Marcel who was really taking her in.

'Buzzy, have you told Abdul what you are?'

'What I am?' she repeated, already feeling a little helpless.

'Buzzy is a writer.'

'Uh-huh.' Abdul nodded expectantly, to show he hadn't entirely rejected the possibility this might prove interesting.

'Actually, there's a good story about why she's chosen this path. Buzzy, may I tell it?'

107

She was fairly sure Marcel knew she'd never told this self-regarding little confession to anyone other than him. The idea of sharing it with Abdul was humiliating, but she said nothing. He continued, 'When Buzzy was a little girl, she wasn't terribly pretty or popular.'

'How old are we talking about?'

'Perhaps nine, ten?'

Buzzy gave a nod.

'At school one day, it must have been in December, the teacher asked the class to write a story. Buzzy wrote about Father Christmas and his elves and reindeer – so did everyone, probably, but the teacher loved Buzzy's story, especially the opening, so much that she read the first sentence to the entire class. These words were so perfect, the teacher said, so wonderful and beautiful that they could have been taken from a real novel. You cannot imagine how proud Buzzy was when she was told that, in front of everyone. Her parents don't read, you see, or know anything about books. So really, Buzzy's artistic ambition, maybe even her life's quest, is to write another sentence like that.'

'What was the sentence?'

'Far away in Lapland, the snow was falling gently.'

'It doesn't seem *that* good.'

Marcel reached casually for the packet of cigarettes. 'Perhaps the teacher should have been more sparing with her compliments.'

Abdul looked blank at first; then, assuming the joke was on him, gave a defensive giggle.

'You're both right. I'm not really a writer at all. In the last six years I've produced a grand total of four poems.'

'You just need to find something to write about,' said Abdul encouragingly, perhaps wishing to make up for his earlier remark. 'And you already know so much stuff about books and history and buildings – everything really!'

'Oh, yes,' said Marcel, smiling. '*En tout cas*, the Price of everything.'

108

'You mean because that's her name!' said Abdul, and laughed triumphantly.

Buzzy laughed too, to pretend it was all harmless fun, as Abdul thought. It was sometimes Marcel's method to say something kind and then later punish her for it, and she wondered if his flattery earlier in the club, which she'd found exhilarating, was connected to him now implying that she was a classless, talentless narcissist. The comment cut her, of course, but there was something intoxicating about being so finely understood. The clarity of his perception! Anyway, was it so wicked of him to say the truth? But then, in deciding to have one last go at writing, perhaps she isn't quite prepared to accept his assessment after all.

If only she could prove him wrong, or at least surprise him in some way. The taxi ride after the Sullivans Christmas ball is the only time she has known Marcel show any interest in her personal affairs (except the silly Henry kiss, but he could hardly be jealous of that). If she accepts that Marcel's drunken warning about Philip also wasn't made out of jealousy, as Afua jokingly claimed, she half wonders if he wasn't laying down an obscure challenge for her. That she will, at the very least and however fleetingly, get Marcel's attention is the main reason for putting herself in Devereux's path.

After a fruitless, procrastinating search through her purse for the business card Philip gave her she Googles the law firm and finds its number in seconds.

'Sullivan and Ball,' the lady on the switchboard announces in a breathy, faintly challenging manner that makes Buzzy's heart thump.

'Oh, hello – I was hoping to speak to Philip Devereux?'

'Who's calling, please?' the lady asks, sounding marginally more relaxed, as if deciding it wasn't her fault if people like Buzzy were allowed telephones, and when it arrives the 'Hold on, please' is almost warm. While classical music plays, Buzzy tries to recall the original, slightly drunken conversation about the Eliot letters. Was it really a 'promise' that Devereux made, or was it more like an offer? Or was it, in fact, more along the lines of a hypothetical statement that he *could* arrange for a private viewing, made with the vague intention of impressing her, or possibly just to fill a silence in the conversation, without imagining she would be so unworldly as to mistake it for something they might actually do?

By the time he finally comes on the line, only a lightheaded curiosity as to how the humiliation will play itself out is stopping her from hanging up. 'Devereux,' he says in a clipped voice, far worse than anything Buzzy had been anticipating. Surely the woman on the switchboard told him who was calling? She wonders for a moment if there's been some terrible misunderstanding.

'Hi – Philip? It's, um, Elizabeth Price speaking?'

'Yes?'

'We met at the Sullivan and Ball ball?' she prompts, feeling stupid and stuttery.

'Oh, of course. Dorothea. Ha!'

Blushing, Buzzy smiles weakly into the receiver.

'And you're well?'

Despite his friendlier tone, Buzzy detects in the phrasing of the question a hint of doubt in her ability not to be a bore. 'Oh, yes. Super!' she assures him, determined to be Great Fun, but feeling so overpowered she can't bring herself to return the pleasantry.

'Now, I'm glad I've got you,' he continues, as if this were all his doing, 'I wanted to thank you for inspiring somewhat indirectly, via your magnificent beer-as-art story, our little exhibition. Yes, it's curated by our friend Sherard Howe, and takes the theme of "turmoil" – actually that was my modest contribution. Anyway, the idea seems to have gone down rather well. If you'll just hold on a second—' Slightly muffled, she hears him ask someone (her stomach shrinks at the thought it might be Marcel) to pass him *City A.M.* After a few moments' ruffling of pages, seemingly unhurried, he says, 'From the City diary: *Next month, blue-chip firm Sullivan and Ball will defy its stuffy reputation by hosting an exhibition of conceptual art responding to the financial crisis. With original pieces from Tracey Emin, Ignacio Villarroel and Jackson Reid, among others, and a percentage of works sold going to charity, Sullivans certainly do nothing by half-measures.*

110

But the hippest firm in the City? Who knew? So there we are. You have made us hip.'

'Well, that's great!' she exclaims, too tense still to enter into the ironic spirit of things.

'Quite. Now, I'm afraid you'll have to excuse me: when my secretary flaps her arms like that it usually means I'm due on a conference call. Either that or I'm about to beat her to death with the Companies Act.'

Again she hears that laugh, so *convincing* it makes her believe its brashness is somehow urbane. It suddenly seems absurd that she has interrupted this important man's day – even inspired, in a roundabout way, a Tracey Emin artwork – because of her obsession with Marcel. Absurd and not altogether unpleasing. 'Of course, I understand—'

'But you must join me for a glass of champagne soon. If you're able to hang on for a moment, my secretary will find a date with you.'

The secretary turns out to be as unfeasibly well-spoken as the switchboard operator, only more ingratiating. In a state of heady relief, Buzzy agrees to the first date she suggests: the beginning of February feels reassuringly remote, and there's no point pretending she might have something else planned. She is less keen about the six o'clock meeting time. Normally in a date situation (which this isn't), she has exhausted most avenues of conversation by about nine, and is ready to shoot herself at the prospect of having to draw the evening out to a respectable elevenish close. Then it occurs to her that, being considerably suaver than the sort of boy-men with whom she has previously met for a drink, he will probably have an engagement later and won't wish to spend longer than an hour with her, at most. It isn't until she is returning home with a box from the Buttercup cake shop, in defiance of its contents' frightening calorie count (and presumably the credit-card letters her father forwards to her 'address' on the Kingsland Road), that it dawns on her that neither of them mentioned the Eliot letters.

Later that afternoon, when the box of cupcakes is shamefully diminished, Afua calls her mobile. Had she not had the Devereux

111

triumph in reserve, Buzzy would perhaps have let it ring out. Instead she finds herself agreeing to meet for dinner with a readiness that slightly surprises them both. Afua suggests the restaurant of the new Saatchi Gallery near Sloane Square – 'My treat, of course,' she adds, as if trying to match her friend's unexpected goodwill.

When Buzzy arrives at the restaurant, a little early as usual, she is astonished to find Afua, with a vodka tonic before her, reading the menu. Wrestling her way out of her navy overcoat, feeling flushed from the steamy bus, she absorbs the familiar curious glances from being Afua's companion and notes for the millionth time how satisfying it must be for men who find themselves in this position.

'Hi, darling.'

'This is a surprise,' says Buzzy. 'You're *here*. And I can't even see your BlackBerry thing.'

'I'm taking a break. I want to talk to someone with no knowledge of or interest in what Mervyn's people are briefing about Adair's people, you know, or the optimum size of a stimulus package.'

'Well, that's me.'

Afua gives a contained smile. 'Bad example. Anyway, I want to hear your news. I haven't seen you since that quick coffee before Christmas.'

The waiter arrives, an attentive Australian whose disfiguring frown line is surely a consequence of the job. Perhaps he could sue the restaurant, or Charles Saatchi? She'd know the answer if she'd gone to law school, like everyone else. After a slightly panicked scan, at least on Buzzy's part, they give their orders. Afua frowns encouragingly as they discuss the good health of Buzzy's parents, the slow (but steady!) progress of her poetry writing, and the New Year's Eve debacle. Only once does Buzzy catch her friend gazing past her shoulder after asking a question. Nevertheless, she has the familiar sense when talking with Afua that if this was a job interview, she wouldn't count on going through to the next round.

'So, what else is happening?'

At this second prompt, which hangs in the air invitingly as the waiter deposits a G and T for Buzzy, she can no longer contain herself. But when she stares at the table's gleaming linen cover and blurts that she's meeting Philip Devereux for a drink, Afua's response is disappointing, even after she has been reminded of how Buzzy met him. 'That's great, if you think you like him. I suppose I'm biased.'

'Biased?'

'Well, Sherard does loathe Philip.'

'That hardly puts him in a minority! Anyway, I thought Sherard is organising some exhibition with him.' She doesn't mention Devereux's crediting of her role in the genesis of *Turmoil*, since the episode with the Hirst bottle, including the real reason why she drank it, is not one she plans to revisit.

'It's true, he is. But I think he only wants to impress Philip with the exhibition because he detests him so much . . .' She shrugs in calm acceptance of the bizarreness of male relations. 'Alec also implied that he has a slightly brutish side. Even Marcel, who actually quite admires Philip, professionally at least, is pretty wary of him.'

'I never said I liked him, just that he invited me for a drink. You asked me for what's new; well, that's what's new.'

'Of course, darling,' says Afua, with a thoughtful smile – Buzzy can't remember if she's spoken so curtly to her friend before. In a voice that's slightly giddy and still tinged with defiance, Buzzy asks, 'Anyway, what's going on with *you*?'

'Oh, just the usual,' says Afua, with the lightness of one whose day-to-day existence isn't at all ordinary. 'Actually, I'm thinking of going to work directly for the Party. There's a vacancy for deputy head of press, but I haven't told anyone else yet, so it's our secret.'

Buzzy wonders with surging interest if it's one that's to be kept from Marcel; and if so, if it mightn't imply a loosening of their intimacy. 'It doesn't feel like you've been working for Alec Merton very long. I thought you were enjoying it? And wouldn't it be complicated, with your MP application going on at the same time?'

'Not particularly,' she says with a little shrug. 'I wouldn't have to start the press job immediately – I could wait a few months if necessary.'

'Mightn't someone else have taken it by then?'

'No, they want me,' she says matter-of-factly.

Buzzy is jealous, not of the job, which sounds awful, but of Afua's eternal failure to panic when opportunities fall in her lap. 'As I say, I was under the impression Merton was a bit of a guru figure.'

'I like Alec,' she says, with a cautious glance at the waiter, who has appeared with their starters, 'or he's fine . . . It's more the thing about being an adviser to someone else. I feel ready to be that someone in the arena. What was it Roosevelt said? Covered "in blood and sweat and dust".'

Having set down her steamed mussels, the waiter's withdrawing hand knocks against Afua's drink. He rights it before any contents are spilled, and with a faint blush wishes them bon appétit.

'Clearly that's an arresting image.'

Afua performs an eye-roll. 'Yah. Maybe I should use it for my campaign posters – though actually it seems I'm not going to have any of those.'

'Shame! But seriously, if that's how you feel, go for the spin-doctor job,' says Buzzy, keen to foster this spirit of uncoupled independence. 'I honestly think you'll be brilliant at it. I mean that in a good way.'

'I know you do.'

Buzzy turns her attention to her dreary pea soup: the combination of rushed decision-making, a conservative palate (a subject of amusement to the more adventurous Afua) and a seafood-heavy menu has so far prevented her from making the most of Afua's offer to pay for the meal, and she's not excited about the butternut squash risotto she chose for the main course. When Afua raises the subject of the 'favour', Buzzy is watching her friend closely for signs of interest in her mouth area, where she is convinced there's a sludge-green beauty spot she's somehow managed to miss with her napkin. The news that this favour is connected with the vote for the Islington seat prompts visions of trudging around Barnsbury in a rosette praising Afua to million-aire *Guardian* readers, and then hearing their enraptured responses to the news of this beautiful half-black prospective candidate, with her thoroughly laudable views on compulsory recycling and nuisance speed-bumps.

The soup; sanctimonious Islingtonians; Afua's barely touched vodka tonic across from Buzzy's glass, empty apart from two melting ice cubes and a slumped slice of lemon, are among her thoughts while she half listens to Afua talk about the prospective candidates' hustings next month. It all sounds democratic enough – all local Labour Party members are eligible to attend and cast a vote – though she imagines the Howes will have stacked things in Afua's favour one way or the other, especially given the alleged enthusiasm of Mandelson and other big-wigs for her cause. Buzzy can't help feeling it would be easier to root for her friend more vigorously if she didn't already have so many powerful admirers.

'The problem,' Afua is saying, 'is that Marcel's dad is getting remarried on the same Saturday. The seventh of February?'

Buzzy catches the waiter's eye and, with an apologetic grin, taps the rim of her empty drink. He nods as he dashes past. 'Right,' she says.

'You can imagine how I feel, not being there for Marcel. It's not as if it's going to be an easy occasion for him.'

'No, absolutely,' Buzzy agrees, wishing very much for the appearance of her G and T. Why has Marcel not said anything to her about his father's imminent remarriage? What right has Afua to know before her? Doesn't he know there is nothing Buzzy would not have done – crossed the Atlantic, quit her job if she'd had one – to be there for him?

'I mean because of his mother. Obviously it's not something he talks about, but I'm assuming you know.'

Buzzy could slap her. Know what? 'I heard she was in France somewhere . . .'

'She's in a psychiatric hospital. Or she was; he hasn't heard from her in a few years.'

'Oh, I see.' Buzzy also sees, from Afua's air of suppressed triumph, the fullness of her friend's awareness of her infatuation with Marcel, and Afua's very recent accommodation with this. She is as unable to think of a question that doesn't implicate her any further vis-à-vis. Marcel, or sound prying or mawkish, as she is to transfer her selfish shock at the clandestine activities of Marcel's parents to the larger, more sympathetic kind she would wish for.

'He won't be angry, of course – Marcel, that is. But I think it would really sweeten the news if he knew you could accompany him to the wedding in my place.'

It is not lost on Buzzy that Afua has managed to ask this favour without actually framing it as a question. But then, she reflects, it's perhaps not lost on her friend that she isn't asking for much of a sacrifice on Buzzy's part.

Afua takes a sip of her vodka tonic, observed with a certain wariness by the waiter, who has at last brought Buzzy's second gin and tonic.

'Cheers,' Buzzy says, inappropriately.

Buzzy hurries past the bus stop, pitying the freezing Filipino lady who will not be attending the wedding of Belgium's former interior minister. She charges her Oyster card in the warmth of Sloane Square Tube station without feeling the usual pang at the cost of travelling two stops on the District Line. Even when the Tube breaks down for fifteen minutes outside of South Kensington, she doesn't dwell on the fact that it would have been quicker to get the 452 or, quite possibly, to walk. Allowing her thoughts time to settle, she scans an abandoned copy of the *Evening Standard*. It seems to hold little New Year cheer. She finds herself oddly interested in the report of an Icelandic bank announcing its intention to sue the UK government for using anti-terror legislation to seize the bank's assets. In another article, important-sounding experts are criticising the government's economic policies – one grandly warns that 'fiscal profligacy will soon come to be rued'. Although the sentences swim a little and she finds she has to re-read each paragraph, the tumultuous financial situation, which she has mostly left for other people to worry about, makes an impression on her. Fiscal prodigacy sounds as undesirable as it does irresponsible, especially when she thinks of her father, worried about the depressed housing market and people's new reluctance to purchase furniture on credit. She remembers guiltily that she didn't really listen when, at her mother's gentle prompting, he told her about this over Christmas – or if she did, secretly dismissed it as trivial and *Daily Mail*ish. Alec Merton is quoted in the piece: *These are exceptional measures to get money flowing into the economy in a period of great global instability. Of course we can reduce borrowing once growth returns.* The words seem reassuring – as from the inset photo does Merton himself, quite handsome in a boring sort of way – though she wonders if they were in fact drafted by Afua, who has never learned economics or worked in a business.

Her new-found interest in current affairs feels quickly exposed during the chilly walk from Gloucester Road Tube. She takes in the raucous throb of a brasserie pub, where she once aggrievedly nursed a seven-pound pint of strawberry beer. Turning off Gloucester Road, she navigates the now familiar side-streets, with their chichi galleries and refined terraces offering comforting glimpsed scenes of domestic life. By the time she's arrived home all the fuss about financial chaos feels rather unconvincing, like the yerba mate gourd she brought back from Argentina and now reaches past to drop a tea bag into her favourite Rothko mug.

At the dining-room table she taps the aged laptop, hears the familiar whirr as it struggles to life. Every now and again, she has a sense of Marcel's failure to tell her of his mother's illness as a space, as yet painless, forming within her. There is still the possibility that the numbness won't wear off, in particular if she focuses on the exciting prospect of a whole weekend at his side and on the chance that if she really forces herself to put some words on the screen something promising may start to take shape.

The abandoned email to Philip Devereux is still open. Its contents appear even more awkward after her conversation with the man himself: the thought of Devereux reciting it to someone (Marcel!) in the dry tone he used for the *City A.M.* extract makes her clench up in horror. She deletes the unsent message, pleased that she did the brave thing for once by telephoning him, as a result of which she now has a firm date.

'Fuck,' she whispers. 'Fuck fuck fuck.' Abandoning the laptop, she goes in search of her mobile. In the kitchen, she scowls at the tattered paperback of *The House of Mirth* on the worktop and the unwashed dishes in the sink. She seizes her coat from where it lies on the table and gropes the first pocket, where she finds a familiar plastic bulge. She calls Afua, who answers with mildly reproaching swiftness, so that for a moment Buzzy feels she is the one being interrupted. She checks her watch: eleven fifty.

'Sorry, I know it's late,' she begins, 'but I've just realised that my date, I mean *drink*, with Devereux is on the first Friday of February. That's not a problem or anything, is it?'

'It might be a little tricky, actually. There's a big family break-fast on the Saturday morning, so the plan was to travel on Friday evening. I think Marcel's already booked the Eurostar.'

'What time does it leave?'

'I really can't remember,' says Afua, with a yawn. 'Nineish, perhaps? I'm pretty sure it's around then.'

'Well, in that case it'll be fine,' says Buzzy, doing her best now to sound unconcerned. 'I'm sure the drink won't take long. Even if I miss Marcel's train, I could get a later one that evening, or first thing Saturday morning. Or I could just rearrange Philip for another time . . .'

'No, darling, you mustn't do that – he wouldn't be pleased. I feel bad enough at the thought of you rushing through your date.'

'Really, I don't mind at all,' Buzzy says sincerely.

'Look, don't worry about Brussels. I'm sure Henry could go, or someone else.'

'No, *really*, it's fine.' She is seriously regretting phoning Afua without first thinking the conversation through. 'I'm definitely going. Definitely. The Philip thing will just have to fit around that.'

It's simply a matter of making sure the early evening drink is finished in time to make the nine p.m. Eurostar. She won't even mention Brussels to Philip, if the thought of her having a later engagement with his trainee would be offensive to the lawyer's ego.

'Well, if you're sure . . .' Afua yawns again. 'It's wonderfully selfless of you.'

'Not at all.'

16

Prodigious cheek!

Private Eye, 28 January 2009

In an admittedly thinning field, is there a member of the old Islington mafia more brass-necked than the ubiquitous journalist and, ahem, 'feminist philosopher', Daphne Depree?

Ten years ago, *Eye* readers may recall, Ms Depree (aka the wife of millionaire publisher and *Liberal Review* owner, Sherard Howe) wrote *The Third Sex*. As clunking as its title suggests, it was as if the author had studied New Labour's crude, ahistorical and entirely vacuous reinterpretation of the British labour movement and decided to do precisely the same thing to feminism. The key 'insight' of the book was that feminists, and indeed women generally, must come in from the margins and embrace their empowerment. They must do this by becoming what Depree meaninglessly termed the 'radical centre'. In other words, it doesn't really matter what women believe (we're beyond left and right now, remember?) or even do, just so long as they're in charge: making porn films; screaming at their secretaries; bombing third-world countries; whatever.

Now that the consequences of this kind of principle-free drivel are plain for all to see, from careerist Blair babes in government to ladettes weeing in the streets, Depree has published a new book in which she admits: oops, sorry guys! Boy did I get that one wrong! Ideology, we learn in *The Prodigal Sister*, turns out to matter after all. Thus the relationship between sisters and capital is described as an 'abusive marriage' – she is particularly scathing about the retrospective justification of Bush's wars in the name of women's rights – and the Labour government is accused of being in hock to a failed neoliberal consensus.

It seems the cognoscenti have once again fallen for Depree's pseudo-theorising. Or rather, given the disasters of Iraq and Afghanistan and now the crisis of capitalism, they are keen to lend her stunning volte-face maximum intellectual respectability before performing their own. 'A virtuosic deconstruction of third-way politics from one of its intellectual architects,' wrote one breathless reviewer, no doubt keen to be invited to the next Howe soirée.

Amid all the applause for Depree's zeitgeisty tome, no one has mentioned that her adopted daughter, Afua Nelson, is currently working as special adviser to Alec Merton, the ambitious – and distinctly bourgeois – City minister. Or that said City minister is a friend of the Howes. Or, indeed, that after the cash for peerages scandal, Sherard Howe is one of the few remaining non-union Party donors, and as such a highly influential figure in Labour circles.

When it comes to Depree's lofty rhetoric about rejecting the Westminster hegemon, it seems to be a case of do as I say not as I do, Comrades. There are even rumours that Labour's high command want to parachute the glamorous Ms Nelson into the soon-to-be-vacant Islington South seat. The mechanism? An all-wimmin shortlist. Watch this space . . .

17

'. . . Yes, and the final piece I found in La Maison Rouge, on the rue Charlot. Do you know the Marais well?'

'Not *well* well . . .'

Sherard, who has a hunch that Graham is not completely sure the Marais is in Paris, chooses this moment to relight his cigar, latterly (and quite pleasingly) an illegal activity, but these are his offices and he will do what he likes in them. The hunch remains just that, however, as Graham rescues himself by asking Sherard to describe the fourteenth and final artwork in the *Turmoil* exhibition.

'Oh, it's called *The gods of finance*: a horizontal sundial with the usual protruding gnomon, I believe they're called, but the hour lines lead mostly to exotic financial acronyms: SIV, MTN, ABS and so on. Occasionally the inscription is something more dramatic, "Crash" or "War" – I think you get the idea.'

Graham gives a hesitant sort of nod. He is the son of a Liverpudlian train driver, and Sherard finds him charmless and physically quite disgusting, with his grimy glasses and constantly peeling facial skin. The only reason he hasn't long ago fired him is his sentimental conviction that, in different circumstances, Graham would not only be content to see him lined up against the wall but would pull the trigger himself.

'Anyway, I was in the area, more or less, so I thought I'd see how we're looking for next week.'

'Oh yes. No, we're looking very good.'

'Might I know the line-up?'

'Of course, of course,' says Graham, who deeply resents Sherard's editorial prying. 'We're going with Gaza for the cover story.'

'And what are we saying?'

'Well, Ari's article, in essential terms—'

'—calls what's happening a Nazi-style genocide; supports this with quotations from some Ivy League law professor or high-level UN report; draws parallels between Israeli government policy and the ideology of apartheid; and decries the Anglo-American support for the tired old "right to exist" mantra.'

'That's more or less it.'

'I suppose I'm just wondering how this is in any way different to what Pilger will write in the *New Statesman*. What's the cover image?'

'We've got the angel of death passing over Gaza. A little provocative, perhaps, but justified we think in the circumstances.'

'Yes, it's hard to keep up. Do you recall the Goya cartoon of Sharon biting off the Arab baby's head in the *Guardian*?'

'Oh, the Dave Brown one? Yes, I remember that.'

'Now, what else? You've remembered to review *The Prodigal Sister*, I hope . . .'

The MI6 building lights up the Vauxhall sky like a gaudy Las Vegas hotel. 'My dear boy,' Sherard tells himself, 'the things you could have been.' He passes the Tube station, where there is a definite and almost invigorating sense that any of the loiterers might be a throat-cutting schizophrenic. After the railway arches, which appear to be deserted, he checks his watch with a prick of anticipation: Daphne is appearing on *Newsnight* and won't be home until almost midnight, meaning he has at least three, maybe four hours to spare.

The bathhouse is next to a mini-cab office that efficiently doubles as a meeting place for resentful Turks. The gleaming strip-lit entrance area is curiously salubrious; identical no doubt to many a provincial leisure centre, with its lingering chlorine smell and bossy locker-room instructions. What sets it apart perhaps is the black receptionist, a magnificent specimen with the brutal evaluative regard of a slave trader. Sherard wonders how many men have stood here and acquired a new perspective on their aesthetic worth. Fortunately he doesn't suffer from any self-delusion in that area, or particularly mourn the passing of his looks, which he never really felt should be up to him to provide. In any case, he wouldn't claim that his egalitarian beliefs, based as they are on hating the people he went to school with, stretch as far as caring what anyone in Vauxhall might think of him. That includes the head of the Secret Intelligence Service, whom he once met and found a complete bore.

He pays the entrance fee – fifteen pounds for an indefinite stay – and takes a towel from the receptionist, who doesn't respond when Sherard says, 'Through there, is it? Ah, yes . . .'

The changing room has a school feel of wet scalps and stolen glances, making Sherard half thankful not to be swimming forty lengths of an unheated pool before running along to Chapel. He was something of a chorister in his pre-pubescent days; sang the Nunc Dimittis at Tripp's memorial service after his heart attack in the middle of a music lesson. 'I didn't know I was *that* bad,' he remembers Grewcock later joking about the dramatic interruption of his trumpet solo. Of course he drank a lot, Tripp, looking back on it, which was perhaps why he wasn't as foul as some of the other masters, really quite witty at times, though Sherard presumes the groping would have got him in hot water these days. 'A little too hurried, I thought, but perhaps it was just me,' was his mother's verdict on the Nunc Dimittis.

He undresses and fastens the towel underneath his sagging stomach. A pale ginger man with the squint of a habitual glasses-wearer sends coins flying across the floor as he removes his trousers from his locker. The other denizens look on as he scurries around picking them up. 'Actually, there's one down here,' Sherard says, pointing to where a penny has rolled under a bench not far from him. The man turns to Sherard with an eager smile that lays bare his wasted evening and at this stage more or less unreserved preparedness to compromise.

Sherard finds the steam room first; hands cautiously raised in front, his throat burning until he adjusts to taking shallower breaths. There is a sharp pine and chemical smell. The silence is remarkable only when he starts to make out the dark shapes around him, and even then isn't oppressive, since it's tacitly understood that the mist hanging like cigar smoke absolves everyone from the usual social obligations. He finds a free spot on a wooden bench and slowly relaxes his back against the scorching wall. Save the odd detail, the experience reminds Sherard of Antony Gormley's recent cloud chamber installation at the Hayward; or even the early afternoon lull in the drawing room of the Reform Club, where occasionally as a young man he'd be invited to join his father for an afternoon whisky.

Sherard slowly becomes aware of the interest of the man next to him. He decides to ignore him, preferring to study the really quite shameful acts occurring across from him, which the steam renders in a satisfying Degas sort of smudge.

''Scuse me,' says the neighbour, 'but you're not Sherard Howe, are you?'

The effect of these words, spoken in loud Estuary English, is to cause the Degas blur of movement abruptly to cease – Sherard has the momentary and melodramatic impression that time itself has been suspended. He is furious, but aware too of sharing with his neighbour the shocked attention of the room. Turning to the source of his anger, he realises the man's face is indeed familiar – those porcine eyes; the thin-lipped smirk, possibly not unrelated to his thick brown hair and impressively matted chest – though he cannot recall from where. He is almost certain they have never actually been introduced.

'Sadly not,' he says icily.

'Why sadly?'

'I'm sure I would have enjoyed the chance to make small-talk.'

There are disembodied titters around the room. His pleasure at the smooth manner in which he has dealt with this potentially dangerous situation is tempered by a distinct and gathering pressure at his left temple.

'Right, I gotcha.'

Sherard thinks the man winks at him at this point; either way he seems maddeningly unoffended, even quite gratified by the put-down. Perhaps he's that type. It occurs to Sherard that someone who *wants* to be humiliated might be his nemesis.

'I'm sorry for getting you mixed up with someone else,' the man starts up again, his smirk unextinguished.

'I would really think nothing of it.'

The pause before Sherard's reply is not as telling as he would have hoped, because the neighbour goes on immediately. 'To be honest, I'm not sure I'd want anyone mistaking me for Sherard Howe.' Now it's his turn to leave a meaningful silence, interrupted by the huffy exit of the performers.

'Why's that?'

'Oh, he's one of those awful public school luvvies who bankrolls Labour. Of course, everyone pretends to take him seriously – or at least they did. It's all about Notting Hill Tories these days, isn't it?'

'I really couldn't say . . .'

'Politics not your thing? Sensible man.' He leans toward Sherard in a confidential manner. 'I'm a journo, for my sins, so I need to keep my eye on all sorts of bollocks.'

'You've chosen a good spot.'

'Nah, this is just to relax, maybe have a little fun. Though it's true we're not far from Westminster: I bet you'd be surprised the number of ministers and mandarins, even peers of the realm, I've seen in here.'

Sherard pointedly does not respond. The close atmosphere of the steam room is not assisting the pain at his temple. He leans forward, partly to disassociate himself from the hack. Tributaries of hot sweat flow down his back, joining above the buttocks.

'Actually, I heard there's some trouble brewing there.'

'What did you say?'

The hack brushes his hand over Sherard's forearm. 'Sorry, with that Sherard bloke, I mean. Something to do with his adopted daughter. Wanna go somewhere more private?'

Sherard cannot read the man's face, and not only because it is partially obscured by the steam. The challenging leer at his lips might denote sexual insecurity, a plea for punishment, or the more ordinary sadism of his profession. If it is all a malign act, he plays an extremely convincing idiot, though Sherard notes he hasn't forgotten the local etiquette so far as to introduce himself.

In the end, his instinct tells him this has gone far enough and it is time to fold. 'No, I think not,' he says, 'I was just leaving.'

The act of standing up makes the pounding in his head increase. His vision dims momentarily, as if in a bunker with power shortages, but not wishing to delay his exit he stumbles towards the door, or at least towards where he thinks that must be. He has only taken a few steps when the moisture underfoot causes him to slip. He manages to avoid falling by throwing out an arm, and is fortunate to make contact with someone's head, which he continues to clutch while righting himself. 'Sorry about that,' he says, and then, '*Fuck!*' as he stubs his toe on the way out.

The coolness of the corridor is quickly unpleasant; his towel has become sodden with sweat and steam and slightly chafes against his thighs as, limping briskly, he attempts to retrace his steps to the locker room. In his hurry – the hack has pursued him out of the steam room, and is calling after him – he takes a wrong turn and heads deeper into the baths, whose layout turns out to resemble a nightmarish psychiatric ward: a warren of dimly lit and near-identical corridors stalked by silent men in white towels. Still followed by the journalist, he hobbles past a Jacuzzi room, a shower room, a lounge-area-cum-porn-cinema.

Sherard rounds another corner and ducks into one of the wooden saunas. Ignoring the objections of the stewed occupants, he holds the door open a crack and watches for his pursuer. At the same time he tries to visualise the route back to the changing rooms. Orienteering has never been one of his strong points: at seventeen, he got his CCF detachment badly lost in the Brecon Beacons. A hungry cadet was almost expelled for shooting (though not eating) a sheep, an act which didn't improve the farmer's opinion of public school boys. It is no use, he decides; he will simply wait another minute or two, to be sure that the odious journalist has moved on, and then ask someone for directions.

In the corridor he stops a man of about his own age and proportions. The latter gazes past Sherard at an eighteen-year-old Latino's vanishing calves with an annoyed look that suggests a chase rudely interrupted.

'Excuse me, which is the way out of here?'

'Who knows, darling,' he replies, sidling past Sherard. 'Not God in my experience.'

The journalist is coming towards him, grinning with satisfaction: he must have gone on ahead before realising he'd been given the slip and doubling back. Flustered, Sherard sets off down an intersecting corridor which is definitely new to him. It's narrow, and on either side are rows of thin cubicle doors of the kind common in public loos. He rattles a few of the door handles – all locked. Behind him he hears footsteps and 'Hold up, mate!'

Sherard breaks into a trot, shaking doors to his left and right. Finally he sees one that is open a fraction: the footsteps have almost caught up with him as he bounds inside and straightaway tumbles over and becomes enmeshed in a surprised pair occupying some sort of gym mat on the floor.

The hack leans against the door frame. 'My kingdom for a camera phone, eh Sherard?'

'My dear boy, I have absolutely no idea who you are.' There is a good deal of squirming going on underneath him, and in the mêlée his towel has become dislodged, so that considerable effort is required to summon his usual hauteur. 'But I should tell you that, *if* your editor is Fleet Street, you can be sure I know him somewhat better than you do.'

'That wasn't a threat, was it, Sherard?' He gives the name of the formidable mid-market tabloid he writes for.

Sherard struggles to his feet, ignoring the vulgar commentary from below. 'Oh, do shut up! And pass me my towel.' Robed again, he marches past the journalist, whose grotesque chuckle stays with him to the end of the corridor, where he emerges, through some geographical miracle, near the entrance to the changing rooms. He finds his locker without difficulty.

'What is this so-called "trouble", anyway?' Sherard asks while rapidly buttoning his shirt.

The journalist is admiring himself in the mirror, raking at his thick wet hair. Hearing this his eyes crinkle in the reflection. 'It's about Afua's election for Islington North.'

Sherard breathes a sigh of relief. 'Islington *South*. And if you're referring to that silly thing in *Private Eye*—'

'I'm not.' He turns around to face Sherard. 'Someone is going around briefing that you lent on the NEC.'

'And why did I do that?'

'To make sure your girl was on the shortlist, and that the short-list was all-women.'

Sherard is now lacing his shoes. 'What a thoroughly tedious little tale. I'm sure the Surrey secretaries or whatever could not be less interested. By the way, it's also not true.'

'Personally, I agree,' the hack says, with a shrug, 'I couldn't care less what smug Islington cunts get up to. Maybe we won't bother to run it. But if we do, I doubt the rank and file will like it, up there in the People's Republic. Nor will Gordon, if he thinks the story's going anywhere near him.'

Sherard stands up. He is ready to depart. 'Who is this source of yours?'

'*Sherard*,' the hack scoffs. 'You're off, are you? Maybe see you around here soon.'

'I shouldn't rely on it.'

'It's pretty funny, really,' he calls after him, 'what with your wife the famous feminist.'

Outside, ignoring the Turks, Sherard hails a black cab. 'Canonbury,' he tells the driver. He closes the screen and then sinks back in his seat, massaging his throbbing temple. His mood starts to brighten when they cross over Vauxhall Bridge. The sky glows orange, giving the impression, regrettably misleading, that behind him South London is ablaze.

18

Boy hearts aunt

Henry tries not to look at his watch. He has memorised the route from High Street Kensington Tube station to the Royal Garden Hotel, and takes comfort from Google Maps' calculation that it's only a seven-minute walk: when he last checked the time, less than a minute ago, it was ten to four. Still, he does wonder if it is absolutely essential that Abdul buy a pack of gum now, on their way to afternoon tea, where chewing is not a good idea. He fears he will be obliged to point this out, and then have to decide what to do if Abdul adopts his increasingly familiar tactic of ignoring him.

Though at no stage has Abdul hung off Henry's every word, since New Year this dismissive attitude has become a defining feature of their exchanges. In Friday's tutorial, he outright refused to read *Can You Forgive Her?*, the next book on Henry's reading list after *Vanity Fair*, on the ground that it 'looked even more boring' than the Thackeray. Instead Abdul made the rather alarming suggestion of substituting it with *A Clockwork Orange*. Mindful in particular of today's meeting with Abdul's aunt, the importance of which Louise Ryder had been keen to impress on him, Henry tried to explain that he did not think a book dealing with extreme sexual violence was the sort of thing with which he was paid to ensure his mentee was familiar. 'I don't want at all to suggest that this is the only point of reading the literary classics,' he reasoned, 'but *A Clockwork Orange* would hardly be a book to bring up if you found yourself in conversation with, I don't know, the wife of the American ambassador. Whereas the Trollope, you see, deals with great themes – love and politics and what a woman should do with her life.' As he said this, it occurred to Henry that the last was perhaps not an animating subject in Saudi Arabian culture, and in the end they compromised on *The Turn of the Screw*, which Henry found quite an easy sell once he mentioned that it was extremely short and a ghost story.

If he is not exactly grateful for Abdul's disdain, to be treated with respect would make him more uncomfortable. It's not just his culpability over Buzzy and the house; or his exposing Abdul, however unwittingly, to Conrad's drug abuse. Since the disaster of New Year's Eve, Abdul has more than once spoken admiringly of Marcel. 'He doesn't talk much,' Henry recalls him saying on one of these occasions, 'but when he does you really want to listen.' He could not help but feel an implicit contrast was being drawn in this observation. This would be harmless enough – Henry is not so petty as to be jealous of some light hero-worship – except, and he is loath to acknowledge this of someone who has suffered the mental disintegration of a parent, he suspects the Belgian is not a wholly benign influence on the young Saudi.

'Ready then?' He wonders if there is something too funereal about his pupil's black tie, or sharp about the cut of his grey suit. Might Abdul's aunt observe this too, and consider it precisely the sort of thing that Henry, as his lifestyle mentor, was meant to address? But even had he known more about clothes, it was too excruciatingly personal to tell another man what to wear. As it is, he cannot say with any certainty that his hand-me-down Aquascutum suit, a relic of his father's trimmer days, is 'better' than his pupil's Giorgio Armani.

They proceed down Kensington High Street, Abdul peering in the shop windows or admiring his reflection, but either way strolling. Suddenly the boy stops in his tracks, forcing the chattering Italian family behind to divide around him. This time Henry cannot stop himself checking his watch: six minutes to four.

'I forgot to get some water.'

'Oh dear . . . Still, perhaps we should press on? We don't want to be late for your aunt.'

'But I need it.'

131

There is a note of mischief here that Henry does not enjoy. He looks at his watch again. 'Do you mean you can't wait until we get to the hotel? Because I think it's only a few minutes' walk.'

'It's not that I'm thirsty *now*. But I definitely will be *soon*.'

Henry remains motionless for a few precious seconds. Surprised at his own calmness, he asks, 'Abdul, have you swallowed some Ecstasy?'

Abdul presses his lips together, trying not to smile. 'Maybe.'

'When did this happen?'

'Just before we left,' he confirms. 'You're, like, blinking. That means you're angry with me.'

'I suppose I'm just wondering what to do. We could turn around now, and say you were feeling ill. Or perhaps I got the dates mixed up. Otherwise, we go and meet your aunt as planned, and hope the drug doesn't kick in before the end of afternoon tea. I have to say the former option is more tempting. Would she be very angry, do you think?'

'Like, to tell the truth? Ya, she'd be pissed.'

'Then I think we better hurry – it's five minutes to four.'

They move between drifting groups of Sunday afternoon shoppers, Henry always a step or two ahead of Abdul. The pedestrian crossing is on red. 'Where did you get it?' Henry asks, careful to keep his voice only just audible over the traffic. 'The pill, I mean.'

'Marcel.' Warily, he adds, 'Only 'cos he didn't want to take them with him to the hospital. Dude, the light's green.'

'How many did he give you?'

'Four? This is the last.'

The short walk along Kensington Road is spent in silence. At three minutes after four, they hurry past the doormen outside the Royal Garden Hotel. The foyer is busy, with an atmosphere of quiet panic that Henry has noticed before in luxury hotels, though it's possible each time he has been merely projecting his own mood.

'Can you see your aunt?'

'Uh-uh.'

'Well, that's something at least.'

Abdul finds an unoccupied sofa, into which he settles with his iPhone, knees swung dramatically apart. Henry remains where he is a minute or two, too nervous to sit down, before realising it wouldn't make a good impression to be discovered waiting separately from his charge. Keeping his eyes trained on the entrance, he perches next to Abdul. 'It was definitely four o'clock,' he affirms, mostly to himself. The Saudi is absorbed in a snowboarding game, tilting the gadget one way and the other.

'I was just wondering,' Henry ventures, 'why you left Switzerland. Riyad mentioned something about getting in with the wrong crowd . . .'

'Riyad is a douche.'

'Nevertheless . . .'

Abdul shoots an elbow in the air, launching himself off the edge of a half-pipe. 'It was nothing. There was this party, my aunt found out.'

'What happened at the party?'

'*Nothing*, I told you.'

'So there weren't any drugs? Any . . . girls?'

Abdul breaks off from the game to give Henry a searching glance. 'Nothing like that.'

'But you've been *drunk* before,' says Henry, slightly desperately. 'Haven't you?'

'Of course!'

An Arab woman in a cream suit enters the foyer and now approaches them. The tip of her nose has an upwards flourish that Henry recognises immediately. With her swept black hair and oval eyes, he thinks she is rather fiercely beautiful.

'In Soho that time,' continues his mentee, who is focusing once more on his snowboarding game. 'Don't you remember? With Buzzy.'

'This is a terrific treat,' announces Henry, referring to the pyramids of cakes and scones. 'I really can't remember the last time I had afternoon tea.' They are sitting in a corner of the Park Terrace restaurant, the great advantage of which – the view of Kensington Gardens – is fading into wintry darkness.

'I thought it was a famous English ritual,' Sanaa says with the faint suspicion that has so far featured in all her remarks to Henry, apart from when he confirmed he'd graduated from Cambridge.

'No, it is. It's just that my family is not especially keen on tradition, at least not the English sort.'

'*We* think it is very important.' She glances inclusively at Abdul, who seems to be lost in intense, almost transcendental thought. Henry would be impressed if he wasn't sure the teen wasn't trying to gauge the internal effects of the drug he'd swallowed. Fortunately thus far they seem to be minimal. Unsure of the etiquette (he is the man, but not he assumes paying for the tea – or is he?), Henry offers Sanaa a raisin and cinnamon scone, which she accepts after some hesitation, only to glower at the offer of clotted cream. Abdul waves everything away.

'You aren't hungry?'

'Not really.'

'No tea, even?'

'Water is okay, Aunt. Maybe a whole jug.'

'But you haven't had one sip yet! I find this unbelievable,' she tells Henry, who smiles weakly. 'Abdul-Latif is the greediest of all my nephews. Are you sick?'

He shakes his head.

'Sad then?'

'Totally the opposite, actually.' He takes a sip of water and at the last second his lips dip into a smirk. Realising whom his mentee is inexpertly trying to imitate, Henry observes this little act with alarm.

'Well . . . I can't imagine . . .'

'I understand your name means "brilliance" in Arabic. It's also the capital of Yemen.'

Sanaa turns to Henry with an expression of high scrutiny. 'I know.'

'No, of course. Arabic is such a beautiful script, isn't it? Much more elegant I always think than the Roman alphabet.' Though

134

Henry addresses this to his pastry selection, he feels Sanaa's doubtful eyes floating like orbs outside his vision.

'What is your opinion, Abdul-Latif?'

'Ya, it's okay. I never thought about it.'

'Think about it now.'

Henry has time to raise a slightly trembling cup of tea to his lips and replace it on its saucer before Abdul, prefacing his reply with a sigh, responds to his aunt. 'I guess English is easier. Specially for messaging and stuff.'

'There: an opinion.' To Henry, she says, 'On the subject of English, how are my nephew's studies progressing?'

'Very well, thank you. I thought we'd aim for a brief *tour d'horizon* of the psychological novel, starting with the nineteenth-century masters – William Thackeray, George Eliot, Henry James and so on.'

'Oh! That sounds . . .' Saana flails, and Henry understands he has rather artlessly misjudged his reply. 'Who is your favourite?' she asks her nephew.

There is another excruciating pause in which Henry hopes the boy is thinking about the question. 'If I *had* to choose,' he says eventually, 'I guess George Eliot? At least some of his characters are quite funny, like Fred Vincy. But still, if it was a movie you'd probably cut like ninety per cent of it. What's the time?'

'Quarter past four. These cucumber sandwiches are delicious: could I tempt you with one, Sanaa?'

'No, I won't. For me English food either makes you fat or has no flavour at all.'

'Yes, I see what you mean.' Henry casts an anguished glance at the spread before them: it might speed things along if he could somehow eat a lot of the scones and pastries and sandwiches, only the pool of adrenaline in his stomach has mostly robbed him of his appetite.

'Riyad tells me that your parents are also well-known writers.'

'Well, my mother is. Actually, her new book is published on Thursday.'

'Too late,' Sanaa says, 'I will have left the country. What is it about?'

'In essence, I suppose, it's rejecting the alliance between feminism and neoliberalism that she advocated in her previous book.'

Sanaa looks rather cross at this, though Henry is not sure if it's due to his mother's thesis or his failure, once again, to speak in a more appropriate register. 'And do you have any brothers or sisters?'

'No. Well, there's Afua, whom my parents haven't adopted, at any rate in the legal sense, but she's lived with us since she was sixteen.'

Sanaa's brow remains pursed. 'Her name is . . . Afua?'

'Yes, that's right. It's Ghanaian.'

'I don't understand. Why does she live with you?'

'Oh, well . . .' He wonders how much detail he ought to go into. 'She always had a difficult relationship with her mother. My family has known Afua a long time, you see: she and I attended the same primary and then secondary school, though she was a couple of years ahead. I don't know why – no one asked her to – but she always shielded me from the bullies. My parents were very grateful for that: Afua was extremely popular, and I . . . well, I think they sometimes felt slightly guilty for not sending me to a private school.' Henry's explanation is punctuated by a series of regular and vulgar gulping noises from Abdul. 'Over time she became part of our lives: I suppose my parents started looking out for her the same way she was looking out for me. In the end her moving in just sort of happened organically, as it were.'

If, because of his dark brown irises, the sudden and radical dilation of the boy's pupils is not instantly noticeable, Henry cannot imagine it will be long before Sanaa raises the subject. Tremors reverberate up Henry's body, starting from his foot, resting against a table leg: Abdul is twitching uncontrollably. Through a grin, he mutters something like '*Yalla*!'

'More tea, Sanaa?'

'I've seen a picture of Afua. She's really pretty. Actually, she looks a bit like you, Aunt, except younger and black.'

'No milk, still?'

'I take tea with a slice of lemon. My mind has not changed on this point.' Henry strains to catch a note of good-natured teasing, but is instead left with an impression of other decisions being revisited. It's clear that she feels insulted and that he is obscurely to blame.

'Aunt Sanaa,' says Abdul, reaching over and gripping her palm, 'I hope you never change. I mean it. You're like my mom or something.'

Sanaa studies her hand as if some fascinating reptile has crawled into it. 'What a strange mood you are in! Riyad should have mentioned that you have gone mad,' she says, though Henry thinks he catches a watery glint in her eyes. 'Since you don't want to eat, why don't you go for a walk or something? I'd like to talk to Mr Howe.'

Abdul finishes another glass of water before striding beamingly off with a promise not to stray from High Street Kensington. Sensing that Sanaa would like a little time to gather herself, Henry braves a scone: he finds swallowing each over-chewed mouthful a minor ordeal.

The maître d' approaches. Addressing Sanaa, he asks if everything is satisfactory, and could he offer a glass of champagne or perhaps a raspberry Bellini? They both decline, Henry as resolutely as manners will permit.

'Talking of Bellini,' says Henry, when they are alone again, 'we recently saw the *Renaissance Faces* exhibition at the National Gallery. It's a shame Abdul is not here or he could have told you about it.' In fact Henry is greatly relieved: the boy discovered he had a low opinion of Renaissance portraiture, with the possible exception of the snigger-inducing *Ugly Duchess*.

'Yes . . . That's good. But really, what do you propose to *do*?' she asks, with sudden urgency.

'Do about what?'

'Abdul-Latif, of course! I'm talking about his behaviour today. The sudden mood swings, not eating his food . . . It's unacceptable.'

'Yes,' says Henry, glimpsing imminent shame and relief. 'I'll resign, of course.'

'Resign? No, that would only make it worse.'

'I'm afraid I don't see how.'

'Perhaps,' she observes, with grim satisfaction, 'this is one subject you don't understand so well.'

'No,' he agrees. 'I'm sorry, which "subject" are we talking about?'

'Love,' she says disapprovingly. 'He has obviously fallen for the African.'

'I'm not *sure* that's . . . He's only seen Afua's photo on Facebook.'

'Do you think that is not enough?' For the first time Henry wonders why she lives in Switzerland, unmarried and without children of her own. 'We shall have to be very careful how we proceed. Never speak of her. When he asks to meet her, don't forbid it, but you must inform me immediately.' She sighs. 'For the young, this feeling of romantic love can be . . .'

Henry thinks of a recent acquisition with which his father is very pleased. 'Turmoil?'

'Yes!' Sanaa says. 'Yes, exactly.'

19

Clockwise from right

ES magazine, *23 January 2009*

Photos (left to right): Mark Lawson with Daphne Depree and Kathy Lette; sometimes a cigar ... The uxorious Sherard Howe lights up outside Quo Vadis.

20

Upstairs at Rules

'Oh, do you like it? I'm afraid it's not in the least fashionable, but I thought it would do, what with the Savoy shut . . .'

Philip Devereux furnishes Buzzy with a pleased and proprietorial smile. Upstairs at Rules it's miraculously quiet for six o'clock on a Friday evening: like the gin cocktails he orders them (he had promised champagne, but she's willing to let this slide), it's an unfamiliar yet comforting choice – shades of a Cambridge college bar, with its panelled walls and claret leather chairs and atmosphere of suppressed male naughtiness. Even the jowly barman might be a college porter. Buzzy catches a whiff of barber's lotion and cigarettes as he arrives with their Charles IIs, praising Philip's choice with hedging informality, as if perceiving the technical matter of whether they have met before will be less important to the lawyer than the sense that he's the sort of person one would remember.

'Well, cheers!'

Philip tilts his cocktail glass, gravely, without the self-conscious exaggeration of one of Buzzy's peers. Earlier, walking up from Embankment, suppressing a shudder as she passed the Italian restaurant where she ate with Charlie and Fiona, she wondered if at his next engagement Philip would make a humorous allusion to the circumstances of his aperitif: 'Do you know, it's a funny thing but I was with a young lady from Orpington!' She sees this is very far from the mark; there can be nothing absurd about her now they are having a drink together. How comforting it feels to be shielded by Philip's vanity! What a blissful holiday from her own self-contempt!

A group of lads shout their way down Maiden Lane: Friday happy hour will soon be in full swing. 'It's so tranquil up here,' Buzzy says, with a relieved smile.

Philip unabashedly inspects her while taking a sip of his Charles II, ignoring the cherry lurking at the bottom of the cocktail. It's slightly silly, but she has never known anyone *own* their drink as he does: the way he bears the glass against his chest, clutching it by its stem so as to reveal his knuckles. She is unable to savour this observation, though, since it's quickly overwhelmed by the same disconcerting sense she had at the Sullivans ball of his usual talkativeness going astray in her presence, as if she were a new species that he is content, at first, just to observe.

There is a humming from his jacket pocket. He fishes out his BlackBerry, a sleek model she hasn't seen before. 'Sorry,' he says, scrolling through the text of an email. He taps out a reply, something terrifically significant and authoritative, Buzzy imagines, while she peeks at his nape. She suspects her father, whose grey hair is always shaved to a fine buzz at the back, would disapprove of the way Philip's coloured curls hang over his collar – consider it 'spivvish', even. Perhaps it's another of those strange instances of inversion, like the upper-class habit of saying 'lavatory', which she was brought up to consider slightly common; or perhaps it's just to conceal the faint crease lines in his neck.

He places the device on the table with a heavy, satisfied thud. 'Some fucking idiot in Hong Kong,' he explains, with a Clintonian smile, wicked and engulfing. Buzzy is startled – not because she is so squeamish as to be offended; it's just that the Philip Devereux of her imagination doesn't swear in front of young women he has invited for a drink.

'I know the feeling,' she says, trying to sound game.

'Oh yes?'

'I keep getting emails from a Patrick Chan, telling me about a 'lucrative business venture' in Hong Kong. It involves him transferring a lot of money into my bank account, or something.' Philip gives a polite laugh, nothing like the lionish roar she heard at the ball, when she told him about drinking Sherard's artwork.

'But it must be hard having to take your BlackBerry everywhere. My friend Afua is the same; it's the bane of her life. You sat next to her, I think, at the Christmas ball?'

'Afua . . . Yes – who works for the minister chap?' Buzzy notes with a frisson of delight that he says this as though referring to some junior curate.

'That's right. Sherard Howe's adopted daughter, or sort of adopted.'

'*Is* she?' – the emphasis, Buzzy feels, relates mostly to his indifference – 'I don't think I knew that.'

There is no point insisting she has told him this already; she is already irritated with herself for bringing up the Howes, at once a lazy and masochistic choice of conversation.

'Sherard and I have been getting a little reacquainted lately, with this art exhibition. Actually, we've known each other on and off for years. We were at school together, you know. It's odd. I treated him rather badly – as his senior, it was only the done thing, though I sometimes wondered if he had a bit of a crush on me. Of course, it was a more innocent era back then . . .' He raises his drink, a little wistfully perhaps. Buzzy wonders if all those who feature in these memories look back at them through the same halcyon lens. 'He does seem to have made himself rather famous among, how can one put it, *le tout*—'

'Among the sort of people who say *le tout*?'

Philip's face darkens and Buzzy is afraid her desire to amuse him has ended with her causing offence, first by interrupting him and then including him in the category of person he was about to ridicule. Then suddenly his laughter fills the room, so that the fur-clad elderly lady who emerges puffing her cheeks at the threshold, clutched by her waif-like husband, shoots him a look of bulging animosity. 'Yes, I see what you mean! Though it's funny, I assumed at first Sherard really was interested in that art he collects, whereas now I'm not so sure. It's possible, I think, that no one could find it more awful than him – that attracting admiration in certain quarters for collecting it is some hilarious private joke. I don't remember him having an impish side: at school he was a bit of a weakling. Anyway, I'm quite impressed.'

'Oh, well that's nice,' Buzzy says blandly. She wonders where this leaves her relations with Philip, seeing as they were founded on shared animosity towards Sherard.

'That went down rather well,' he says, of his drink. 'I think I might try another. Would you . . .?'

Buzzy palms at her unfinished glass. 'I'm fine for the moment, thanks.' She resists an urge to check her watch. It can't be much after six. She hasn't mentioned anything about Brussels to Philip, certain they'll have parted ways before she needs to make the journey to St Pancras by around eight. 'I'm enjoying it though – it's interestingly spicy.'

'Isn't it,' he replies, catching the barman's eye. 'Now, I haven't asked how things are with you.'

Buzzy's buoyant mood suddenly sinks as it dawns on her that he required a gin cocktail, and the knowledge that another is en route, before broaching this elementary subject. Or is she being absurdly over-sensitive? 'Fine, thank you,' she shrugs. 'And you – are you working on any big deals at the moment?'

'Not many of those around, I'm afraid. At the moment I'm knee-deep in restructuring and insolvency proceedings – as you might have read, some of my banking clients have had a few existential difficulties. It's hideously complicated,' he says brightly. The second Charles II arrives. 'Oh, good man!'

'I'm not sure I understand. Do you mean that you advised the banks while they were getting into a mess, and now you're advising them on how to finish themselves off?'

A python-skin loafer jigs up and down at the end of Philip's crossed leg. 'You do have an interesting perspective on things, Elizabeth.'

Buzzy, who would have assumed her perspective was fairly conventional, feels herself blush. 'Do I?'

'You know, you never got in touch with me about those Eliot letters,' he says, sounding faintly hurt. 'I admit I assumed you would.'

'Oh, but I thought *you'd* forgotten. Or didn't really mean it when you offered to arrange the viewing.'

'I don't make an offer if I don't mean it,' he says pompously. 'Well, anyway. Perhaps we'll get round to it next time, if you're interested.'

'I definitely am.' She wonders who this man is, exactly. Is his inauthenticity – she doesn't think real gentlemen swear and dye their hair – part of his roguish charm? Or is the charm inauthentic? The latter feels more likely. It remains highly possible that her interest in Philip Devereux is based on nothing more than Marcel's and Afua's disapproval of her consorting with him. Yet she is quite enjoying herself.

'Damn,' Philip mutters, regarding another couple entering the bar. 'Murray, hi!'

'Philip, what a pleasure. We were a little early for our table downstairs and I said to Jane: wouldn't it be fun to have a quick drink first?' Murray, who is South African, delivers this from the side of his mouth as though telling a joke.

'Do come and join us.'

Mousy blonde Jane, whose hands are diffidently stuffed in the pockets of her trench coat, gives Buzzy an apologetic smile. A minor fuss follows while introductions are made and they decide to switch to a larger table. When they are at last settled, there is a throat-clearing pause which Buzzy doesn't mind, for once, since it won't be up to her to start the conversation.

'What's that you're drinking?' asks Murray, looking at but not addressing Buzzy.

'I believe it's called a Charles II.'

'I wonder why they named a drink after him. Wasn't he a complete nuisance?'

'If you mean he dissolved parliament and sired a dozen bastards. But given parliament had had his father's head chopped off, one has to admire the *joie de vivre*.' Philip's laugh again fills the room.

'You're probably related to him somewhere along the line,' Murray suggests mischievously. Philip emits a modest 'ha!' that leaves the idea not quite refuted.

'I think I'll have a martini, even so,' Jane says, with a quick uncertain smile.

The barman arrives and drinks are ordered, Buzzy sticking loyally with the Charles II. Murray makes an impenetrable reference to the collapse of something or other – she gathers he's with a rival law firm – and Philip answers in vague, upbeat terms, making sure to smile at the ladies in a *pas devant les enfants* manner that's nonetheless appreciated by Buzzy. Jane too, perhaps, as she turns to Buzzy and asks what she does.

'Elizabeth is a brilliant young writer, from Oxford.'

'Are you, gosh.'

'Hardly!' says Buzzy, though she is starting to feel as if she really might be a brilliant young writer, if not from Oxford. She has, after all, recently commenced her fifth poem, so it is not entirely a lie when Buzzy explains that she is working on her first collection, and nor when she says some of her work has already been published: 'A, B, C' did feature, pseudonymously, in the 2006 *Mays Anthology*. Jane is such an encouraging listener, and emits such a constant stream of nods and *wows!* and *wonderfuls!*, that by the time Buzzy touches on 'Portraits of Ladies', her undergraduate dissertation, she wonders if she hasn't got a little carried away. She glances at Philip and is reassured to find that his expression is relaxed, if inattentive. When Buzzy comes to asking Jane if she works at all, it's with a certain amount of compassionate trepidation.

'Are you really?' she asks, feeling herself blush, on learning that Jane is a psychologist. 'What sort?'

'I see quite a range of patients in my clinical work. But in research terms, I'm mainly interested in psychopaths.'

'Evidently,' Philip jokes.

Murray rolls his eyes. 'Yaw, yaw,' he says, enjoying the attention, while Jane smiles at them both.

The conversation moves on to other topics: the old-world charm of Rules and some fabulous restaurant in Copenhagen; the new Kevin Spacey play at the Old Vic; a lack of snowfall in Gstaad. Buzzy checks the time and is surprised to find it's almost seven thirty. She smiles achily, trying to think what excuse she might make to Philip if Murray and Jane are still chatting away in another half an hour; except after two gin cocktails she has lost the willpower not to dwell on Marcel and the impending weekend, and fails to come up with anything convincing. She is so excited about the next couple of days she dreads them arriving, because then Monday will roll around and she will be alone again in Kensington, weighed down by the same dull preoccupation – that she is neither Dorothea nor Celia but a sort of Casaubon, less than her ambition – and she isn't sure she can face this without any distracting fantasy.

'I'm sure it won't be a problem,' Murray is saying, 'we dine here quite often.'

Having forgotten Buzzy, the others now seem to be awaiting some kind of response from her. She guesses they are discussing the possibility of going downstairs for dinner. 'I can't.' In the end the shock of landing so firmly on the last word, and her sudden powerful hatred of these people who would so casually risk her missing Marcel and the Eurostar, prevent her from making any attempt at an explanation.

To her surprise, and as though accustomed to speaking on her behalf, Philip says, 'Elizabeth has to go to Brussels this evening.'

Marcel must have told him she was going to the wedding. Since all their recent communications have been filtered through Afua, Buzzy hasn't directly discussed with Marcel either her drink with Philip or the trip to Brussels. So it's not as if Buzzy has asked him to keep their St Pancras rendezvous a secret. But he has too fine an appreciation of human weakness not to see perfectly well why Buzzy might have preferred to shield Philip from the knowledge that she had a more significant engagement with his trainee later the same evening. The remote possibility that Marcel is jealous of Philip after all – that this and not idle competitiveness explains why he has chosen to humiliate the senior man, by revealing the length to which Buzzy has gone to protect his self-importance – more than compensates for her present embarrassment. Murray and Jane mistake the source of the latter and respond with sympathetic murmurs.

'Actually, I'm quite looking forward to it. I've never been on the Eurostar before.'

146

'Oh, it's marvellous,' says Philip gallantly, 'absolutely the most civilised way to travel. Makes arriving in Belgium almost worth it.'

Despite its unfashionable Victorian façade, which Buzzy finds in any case impressive, the interior of St Pancras International has an air of modern continental sophistication, with its unusual cleanliness, multilingual signs and elegant arcade of shops with names like Neuhaus and Le Pain Quotidien. The people, too, give off an enhancing cross-border glow compared with the tired swarm of commuters over the road at King's Cross.

Arriving a good quarter of an hour early, she ought to buy some sort of snack to soak up the gin cocktails but finds herself gliding past Marks & Spencer. It's not that she isn't hungry; more that eating a sandwich would feel an overly prosaic thing to do at this moment in her life. A familiar figure is waiting by the ticket machines, clutching the extended handle of a scuffed and, she happens to know, inexpensive suitcase. Staring at the ground in front of him, his other hand resting on his hip, his overall pose resembles a bloated and cruel parody of Donatello's *David*.

'Hen!' She kisses his cheek. 'Thanks so much: you've literally saved my life. Well, not literally,' she adds, seeing Henry's eyes widen.

'Really, I was glad to help. How was your drink?'

'It could have been worse. We went to the cocktail bar at Rules, do you know it?'

Henry's response is delivered with an air of tragic inevitability. More cheerfully, he adds, 'Perhaps you'll need another hand on Sunday evening, when you return?'

'I hadn't really thought about Sunday – I don't think so.'

'No, it was just, if you wanted help with your suitcase. It's quite heavy.'

'Thanks, but I hope I'm not that much of a diva yet. Though you're right,' Buzzy muses, 'I *have* packed a lot for one weekend. In my defence there is a wedding. Also, apparently it rains all the

147

time in Brussels, so I thought I'd better bring a few changes of clothes.'

'I went to Bruges once. It certainly rained buckets, not that that really proves anything.'

'I'm sure it proves something,' says Buzzy, though she can't think what. 'I suppose Marcel isn't here yet?'

'Actually, he is. He's already gone through to the departure area.'

'Oh, did he?'

'I suppose he's a little anxious, with the ceremony tomorrow.'

'Yes, you're probably right about that,' she says gratefully. 'I wonder what she's like – the new mother-in-law.'

'Quite young, I gather.'

'Hen, did you know about Marcel's mother?'

'The psychiatric, ah, history? Afua did mention it once. It must have been very hard on Marcel; I gather he was a teenager when she was committed.'

'You're right, it must,' she says, a little ashamed to have raised the subject. Ashamed, too, for her earlier hardness when he offered – innocently, chivalrously – to do her yet another favour. How was Henry to know that she couldn't bear to think of Sunday arriving? 'I suppose I'll go through to departures. Thanks again, Hen.'

'Not at all. Bon voyage!' he adds, with a modest jocular flourish.

'Perhaps I'll see you next week – at the private view of this art exhibition?'

'Oh, you're going to that? Fantastic, well, yes, I'll definitely see you then.'

'I haven't completely decided,' Buzzy says. 'Philip invited me, but do you think your father would be furious? I really never meant to drink his Damien Hirst beer; it was all just a terrible mix-up.'

'I don't think my father would object to your presence in any ostensible fashion,' Henry says carefully. 'He's actually been quite cheerful lately. I think it's the exhibition, he's looking forward to it.'

148

'Great,' Buzzy says, really not interested in Sherard Howe's mood swings. 'Well, until Thursday then, I expect.'

'I'll pass on your good wishes to Afua, for the vote tomorrow.'

'Of course, yes, please do. Au revoir!'

21

Labour family

'*Labour donor tells nepotism critics to "shut up"*',
Evening Standard, *6 February 2009*

A Labour donor today hit back at a 'dishonourable' attempt to sabotage his adopted daughter's hopes of becoming an MP.

Afua Nelson, a 25-year-old Treasury adviser, has been caught up in a nepotism row amid allegations that the Party hierarchy is trying to parachute her into the Islington South seat.

One MP called the process a 'stitch-up', claiming that Sherard Howe, 50, has 'blatantly and shamelessly' used his influence as a prominent donor to ensure the Party machine swung behind his adopted daughter.

Ms Nelson has lived with Mr Howe and his wife, writer and broadcaster Daphne Depree, in their Canonbury home since the age of sixteen. Before then she was raised on an Islington council estate by her mother, an alcoholic.

The row began last month when the incumbent MP, Labour's Ruth Beggs, made the surprise announcement that she intended to retire at the next election. Critics, including the unions and some backbenchers, accused the Party of holding the selection process to an accelerated timetable expressly to discourage other candidates from putting themselves forward. The decision to impose an all-women shortlist has also been controversial.

A Cambridge graduate, Ms Nelson wrote a successful blog for the *Liberal Review*, the left-wing magazine owned by Mr Howe. She quit journalism last year to work as an adviser to Treasury minister Alec Merton, and is seen by many as a rising star in the Party. Her boyfriend, lawyer Marcel Moreau, is the son of Belgian politician Anatole Moreau.

The actress Rowan Harwood, a family friend of the Howes, said: 'This is a talented and serious young lady who comes from a troubled background and whom Sherard and Daphne love as their own daughter. To see her targeted in a smear campaign like this is disgraceful.'

Mr Howe told the *Standard*: 'If any of these dishonourable briefers has the courage to go on the record, my lawyers would be delighted to make their acquaintance. If not, I hope they will do the decent thing and shut up.'

Daphne Depree's latest book, *The Prodigal Sister*, published last month, contains trenchant criticisms of Labour's record in power. It calls for a fundamental rethink of capitalism and the forming of a new 'progressive alliance' including feminists and the trade unions.

22

Marcel (1)

The 'apartment' – it consists of three floors, but that's what Marcel calls it – shows signs of life: cisterns flushing; floorboards creaking; the odd bark of French that makes her stomach tighten. Late last night he mentioned something about a family breakfast, but by then Buzzy was convinced he saw her presence this weekend as an annoyance, and decided against asking for any tiresome details. The upshot is that she now wonders when she ought to emerge from her guestroom. The church service is at two o'clock, she's sure at least of that. But does it imply they will have lunch around noon, and want an early breakfast? Or will lunch follow the service, meaning 'breakfast' will be more a hearty mid-morning brunch? She's torn between not wanting to miss a second in Marcel's company, however agonising, and the fear that he won't materialise for a while yet. This would leave her to make conversation with his relatives, including his father, whom she would think of as terrifying even if he wasn't a famously (to those who have researched him on the internet) austere politician.

She curls up in the centre of the large bed. Despite the freezing February temperature the room does not seem to be heated at all, so that the sound of her own chattering would have kept her awake even if her brain hadn't been whirring about what a disappointment the trip had been so far.

Their conversation on the Eurostar was brief and unspectacular. (He couldn't conceal a slight grimace when she told him how exciting it was to travel first class.) As soon as it was polite to do so, he brought out his book, Flaubert's *L'Éducation sentimentale*, which, despite his turning of the pages every now and again, she suspected he wasn't really taking in. The only time he showed any enthusiasm was when the drinks trolley passed by, and the redhead stewardess reached across Buzzy to hand him two miniature wine bottles. They finally arrived at the apartment at almost one in the morning, at which time he suggested they get some sleep. About ten minutes later, on her way to the bathroom, she met him on the landing clutching the stem of a wine glass and a not-so-miniature bottle of red. Buzzy received the same vacantly courteous smile he'd given the stewardess.

She checks her phone: it's coming up to quarter past seven, quarter past eight Brussels time. Evidently she can't lie here indefinitely; for one thing she might die of cold, and the matter is settled by the sight of her purplish fingernails and her certainty that there must be some warmth to be found in the kitchen. Where's the pleasure of living in such grand neoclassical elegance if you can't afford to heat the place? Except that's not really the issue, she reflects, while pulling on riskily casual jeans and a light-blue V-neck. Keeping a cold house is an upper-class habit she knows she could never acquire.

Buzzy twists the cut-glass door knob, wincing when she hears the thud of the sprung latch. In the corridor she catches herself in the Louis XVI mirror: she looks a little startled amid the gold-leaf gilding. She retraces her steps from the night before, passing Marcel's door, firmly shut, as she heads for the marble stairs. This must be the middle floor of the Moreau apartment, she decides; the sixth and penultimate of the building. *Je m'appelle Elizabeth. Enchantée* . . . She wonders if they actually say *enchantée*, or if it sounds as old-fashioned as 'enchanted' in English.

The corridor at the bottom of the stair leads directly to the kitchen. Slowing her pace, she notices the oil paintings on the walls: a shipwreck and several verdant landscapes, she guesses in the Romantic style, feeling dimly that Flemish painting has been important at certain periods and that she might have done well to have investigated this a little more.

The clatter of cutlery is coming from somewhere on this floor, but Buzzy finds no one in the kitchen, and only briefly considers investigating further. The room is about the same size as the Howes' but with more natural light. On one wall a muted flat-screen TV shows America's new president at a news conference, looking grave and faintly distempered.

Buzzy wonders, a little Henryishly, if it would be impolite to help herself to a glass of water. She finds a tall slim Pernod glass in a cupboard given over to miscellany (an ashtray, cooker instructions): it's not quite what she was looking for but she is in a hurry – she doesn't want to be discovered rootling around in someone else's kitchen – and it will do.

The tap water has the same alkaline taste she remembers from Argentina. She gazes down on Avenue Louise, as if she might glean some insight into him from the line of chestnut trees and grey mansions which Marcel must have looked on so often. Her phone bleeps in her pocket, a message from her network provider belatedly welcoming her to Belgium. 'Shit,' she says, at the sound of the glass of water, which she left balanced on top of the radiator, smashing against the floor. The height of the glass has at least meant the break was relatively clean. It lies in a little puddle of water, divided into an upper and lower half, with just a few smaller shards around the central break. Buzzy kneels down and carefully picks up the pieces.

She's almost finished when she hears an aged female voice and the approaching sound of the speaker's footsteps. Panicking, she grabs the remaining bits, all except one or two of the very smallest, which she leaves as little glinting diamonds to crunch under some-one's foot. In vain Buzzy whirls around in search of a dustbin, knowing the speaker will arrive in the kitchen any second. Holding the pieces of broken glass to her chest, she uses her other arm to pull open drawers. The first is full of cutlery. The one beneath contains a small mound of neatly folded drying towels, into which Buzzy tips the fragments of Pernod glass. She gives her jumper a few rapid brushes to make sure nothing incriminating is stuck in the wool, pushes the drawer shut with her hip and swivels round to the face the new arrival.

The lady, presumably Marcel's grandmother, is glamorously shrunken inside a fuchsia skirt-suit. Her face is framed by white hair that's raised in a bouffant of equal height to the distance separating her eyebrows from her chin, and arranged into curls at the temples. It gives an impression of lustrousness and, Buzzy assumes less intentionally, the Old Bailey.

'*Enchantée, Madame.*'

The old lady peers at Buzzy uncertainly. Four rows of pearls round her neck seem to account for a slight stoop in her walk. '*Mademoiselle?*'

'*Je m'appelle Elizabeth. Je suis l'amie de Marcel.*'

The lady still looks confused: perhaps she has dementia and doesn't remember her grandson. Feeling it up to her to take charge in this situation, Buzzy takes the lady's hand and shakes it in a manner that she hopes is firmly reassuring. '*Comment t'appelles-tu?*' she asks slowly, with a wide smile.

'*Marguerite, enchantée.*'

She releases Marguerite's fingers, feeling a fresh lurch of sympathy at their refrigerated prune texture. The elderly lady's hand is left hanging momentarily and Buzzy finds herself studying Marguerite's nougat skin, her compassion slightly tempered now by a gasp-worthy collection of rings. Buzzy is trying to compose her next sentence of French when she notices a smear of blood over the last knuckle, where Marguerite must have cut herself without noticing. Delicately, she points at it and says, '*Je pense que . . . sangre?*'

'*Sans gré?*' The Spanish word was not entirely unhelpful, however, as Marguerite follows this with, '*Ah, du sang! Mais regardez, mademoiselle.*' It's the grandmother's turn to point, and Buzzy duly observes a red smear down the front of her V-neck. Near the top of her fourth finger is a half-centimetre long flap of skin. Buzzy holds it up for inspection and several drops of blood fall, as if on cue, onto the kitchen floor.

'*Merde,*' she says, despite everything a little pleased to have identified the correct word.

After Marguerite has found and applied a small plaster, it is evident some sort of explanation is required. Buzzy mimes the breaking of a glass, wishing very much that she could remember the word for 'sorry'.

'*Ah!*' says Marguerite, in satisfied comprehension. '*Mais où est le verre? Attendez*,' she mutters to herself, 'where is now *le verre* . . .?'

'Oh, you mean "where is the glass?" I put it in here,' Buzzy explains confidently, as though it were the most natural decision in the world. She cannot quite bear to check the look on Marguerite's face as the shattered item is revealed lying on its cushion of towels.

'*Vous êtes bien l'amie de mon petit-fils*,' says the older lady, in the studied tone of one who has grasped a prank rather belatedly and doesn't want to reveal as much.

'I think I'll just change my jumper,' says Buzzy, who has an idea she has not been paid a compliment. 'It was lovely to meet you.'

The conversation has slipped back into French and Anatole Moreau is discoursing on something or other – the traytay de rom, which from Buzzy's hazy recollection of citizenship studies might be the Treaty of Rome. It seems an unusual topic for a wedding day, but he is so much her idea of a European founding father, and he looks so aged (more so, almost, than his mother), that she could believe he wrote it. Less credible is the idea that this desiccated man, with his unceasing rasping voice and close-set eyes and elongated skull, should have had any role in the establishment of Marcel.

She was pleased to discover that the breakfast was a small affair, if not exactly informal – she is getting the impression nothing involving Anatole would be that – and was relieved to have changed out of the blood-stained V-neck and into her wedding outfit. Given Buzzy's shallow grasp of continental politics and unreliable French, which segues at unexpected moments into Spanish, she'd rather not imagine what would be made of her presence at the coffee table if she were still wearing jeans. Next to Buzzy is a plump man whose name remains as unclear to her as his relation to Anatole and Marguerite. 'Contan' is how it sounded when they were introduced, but never addressing him seems the most practical solution, especially as his attention is focused exclusively on Anatole, to whom aside from the occasional grunt of agreement he listens in silence. Marguerite too is mute except to urge more pastries and coffee on the men, giving Buzzy hope that the smashed glass incident has not been relayed to Marcel's father. With the obvious exception of her friend, no one else appears to be expected. There is no sign of the bride. Buzzy has a vision of her as a redhead like the Eurostar stewardess, wearing the ripped remains of her wedding dress and engaged in frenzied coitus in Marcel's bedroom.

She sips her orange juice and attempts to look interested in whatever Anatole is saying, though by now she has completely lost the thread. On the Eurostar, she asked Marcel what his father does these days. He replied he was a politician. When she persisted, asking what *sort* of politician – she knew that he knew that she knew, after all, that Anatole served as interior minister in two Belgian administrations in the nineties – he carefully marked his place in the Flaubert. He explained that his father has retired from national politics and now presides over a special committee representing the group of European Union member states who are signatories to the borderless Schengen Area. Marcel went into some detail as to the purpose of the committee, and Buzzy struggled to follow at times, though that wasn't why she felt hollowed out by the time he'd finished speaking. She thanked him, and he smiled and returned to his book.

When Marcel finally appears for breakfast, he is wearing a charcoal suit and dazzling white dress shirt. Were it not worn by him, she might have said his green silk tie, with its curious emblem of a spread of playing cards at the line of his heart, was a little tasteless. Anatole continues with his impenetrable speech as though he hasn't noticed his son's arrival. Buzzy watches Marcel quietly close the door of the breakfast room and approach the table, his eyes fixed modestly on the floor in front of him. He pulls his chair back, careful to avoid it scraping, and sits down. He unfolds his napkin in his lap and, still without looking at anyone, traces his fingers along the handles of his cutlery, like a pianist gathering himself.

After what seems to Buzzy an excruciating length of time, Anatole at last pauses in his argument. He says something she doesn't quite catch, without addressing Marcel directly, but she understands from '*jeune homme*' that he has made a reference to his son's entrance.

'*Bonjour Papa, Grand-mère, Quentin,*' Marcel replies, regarding each solemnly. When, last of all, he glances at Buzzy, there is a ghost of a grin at his lips, lesser and more magnificent than any he's given her since the start of the trip.

As if she has been waiting for permission, Marguerite gets up to pour her grandson a coffee and offer him a trembling plate of croissants and glazed pastries. Buzzy notices she has not touched any of them herself; no doubt she would sooner die than allow a mouthful of custard-filled apple cake or chocolate-coated waffle to pass her lips. He too declines, politely, in favour of fruit salad.

Father and son exchange a few remarks in French; or rather, Marcel answers Anatole's questions. His tone is respectful (he uses the '*vous*' form of address, something that Buzzy, in her general panic to make herself understood, has forgotten to do herself), but increasingly Anatole seems displeased by what he hears.

The discussion has not lasted long when, to her surprise, Anatole turns to Buzzy. 'I understand you have known my son for some years now,' he says, in accented English. She nods, wondering if he could possibly be mistaking her for Afua: she had tried to explain who she was earlier, but his boredom seemed immediate and comprehensive. 'Perhaps you think he has become more like you, more British, in that time? In fact, this is not true. He has always had a British side. Always polite, as you see, always reserved. Perhaps "Britishness" is more than that – perhaps less, since those attributes are increasingly rare in your island. But this is exactly the word, because for us Britishness is still characterised above all by a certain in-sul-ar-it-y,' he says, separating each phoneme. 'I find it ironic that it was an English poet who wrote "No man is an island"—'

'*C'était John Donne, je crois,*' Quentin says.

'When this statement is true,' – he holds up a bony finger – 'with one exception: the Englishman!' He stares at Buzzy with a forbearing smile, as if waiting for the laughter in the chamber to subside. '*Alors*. What form, beyond a polite and reserved disposition, does this insularity take?'

'I suppose you could say—' begins Buzzy, half realising the question is rhetorical but having an urge to hear her own voice for the first time in what feels likes an age.

'—I refer not,' continues Anatole loftily, 'or not just, to a metaphysical insularity. Rather, to a metaphysical insularity that also reveals itself in the political domain. Look at my son: does he believe in solidarity? Or is he an individualist? It's the latter, of course. I say "of course" – he has not told me this, still less argued with me. Never in his life. So I make inferences, based on the choices he makes.' He takes a sip of coffee. 'Insularity,' he repeats, with disgust.

'Europe must turn its back on neoliberalism,' Quentin affirms. Buzzy wonders if he's tin-eared or if this is also some oblique rejection of Marcel.

'Quite so,' says Anatole, who goes on to explain that the great existential threat to Europe is Protestant, not Islamist, ideology. The Anglo-Saxon credos of multiculturalism, after the London Underground attacks of 2005, and unfettered capitalism, after the financial crisis of 2008, have collapsed 'in Hegelian style'. Europe is a Catholic club or it is nothing; Turkey's application to join the EU must be rejected at all costs. Occasionally Quentin breaks in with an *exactement* or *c'est ça*.

If the purpose of all this is to goad Marcel, it's a spectacular failure, as she could have predicted. Back erect, he listens to his father with the same practised, far-off smile as his grandmother. Every now and again, his dark eyes dip a fraction and Buzzy wonders if he is fighting a desire to check his watch. If so, he never succumbs; they always swerve back to Anatole's face.

'I'm sure you're right,' Buzzy says at one point, taking her cue from Marcel. 'We *are* very immoral and greedy. It's almost as if we've been encouraged to behave like children who must have whatever we want. I mean, I can't remember how many credit cards I own and I'm definitely not rich. To be honest, I'm not even *poor*: that would imply there was a small amount of actual money to my name.'

Anatole's glassy expression causes Buzzy to redden: evidently Avenue Louise eurocrats do not expect guests to lay out their indigence for comic effect. She stares at the scattered shells of pain au chocolat on her plate, though in truth her shame is undermined by guessing how much her remarks will have pleased Marcel.

'Marie-Thérèse is not joining us?'

Marguerite gives a wincing shake of her head. It's not clear to Buzzy if she's understood Marcel's question, delivered in English, or if it's a reaction to hearing her future daughter-in-law's name.

'Impossible,' says Quentin, since Anatole doesn't seem inclined to answer. 'It means bad luck for the marriage.'

'Bad luck. Yes, of course.'

'For one thing,' Anatole adds caustically – previous encounters between Marcel and Marie-Thérèse have evidently not been a success. In the same tone, he asks, 'Do you intend to wear that tie in church?'

'I can wear something else, *Papa*, if you prefer.'

Anatole nods sniffily, and drains the rest of his coffee.

'I've had this tie for years,' Marcel continues. '*Maman* gave it to me.' There is no obvious note of triumph, but Buzzy wonders if she is the only one to spot his sardonic glint, as if the minor vulgarity of those four playing cards, barely visible from a distance, was a sure sign of the poor woman's madness.

When they should be inside St Boniface church, observing Anatole's nuptials, they are wandering the streets of Brussels. After a considerable silence, Buzzy praises the grandeur of Avenue Louise. Marcel replies it was where the Nazis chose to locate the Gestapo's headquarters during the Second World War. She doesn't want to dwell on whether he is subtly highlighting her lack of taste, as he had earlier with his mother: she has a terrible feeling that he isn't, that he rather admires the Third Reich's aesthetic

160

elan. After another silence, he talks, stiffly at first, about the city's architecture; its mix of Second Empire and Flemish Gothic styles. Passing Hôtel Solvay, he mentions Victor Horta and the art nouveau movement. He suggests, and Buzzy readily agrees, that they may as well wander over to nearby Hôtel Tassel, also designed by Horta. There he points out the curved bay window, the fertile shape of which incensed early Catholic critics ('Because pregnant women can think of *nothing else* but getting a man into their bed,' she observes, with sham-outrage), and its columns that finish eccentrically in sets of claws. He explains that art nouveau was a rebellion sponsored by the haute bourgeoisie.

'Oh dear – Belgian Sherards.'

'*T'es vachement méchante aujourd'hui.*'

'Cowishly naughty, did you say?'

'*Exactement.*'

She is just coming to the conclusion that Marcel is almost enjoying himself, when – as though he were reading her thoughts and timing the thing to perfection – he announces that Brussels is tedious and provincial and really there is nothing much to see. Secretly, she can see his point: the city resembles to her a smaller, shabbier, more melancholic Paris. But since she feels she is responsible for their current rather aimless predicament, and by extension his state of mind, and since the latter is in any case the central preoccupation of her existence, it seems important that they find something fun to do.

The initial rush that followed their escape dissipated fairly quickly. For Buzzy, at least, it was replaced by more practical questions: where were they going to sleep tonight? How was she ever going to retrieve her suitcase, her passport?

The proposal to skip Anatole's wedding was simply a nervous joke, something to say when Marcel came to collect her from the guestroom. At least, that's what she's telling herself, now that Marcel might have ended his relationship with his father so she could avoid a difficult social occasion. How could she have anticipated that his beautiful slender lip would first curl in bemusement and then, when it should have continued rising upwards, harden into a flat line? The way he looked at her! It was disturbing and exciting. 'Sure,' he said, 'if you want' – and proceeded calmly to exit the apartment, ten minutes before the taxi was supposed to take them to Place Boniface.

If you want. Meaning Buzzy will bear the consequences. The worst part is that, though increasingly anxious, she still doesn't wholly regret the situation. They are bound to each other now.

Only a few streets from the fashion boutiques and luxury hotels, she is surprised to find they are in a grimy, pot holed quarter that if it wasn't for all the halal shops wouldn't have felt out of place in Latin America. The plan is to visit someone called Jean-Michel, whom Marcel refers to vaguely as a friend. Every now and again he points out a landmark – a large soulless square called Place Flagey; the art deco National Broadcasting Institute; the Ixelles ponds – but after a while these either dry up or he is too busy concentrating on trying to remember where Jean-Michel lives. '*Oui, par ici,*' he says to himself, and turns abruptly into a rank-smelling side-street. Buzzy buries her resentment that he has chosen to take her here over the gold-trimmed splendour of the Grand Place.

Jean-Michel lives above a butcher's shop; going up the stairs there is a powerful smell of dried blood. He glares at Marcel in a manner that Buzzy considers distinctly unfriendly. He's tall and rangy, with a little potbelly: she knows this because despite the freezing temperature of the building he's wearing a close-fitting T-shirt. It bears an image of a Chinese baby riding a dragon and the name of a band, Stone Temple Pilots. She's never heard of them.

'*Ça va? C'est moi – Marcel.*'

'*Oui, bien sûr,*' Jean-Michel says eventually, without enthusiasm.

The décor of the flat is strongly uninspired by art nouveau whimsy; the centrepiece is a small, ineffective convection heater. Several junkies are bunched up on a cheap-looking brown sofa. They gaze up at the pair's entrance, confused at but not interested in the sight of Marcel in his suit and Buzzy in her make-up and old Karen Millen dress and too-thin navy overcoat.

Marcel and Jean-Michel have a brief hushed conversation, after which Jean-Michel disappears into a backroom. When he returns he seems much more relaxed. He introduces himself to Buzzy. When Marcel explains she is English, he seems pleased for some reason.

'You are from London?'

Buzzy says yes.

'A big place.'

'Oh, yes, it is!' she replies, with a nervous laugh. 'I'm hoping to see your own big place – the Grand Place – while I'm here.'

This earns her a look of mild suspicion. Gesturing at their clothes, Jean-Michel says, 'Eh, why you . . .?'

Marcel explains that his father is getting married today, repeating himself in French when it's clear Jean-Michel has not understood.

'When?'

He looks at his watch, flicking a lock of black hair from his eyes with a slight sideways motion of his head. 'Now, in fact. *Maintenant.*'

The dealer pinches his crooked nose. '*C'est comme ça?*'

'*C'est comme ça.*'

Marcel takes several banknotes from his wallet. Ignoring his outstretched palm, Jean-Michel retrieves three wraps from his jeans back pocket and holds them aloft between his fingers like a winning hand of cards. Turning to the figures on the sofa, he says, '*Vouz savez qui est son père?*' Buzzy feels Marcel tense slightly. '*L'ancien ministre de l'intérieur, Anatole Moreau!*'

There are one or two hollow grins. Bored with them now, Jean-Michel concludes the exchange and to Buzzy's relief they are ushered to the front door, still slightly ajar. They are almost there when one of the junkies – she thinks it's a wizened North African – calls out gruffly, '*Moreau: je me souviens de ce mec. C'était un fils de pute.*' She hears him clear his throat, then the soft slap of his spit against the floor.

163

Marcel turns round. His neutral expression gives way to a bleak smile. '*Il n'a pas changé, en fait.*'

Feeling reckless after two pints of Trappist beer, it's Buzzy's idea that they go for a drink in Matongé. It surprises her he's never been to one of the bars around here; it's not that far from the Moreau residence and she is already getting a sense of Brussels' smallness.

'It's the Congolese area,' Marcel shrugs, as if this weren't obvious. In London, he would never say, 'It's the Bengali area' about Brick Lane or 'It's the Chinese area' about Chinatown (though it's true he'd be unlikely to dine in either). And isn't his girlfriend half-African, when it comes down to it? Perhaps he has a more Anatolian attitude to multiculturalism in his own city.

'Afua is not African. Not at all.' He sounds more amused than indignant.

'You make it sound as though I'm trying to be offensive about Afua.'

'*C'est plutôt* . . . Maybe you will see what I mean.'

'Is the "maybe" because you might be wrong, or because I might be too much of an idiot?'

Marcel has stopped walking. 'Perhaps this one?'

The walls of Chez Doudou are dark cherry. The place is scarcely lit apart from the bar area, which is festooned with fairy lights. Above the bottles of spirits, in pride of place, is a large photo of a black woman in a head-dress, her full lips parted a fraction. It vaguely reminds Buzzy of Vermeer's *Girl with a Pearl Earring*, except the African lady is facing in the other direction, and has an ethereal greenish glow from the UV strip light above her.

The few patrons, all male, display none of the horror-inflected jollity she has been expecting. Certainly they don't seem grateful that a young white pair is so broadminded as to stop by their drinking spot.

They choose a table in the corner. Buzzy is left on her own while Marcel goes to the bar, returning with a beer and a rum and coke before heading for the loos.

While he is gone the place starts to fill up. In a moment of paranoia, as a lithe man in a singlet settles at a nearby table and stares at her, she wonders if word has got out of the white girl sitting all by herself. She feels immediately ashamed. But Marcel was right, she realises: Afua is not African, not in the way these people are. Nor, even, was the footballer's cousin she met in La Collezione, with his designer clothes and expensive taste in champagne.

She distracts herself by thinking of Marcel and the hours stretching ahead of them. Again she wonders where the two of them are going to sleep tonight.

The man observing her gets up and in a few jangling strides is at Buzzy's table. An unlit cigarette is stuck in the corner of his mouth; he asks her for a light.

She shrugs apologetically. 'Sorry,' she replies in English, 'I don't smoke.'

He removes the cigarette, his teeth iridescent under the ultraviolet. 'Okay,' he beams, with that childish French pronunciation, and is about to say something else when Marcel returns and offers his lighter. He wears the mask of cold civility Buzzy has seen so often. The guy hovers for a couple of deep drags, dipping his shoulder in rhythm with the rumba music, and eventually departs with an upturned thumb.

'Everything fine?'

'Quite good, in fact,' he replies, though nothing in his manner gives away that he has just snorted several lines of Jean-Michel's product. She earlier declined Marcel's offer to try this herself, having taken cocaine only once, at a May Ball, and found it made her embarrassingly weepy.

'At the ball, Panos mentioned something about your family's "illustrious Congolese heritage" . . .'

'It's true my grandfather was a magistrate in Léopoldville – Kinshasa now. I don't know how he knew that.'

'I expect he has his sources. He assured me people always tell him everything.' Marcel lights a cigarette of his own, raises his eyebrow. She goes on, 'Léopoldville . . . wasn't there a King Léopold? I don't mind the idea of having a place named after me.'

'I believe there's an Elizabethtown in Kentucky.'

'Damn, is there? "Buzzyville" doesn't quite have the same ring.'

'One could say it wasn't worse than Orpington,' he offers diplomatically.

'That's a qualified endorsement, but thanks anyway. As for Marcelville . . .'

'I can't imagine anyone would want to live there.'

'Oh, I don't know. I think it sounds quite nice, really; like somewhere you might find on the Côte d'Azur.' Hastily, she adds, '*Mar* makes me think of the sea.'

By the time Marcel has made another couple of visits to the bar and lavatory, dancing has started in the spaces between the tables around them. Buzzy notes the odd white face in the crowd.

'I'm sorry about today – with your father, I mean.'

'It doesn't matter,' he says, extinguishing a cigarette. 'It was a big event, with lots of important people. By now he's probably forgotten I wasn't there.'

'You never told me about your mother,' she says quietly. 'I'm sorry.'

She wonders if the words have been drowned out by the sound of the music and dancing, and is trying to think of a new topic, when he replies, 'When I was younger, I could be' – he pauses, bites his lips, gives up – '*très con.*'

'When you were *younger* . . .' Buzzy says, in a hopeless attempt at levity.

'Even more than now. With my mother, we were close, but sometimes I was . . . unkind.' He steals a cautious glance at her.

'You were a teenage boy and your mother was ill. How could you have known what to do? *All* guys are horrible at that age – it's genetically encoded or something.' She wishes she could sound more useful and authoritative, that she'd actually read one of those Richard Dawkins books she used to spot on other undergraduates' bookshelves. 'What I mean is, you mustn't blame yourself or anything like that.'

'I don't blame myself,' he says, the trace of mockery back in his voice.

'No, of course – good,' says Buzzy, confused. For a few rapturous moments, she thought they were finally speaking sincerely, in the same manner as everyone else in this bar. But isn't he entitled to feel she doesn't understand anything – that it was gauche, even despicable of her to imply he might somehow feel responsible for his mother's illness? 'I think it's about time I bought the drinks. Another beer?'

Marcel looks at his half-full glass and shrugs. She'll take it as a yes. She is suddenly apprehensive he'll yawn and suggest they call it a night, perhaps even catch the last Eurostar back to London. If it'll prolong things, she is prepared to get very drunk.

She feels a little unsteady on her feet. The rum and cokes were deceptively easy – certainly compared with the beers in the afternoon; she had no idea the monks would brew something so maliciously strong – and she finished all three of them quickly.

Buzzy prepares to swerve past a voluptuous dancer in a black cotton dress. The girl's forehead is vast, a Canada above the United States of her face. Buzzy is thinking how fascinating she looks, an African Habsburg, when the dancer grabs her by the wrists and starts gyrating. A circle quickly forms around them.

Continuing to clasp Buzz (who fears her purse is going to spill onto the floor), the girl goes floppy, her head and shoulders hunched forwards. Buzzy is wondering if her new friend is about to be sick when to whoops of appreciation she commences rolling her buttocks in extravagant horizontal and vertical arcs. A man appears by the girl's side and before Buzzy knows it there are four of them in a line, the singleted guy from earlier having appeared next to Buzzy. Wishing to extricate herself without appearing too much of a bad sport, she shrugs and waves her purse at him. 'C'est bon, c'est bon.' He takes her purse and, grinning rather madly, slides it in the back pocket of his jeans. He raises his arms in a *voilà* gesture before thrusting his behind in Buzzy's direction.

The music consists of the same urging phrase – not French, as far as she can tell – over a tinny synth hook and conga beat that seems to be speeding up. Marcel has been out of her thoughts for

167

an improbable stretch of time, at least a few minutes. Now she flushes at the sight of him watching her. The singlet guy's arms are raised above her shoulders and he's shaking his tightly drawn chest. She catches his warm earth odour as he bends his arms and lifts his elbows level with his ears, which is odd because she feels his hands at her sides. These turn out to belong to someone behind her, curving himself against her and almost pushing her off her feet with his meaty thighs, so that she has to reach out and grab hold of the singlet guy, who interprets this as a signal that she is finally getting into the spirit of things, and presses in close enough that his knees jostle with those of the man at her back.

He has tobacco breath. 'You like this music?'

These are difficult circumstances in which to hold a conversation, and her opinion on the music is not settled. She nods.

'*Ndombolo*,' he pants, in uncomfortable proximity to her lips.

Buzzy tries to push her palm discouragingly against the thigh of the unknown man behind her. She hears a throaty reaction at her nape (he must be short) and feels her hand being moved further up his thigh.

She has missed some further remark from the singlet guy. 'I'm sorry, what?'

'What iz your name?'

'I'm sorry; I really think I need to get back to—'

'I am Marcel.'

Before Buzzy can process this questionable statement, the real one is next to her. He holds out his palm. She seizes it with as much dignity as she can muster, hardly noticing the other Marcel and his shorter compatriot slipping back into the crowd.

'May I have the honour?'

'I thought you'd never ask,' she says wryly, with a thumping heart.

'It's true I don't like to dance. But I can make exceptions.'

Their movements are a little stuttering at first. It would be impossible for Buzzy to conceive of Marcel as being truly bad at anything, but he is not a natural lead. After a few missteps in which they are clearly out of synch with the drumbeat, he finally

168

settles into a slower rhythm and modest hip slide which Buzzy can follow easily enough. She holds close to him, savouring the delicate brush of his legs. Boldly she lets her arms trail down his back. She feels the faint ridge of his spine through his dress shirt, now slightly damp, unless the moisture is from her own palm.

For a while they are silent, and she senses he is concentrating on the music. This prompts her to wonder if his initial awkwardness was perhaps terribly injurious to his pride, and if so – but she can't quite believe it, if only she could be sure! – what it meant that he asked her to dance. His cheek brushes against her. 'This is not how I pictured it.'

'What isn't?'

'My father's wedding day. Trying to dance *kwassa kwassa* in Matongé, with you.'

'I think we're doing pretty well, as it happens.' Buzzy allows herself to note that if he doesn't agree with this assessment, he doesn't disagree either.

When the song finishes, they drift to the edge of the improvised dance area, Marcel seemingly content to stand among the raucous crowd. She feels his subtle heat at her arm.

'So what are we seeing tomorrow? Oh, please,' Buzzy says, of the exaggerated creases on his forehead, 'I come from North Kent. Why is everyone so rude about Brussels?'

'There is the Musée des Beaux-Arts, I suppose. Of course it's much smaller than the National Gallery, but there are some pieces worth seeing. I used to go quite often to look at the Bruegels.'

'It sounds perfect. Wait a minute: Bruegel's *Icarus*!'

'Oh – well, yes – that's one of them . . .'

'I mean as in the Auden poem. You know: the one where the ploughman is minding his own business, while Icarus falls into the sea?'

'I never knew about this poem.' There is a slight suggestion this is more noteworthy than a boy tumbling out of the sky. But he doesn't sound resentful; indeed, he smiles as if pleased to be caught out. 'Actually, there's another example of art nouveau not far from the Musée des Beaux-Arts. It's a museum of musical instruments, but there's a rooftop restaurant with quite a decent view of the city. Perhaps we could have breakfast there – if you want to, that is. It's nothing very exciting.'

'I would love to. Really, let's do it.'

He moves his thumb along her finger, as far as the plaster. He gives it an exploratory press. 'I meant to ask what happened with this.'

'It's nothing. I smashed a glass at your house.'

'Well, I probably had that coming.'

They are climbing into a taxi when the Congolese Marcel emerges from the bar, shouting and waving something at them. Buzzy pauses before winding the window down. It's her purse, which she forgot was still in his back pocket.

The hotel is not far from the European parliament. In the lift Buzzy says she supposes one never knows the nice places to stay in one's own city, knowing how false she must sound (there *are* no nice hotels in Orpington) and how unimpressed Marcel will be at her attempt to justify his choice. The receptionist asked if they wanted a double room. He said yes, casually, without consulting her, and now she doesn't know if she feels nauseous from nerves or all the alcohol on an empty stomach. He did enquire more than once if she wanted to eat, but she knew the coke had killed his appetite and he'd find it a bore.

On entering the bedroom, it isn't the undeniable presence of the matrimonial bed that catches Buzzy's eye, but the shower chamber in the centre of the room. The door and two of its walls are entirely translucent; the only side that's not is connected to one of the main walls.

'It's not very British, is it?'

He is referring, she realises, to himself: he's so guarded about his body that Buzzy's never even seen him in a T-shirt. He will detest the idea of bathing himself in front of her, yet she's pretty sure he'd find the idea of going a day without washing too barbaric.

'I think I'm going to be sick.'

Marcel tilts his head slightly. For once it's him who isn't certain on what level they're speaking, though Buzzy's dash for the sink hardly feels victorious.

When she wakes she is in bed. A slight gap between the curtains allows her to trace Marcel's shoulder blade and upper arm, which she stares at for as long as she can, until the whiteness of his skin starts to leak into the space around it and the shape of him is lost. Only then does her consciousness extend to her own body: she is wearing nothing but her bra and pants.

Any question that she has died and gone to heaven is settled by her parched throat and the surly promise of a headache. Blood thumping in her ears, she eases out of the bed in search of water. The journey to the sink is complicated by the darkness and not having seen the room sober. Creeping along, at one point she gropes what must be the door of the wardrobe. She opens it with an anxious grimace; fortunately the hinges don't creak. She can just make out the outlines of her dress and Marcel's suit hanging next to each other.

The sink is on the other side of the shower installation. Further to the right is a small loo. Without entering it, she turns the light on and leaves the door slightly ajar, so that the rest of the bedroom comes into low-beam relief. Buzzy pours a glass of water, ignoring the memory it stirs of Marguerite. She is surprised to find her face in the mirror is not a horrible smudgy mess. She bends over and checks the bin: there are clumps of sodden tissue at the bottom. She collects one of these and holds it up against the illuminated crack of the loo door. It's streaked with the same red as her lipstick. Buzzy notices too that the acidic taste of vomit in her mouth is partially hidden by mint. She has no recollection of removing her make-up or brushing her teeth, and she's almost certain she wasn't in a state to perform either activity, at least by herself, before she passed out.

Back in the bed, she lies staring at the ceiling for a long time. When the first hint of grey morning is already sneaking under the

171

curtains, he turns over to face her, still asleep. Buzzy mirrors his position. There are little stubble marks on his chin and upper lip which she has never dared to gaze at as she does now. His mouth is parted slightly, giving him a guileless expression. She inches closer in a series of feigned unconscious shuffles, until she can feel his warm breaths lapping against her nose. She shifts her head upwards – a more obviously premeditated movement – to take in a mouthful of it. The first soft rush over her tongue provokes a juddering involuntary exhalation, like spluttering on a joint. For an awful second she thinks she might have woken him, but the rhythmic shushing continues. Emboldened by this escape, or simply unable to stop herself, she closes her eyes and leans forward to find his hard thin lips – she worries that her own are trembling too much, but breathing insufficiently, refusing even to swallow, she leaves them there. At some point the little rushes of air cease: she imagines Marcel opening his eyes (her own are scrunched shut); then, after an agonising pause, they resume, shallower, before returning to their original tempo, or an approximation of it. Not long after they make love.

It must be six or seven when Buzzy wakes up to Marcel's leg hairs scratching against her calf. Her cheek has adhered slightly to his chest: she actually has to peel herself off him, then immediately regrets doing so. His nipples are as she imagined: small and neat, no larger than one-centime coins. She is still absorbed by them when his mobile phone starts thrumming wildly across the dressing table. She feels him stir and at the same moment rolls back onto her side of the bed, facing away from him. The alarm goes silent. She maintains the ludicrous charade of being asleep while he gets up and moves around the room, refusing to open her eyes or shift her position even when she hears the loo door shutting. There follows a discreet hiss as he relieves himself against the inside of the bowl, and not directly into the water as another sort of man would have done.

For once she has no desire to know what's going on inside Marcel's head even after he has dressed and left the room. The

172

buzz of being left on her own has started to wear off by the time an extended stomach rumble reminds her that she has not eaten since breakfast yesterday: that and last night's vomiting have left her with a sharp craving for food, preferably fried.

After about an hour and a half, during which her phone is inactive apart from the frequent occasions when she powers up the screen to check for new calls or messages, she decides to have a shower. This is a deliberate tempting of fate – by waiting until now, she has increased the chances of Marcel walking in on her. But the potential embarrassment of this, compounded with the uncertainty of how or whether they might broach the subject of last night, is something she is starting to dread less than his continued absence.

Entering the transparent cubicle is like walking into a piece of installation art. She gives herself a perfunctory wash with the hotel shower gel, glancing often at the bedroom door in case Marcel or maybe a chambermaid walks in. Neither does. Perhaps he is back at Avenue Louise having breakfast, coolly telling his father about his unstable friend who refused to attend the wedding and who might have done who knows what if he'd left her alone in a foreign city. She imagines him accepting a sugary pastry from Marguerite, who adds that she's not surprised, the girl's behaviour was very strange indeed.

Buzzy turns off the water and stands naked and dripping for a few seconds, though not in the exhibitionist spirit encouraged by the designer of the room – she can't remember if she has shampooed her hair. She yanks the shower lever back, and under a fierce jet stream lathers gel into her bedraggled curls.

She forces herself through the routine of drying herself and putting her dress back on and rubbing more toothpaste into her gums. Her hangover has migrated from her head to the base of her throat. Carefully she makes the bed, smoothing out the rumpled sheets and tucking the ends tightly under the mattress in the hotel style. She turns on CNN and a few seconds later switches it off. She sits and waits. Her phone bleeps once to warn the battery is running low.

Perhaps he isn't going to return. Her passport and Eurostar tickets are in her luggage, which is in the Moreau apartment. The train back to London is not until mid-afternoon, but even if she could find her way back to Avenue Louise, would she be able to press the buzzer, face Anatole again? There's a chance he might be on his honeymoon, but he doesn't seem the type to go in for that, certainly not the second time around. Even if he has taken Marie-Thérèse to Tahiti or wherever, could Buzzy bear to speak to Marcel's grandmother, or worst of all Marcel himself, if he has gone there specifically to avoid her? If not, what are the options? She has her wallet, but surely not enough credit on any of her cards to fund a ticket home at such short notice. Flippantly she imagines a new life as a Belgian sex-worker. Then, as the flicker of mirth dies out, she sees the gravity of the thing she has done, the wrong she has committed. She resolves to phone Henry, who she realises is the only person she can imagine confessing to, and the only person who might be willing to come and rescue her.

But instead she calls Marcel's number, which goes straight to answerphone. He hasn't recorded a personalised message; a piti-less female voice tells her that he isn't available to take her call. She fires up the screen again, pointlessly, and as soon as she does so the phone dies.

Finally, the door opens and there he is, looking fresh and smartly European in chinos and a Lacoste jumper beneath his mackintosh. He takes in the absurd room and then Buzzy. Her heart sinks.

'You've brought my luggage; thanks.'

'Yes. I thought it'd be better if I fetched it before anyone was up,' he replies in a friendly voice, and she knows there will be no discussion of last night.

He goes over to the window to light a cigarette. 'I have good news.' Buzzy notices the tip of his nose is red; it must be cold outside. 'Afua got selected for Islington South yesterday evening. She's the official Labour candidate at the next election.'

'That is good news. How do you know?'

174

'I called her this morning. It seems last night was hectic, with lots of people to thank and so on. The local Party took her to Pizza Express to celebrate; apparently the prime minister phoned to congratulate her during the meal. I suppose she'll have to get used to that sort of thing. Anyway.' He takes a drag on his cigarette, glances at the bed. 'Sherard's taking the family to lunch at the Wolseley.'

'That's nice of him. Well, he can afford it. He's rich – like you'll be. And Afua will be famous, just like Daphne.'

He finishes his cigarette. She has an unnerving sense that from now on jokes about Sherard and Daphne, if that was what her remark was, are less certain to be indulged.

'I just think you – I mean both of you – could aim higher than that.'

'Like Philip Devereux, you mean?' Buzzy is taken aback by the bitterness in his voice. Collecting himself, he says smoothly, 'No doubt you'd like to change your clothes; I'll wait for you downstairs.'

'Are we still having breakfast at the musical instrument museum?'

'I would love to,' he says, and for a moment she feels enormous relief. 'But I wondered, would you mind terribly if we went straight to the station and caught an earlier train? It's this lunch. I promised Afua I'd try and make it for the coffee and dessert.'

'Of course, it was a silly thing to say. Sorry.'

'Obviously I'll pay for the new ticket. Unless you'd prefer it if I didn't?'

Buzzy nods, indistinctly, but she is too choked to speak. In any case Marcel, who himself nods once before turning and leaving the room, has evidently understood.

23

Turmoil

'Yes. Well, we're missing Gilberto, of course.'

'Gilberto! We're missing *Vieira*; we're missing Tony fucking *Adams*. And the whole Gallas thing . . .'

'I rather like Gallas. As I said to Arsène before Christmas . . .'

He realises his advice to Arsenal's manager will have to wait for another occasion: Gijs's attention has been diverted by the arrival of a tall and svelte blonde. Her expression, which ought to be directed at her own decision to wear a negligée to an art exhibition, indicates puzzlement at finding Sherard discussing football. In fact, it's one of his favourite topics. He admires the sheer scale of its pointlessness, and encourages others to devote their thoughts to it as often as possible. 'I see that Barcelona has trumped Arsenal once again. Esther, my dear: have you met Gijs de Vocht?'

'I've heard all about you.'

'Likewise.' Gijs accepts her outstretched hand only for balance, as he raises himself onto tiptoes to kiss her cheeks.

'Gijs was telling me what a huge fan he is of your collection,' Sherard says, a little mischievously, but he's annoyed that neither has yet congratulated him for *Turmoil*.

'Oh – how kind!'

'Sure. It's just so disparate, and . . .' he wilts slightly under her expectant, Paltrowesque visage, 'brutal.'

'You know, I never thought of it like that, but you're so right. I guess my taste *is* disparate and brutal.'

Sherard accepts a refill of champagne from a passing waitress. He's pleased to note it's Veuve Clicquot: Devereux hasn't insulted him, or at least not yet, not in such a petty manner. 'My mind is rather leaping to your *Sheep Clones* phase.'

Esther's smoky continental laugh sends a stir among the Englishmen around them. 'Sherard is always teasing, but he doesn't mean it.'

'Anyway, this show is great,' Gijs says, cottoning on at last.

'Oh, this,' – Sherard looks around disapprovingly – 'it's very thrown-together. And the space is hardly ideal.'

Esther touches his wrist. 'It's perfect! No, really. I even love the way we're on this lower floor – *bajo tierra*. Like we're in the belly of the beast.'

'The great Sullivan and Ball,' Gijs chuckles.

'Seriously, Sherard, this is the zeitgeist – the beginning of the end of capitalism, or the West, or something. You've totally captured it. Also, everyone is here.'

'I don't know about that.' She's right, he reflects; he ought to be mingling. 'There's Sam. I think I'll just . . .'

Leaving Esther in the not entirely safe hands of Gijs, he has barely taken two steps before someone blocks his path.

'Hello, Sherard,' the man says familiarly, though they've never met before, 'Alan Lyle-Smith.'

'Ah, yes – you're the school captain, I understand.'

They shake hands. Lyle-Smith is slight, with a thin, forgettable face. Though Sherard was expecting someone more like Devereux, it makes sense that this man has ended up as senior partner of Sullivans. Like some Russian *silovik* turned frontman, his role is clearly to manage his more breast-beating colleagues.

'This is my wife, Annabel. She's terribly interested in art; you can imagine how pleased she was to hear we were doing something cultural for once.'

There is no obvious sign that the large Annabel, who is staring past Sherard at Esther, is filled with contentment.

'Not a great fan of work shindigs?'

'I'm hoping this is going to go better than the last one,' she says, now eyeing him keenly.

'Poor Annabel got quite badly injured on her last outing.'

'Ah.'

'It was at the firm ball. She had an unfortunate collision with a young man on the dance floor.'

'*He* collided with *me*. I'm only just out of crutches.'

'You must watch out for the sundial, in that case. It would be awful if you tripped and fell on that next.'

'We saw that, didn't we, darling? *The gods of finance . . .*'

With a feeling he is going to enjoy this, Sherard asks her what she thought of it.

'The central idea, I gather, is that the financial system is arbitrary.'

'That is, as you say, the essence of it.'

'I wasn't congratulating myself. As observations go, I shouldn't think it was much beyond my Labrador. Only the artist, whoever he is, seems to be linking the sun with polytheism. I suppose this would make a little more sense if he had presented us with a Mayan sundial; except I'm not sure that even those had anything to do with divine worship. Their basic purpose was empirical, wasn't it? To tell the time. The sundial face itself seems a competent replica; whether the artist had any role in the making of it, I don't know.'

'None at all, I can assure you.'

Lyle-Smith beams at them. 'I don't claim to know anything about modern art, but I think it's all fantastic. Tell me: is that the Tracey Emin?'

The basement conference facilities comprise a reception area, where they are presently standing, and two large conference rooms to its right and left. The walls have been repainted white for the exhibition. The first thing visitors see on descending the stairs – the *only* thing they can see without leaving the reception area – is Emin's sky-blue neon scrawl, *Turmoil . . . (love is).*

'It looks like the graffiti at London Bridge.'

'Or the sign above a Thai strip bar.'

'Rather expensive graffiti, darling. Before you go, Sherard, I understand the minister is intending to say a few words. So, I imagine, is Philip. Are you . . .?'

'If it's not too inconvenient,' says Sherard, with *froideur*.

'Of course! It's your show. Oh look, speak of the devil. Well done the pair of you.'

Philip Devereux's tailored pinstripe is at odds, in Sherard's view, with his decision to go tieless. Before she limps away Devereux makes a great fuss over Annabel. In doing so he ignores her evident loathing of him, apparently of an order Sherard can only aspire to.

'So you've met *il duce*, with his first wife.'

'I didn't realise they were divorced.'

Philip grins wolfishly at no one in particular. 'They're not. But you know. She's so ghastly, isn't she? *Hi.*' He shakes hands with a trim FTSE type in steel-rimmed glasses. 'Your son bumped into her recently, I don't know if she told you.'

A photographer appears and asks them to stand next to the Emin.

'Perhaps they'll reconnect this evening. Henry is floating around somewhere, if that's the word,' Sherard adds, tilting his flute at a passing waitress.

'Is she here – the Emin woman?'

'No, couldn't make it.'

Another photographer comes up to them. 'Such a bore,' says Devereux, looking relaxed. 'Shall we do a little circuit? Let's start in here.'

As they walk, or rather process, accepting praise from their respective camps of art and commerce, Sherard thumbs a Romeo y Julieta tube in his pocket. 'I suppose I can't smoke in here.'

'I do love this little chap.' Devereux points to the fibreglass model of a besuited banker, slumped drunkenly in a corner. 'He looks so real, I keep wanting to fire him.'

Sherard feels a hand on his arm. 'Someone from the Gagosian is looking for you.'

'Cressida? I've spoken to her already.'

In her sleek leather jacket, her silver hair erect, Daphne looks striking. 'Not London,' she says impatiently, 'one of the US branches.'

'My dear, it's not Wal-Mart. Which one is it?'

'Miami, perhaps? He didn't say.'

'There is no Gagosian in Florida,' he says censoriously, though secretly amused. She is not normally so witty.

'California then. Sherard, I really don't know.' She releases his arm. 'I'm going to say hello to Alastair.'

'Daphne, have you met . . .' he begins, but his wife is already raising her arms, preparing to kiss the young documentary-maker on both cheeks. 'Sorry,' Sherard says to Devereux, not minding how unconvincing he sounds. He is tremendously pleased with his wife's little performance. Her magnanimity seems to have something to do with his reaction to the commentariat's reaction to *The Prodigal Sister*, neither of which, it seems, was what she was expecting.

'Not at all, it's only a shame not to have congratulated her on the new book. I heard it being discussed on Radio 4 the other day.'

'That's no great triumph. They were my wife's friends.'

'Even so . . .' Devereux seems disinclined to proceed with his thought, or indeed their stroll, and stops in the centre of the room. 'You know I met your father once. It was on your first day at the beloved gulag. Turnbull had probably had him in for a sherry or two; he must have been leaving when he poked his head round my door. Possibly he was looking for you. Anyway, I remember I had some Wagner on my record player. He told me he'd love to be seventeen years old and listening to *The Ride of the Valkyries*. I don't think I paid much attention at the time; I'd probably only put the thing on to show off, and didn't see what difference it made listening to something at seventeen or seven hundred. We talked a little more: he grilled me on what books I was reading. A very cultured man, I remember.'

'He was a publisher.'

'So I gather. Anyway, when he was about to leave, he fixed me with a rather stern look. The first week could be rough; he said he knew that because he'd been a new boy himself once. Fagged for a chap in the very dorm room we were standing in. He said perhaps I would look out for you, as you might find it hard to be apart from your mother.' Devereux gives the remains of his champagne a quick swirl, finishes the glass. 'I did look out for you. Not in a sympathetic way, I fear.'

'I shouldn't worry; he probably knew what he was doing.'

'Yes, perhaps you're right.'

'I suppose it *was* rough at first.' He wonders if Devereux remembers the trunk incident, how matron almost fainted at the sight of his arm. 'But I didn't miss my mother. He was wrong about that.'

Devereux chooses a point beneath Sherard's mouth, making the latter feel unusually conscious of his jowls. 'Anyway, things turned out all right in the end. Look at your little empire: publisher, proprietor, art mogul . . .' He gestures vaguely at the walls and general hubbub. '. . . A philosopher wife, an adopted daughter headed for the Green Benches . . . I hear you'll even have my young protégé, Marcel Moreau, as a son-in-law. One could say your old man did you a favour.'

Sherard grunts. Despite his irritation at Devereux's sly attempt to claim credit for his success, itself slyly reduced to a 'little empire', this has been a satisfying encounter. A server approaches: a young man with Slavic cheekbones and a pale, faintly sickly pallor. They glare at him idly. 'Nice to see a chap get some colour in his cheeks,' observes Devereux of the boy's rising blush. Sherard advances his champagne flute and the boy busies himself with refilling it. 'Good idea,' Devereux continues, looking at his watch. 'Any minute now they're going to switch to some vile sparkling wine.'

Sherard wants to get the speeches over with before the event reaches its peak. Irritated not to spot Merton anywhere, he ignores the impertinent Greek lawyer who seems to think they are acquainted.

'I was at the Biennale last year. Well, I didn't go specifically, I happened to be there with my mother. It was our little joke: a sojourn in Venice. Well, my joke, she's never read Proust. But I couldn't stand it: so eurotrashy – so *Russian*. The sight of their enormous yachts lined up along the Grand Canal made one weep. One wouldn't mind – well, perhaps one would – but they don't even *pretend* to take an interest in the art. Many of them are our clients, of course, so I shouldn't really be saying this. Some are here this evening.'

Sherard decides he looks vaguely familiar; perhaps they have met somewhere before. 'Have you seen Afua? Or Marcel, even?'

'I'm taking up your time, how rude of me.' The Greek pauses and Sherard, who is perfectly immune to the young man's bristling tone, does not demur. 'Last time I saw Marcel Moreau he was in the men's room. I haven't seen *la fidanzata* – Afua, is it?'

Sherard scans the room, but there are too many people, or he is too bloody short. The silly Greek seems to be expecting a response. 'What was that?'

'I was saying that my merger notification won't write itself.'

'No, I imagine it won't. Goodbye then.'

He makes his way through the crowd; his you're-too-kinds and so-glad-you-cames sound, even to him, decreasingly sincere. He finds his son, who says he hasn't seen Alec Merton or Afua, but thinks Marcel might be in the other conference room. 'It all seems to be going tremendously well,' Henry adds brightly.

Sweat is starting to dampen Sherard's shirt as he beats a path back through the room and past the Tracey Emin again. The lighting in the other exhibition space is unhelpfully dim, thanks to the video installation of the cow in the tornado on the far wall. Next to Marcel a figure is slightly encroaching on where the video is being projected, so that the curved tip of his nose is caught up in the outer swirl of branches and road signs. Transfixed, Sherard floats towards the young man. He clears his throat. 'Now, I need your help.'

'Hello, Sherard. Of course.'

'Merton is late. Can you get hold of Afua, find out what's going on?'

'Actually, I spoke to her perhaps twenty minutes ago. She said they were en route.'

'That could mean anything, as you know,' he says sharply, then checks himself. His heart is beating foolishly. 'If you could impress some sense of urgency on her, I'd be most grateful.' Turning from Marcel to the figure, who stills seems engrossed by the whirling cow, Sherard chuckles and says, a little louder than he planned, 'I thought you were my wife.'

The boy swivels to face him. He looks surprised, and slightly offended. 'Huh?'

'No,' Sherard laughs, falsely, 'I meant that she has a leather jacket just like that.'

The boy glares down at his jacket, and Sherard is relieved when Marcel, apparently unruffled by this conversation, steps in. 'I'm sorry. Abdul, have you met Sherard Howe? Sherard has organised this exhibition – he's Henry's father.'

'Oh. Hello.'

'I see you're interested in the Aoyamaai piece. The cow.'

Abdul glances towards Marcel, who has discreetly moved away to telephone Afua. 'It's cool. I think I already saw it on YouTube though.'

Sherard clears his throat. 'You like the internet, then?'

'Of course.'

'I see you're drinking orange juice.'

This time Abdul's response is to suck on his cheek: without it troubling him especially, he seems to have concluded he is dealing with a mental defective. Sherard, meanwhile, feels a stirring sensation in his trousers.

'Are you sure you wouldn't like some champagne? I often find it improves the art.'

Abdul jerks his head away, like a sleek Barbary foal, with Sherard the fly. 'I promised Henry I wouldn't.'

Already gesturing for a flute, Sherard says, 'I didn't realise my son was such a disciplinarian. One glass won't hurt, unless you have a particularly exigent palate: I'm afraid I can't guarantee its quality now we're past the hour mark. Unless it's forbidden, for, ah' – it pains Sherard to say the word – 'religious reasons?'

'It's not that . . .'

Marcel rejoins them. 'Afua and Alec Merton have just arrived.'

'What? Good.'

'I saw you chatting to Philip earlier.'

'Yes, we're terribly friendly these days, didn't you know? It only took us thirty years.'

'It's nice to have friends,' Abdul says, after a firm gulp of what Sherard hopes is Veuve Cliquot.

'Do you think so? I've always thought there were two kinds of male friendships: those where you secretly despise each other, and those where you secretly like each other. Most, if not all, are in the first category.'

'I don't get it. If liking *and* hating are a secret, what's the other guy supposed to think you think?' Abdul frowns, puzzled by his own question.

'Indifference.' Sherard is relieved there are no Englishmen within hearing distance. He smiles: 'No doubt it's different in Saudi Arabia. You know, if you're interested in learning something about contemporary art, I could show you my private collection some time. It's not unimportant, in its way. Perhaps we'll get Henry to arrange a date.'

Attempting to hook one foot around the other, Abdul loses balance and almost treads on Marcel, who ignores this and says, 'I think it sounds an excellent idea.'

The boy runs a hand through matted hair: he has evidently been wearing a hat of some description. 'I guess that might be okay,' he says, a shade sulkily.

'Well then.' Sherard observes the approach of Merton and Afua. 'Almost time to address the adoring crowd.'

24

Credit where credit's due

It occurs to Alec, in his brief post-speech low, that the pun connecting his remarks on the banking crisis with thanking Philip and Sherard for organising the exhibition was not quite as witty as it had seemed minutes earlier, in his head. Had he made the same joke at the same gathering a few months ago, he'd probably have thought nothing of it. After all, no obvious embarrassing silence followed it; on the contrary, there was a healthy ripple of laughter. The suspicion arose out of glancing at Afua and noticing the extra clench in her smile – he has come to interpret these impressive delineations of her cheekbones as an unhappy sign.

Not that he, for his part, has reason to be pleased with her. The ministerial car was waiting to take them to the exhibition when she closed the door of his private office and told him she'd received two proposals, one romantic and the other professional, the latter to take up a communications role at Labour HQ. (He understood from the ensuing silence that both offers had been accepted.) It was probably to be expected that she would wish to manage the delivery of these pieces of bad news, so it wasn't the slyness of the timing per se that struck Alec as objectionable. It was that it was so *obviously* sly, suggesting that when it came to it, she didn't mind him seeing her treat him like some poor press dupe.

Alec poured himself a whisky, without offering any to Afua. 'What can I say? Congratulations, for the engagement at least. Where's the ring?'

'Marcel is having it refitted. It wasn't really necessary, but he's particular about these things.'

185

Alec's first instinct was to punish her. Except that isn't really his style, and anyway, he realises he has startlingly few options there. Part of Afua's job, at which she has proved to be highly adept, is to use her media contacts against her opponents – *his* opponents, until now. But as much as her communication skills; as much as Sherard Howe's patronage or her support from the Party hierarchy, what makes Afua truly formidable is her fearlessness. When Alec started bringing her to the high-level briefings on the financial crisis, she seemed as impervious to the pre-meeting apprehension among the assembled ministers as she was to the beery, sweary banter of the Downing Street advisers. The latter, of course, are not impervious to her. Alec has noticed fewer references to football of late. When Keith recently asked if she had seen the *Maeght* exhibition at the Royal Academy, Afua seemed the only person in the room not astonished by the question. 'I feel like I've seen enough Bonnards and Matisses. Also, I think it's pronounced "Mag", not "maggot".' A flicker of a smile crossed the face of the chancellor as he turned the page of a strategy paper.

Neither was she fazed by the Treasury officials when they switched into the local dialect. 'Sorry,' she'd tell them, of a particularly obscure section of an internal document that even Alec could not easily follow, 'but I really didn't understand this part.' At first the civil servants feigned regretful surprise, as though it had been very much their intention to render it intelligible. But then Afua began routinely to interrupt when their speech was too pregnant with jargon – 'bottom-up due diligence' or 'ventilate the monetary transmission mechanism' – or to take issue with the substance of their advice, always prefacing her remarks with a languorous apology. Finally the officials' patience snapped. 'I thought you weren't quite *clear* as to how it would function,' one of them replied, after Afua said she thought the proposed toxic asset insurance plan was untenable in its current form. She allowed herself a brief, knee-weakening smile at the document in front of her. 'I'm looking at the top of page one, where it says this plan was devised by an investment bank. How much did we pay them for this?' The mandarins knew better than to answer. 'Because this looks like taxpayers' money going to one bank for advising the Treasury on how to risk more taxpayers' money on insuring another bank's disastrous investments.' The plan was tweaked and presented as a Treasury idea. It was well received by the commentariat.

Since there is nothing he can do to stop Afua leaving, he might as well try to be graceful about it. He has a knack for getting over these things and besides, according to the newspapers, she is the 'future of the Labour Party'. Whether or not that proves accurate, Alec knows she already has a firmer place than him in the public imagination. The precise details of the spat about the Islington seat might quickly fade, but not the photo the press 'found' of her at one of the Howes' parties, looking like a film star in a black gown and crimson shawl.

'For the City minister, you don't seem to be enjoying the present company much.'

'Hello, Daphne,' he says, kissing her on each cheek. 'For a moment I thought I was surrounded by sharks, yet here you are.'

'Darlin', I eat the sharks. I'm a killer whale.' She sounds unusually Kiwi, not to mention relaxed.

'I very much enjoyed your book.'

'Liar. You haven't read a word of it.'

'Well, no. But my wife has, or she's bought it. It seems to be making great waves at any rate.'

'How is Rebecca?'

'Very well, thank you. Still slightly adjusting to life in Grimsby – the whole family is, really.'

'Except you're here; drinking champagne.'

'I'm not sure I'd call this champagne.'

Daphne's laugh is scratchy. 'They must love you in Grimsby.'

'Speaking of constituencies,' says Alec, whose slim majority is in fact a matter of some anguish, 'isn't it good news?' As he utters the words he wonders if he has subconsciously foreseen their effect: he finds he is not surprised by the slight tightening at Daphne's mouth.

'Afua, you mean? We're delighted, of course – look out, a shark is moving in for the kill.'

'Bugger, I knew my luck couldn't last.'

'That was the good news,' she says, giving his arm a quick departing squeeze. 'The shark's wife has a face like a slapped arse.'

In conversation with yet another High Net Worth Individual – if Alec were Russian, and they held proper elections in Russia, the evening might have been more useful – he spots the one woman in the room whose upper arms are as sculpted as Afua's, or almost. She's dyed-blonde, mid-thirties, Mediterranean-looking, with a commendably minimal approach to clothes-wearing. She is also endearingly self-conscious. One of her arms is wrapped protectively around her waist, and her long, tanned legs are planted perhaps a fraction too far apart. Ostensibly she is listening to a pudgy-faced man, her age or a little younger, in whom Alec can tell, even at this distance and for reasons he could not put into words, she isn't sexually interested.

He nods at the Russian, who keeps racehorses and seems to have assumed so must a government minister, or at least be friends with people who do.

'Do you shoot them yourself? When they get injured, I mean?'

He is relieved when Vladislav replies casually, 'In Russia, I have done this. Here you prefer injections.'

'I suppose as an owner it's something one ought to be prepared to do, in theory at least.' He is conscious of prattling rather meaninglessly – he is definitely below par today, even without the distraction of the Mediterranean girl, with whom he at last makes eye contact – but Vladislav grunts, briefly recollecting.

A young Pole arrives and with an oddly determined grimace extends a tray of satay chicken sticks. The Russian takes one. 'These again.'

'Have you had a look at any of this art?'

'Art?'

'Yes, on the walls, and the floor. I really ought to do a quick tour before it's too late. It was great to meet you.' He tries a Daphne-like valedictory arm-grip that results in Vladislav's chicken stick and silk tie coming into contact. The Russian doesn't notice, and for a moment Alec considers saying something: the stain will be worse if the blob of satay is left to seep into the silk. Instead he turns and wanders with calculated insouciance towards a large-scale photograph of a bullfight. The bloodied bull appears to be on the verge of goring a matador whose cape, raised high above his head, is emblazoned with a rippling Coca-Cola logo.

He chooses a spot not far from where the girl is standing. He can hear her companion describing a visit to the *corrida* in Seville; to Alec's relief it doesn't seem to have been notably different to any other bullfight. At any moment someone might resume lobbying him against EU hedge fund directives, and he'd be powerless to prevent her drifting away, or leaving the exhibition altogether. Already the crowd is thinning out now the speeches are over. Next to him is a couple who seem not to belong to either the business or the bohemian world, but have an air of clinging to each other. Alec realises he knows one of them.

'Hello there – Henry, isn't it?' He pretends not to notice when the young man flushes. 'I think we met at one of your parents' parties.'

'Of course, hello. I didn't mean to be rude just now; I didn't think you'd remember me. This is my friend—'

'Elizabeth.'

'Hello, Elizabeth.' The girl's hand in his is limp. There is something virginal yet strangely unappealing about her. Perhaps it's the effect of the beautiful Spanish or Italian woman in the background.

Since no one else volunteers a topic of conversation, Alec asks Henry how he's finding life at the Bar.

'I didn't finish the BVC,' Henry says, blushing again.

'I'm sorry; I'm behind the times. What are you doing now?'

'I've been doing some private tutoring, actually,' he says, with forced brightness.

'Great – you don't do the Common Entrance, do you? I know a pair of ferociously idle twelve-year-olds who could do with some help.'

189

Alec is mildly annoyed when Henry answers him in earnest. 'I'm afraid it sounds like I'd be out of my depth there. Also, I'm not sure if I'll be doing it for much longer.'

'Oh? What are you thinking of doing instead?'

'I haven't entirely decided.' After a sheepish glance at Elizabeth, 'I thought perhaps I might apply for the civil service.'

'That's a great idea, Hen,' she says, distantly supportive and somehow pained, as though it was costing her to speak. They're not a couple, Alec realises, or not yet. Probably Henry is not a fast-mover in that department.

'Who knows, perhaps I'll see you in the Treasury; that's if I'm not shuffled off the ministerial coil. And what do you do?'

'Nothing really.'

He is almost relieved to have his suspicion confirmed that this girl is too thoroughly morose for him. Still, there is something to be said for her thick auburn curls. 'Another NEET? That isn't good for our statistics, you know. "Not in Education, Employment or Training",' he adds, on noticing their puzzled faces. His spirits are starting to flag when once again he catches the beautiful Mediterranean woman glance at him. 'But no, I thought I was going to be a singer at your age. Speaking of the arts, Henry, your father will be annoyed with me if I don't have a quick look at his collection, since that's what we're here for. What do you make of it?'

'As a matter of fact, we were just discussing this before you arrived . . .' He seems to hope this will suffice as an opinion.

'My taste in art is dreadfully conventional, I'm afraid. But I can see Sherard's sense of humour in these pieces. It's all very *fun*.'

'If art does not enlarge men's sympathies, it does nothing morally.' The articulate remark seems to burst out of Henry in spite of himself, and he blushes for the third time in as many minutes. 'It's something George Eliot said – I've been reading her with my student. Probably it's not applicable here.'

'No, it sounds very pertinent. Except what about the viewers, or readers, in the case of Eliot?' asks Alec, thinking of voters. 'Don't they also have some moral responsibility? You can lead a horse to water and so on.'

'You're right. If you read a book and the characters do things that are stupid or wrong, and the reader *knows* that but then she makes the same mistakes in her own life, that's hardly the fault of art.'

'Precisely,' says Alec, surprised at Elizabeth's vehemence.

With miserable resolve, as if this modest exchange has helped her decide, unhappily, an important matter, she tells Henry she is leaving. He offers to escort her home and she leaves him hanging for a moment before accepting. Would she mind terribly waiting a few minutes, Henry asks, while he says his goodbyes? She says she'll wait outside.

Alec, who has been forgotten during this exchange, discovers his phone is ringing. It's his wife. 'Hello, darling,' he whispers. 'There's rather a lot of shouting.'

'Is there? Andrew hid one of Alison's soiled nappies in William's bed, so it's probably . . . What are you up to?'

'Just at Sherard Howe's art exhibition.'

'Oh, yes, I remember you saying. Any good?'

'Absolutely not,' he says, cheerily.

'You can't talk now.'

'Yes, let's catch up later.'

'All right then,' Rebecca yawns, 'well, do try and have fun.'

'Bye, darling – tell Andrew I'm extremely vexed and will deal with him this weekend.'

'You're vexed, I'll pass it on. Bye then, darling.'

Both the young couple and the Latin lady have disappeared while Alec had his back turned. A moment of keen resentment subsides into resignation: her presence provided his evening with a sense of intrigue and purpose, but the evening is now over, judging by the steady stream towards the cloakroom. There's a Commons vote in about an hour or so. Rather than pretend to get some work done at the Treasury, he'll skulk around in the Stranger's Bar; perhaps he'll bump into the Conservative silk who recently lent him *Trial by Battle*. He is wondering where Afua has got to when Philip Devereux comes striding up to him.

'Back to HMT?'

''Fraid so.'

'Anyway, thanks so much for coming. I know how busy you are.'

Alec is not in the mood for Devereux's aggressive conviviality. His speech this evening was commanding without conveying much about anything other than the supreme self-assurance of the speaker. Alec could sense the audience giving in to it, which was why he was unusually doubtful about his own remarks. He has the impression Philip is very much enjoying having the minister in his domain.

'It's not quite the round-the-clock operation you have here.'

'Don't be fooled, it's mainly night secretaries reading *Hello!* or whatever. I hope the evening hasn't been too painful?'

'Not at all, I've enjoyed myself. If only I always discussed financial regulation with a glass of champagne in my hand.'

'Quite,' Devereux says, with a bark of a laugh. 'Besides, I hope you weren't paying any attention to my clients. I'd hate to think you were planning to *reduce* the volume and complexity of government legislation.'

'What's the Labour Party for, if not to keep Sullivan and Ball busy?'

'Incidentally, have you seen a young lady around – curly hair, dark reddish?'

A flutter of Spanish quite miraculously announces that the woman with the sculpted arms has not gone after all. Having said farewell to a compatriot she is wandering slowly, leggily, in his direction, rummaging for something in her handbag, or pretending to. 'As a matter of fact I was speaking with her just now. Elizabeth something? She was going to wait outside, you might still catch her.'

'Waiting for whom?'

'Henry Howe – Sherard's son. He was going to escort her home.'

'Oh, was he?' Devereux finishes the last of his champagne. He seems vaguely insulted. 'Perhaps I'll see if she'd prefer a quick drink.'

Part II

25

'Afghanistan and the Myth of the Feminist Gunslinger' by Daphne Depree

Guardian, *13 August 2011*

'La Guerre du Golfe n'a pas eu lieu.'
(The Gulf War did not take place.)
Jean Baudrillard, 29 March 1991

'There's an old poster out West, I recall, that says,
"Wanted: Dead or Alive."'
George W. Bush, 17 September 2001

Next month marks ten years of Western military operations in Afghanistan. The woman on the street might be forgiven for wondering why this faraway war isn't over yet. But one could equally ask: did it even take place?

Yes, the Americans finally found and executed bin Laden – in Pakistan, the West's 'ally' in the War on Terror. Back in Afghanistan, however, Mullah Omar is still alive and the Taliban resurgent. Opium production is at record levels. The warlords, rich on US contracts, are more powerful than ever.

A single extra-judicial killing does not authenticate a conflict that has already lasted longer than the two World Wars combined. Clearly I'm not suggesting the over 30,000 Afghan dead are a fiction – that would be absurd as well as offensive. Nor am I denying George 'austerity' Osborne bankrolls our involvement in the campaign to the tune of £12 million a day, even as the coalition government slashes vital services for the most vulnerable at home.

When Baudrillard wrote that the first Gulf war 'did not take place', he was observing how the stylised packaging of the conflict by the rolling news networks reduced it to a type of 'virtual' media spectacle for

Western audiences. This simulation or Hollywoodising of reality also applies to the war in Afghanistan, only here the sense of illusion is as much to do with the overall narrative as the images themselves.

Unforgiven is a 1992 western which earned Clint Eastwood, who directed and produced as well as starred in the film, Oscars for Best Director and Best Picture. Eastwood (a notorious Republican, don't forget) plays an ageing gunslinger with a heavy-drinking, possibly psychotic past. He is persuaded to come out of retirement for a final bounty hunt where the wanted are two cowboys accused of brutally disfiguring a prostitute.

To put it another way, the audience is licensed to cheer Eastwood's rediscovery of his killer instinct – it turns out his old sharp-shooting skills are undimmed by whiskey or advancing years – because he is apparently avenging a savage attack against a defenceless woman. The matter of the reward money, made up of the savings of the victim's fellow sex-workers, is somewhat glossed over.

Similar audience manipulation could be detected in the build-up to military intervention in Afghanistan. There was the imperial West, grown weak from its decadence and having renounced its violent ways. Then along came 9/11 and bin Laden. Unlike Iraq, the Afghan campaign was the 'good' war, with simple motives: to saddle up once more and capture the bad guys, dead or alive.

As with *Unforgiven*, the theme of injustice against women was part of the backdrop of the War on Terror from the start. 'The brutal oppression of women is the central goal of the terrorists,' said Laura Bush in a White House radio address in 2001. 'Civilised people throughout the world are speaking out in horror, because . . . in Afghanistan, we see the world the terrorists would like to impose on the rest of us.'

In reality, of course, the treatment of women in that country has for a long time been brutal, including under the US-backed warlords. It could even be argued that the Taliban brought some stability to the lives of Afghan women, albeit at some cost.

The neoconservatives' motives for conflating the struggle for women's rights and Operation Enduring Freedom are dubious, to put it kindly. If it is true, as Laura Bush claimed in her radio address, that 'the fight against terrorism is also a fight for the rights and dignity of women', why does the Western-backed Karzai regime today stand accused of bartering women's rights in its bid to strike a peace deal with the Taliban?

We should reject the notion that the war in Afghanistan as presented to us by Washington – the fantasy of imperial cowboys riding to the rescue of weak women – ever happened. We should go further, and reject the fantasy itself – that disregarding legal frameworks, Western gunmen can solve injustices in complex societies that are deeply suspicious of outside interference.

26

A disagreeable prospect

A summery, slightly semenish smell wafts in through the open
window of the downstairs study. At half past eight in the morning, the sun is already warming Daphne's eyelids: one might easily
imagine oneself in Tuscany rather than Islington. She wonders if
the weather will be so Tuscan when they are actually there next
Saturday, and then if she wouldn't mind too much if it wasn't,
if only to witness the fury of the bride.

Saturday's *Guardian* is taken up with coverage of the aftermath
of the English riots. She has already written about the lootings in
Hackney, what Sherard would have called one of her 'no excuses,
but . . .' articles. No doubt she will return to the subject; but for
now, while public interest is at its zenith, there is a pleasing anti-
parochialism in focusing her latest piece on Afghanistan.

The news section is a fraction more interesting for knowing
that her article occupies the prime space next to the editorial.
Daphne always closely re-reads her work when it appears in the
paper. When teased by Sherard about this, she would tartly reply,
and it was partly true, that she wanted to check some moron sub-
editor hadn't missed a typo or changed the meaning of a crucial
sentence. It's also true that seeing her words in print and imagining the reader coming across them for the first time is something
she still savours, even after more than two decades as a commen-
tator. Most of this time has been freelance, punctuated by brief
happy periods with her own column in the *Independent* and *New
Statesman* and, least successfully, the *Evening Standard*. It's only
in the last two years, thanks to *The Prodigal Sister*, that she has
attained the Holy Grail of a contract for a weekly *Guardian*

op-ed. She doesn't miss the regular humiliations that come with being a pen-for-hire: pitching the same article to bored editors half her age in Sydney and Dublin and New York – anywhere, frankly, in the anglosphere – or endlessly chasing up payments with accounts departments (she never *needs* the money, that's not the point) for pieces she wrote months previously. How Sherard must have enjoyed putting Afua, at the age of twenty-one, straight on the *Liberal Review* payroll for her silly little blog!

Since she has nothing else especially exciting to look forward to today, Daphne decides against skipping straight to her article. Instead she puts the main paper aside and flicks through the other sections. Binning the sports and family supplements without a second glance, she unfolds the *Saturday Review* and smoothes out the central fold. Dutifully she reads up on the Edinburgh book festival. She's having a year off, having been up the last two summers to promote the hard then paperback release of *The Prodigal Sister*, the worldwide sales of which have recently overtaken *The Third Sex*. (Pleasingly, vis-à-vis a certain rival, the book is making waves in Australia, where the prime minister has let it be known she kept a copy on her bedside table.)

Among the round-ups she notices a short review of *The Bathers*, a debut collection by a poet whose name sounds familiar but which she can't at first place. In the sentence that remains after recording that Cambridge-educated Elizabeth Price is still in her twenties and a contributing editor to the *Spectator*, the poet's 'youthful, at times violent lyricism' is noted along with, more approvingly, her progression towards a sparer style, at once enigmatic and conversational. Daphne notes with mild interest that the publisher of the volume is Howe & Steen.

Returning to the main paper, naturally she feels for these Asian shopkeepers, whose windows have been smashed in and whose stock has been looted. Though in the end, for all the distress and practical inconvenience, won't their losses be covered by insurance? Daphne's eyes are drawn to the police stills of handsome, skunk-glazed Caribbean boys abandoned by the new, Education Maintenance Allowance-cutting Tory government; by their own fathers, most likely – by everyone except the multinationals, with their vast marketing budgets devoted to ensuring these kids' self-worth depends on owning their over-priced products. The fact she can write the article in her sleep doesn't mean it's not true, whatever nonsense of Afua's she has heard and read in the last few days.

The baby is crying again. It's one reason why she's taken to using this study – even though it is a mess, with books spilling everywhere – over her upstairs writing room. Out of infuriating loyalty to Sherard, Marta has only done a partial job of replacing the contents of the library shelves, forcing Daphne to stare at *Father Goriot* and *The Gathering Storm* and other pompously patrician tomes that belonged to her father-in-law. Although when Henry was here she'd frequently forget about him, so that, enveloped in a writing-cocoon, she might be scraping some half-eaten dish of Marta's into the bin when he'd emerge wondering what time dinner was, the house feels emptier since he left. Or rather, it feels ever more cluttered with objects that have nothing to do with her, beginning at the start of the year with shadow cabinet policy documents, and followed in the spring by nappies and Babygros and milk formula. Admittedly, Marcel is scrupulously tidy. He never leaves a tennis racquet or even so much as a stray pair of cufflinks lying around, but then he's so seldom in the house Daphne wonders if there's an unspoken competition between him and Afua as to which of them can work the most punishing hours. Nevertheless, there are times such as this morning when the house is thrumming with life yet no one seems to know or care that she is in residence.

'Please?'

'Marta. How long have you been standing there?'

'You will take breakfast in here?'

'No, I don't think so. No breakfast for me anywhere,' she clarifies. 'Will you have to stay long?'

'Till five o'clock,' Marta says, bristling. 'New contract.'

'I just meant it's a shame to be stuck inside on a Saturday. It's going to be sunny.'

This is as much as they've spoken to each other in a while. She doesn't go around referring to Marta as her 'friend' or any of that patronising bullshit. The housekeeper has worked at Canonbury Lane for so many years it would be ridiculous to start asking her now what her son does for a living, or what exactly, since Marta is a widow, she does with herself when she's not cleaning after them or cooking their meals or (latterly) acting as nanny to Benjamin. On the other hand, Daphne's current conversational options are very limited.

'I have an article in there.' She gestures at the *Guardian*, and instantly regrets it.

'Yes.'

'It's about Afghanistan – how we used the issue of women's rights there as a pretext for the War on Terror.'

Marta reaches behind her neck and tugs at her silver-streaked ponytail. With her high cheekbones, she was probably once popular with the boys. 'Afghanistan, yes.'

'Look, while you're here, there's been a lot of change in this house in the last year or two, as I'm sure you've noticed.' How much does Marta know about the Sherard situation? Not a lot, in all likelihood, given Daphne has never once spotted her reading a newspaper in a house that's usually overflowing with them. 'Afua and Marcel – all of us – would have struggled without your help with the baby. Certainly Afua wouldn't have been able to go back to work so soon. Well, soon for these days.'

When Afua is asked in interviews about her single month's maternity leave, she smilingly notes this is four times longer than the French interior minister gave herself. It's a characteristically nuanced line, managing both to seem self-deprecating and to refute the charge she is un-maternal.

'It's not a problem; he is a good boy.'

'Most of the time . . .'

Marta joins her in staring up at the ceiling. 'He is hungry. I will make his bottle now.'

'You know, if we could find you a ladder, those corners could probably do with a dusting. Remember we're away from Friday for Henry's wedding. It might be a good opportunity to get in here and really sort this room out. What needs to happen is for these boxes of books to go on the shelves.'

'But I think there are already too many books on the shelves.'

'There won't be too many books, Marta, when you've finished taking the books that are on the shelves off the shelves.'

'Where will I put them?'

'They can be probably go in the garage for now. I don't really care, frankly.'

After Marta has left, Daphne returns to the *Guardian*. Her patience is now exhausted and she quickly flicks through the pages until she finds her article. How rude of Marta not to congratulate her on behalf of Henry! Especially after Daphne went out of her way to show appreciation for all her housekeeper's assistance over the last few months. It's not as if Marta has the excuse of having met the fiancée.

She rubs the wretched pouches under her eyes. Steve's cartoon is spot-on as usual: a drone aeroplane releases a fat missile bearing the words WOMEN'S LIB, INC, while on the ground below a huddle of burqa-clad women wait to be obliterated.

For once Daphne can't interest herself in re-reading her piece. She's distracted by the wailing baby and the muffled discussion between Marta and Afua. Distracted, too, by the thought of the empty day ahead. Perhaps she'll give Henry a call. They could meet for lunch; she might even go over to Ealing. For a moment Daphne is very happy at the idea, before it occurs that Henry would be sure to involve Fiona, and she thinks better of it.

Next month marks ten years of Western military operations in Afghanistan . . . Daphne tuts softly: 'a decade' would have been more concise. Why does she only spot these things when it's too late, and why can she never rely on anyone else?

27
Renaissance men

'*Buona sera.*'

The concierge echoes the phrase, adding *signorina*. Since Buzzy is always half expecting strangers to allude to the fact that she is nearing thirty and unmarried, there is something reassuring about being in a country where they will do so immediately.

'I have a reservation for two nights. The name of Price.'

The Italian consults his computer. Rather loudly, and with a hint of pride on her behalf, he says, 'The Michelangelo suite?'

'Possibly,' she replies, 'someone else made the booking.'

The concierge nods approvingly, and returns to his computer with renewed zeal. His black hair is prematurely flecked with grey at the temples – he can't be more than a few years older than Buzzy. She decides it suits him.

After she signs a form and hands over her passport, he presents her with an electronic key-card. 'Welcome to Arezzo, *signorina* Price. This is Vincenzo.' A trim youth in a blazer has appeared from nowhere and is hovering unctuously. 'He will show you to your room. Will *signorina* be dining with us this evening?'

'I haven't decided yet. Actually, can you tell me where the Piazza Grande is? I need to meet someone there.'

'The Piazza Grande is very close: left outside the hotel and another left on Corso Italia. After ten minutes you arrive. When is your meeting time?'

'Now, I think.'

'But there are taxis outside. Vincenzo!'

'No, it's fine. I'll walk – after I've been to my room.'

'*Certo.*'

Vincenzo takes charge of Buzzy's luggage (she feels a twinge of reluctance handing over her Smythson bag) and escorts her to the lift, where they wait beside a gold-painted cherub. The décor is unrestrainedly baroque, even for Italy; but when Philip mentioned he knew somewhere right in the centre of the old town she knew there was no question of her staying anywhere else.

'Isn't it selfish to have your wedding in Italy?' Buzzy had said to her mother, during her visit home last weekend. 'I dread to think how much it's all costing, what with plane tickets and two nights in a hotel and the new dress. Anyway, Tuscany is so *ancien régime*.'

'Is it, dear?' her mother replied, with an anxiousness that covered both the existence of a bespoiling element of the wedding and her failure to understand what exactly it was. She was also pained, Buzzy knew, by her daughter's strange silence on whether Philip was planning to accompany her on this trip, and indeed the subject of marriage and children in general.

It might be *ancien régime*, but the spell of the old town, as she enters the sloping main square, is hard to resist. (She wonders vaguely if the Blairs will be there tomorrow. It's hard to keep track of whom Sherard and Daphne have fallen out with, apart from each other.) The sultry air! The crisp shirts, the dark-eyed men! Scanning the piazza for her meeting place, a bar, she ticks off the stretched façade of the Vasari loggia, the quattrocento palazzo, the stumpy bell tower of the Santa Maria della Pieve.

Spying the bar, she heads towards it with her eyes tearing up from the suntan lotion she quickly applied to her face before leaving the hotel. She knew they would – it's the effect of a mild allergy she's always had – but the alternative was to arrive at the wedding tomorrow pink from sunburn. As she crosses the crenellated line of shade an old thrill runs through her. The black pool of Marcel's hair, the shape of his body, one leg casually draped over the other, is achingly familiar. Apart from the baby resting in the dip of his thighs, he is alone.

He hands her a paper napkin. '*Bonjour, tristesse.*'

'It's the stupid lotion, it always does this.'

He nods, suddenly serious. There is a new little wrinkle between his eyebrows that she hasn't noticed before. She would like to reach out and trace her finger down it. 'You're late. I was beginning to think you might have abandoned me again.'

'I didn't abandon you. I've never abandoned you,' she insists, conscious her tone is querulous rather than romantic. 'Where's Afua?'

'She was expecting a telephone call from the Leader's office, so Benjamin and I took a taxi into town. We saw the Piero della Francescas.'

'Did he like them?'

'Actually, he cried a lot.'

There is a hint of genuine disappointment, which Buzzy seizes on. When the waiter comes over, she orders a glass of white wine and Marcel decides to join her.

'Is the coffee no good?'

'Oh,' he says, staring at his abandoned americano in slightly bored surprise. 'No, it's fine. It makes me want to smoke.'

Benjamin is fidgeting: he seems to have the extraordinary desire to remove himself from his father's lap. 'Would you like to hold him?'

She takes the baby from Marcel, seeing in the latter's expression a sudden vulnerable depth. If only she understood what it meant. Is he frightened she will dash his son's head against the medieval stone floor? Or does he realise this is cruel, even by his standards? Though she has tried to avoid picturing Benjamin, now holding her finger trustingly, she has occasionally, often in the early hours of the morning, been unable to resist giving in to the almost pleasurable torment of it. The face before her is the more surprising because his large brown eyes are so widely spaced; for a moment she almost has the impression he is ugly. He starts to blub. Flushed with failure, Buzzy looks pleadingly at Marcel. 'He probably wants his bottle,' he says, when he eventually takes Benjamin back.

Buzzy watches him reach into a brown leather travel bag and retrieve a bottle of prepared milk. He takes a handkerchief from his jacket pocket and wipes the teat. When he's finished, he holds it up for inspection and brushes an imaginary speck away with his index finger. 'Poor thing,' she says, 'I know the feeling.'

The waiter returns. The pearl face of his watch is yellow with age, she notices, as he runs his thumb down Benjamin's cheek rather roughly, as though confirming for himself the incongruous skin tone has not been painted on. He gives Buzzy an impertinent stare disguised as a smile: if she weren't in such need of them, she'd throw the freshly decanted contents of her glass in his face. When they are left alone, she asks, 'Are we near the town hall here?'

'Not far – the Piazza della Libertà. The bride was initially keen to get married in the cathedral,' Marcel adds, with studied casualness. The briefest flicker of his eyes checks if Buzzy has understood he is being droll.

She has. 'How did *that* go down with Daphne?'

'Daphne had some reservations, I think; as did Henry, when he realised he'd have to pretend to be Catholic. But the main obstacle was the Italian bureaucracy – *tu peux imaginer*.'

'Good old Hen. Is Sherard invited?'

Buzzy is slightly irritated when Marcel ignores her question. Instead he says, 'I heard about the *Spectator*. Congratulations.'

'I don't think the pay will be much. And I'm not even sure what a contributing editor does.'

'I shouldn't think you need worry.'

'About which?'

'Either.'

A flushed Dutch family settle at the table next to them. The blond-haired son, who must be ten or so, gawps at the sight of Benjamin suckling his bottle. His mother makes some rapid admonishment and smiles at Marcel, who pretends not to notice. The square is filling with locals on their early evening *passegiatte*.

'Perhaps we should've met somewhere else,' Buzzy says quietly.

As if to prove her point, Henry and Fiona are making their way huffily up the square. The latter's bothered squint at the low sun might be easily mistaken for a grimace, and a sense that Arezzo's Renaissance splendours are rather less than she bargained for. She is a step or two ahead of Henry, but it is the groom-to-be who first spots Buzzy and Marcel in their shaded position.

Buzzy returns his wave. 'They're coming over. Isn't it bad luck for them to be together so close to the wedding?' She dimly worries she has discussed this superstition with Marcel before.

'That's only the wedding day itself. Besides, I'm not sure Fiona is the sort of woman who believes in bad luck.'

Like Afua, Buzzy thinks. 'I've only met Fiona once, for dinner when she was seeing Charlie Wynter. We went to this awful Italian restaurant on the Strand; I remember she insisted on it. I'm pretty sure she loathes me.'

The engaged couple are only yards away, Henry a little in front now. He is wearing a linen jacket that doesn't quite fit, looking boxy at the shoulders and stretched around his stomach, where he has unaccountably chosen to employ both buttons. His smile as he approaches is both sincere and bashful – probably he is embarrassed by whatever bitchy thing Fiona is whispering to him. Seeing him now, for the first time in over a year, Buzzy realises she has missed his hapless faithful presence in her life.

'Hen!' she says, on her feet now, 'I'm so glad to see you.'

28

A matter of education

How slim, how casually elegant she looks in that navy cotton dress!

Henry wonders if there is something wrong – obviously there is something wrong, but if there is something *culpable* – about the fact a hug from Buzzy might be the highlight of his wedding weekend. Aside from inviting her to Italy, it's not as if he has actively sought out this encounter: finding her here is pure luck, even if he might have stacked the odds in his favour a little bit by suggesting, somewhat to Fiona's irritation, that they ascend the main piazza not very long after walking down it.

The larger blame refers to his failure, despite all his best efforts, including denying himself her company for over a year, to repress his feelings for Buzzy. He has gathered from his study of the canon that even the grandest passions fade after a certain passage of time. *All true love must die / Alter at the best / Into some lesser thing*: Henry is mystified why something like this hasn't happened to him yet. It seems less a sign of spiritual amplitude than of his capacity to fail even at unrequited love.

He wonders if the intransigence of these feelings points to a powerful stubborn streak in his subconscious. This could, in turn, explain why it feels as if he's managed consistently to upset those closest to him with his life choices. It started with dropping out of law school. Then there was the disastrous role as Abdul's paid mentor, which led indirectly to his parents' separation. At least Henry had Afua's support for that job: in fact, if he remembers correctly, it was she who suggested he sign up with a private tutoring agency. He senses she is less pleased with his current employment, though she hasn't said anything directly. Certainly as far as Sherard and Daphne are concerned, it's no defence to point out that the political neutrality of civil servants is a constitutional imperative, or that he worked for the previous Labour administration for almost as long as he has for the coalition. They may not be on speaking terms but they share the view that Henry is essentially a collaborator. He hasn't dared tell either of them the exact nature of the latest project he has been tasked with developing, and intends to delay doing so for as long as possible.

What if his parents are right and he is by temperament the thing they most revile, a small 'c' conservative? At the very least he must have what amounts, in Howe terms, to an unacceptable tolerance of Toryism. If not, he wouldn't be marrying a Woldingham alumna with the feistiness to tell his mother that Roger Scruton was Britain's 'greatest living philosopher', while dismissing continental theoreticians as 'pretentious Marxists'. (Henry knew these were two of the lowest qualities Fiona could ascribe to anyone.)

He hasn't altogether given up hope that his separated parents and future wife might find a way of tolerating each other. Don't most families have to make an effort to put aside their differences, to one extent or another? It seems to Henry both his parents might have given Fiona more credit for leaving the *Mail* when her relationship with Henry became 'serious', as she put it. Perhaps she might have stayed if it were a question of the odd snippet in the Ephraim Hardcastle column about, for example, Howe dinner parties doubling as BBC editorial meetings; but after the business with his father and Abdul – which, as a relatively lowly sub-editor, she could hardly veto her employers reporting – she felt that her position at the paper was untenable. (Of course the Bloomberg job came with a pay rise and a permanent contract, but Fiona made it clear that financial news was not what she dreamed of writing about and Henry should consider it a significant sacrifice.)

'God, Henry,' Fiona says, not quite in a whisper, 'is that Buzzy – sorry, *Elizabeth* Price? Did I tell you she once corrected my pronunciation of *bruschetta*?' They have virtually arrived at Buzzy and Marcel's table when she adds, 'You'd really never guess she was from Orpington.'

'I don't think anyone actually bought it. Honestly, the sales figures are embarrassing.'

'Well, Henry did. It's amazing what he finds time for,' Fiona adds, in pointed reference to the neglected *Economist* subscription she bought him for Christmas.

'Thanks, Hen! I'm very touched you'd do that.'

'I thought it was wonderful,' Henry says, with feeling, 'especially the early poems.'

'Oh, I wish I'd left those out; they're so adolescent and *awful*. The critics much preferred the later ones.'

'Right, sorry,' he says, annoyed with himself he's managed to get it so wrong. 'It's probably just that your more recent work is too avant-garde for me to . . .' Henry's heart is beating fast; he fears (not least because Fiona is listening) his voice will start to wobble. 'I really know nothing about modern poetry.'

'I think you've just demonstrated that.' To Buzzy, Fiona says, 'It's a shame you're here on your own; I hear your boyfriend is stuck at the office.' This is ventured with naked scepticism.

'He's a little old to call him my "boyfriend",' Buzzy says, lightly.

'How old is he, if you don't mind me asking?'

'He's remarkably well seasoned,' says Marcel, who until now has confined himself to rocking the sleeping Benjamin's pushchair from a seated position. While on the surface his remark is perfectly intelligible and even gallant, since it spares Buzzy from answering the question, there's likely as not some mischievous hidden connotation. (Since the incident with Abdul and the Ecstasy pills, Henry has found himself slowly caving in to his doubts about Marcel's character.) Buzzy's expression, both stung and searching, seems to confirm as much.

'Well, he must be very rich,' Fiona observes, pretending to strive charitably for a positive. 'Isn't he a partner at Sullivan and Ball? Actually, isn't that where you are, Marcel?'

Marcel confirms it is, and Fiona continues, 'How weirdly incestuous! Do you work together?'

'I work *for* him.'

Henry feels a blush rising: he can't help but be aware of how Fiona must be coming across to his friends. (He's sure he caught them exchanging a look during her description of the arrangements for tomorrow.) Is this the reason why he's avoided Buzzy since he started going out with Fiona: not noble self-denial, but low embarrassment of the first girl to take any real interest in him?

'Where are you staying?' he asks Buzzy.

'I'm not sure if I can remember the hotel's name, but it's very near here. The *Continentale*, perhaps?'

'That's one of the ones we looked at. It's very expensive.'

'It's quite horrible, actually, so you're not missing anything. Besides, I think your villa sounds much more civilised. It must be lovely to wake up in the Tuscan hills.'

'That's what Henry thought,' Fiona says, not by way of endorsement. 'But in practical terms, it's a nightmare getting back and forth into town. Henry refuses to drive.'

'Very sensible, Hen: windy roads and Italians motorists . . .'

'Do you or Afua drive?' Fiona asks abruptly of Marcel.

'Neither, in fact.'

'I suppose the shadow home secretary gets her own chauffeur.'

'Oh, no,' Henry cuts in, 'outside of government, only the Leader of Her Majesty's Opposition is entitled to an official car.'

'Still, it must be very strange for you to have such a famous and important wife.'

'I will have to pass on some advice to Henry.'

'But you must be very ambitious yourself,' she persists, deflecting Marcel's ironic flattery. 'Not that Henry isn't, but you know what I mean. A City lawyer – not many people can take the hours you must work.'

Henry watches Marcel gaze into the pushchair with an expression of paternal forbearance. It occurs to him that his quasi brother-in-law's suave reluctance to talk about himself is due less to modesty than the fact his self-absorption is so limitless he's afraid of drawing attention to it.

'What do you think, Buzzy? Is Marcel too ambitious to be happy in his wife's shadow?'

'The shadow's shadow!' Henry jokes weakly.

'I think what Marcel wants is to triumph on his own terms. I'm not sure he really cares what other people think.'

'Well what *are* those terms?'

'I couldn't say. They vary, I think.'

Buzzy hasn't looked at Marcel while pronouncing on him like this. It strikes Henry as a little presumptuous, given the acuteness of the observation and their friend's special dislike of being acutely observed.

'Talking about jobs, Hen, I hear you were asked to join an important government policy unit.'

'It's only in the Cabinet Office. The one in Number Ten is much more influential.'

'Henry, I can't stand the way you talk yourself down,' Fiona says. 'It's a fantastic position,' she tells Buzzy, 'completely at the heart of government. The Number Ten unit is smaller, and they're all political appointments from outside the civil service – the PM's chums, basically – so Henry couldn't get in there even if he was Brain of Britain, or *not* a member of the Howe family.'

'How did you know?' he asks Buzzy. 'I mean about my getting the job?'

'I think Afua must have told me.'

'Oh, I see . . .'

'It was I who told you,' Marcel says, 'when we met for a drink the other day. Don't you remember?'

'Yes – of course. I haven't spoken to Afua in months, come to think of it. She's so busy these days, isn't she?'

'Terribly busy,' Henry agrees. Somehow he can't imagine Marcel ever mentioning him in his absence, and nothing in the Belgian's present demeanour is encouraging Henry to revise that perception. Also, he hadn't realised that Buzzy and Marcel were in regular touch.

'What are you working on?' Buzzy asks, after a short pause. 'Unless it's confidential . . .'

'No, nothing like that,' he says, perversely, since he's been very careful to keep it a secret. 'We're looking at school reform. There's an idea to lower the age at which students can be selected on academic grounds in certain Free Schools in certain geographic areas – essentially London, to start with.'

'I had the impression selective state schools in England were called "grammar schools",' Marcel says, with unexpected interest. 'They're seen as polemical.'

Henry wonders why Marcel hasn't referred to Buzzy attending a grammar school, since it's surely the basis of his knowledge on the subject; but then someone who spends his whole life suppressing the urge to bring conversations round to Buzzy probably isn't well placed to gauge the significance of this omission. 'Well, we *certainly* wouldn't refer to these schools by that, ah, appellation. For a start, the selection process would be at thirteen rather than eleven. Also, the form of academic testing would very probably be different. Of course,' he adds, hurriedly, 'this is all at a preliminary scoping stage—'

' "Blues skies thinking",' Fiona drawls.

'—before any process of political screening—'

' "Thinking the unthinkable" . . .'

'Do you mean Henry is wasting his time?' Henry is moved to discover Buzzy's cheeks are flushed by more than wine and the late afternoon heat. 'You were just saying this policy unit was influential.'

'What I'm *saying* is that in the end nothing will come of it. Cameron's as spineless as Blair when it comes to taking on the liberal establishment; apparently it's much easier to invade Arab nations.'

'Or marry into it,' Buzzy murmurs. 'I'm probably confused, but I thought they started these foreign wars because they were so keen everyone had a liberal establishment.'

Benjamin, exhibiting his father's sense of timing, interrupts the silence with a little gargle. Henry wonders if he ought to have enquired after him more, but he can't think of a line of questioning beyond the infant's sleep patterns, which seems terribly dull even to him. He dreads the scrupulous application with which Marcel would set about answering.

'I'm afraid *le jeune homme* is becoming restless; maybe it's time to return him to his mother.'

'Are you going back to the villa? We can get a taxi together.'

'Yes, I suppose Granny P and George will be arriving soon,' Henry says.

'George is her boyfriend from the nursing home. It's such a sweet story but it'll have to wait for another time: she'll eat Henry alive if he's not there to greet her.'

'It's really more a *residential* than a nursing home. The inmates – that's not the word – are all quite spritely and, you know, autonomous.'

Marcel raises Benjamin aloft for inspection. 'I must apologise if our conversation is rather primitive.'

'Oh, we won't mind! I'm sure he'll behave beautifully, anyway,' Fiona says, though Henry suspects Marcel was in fact addressing his son.

Perhaps because it's happening in another country and he is still elated from seeing Buzzy, Henry has a dreamy belief that his marriage and his wedding essentially amount to the same thing: a slightly dreadful weekend's socialising.

'Also,' Fiona says that evening, over the gnocchi, 'after making such a thing of swearing me to secrecy, I was surprised to hear you casually mentioning the grammar schools policy. What if Marcel tells Afua?'

Henry doesn't think Marcel would commit such a vulgar betrayal, but isn't sure how to explain this to his soon-to-be-wife.

'In fact, I wouldn't trust either of those two – those three – with *my* career.'

'I don't think it's really a question of, ah—'

Fiona has been reflecting for a moment. 'Buzzy was always pretentious and self-satisfied, but until today I didn't realise she was as *creepy* as Marcel. That stuff about him not caring about the judgements of others: who is she to speak about him like that? Oh what, nothing is lost on her because now she's this famous poet?'

Henry doesn't attempt a response this time.

'Obviously she was implying he's above my sordid opinions. I remember when Charlie and I went for dinner with her and I mentioned I was working for the *Mail*. Even then, before the *Spectator* job and the rich boyfriend and the skinny arms, she looked at me with that superior expression of hers. I'm sorry, Henry, I know she used to be your friend, but Buzzy Price is a snooty bitch. I'm certain of it.'

29

A successful visit

'It's certainly not that they're Tories,' Rebecca says. 'You know I'm not political in that way.'

'I do.'

'They'll talk about London things, and I won't be able to keep up.'

'Where's the f— bloody bottle opener? What sort of moral degenerate charges a thousand pounds a week for a place with no . . .'

'Dad said "fucking". He must really need the booze.'

'I specifically did not say that word, William.'

'You mouthed it.'

'Exactly. I don't know what you mean by "London things", darling. You lived there for fifteen years.'

'Do you have time for that beer, darling? I don't know, like *Jerusalem*, or . . .'

'Jerusalem? Oh, *here's* the stupid thing.'

'Darling, please don't drink that now, they'll be here any minute. It's the play everyone's talking about.'

Alec frowns at the unopened bottle of Doom Bar before replacing it above the fridge, next to one of Alison's dolls. 'Were we going to have a little tidy-up before Lord and Lady Glasson arrive?'

The ringing of the front doorbell stops Rebecca from saying something she might regret.

An hour later, in the kitchen again, Alec whispers, 'What do you think? I quite like him, actually. He's invited me to play tennis at the Hurlingham Club.'

'He's certainly interested in sport.'

'You're right; he was a bit of a bore about the England cricket chairmanship. Anyone would have thought he'd been made the Emperor of India.'

Rebecca is rummaging for more biscuits. 'I thought he was saying it was the Indians who run cricket now.'

'You *were* listening,' Alec says, 'well done.'

'I was sure I bought another packet of those lemon Duchy shortbreads. The trouble with hiding things from the boys is that I can never remember where I've put them.' Lowering her voice further, Rebecca mouths, 'The wife's a bit chilly.'

'Yes ... would you mind taking her for a little walk or something?'

Rebecca sighs, admitting defeat. 'It's so embarrassing to run out of biscuits.'

'I just want to hear whatever it is he has to say.'

'Is he going to ask you to join the coalition?'

'That's what I want to find out.'

'But wouldn't it get you into a lot of trouble with your own side? Also, darling, it's raining.'

'Just take a turn or two round the fields; you don't need to bother going down to the beach or anything.'

'I thought the agent woman said there were bullocks in the fields.'

'Nonsense – Colonel and I did a whole circuit yesterday evening and didn't see any.'

'What about Alison, is she going to stay here?'

'I wondered if she could go with you.'

'No, surely it's too muddy?'

'The boys can take it in turns to carry her. It'll distract them from annoying the bullocks.'

'I thought you said there weren't any bullocks.'

'There aren't. I was joking.'

'Well, all right, but only if she's brought a pair of wellies.'

'Oh, she's bound to have a pair in the car; they holiday here every year, apparently.'

*

'He's got so much energy, sometimes I wonder if he gets bored with the family – or just me, most of the time. Perhaps we ought to find him a nice companion to run around with . . .'

Rebecca listens to herself witter on about the dog. Lady Glasson – Virginia, she insists; wife of a life peer ennobled by the prime minister – advises public companies on something called corporate social responsibility. She's late-forties, gym-toned, childless and transparently bored. In the year since the Mertons acquired Colonel, to 'keep mummy and Alison company during the week', as her husband put it, with the boys boarding (though Sam, still at St James', is back at weekends) and Alec himself in Westminster, Rebecca's conversation has become ever more dominated by the family border terrier. She is not so stupid that she hasn't been aware of this happening; it just isn't something she minds particularly. Not only is she certain Colonel's evolving animal consciousness is a more rewarding subject than corporate social responsibility, or parliamentary politics for that matter, but the dog is her remaining link with William and Andrew. Almost overnight they've decided conversation with her on any other subject is excruciatingly pointless. Of course, this is about the onset of adolescence, but it's hard not to place a tiny bit of the blame on the twins starting at an all-boys' boarding school last year. Now and again, she'd like to remind them that she went to Oxford, or that she has played the organ accompaniment to the *Missa Gaudeamus* at Westminster Cathedral. But that all seems a long time ago and, in any case, these days the twins are impressed by narrow pursuits: 'pulling' girls (such an ugly verb!) and perfecting a new type of cricket shot which their father says ought to be illegal. How many ways can one swing a bat, she wonders, though she hasn't asked for fear of the eye-rolling that would be sure to follow.

'We'd like to take him with us to Padstow tomorrow. Do you know if dogs are allowed on the ferry?'

'Don't worry about that. It's a sort of canine Noah's ark most of the time.'

218

'How wonderful!' Rebecca says, in defiance of Virginia's sarcasm. 'William, did you hear that? We can take Colonel on the ferry tomorrow.'

'Mum, can you tell Andrew to take Alison and give me my football back?'

'Darling, I'm sure he will as soon as we get into the next field. We're so looking forward to seeing Padstow,' Rebecca continues. 'The estuary is so beautiful . . . You must love coming down here every year.'

In the distance, she can see a pair of smudgy figures track across the beach beneath a slate-grey sky. Filmy drizzle sits on her face.

'It's really John's obsession; childhood memories and all that. Dubai in November is my quid pro quo.'

'No need for wellies there, I imagine.'

'Yes, thanks for the boots.'

'Not at all – I hope they fit all right.'

'They do pinch a little, but I think your husband's were too large. It's a shame about your trainers.'

'Oh, it's just a little mud, and we're hardly going to be playing tennis in this weather.'

Virginia lets out an unexpected hiccup of a laugh, and Rebecca nears the end of the first field with a sense of minor accomplishment. A quarter of the way through the walk already; they'll just do a lap of the next field and then straight back to the rented cottage. Of course, she'll have to offer more tea when they get in, but the Glassons will surely decline.

'Yes, we're going to the Rick Stein café tomorrow, which should be a bit of a treat. Alec and I wanted to go to the fish restaurant, but it might be difficult with Alison. And Sam claims to hate seafood, so . . .'

'I thought they were called Andrew and William?'

'No, they are – Sam is my ten-year-old. He's playing with a friend who has a holiday home over at Daymer Bay. Well, his parents have one!'

'Three boys . . .'

'I know,' Rebecca says, with an apologetic smile. She can picture her skin crinkling horribly around the eyes and wonders if they sell Clinique in Cornwall.

'Have you been to the Mowhay yet? That's at Daymer. It's very casual, you might like it – David and Samantha are enormous fans.'

'David and . . . Oh, I see. Andrew, darling, just wait by the stile . . . Andrew, no *please* don't run on ahead . . . It's your brother's turn with the football.'

With Rebecca's inferior height and fitness, and her gripless shoes, it's increasingly a struggle to keep up with the rest of the party. By the time she has negotiated the stile the others are half a dozen paces in front.

'You absolute wanker.'

'*William!*'

'Mum, Andrew just booted the football into the other side of the field. He nearly hit one of the bullocks.'

'It's all right,' Andrew says, 'Colonel's going to fetch it.'

A streak of brown shoots in a curve towards the location of William's prized Jabulani football, which rests in the middle of a small herd of bullocks.

'If Colonel punctures my pissing ball . . .' William strides towards his brother with the same menace with which he enunciates his 'P's. Alison, invisible beneath her waterproof jacket hood, slides joltingly down his hip and starts to whimper.

'*William*, careful darling. You're going to drop Alison. *Colonel*,' she shouts, 'Colonel, come back!'

'I think we should try to keep the noise down,' Virginia says, 'if we don't want to disturb the bullocks any further.'

The twins are heading in the direction of Colonel and the football and the bullocks. From the back, at this distance, the only way to distinguish the boys' lanky frames and dank brown hair – they haven't bothered to put their anorak hoods up – is the sight of Alison's bobbing red boots. She has been hoisted off William's hip and is now clutched against his chest like, Rebecca fears, a rugby ball.

'*Colonel!*' she shouts again, pointlessly, she knows, as the dog's usual anxious attentiveness has been subsumed by an instinctive compulsion to chase the round object. It's another instinct, self-preservation, which to Rebecca's boundless relief causes him to tack hard to the right and complete his arc just in front of the bullocks. She takes a few slippery steps towards the retreating dog, repeating his name approvingly and telling him what a good boy he is. The bullocks have been inscrutably taking in the unfolding uproar; when they start moving towards the trespassers they do so slowly, with an air of vague regret.

'Never mind the bloody dog. Tell your children to get back.'

'Boys! *William!* Leave the ball! I said, leave the ball! They're dangerous.'

They don't believe a herd of provoked beasts would actually try to hurt them. Or at least, she thinks, if *I* believe it, they automatically doubt it. Spreading her arms for balance she starts after her children. The spectacle of the advancing bullocks has distracted Alison from her crying, with the result that Rebecca hears with absurd clarity the slapping of her trainer soles against the muddy surface of the field.

The sight of Colonel racing past them seems to galvanise the twins. The bullocks are no longer lumbering but moving in concerted strides, each a little quicker than the last.

'Shit, they're coming,' Andrew says, excitedly.

Rebecca has almost caught up with her children and is reaching out to take Alison when her foot lands on a mud slick. There is a moment of liberating weightlessness. On all fours, she adjusts to the sensation of her tongue caught between rows of teeth thudding shut.

'I probably wouldn't stay down there,' William says, on his way past. 'Those bulls look pissed off.'

From her view from the ground, she is relieved to see William handing Alison to Virginia, who carries her over the stile to safety. The rumble of the herd is getting louder behind her and the twins are now shouting and making Italianate gestures. How did their faces get so tanned, in this weather? There is something wondrously foreign about her sons: their laddish coarseness and sports madness is so unrelatable to her and even Alec, whose rather superficial knowledge of football is, or was, strictly for professional purposes. He used to quiz the twins on team formations and goal-scoring ratios as if they were ministerial aides (though Rebecca can't imagine his actual adviser – the beautiful one who all of a sudden seems to be the shadow home secretary – taking an interest in the game for the sake of Alec, or anyone else). She wishes she could tell William and Andrew that she is very proud of them; she'd never have imagined it was possible to be shy of one's own children.

'*Run!*' Virginia orders.

Rebecca gets to her feet and launches herself towards the corner of the field, slipping and sliding and falling to her knees every few steps. At least I'm wearing my brown coat, she thinks just before the bullocks break into an all-out charge. She mustn't look back, like Orpheus wasn't it, but how close and how powerful the cattle sound! A large rock flies past, lobbed by Virginia, who is mounted on a concrete step in an impressively bellicose pose. Below her, the twins lean over the stile bar with arms outstretched . . . their confident faces riven with white panic . . . such a relief, she thinks: they do love me after all.

Into their embrace – *oh!* she cries as her sons pull her, roughly, over the metal bar. Her knee bangs painfully against the step vacated by Virginia and she lands cheek first in a basin of mud.

Back at Maiden Over, the men are enormously amused by Rebecca's bedraggled appearance and the twins' breathless account of the crazed bullocks in the farmer's field.

'Lady Glasson was awesome,' William says, to the purse-lipped pleasure of the subject.

Andrew agrees: 'Like Ripley in *Aliens*.'

Afterwards, in bed, Rebecca has taken a broken-spined Anne Tyler from the bookcase, while Alec watches *Newsnight*.

'Are you going to take it? The job offer.'

'I don't know, darling. My side would be furious.'

'You'd be burning your bridges.'

'It's completely obvious what Cameron's trying to do: he wants New Labour's imprimatur on his education reforms.'

Rebecca doesn't want to imply her husband knows nothing about education policy. 'But you were in the Treasury.'

'True, but apparently I'm seen as a quintessential Blairite, even though I've only spoken to TB twice. Possibly what they mean is I'm middle class. Anyway, Lord G made it clear I could only chair the commission if I'd go along with a recommendation to lower the academic selection age from sixteen to thirteen, at least for Free Schools.'

'I don't understand. If it's your commission, how do they already know that's what it's going to recommend?'

'It's just how these things work.' Alec picks up his book, the last volume of a series on the Hundred Years War that he started reading when he was in government. 'On the other hand, I'm not exactly in favour with the Party as it is – stuck in the mud, you could say.'

She pretends not to notice his sly glance, and is disappointed when it's gone.

Alec sighs. 'It *would* be fun to be part of government again.'

'I'm just thinking about the boys being at Tonbridge. It's not as if you're against selective education – no one could call you a hypocrite, could they?'

A self-assured young voice can be heard on *Newsnight*: it's somehow both urban and urbane, which strikes Rebecca as perhaps a very useful political combination. She looks up from her unread page and finds it's Alec's Afua who is talking rather sensibly about the riots, something about accelerated trials and refusing to make excuses for mindless violence. Beside Afua in the studio is Daphne Depree, Sherard Howe's Kiwi wife, making barbed but inaudible interjections. Jeremy Paxman brusquely tells her to wait her turn. Afua stops and laughs, touches Daphne's arm and says it's like being at the breakfast table. Paxman's corrugated expression turns heavenwards and poor Daphne looks crosser than ever.

'. . . Sorry, darling. No, you're absolutely right.'

'God, doesn't Afua look stunning. Hasn't she only just had a baby?'

'Yes, actually let's have this off,' Alec says, reaching for the remote. 'This is supposed to be a holiday, after all.'

30

A trip to town

Buzzy's parents are almost a quarter of an hour late; that this should seem unremarkable to Philip only emphasises how painful the encounter is going to be. It's also one that she's put off as long as she could. At first her tactic was simply to ignore her mother's discreet hints about not having met her new, nebulously older boyfriend. After she moved in with Philip, around the time she confessed he was a year her father's senior, she found herself agreeing to the by then unabashed maternal requests for an introduction, only to cancel on each occasion at the last minute. Buzzy told herself that her mother was secretly as relieved as she was when the arranged time supposedly clashed with a poetry reading at the *London Review* bookshop, or Philip was at a client's board meeting in New York.

Then a month ago, her father, who, she believed, had accepted each of her excuses with cheerful fatalism, announced that Doreen and he were 'coming up to town' on the third Saturday of September. They thought they might drop in on Buzzy and Philip in the afternoon, 'if it wasn't inconvenient'. He spoke in his usual jovial, slightly tremulous voice that whenever she heard disembodied over the telephone made her morbidly distracted by the thought of how much she was going to miss him when he died (because of this, she sometimes missed what he was actually saying). Buzzy replied that it sounded great but she'd have to check her and Philip's diaries, knowing on this occasion she wouldn't try to get out of it. Despite the fact Orpington was twenty-five minutes from Charing Cross on the train, a trip to London by her parents was not a trivial event, and inviting himself to tea not something her father would do lightly.

225

The thought that their lateness is limiting the amount of time Philip will be exposed to her parents, and vice versa, is counterbalanced by Buzzy's concern that something has happened: they've wandered down the wrong West End side street and been mugged; or, that perennial fear, her father has had a heart attack.

Philip examines himself in the wall-to-floor window. 'Remind me what time the parliament thing starts,' he says, plumping his hair unashamedly.

'The invitation said six.' Buzzy wonders if it might have been six thirty for seven, but with Philip it's best to sound certain. In a few minutes, if her parents still haven't arrived, she'll sneak off to consult Afua's email on her new MacBook.

'Right, well if we leave at seven.'

Often he leaves his sentences vaguely unfinished, as if the whole business of speaking to her was rather an effort. 'You've booked a car, have you?'

'I'll do it right now.'

With her parents' visit and then Afua's party, Buzzy is imposing on Philip's time twice today, and she's only too conscious of how deeply he resents this. It won't of course have crossed his mind that she may be dreading both social obligations far more than him.

Ralph and Doreen Price would normally avoid wine in the afternoon, especially before a show. They'll now be unable to watch *The Phantom of the Opera* without worrying about drifting off or needing the loo. However, since Philip's offer is so startlingly grand ('I thought I'd open a Château d'Yquem to go with your biscuits, if you've no objections to something sweet. It's so wonderful to meet you at last . . .'), and since Buzzy, who is already feeling her mother's disappointment at Philip's casual reference to the Fortnum & Mason offering that she will have been fretting about for weeks, doesn't dare suggest tea instead, they accept with only a minimum of hesitation.

'I just can't get over your view.'

Doreen looks flushed, or perhaps she's overdone her rouge today. Buzzy's maternal grandmother was born in Bombay to a Scottish Catholic railwayman and his Anglo-Indian wife, and there's a subtle swarthiness to Doreen's complexion which wasn't passed down to Buzzy, who is aggrieved to have instead inherited her father's freckly Celtic skin.

Philip doesn't look up from pouring the wine. 'We're lucky it's sunny, for once.'

'Oh, yes, isn't it hot today?' Doreen offers, faintly disapprovingly.

'That's the MI6 building, of course. What else . . . Parliament, obviously. And the Eye thing.'

'Actually, we've just been on the London Eye – thank you very much.' Her father accepts Philip's proffered glass, smothering his alarm at the unfamiliar coffee tint of the Château d'Yquem with a wobbly smile. 'If we'd known this was the view waiting for us, we wouldn't've bothered!'

'Ha! No, but I'm sure there's more to see from up there.'

'You haven't been? Well, not surprising when you live somewhere like here . . . It's very impressive – too dear, that'd be my only issue.'

'Ah, well . . . I've had it a while, and property prices weren't quite so *insane* fifteen years— You're talking about the wheel.'

Philip's laugh drowns out her father's embarrassed chuckle.

'Maybe Philip should tell us exactly how many millions Pimlico penthouses are worth,' Buzzy says, annoyed with everyone, 'then we can move on to something else.'

'Your daughter has a very mischievous sense of humour. Do sit down.'

'Thank you. Once again, I'm *so* sorry we were late,' says Buzzy's mother, with a hint of desperation.

'Now, what was it you said you were off to see this evening? *Phantom of the Opera*?'

'I can't understand why you want to see it *again*,' Buzzy says. 'Isn't there a sequel now? Why not watch that?'

Her father is grinning at her: in spite of his present shyness it's a loving expression. But how shrivelled he looks, next to Philip! How forlorn the sparse wisps on his pate! 'We wouldn't know any of the songs, would we? Buzzy loves *Phantom* really,' he tells Philip. 'We used to have the record of the original cast. She used to sing along to all the Sarah Brightman parts.'

'When I was ten or something!' Buzzy protests, cheeks burning. 'Anyway, I preferred *Les Misérables*. Have you seen that?'

'Do you know, I *haven't*,' Philip says. 'It's rather extraordinary, but I don't think I've ever seen a musical in my life. I once found myself sitting next to Andrew Mackintosh at a dinner—'

'Cameron Mackintosh,' Buzzy corrects.

'—Cameron, thank you, darling' – Buzzy's parents smile resiliently through the last word – 'it was dreadfully awkward. But no, I quite understand you, Ralph,' Philip says, pronouncing her father's name *Rafe*. 'One likes to return to what one's grown up with: the music of one's life. I'm more of a Wagner man myself. *The Ring*. I must have been about twelve when I first heard that.'

Ralph, who hasn't heard of Wagner, nods encouragingly.

'But what *I'm* saying is that I heard *Phantom* when I was young and I've definitely moved on from it now. It would be terrible if people were condemned, for sentimental reasons, never to develop their tastes.'

'Do you mean your parents ought to try harder?'

'Well, yes! But only for their own pleasure and, you know, stimulation.' Buzzy addresses this to her mother, hoping to draw her into the conversation. Instead Doreen looks mortified at the ill-chosen word. 'There's so much that art, real art, can reveal about life, and everything . . .'

'My Dorothea!'

'No, you know what I mean,' Buzzy says, surrendering to Philip's teasing.

'I'm just your old Casaubon.'

'Please, you're the least Casaubonish man I've ever met.'

Philip, immensely pleased, roars with laughter.

'We're very proud of our daughter,' Ralph says, using the cover of his host's mirth to slip in the little boast. 'Aren't we, Doreen?'

'She's always loved her books. We went to the EuroDisney once, in Paris—'

'Ah, Paris, yes—'

'—we went all the way round *Pirates of the Caribbean*,' Doreen continues, with a determination that surprises Buzzy, 'without her looking up once from her Nancy Drew. I said to Ralph: "I don't know why we came all this way when she doesn't even know what ride she's on." I'll never forget how *busy* it was for March . . .'

Doreen's habit of concluding with a remark of tangential relevance to the preceding story leaves even Philip briefly floundering for a follow-up.

'Of course, Elizabeth is an extremely talented poet . . .' He seems to say this more mechanically than if he were talking to one of his friends, or indeed (or especially) enemies. Perhaps it's just that he's delivered this line, or something similar, many times in the last couple of years.

'Oh, yes!' Ralph says, satisfied, before tactfully changing the subject and asking Philip how his work is going.

Buzzy silently wills her parents not to show their ignorance too obviously while Philip talks about gearing up for the new regulatory regime for financial services; the round of consolidations related to the slowdown in China and the East; the insolvency work still dragging on three years after the initial bank collapses. 'I'm afraid,' he concludes, 'the crisis has worked out enormously well for the lawyers.'

'We wanted Buzzy to be a solicitor, like you, at one point.'

'Really,' Philip says flatly.

Straightaway Buzzy realises how parochial 'solicitor' sounds in her father's mouth, as though Philip were the local notary. No less offensive is the idea that his profession was the second choice of a Orpington shopworker's daughter. (By not asking after Ralph's employment Philip avoided hearing how badly the furniture business has fared in the last few years.)

'I'm sure I would have been a useless lawyer,' she tries, but it sounds as if she is trying to fish for a compliment.

'We had trouble understanding Buzzy was an artist – you know, with things she needed to say about the world.' He chuckles. 'All the same, we're relieved she doesn't still live in that awful old area.'

'Yes, of course,' Philip says, with a quick arch glance towards Buzzy.

'Her mother used to worry non-stop about her safety. It's the Bohemian lifestyle, I told her . . .'

Philip visited the South Kensington address once. Buzzy had vaguely indicated Henry was letting her use it on a temporary basis, and she was relieved when he didn't seem interested in further details. Naturally she said nothing about pretending to her parents she was living in Dalston. Even though they'd only been seeing each other a month or two, when Buzzy suddenly needed to vacate the mews house – presented as an entirely unrelated turn of events to Sherard Howe's embarrassing incident with Abdul – Philip chivalrously offered to have her stay at his penthouse flat. The plan was for Buzzy to stay 'for a few days' while she made new arrangements. She wasn't sure if he knew all along that she hadn't the money to move anywhere except back in with her parents, but in the event a week became a fortnight and then a month . . . Since Philip worked such gargantuan hours at Sullivan and Ball, he joked that having her living at the apartment was really the only way of them seeing each other, at least during the week.

During this early period they often took trips outside of London on weekends. Philip always had corporate hospitality tickets for something or other: the Henley regatta; the Burghley horse trials; opera at Grange Park. In the winter she finally visited New York. Her initial idea was to present a strategically simplified version of herself – young, artistic, slightly in awe of him – purely on a provisional basis, before she felt sufficiently comfortable with letting him see a more unexpurgated Buzzy, or rather Elizabeth. Except they're now into their third year together and she is still playing basically the same part. The only difference is her performance is increasingly stale, which was why in her more optimistic moments she'd allowed herself to hope that today – by permitting Philip a glimpse, via her parents, of the dreary suburban upbringing she's hitherto been so anxious to hide from him – might represent a belated step forwards in their relationship.

'Did I mention Afua is having a drinks party on the House of Commons terrace this evening? I should probably start getting ready quite soon . . .'

'What was it exactly that made you nervous about the neighbourhood – if you don't mind me asking?'

Buzzy watches helplessly as her parents exchange glances; she doesn't dare try intervening again.

'Quite a few Arabs, I suppose . . .?'

'It's just that she's our daughter, you know,' replies Doreen, gratefully.

'Oh, of course. I can assure you that Elizabeth is very safe here with me.'

Ralph is nodding. 'We can see that, can't we, dear?'

'I've just realised,' Philip grins, 'I never said cheers.'

'Oh!' Doreen says, rather excitedly.

'Well, Dor, Buzzy, Phil – cheers!'

Buzzy answers without thinking. 'It's Philip.'

'I don't mind at all. It's like a glimpse of a different life.'

'We want Black Rod's entrance,' Philip informs their cab driver, without leaning forward. The naturalness of his tone, Buzzy suspects, is both part of the joke and a rehearsal for his demeanour when they arrive: he's never been inside the Houses of Parliament and will probably be keen not to let this show in front of the other guests.

The silence during the five-minute taxi ride from Pimlico has been Philip's version of nerves. Either that or there really is something he needs to read on his BlackBerry accounting for his restless scrolling. Or he's letting her know how much of a sufferance it was entertaining her parents. It's alarming – not least for what it says of her own powers of observation, in a way her only professional qualification – how often her understanding of Philip's moods is guesswork, even after two years of cohabitation. Fundamentally she can't decide if he's not all that reflective (does he, for example, share her anxiety at the thought one of them might let their partnership down this evening?), or if it's she who's superficial for not grasping his complexity.

What Buzzy does realise, which certainly is superficial, is that she's not looking forward to being seen talking with her boyfriend in public, at least by her friends. Afua's mere presence (she can't even think about Marcel) will make her lose faith in the authenticity of her own behaviour; she'll feel hopelessly self-conscious smiling at Philip's jokes or including him in whatever she's saying – which is not fair, because she really *does* think he's sharp in company (too sharp, in the case of her parents), and prefer it when he's drawn into the conversation. It would be much better if Afua were limited to reading about Philip Devereux and Elizabeth Price, or possibly seeing photos of them together. In Buzzy's imagination, neither Afua nor Marcel has missed any of the handful of occasions when her name has appeared in the society columns or culture supplements, even though this would require them to spend much of their time Googling her name, and even though she herself makes a point of immediately skipping any article in which Afua is mentioned.

If Buzzy assiduously searches for the mentions of herself she then pictures her friends reading, at least she is discreet about it. Philip has a habit of leaving the *Financial Times* folded at an article referring to him, or the deal he's working on, somewhere prominent in their (his) flat. Buzzy knows to remark on it, despite the fact that the courtesy isn't reciprocated, and that she finds the *FT*, let alone the Companies & Markets section (let alone *The Lawyer*!), less impressive than, say, the *Guardian Review*, which reviewed (quite positively) *The Bathers*; or even *Slate*, which recently published a new poem of hers.

What she wants is a notable man who would never think of drawing attention to the occasions he is noted. Then again, she thinks, trying now to find fault with Marcel, at least Philip is fundamentally interested in what others think of him. This requires a degree of respect, however modest, for the opinions of his fellow human beings. Marcel only wants to impress himself – with the fineness of his mind, his connectedness to the centre of things. His solipsism is just as well, because mystifyingly to Buzzy (who Googles his name as relentlessly as her own) no one else in fact does seem to take much of an interest in him. He still has no friends, as far as she can tell, and he's never written about other than occasionally in the context of Afua. Buzzy takes some small pleasure in this: lately she has been making an effort to find Marcel tiresome. There are times when this is less challenging than others, such as on those rare occasions when the two of them can meet for dinner – Philip is out with clients and Afua is voting late at the House and Marta is babysitting Benjamin – only for Marcel to go from ordering his food to the arrival of the first course without speaking more than a handful of words. But then he'll be busy at work and stop emailing her, or make some apparently offhand reference to looking for a house to buy or an adequate nursery school for Benjamin, and despite herself she'll be relieved when she feels as desolate as ever. Then she wonders if she ought to be suspicious of that relief, if that in itself is evidence the old obsession is on the wane. Or if in its maturing her obsession has both weakened and strengthened, so that she can acknowledge his limitations, even despise him a little for them, and desire him nonetheless.

Understanding oneself is a vast project, but oughtn't she at least be sure if she's having an inappropriate relationship with a married man? She'd *thought* she was: this is, after all, someone she slept with while he was in a relationship with his now wife; someone with whom she arranges furtive if sporadic meetings, characterised by a charged awkwardness that, whatever else it is, doesn't feel platonic. Yet she realised in Arezzo that not only was Marcel happy to casually tell Henry about their most recent encounter, but from her (deliberately brief) conversations with Afua on the wedding day itself it was clear he'd been keeping her up to date with Buzzy's news. This leads Buzzy to wonder if the secretive aspect of their carryings-on is only in her head, which is marginally less painful than the next thought, that she is the eccentric mutual friend whose latest doings Marcel amusedly recounts to his beautiful wife over a glass of wine.

Her only guiding certainty is that she no longer deserves to give herself the benefit of the doubt on anything. Thus, the reason why Philip and her parents think her modest about the equally modest success of *The Bathers* is not because she's virtuously self-effacing, but because most of the volume was urged into existence to impress an audience of one. When the truly wise (not to mention moral) course would have been to give Marcel up, she'd instead finally eked out enough poems to allow him to contrast her supposedly metaphysical qualities with those of practical, political Afua, never mind that in any measurable terms the latter's successes are of a different magnitude to Buzzy's own.

There is nothing lofty about her artistry, if that's what you called the mundane fragments of verse, verging on the pastiche, that Buzzy wrote hastily, in a state of desperation – so far from the sort of poetry she'd dreamed of publishing, and being admired for! What frightens Buzzy almost as much as her feelings for Marcel ripening and starting to putrefy, is that she might have already lost any creative ambition. What will she do for the rest of her life, having turned her back on the conventional Orpington aspirations of a husband, a joint mortgage, her own car (she doesn't even drive), of children?

The Palace of Westminster comes into view, its Gothic angles sharp against the cloudless September sky. It's entirely consistent that Afua would gamble on an outside drinks party in autumn, only to find the day is record-shatteringly hot.

They stop at the traffic lights before Westminster Green, an odd pause in which they have virtually arrived but remain in the taxi at Philip's silent instigation. He stuffs his BlackBerry back into what seems to Buzzy an alarmingly cream jacket, even if she defers to him in what's sartorially recommendable for middle-aged, upper-middle-class men.

The natural way to break the silence would be to query who or what Black Rod is. Reluctant to expose his ignorance as much as her own, however, she says instead, 'I expect there'll be quite an impressive politico crowd at this.'

'Oh yes?' Philip says, with false cheeriness that's meant to convey his determination to indulge her, despite his personal indifference to the guest list. (Of course it's she who is indulging him, knowing he will be reassured by this remark, however tawdry it was of her to utter it, and however little she enjoys talking up Afua's popularity.)

'Even Blair might pop by, so I hear.'

His head stays turned away from Buzzy, towards the public gardens and line of trees overhanging the river. She can hear his cautious interest when he says, 'Ewan Blair?'

'No, *even* Blair – Tony himself. Apparently he doesn't often appear at these sorts of events, so I think Afua would consider it a bit of a coup.'

'You say "this sort of event" without telling me what it's in aid of. Do I need to congratulate her for something?'

'No, it's just a very late summer party. The Howes always used to hold something similar at their house in Islington. Everyone would arrive very promptly because some ludicrously expensive champagne was always served for the first hour. Probably Afua doesn't need to bribe her guests,' she adds, with an instantly fading smile.

Their car has pulled up opposite the entrance to Black Rod's Garden. Buzzy thanks the driver as she climbs out of the Mercedes, in the obscure hope her good manners will by some mystical process be noted and rewarded by the partygoers on the House of Commons terrace.

'Will whatshecalled be here? Sherard?'

'I don't know . . .' Keen to encourage this suggestion of mischievous good spirits on Philip's part, she adds, 'I think he might still be in disgrace.'

'Ah, yes, now why is that again?'

Buzzy pauses before answering, to allow the bored police officers to hand them passes and send them through the security detectors. Philip has surely not forgotten, since she remembers him enjoying it a great deal, the story of Daphne arriving home to find Sherard foisting himself on his son's pupil when he was supposed to be showing off his art collection. (In Henry's dismal narration of events the fact that Abdul's claim on the Saudi throne was pretty theoretical – a small army of other princes would have to be wiped out first – did not lessen the diplomatic fuss that followed.) The buoyancy of Philip's mood, and from that the success or failure of her entrance to Afua's glittering party, seems to hang on whether she can offer up the incident in a manner that will entertain him as much as it did the first time.

3 1

Connecting dots

Lord knows, she's not a timid person, but Daphne hasn't got used to going to parties by herself. Before she met Sherard she hardly went to any, at least not ones attended by people in her intellectual hemisphere. It's silly the slight clamminess in her palms as she descends the familiar shabby green-carpeted staircase leading off Central Lobby. (She paid no attention to the request in Afua's pompous invitation – what was she doing sending it to Daphne by email, when they lived in the same house? – to use Black Rod's Garden Entrance.) No doubt parliament is usually quiet on a Saturday evening, but the fact it's now in recess for Party conference season seems to heighten the deserted feel of the place.

Daphne realised, after they had gone ahead and left without her, that she had assumed she would be arriving with Afua and Marcel. It was a surprise to wake from her afternoon nap (a new routine, reluctantly acquired) to find the house empty. On the kitchen table she found a short note in Marcel's precise continental handwriting, informing her that they were dropping Benjamin off at Marta's before the party and would see her there.

It's obviously tempting to blame the Belgian for her state of abandonment. He dislikes her, that much is clear, despite his relentless probing of her views on those occasions when he can't evade her presence. His talent for identifying topical items on which she isn't quite certain of her ground is unnerving: Daphne always feels she's lost the argument without him having even deigned to contradict her. Instead it's his readiness to concede, his carefully imperfect pretence of imbibing her wisdom, that alerts her to the flaws or inaccuracies in whatever she has been *induced*

– that's what it feels like – into saying, even if the nature of those only becomes apparent to her hours or even days later.

He seems to read the *Liberal Review* avidly; whether or not this too is part of his casual campaign to drive her mad she couldn't say for sure. Either way he's doubtless quite enjoying her increasing marginalisation in the family – the qualifier here is everything, since Daphne doubts he would pay her the compliment of being fully engaged in her misfortune. In any case, he's too calculating, too *malin* (the French word, she looked it up) to take a position on Daphne that would be dramatically out of step with Afua's, consciously expressed or otherwise.

The Stranger's Bar, which leads through to the terrace, is locked. She stares at the prissy members-only sign on the door, digesting her situation. The idea of phoning Afua for directions when Daphne has been visiting parliament for almost three decades (albeit not frequently, never having been a lobby hack) is not one she's prepared to contemplate. Though maybe she could have printed off the blasted email, or at the minimum finished reading it.

As it turns out, there's another terrace entrance almost immediately to her left, next to the Commons cafeteria. At the opposite end of the terrace from where she emerges, a smattering of early guests stand around clutching drinks outside a marquee extension to the Lords bar, making the most of the late afternoon sunshine. Daphne checks her watch: barely six o'clock. In another life, Sherard would have infuriated her by inviting someone round for an aperitif or insisting they have an early dinner at the Cinnamon Club. By the time they finally arrived, slightly tipsy, the event would have been at its peak, with Daphne experiencing the delicious sense of having far too many people to catch up with before the end of the evening.

Instead, on leaving home she knew she was going to be too early but her boredom made her set aside the fact. In any case, having little practical experience of the first half-hour of someone else's party, she didn't fully understand how necessary it was to skip it, not least when the hostess herself hasn't yet graced the proceedings with her presence.

The first person she recognises is Gareth McKenna, a former minister she would normally have taken great pains to avoid. The conversation that follows is comfortably their longest in the couple of decades she has known him. She's surprised to learn he was in the North East yesterday for a constituency surgery, and has driven down specially to be here this evening. 'But it's only a very casual thing; I doubt even Afua's planning to stay later than ten.' Taking pity on him, she adds, rather stiffly, 'I'll have to let her know you went to such an effort.' This provokes such a cringe-worthy display of gratitude she immediately excuses herself.

The marquee is empty apart from the bar staff. She asks for white wine and drinks down half the glass in three swift gulps. Back outside again, steering carefully clear of McKenna, she finds herself mingling and making introductions, playing the role of hostess by default. At one point Cynthia Scott, the *Indy* columnist, corners her and launches into an extended commiseration about the rampant sexism and ageism in journalism; the relentless and depthless search for novelty among commissioning editors; the barbarism of a new world in which citizens refuse to pay for the written word. 'To tell the truth,' she concludes, 'I was a bit worried you'd be after my job.'

'*Your* job,' Daphne smiles, 'why would I want that?'

'Well, because of your *Guardian* contract.'

'What about it?'

'I heard they weren't planning to renew it.' Realising she has blundered, but not insensible to the pleasurable aspect of the situation, Cynthia adds, 'It's probably just one of those silly rumours.'

'Don't bullshit me, Cynthia. Is it true or not?'

'It was a pretty good source; I'm sorry.'

'Well,' Daphne says, briskly, 'well, fuck.' She finishes her wine in a large gulp.

'You had a good run – well goodish. And there's still the Beeb, for now.'

They both know, because Cynthia is always trying to steal it off her, that this is unpredictable work, and virtually unpaid.

The terrace is now quite thick with bodies awaiting their hostess's arrival. Cynthia smiles and glances around: she seems to be losing interest in this discussion. 'Or you could write another tome.'

'Perhaps I will.'

Daphne is sure she won't publish another book. All the buzz these days is around the new generation of 'feminists' whose style seems, perhaps intentionally, the antithesis of her own: irreverent, anti-theory, apolitical. Moronic would be another word. More fundamentally, however, Daphne knows deep down she has nothing left to say; that the success of *The Prodigal Sister* – an unapologetic return to Marx published at the height of the global economic crisis – was mainly a matter of felicitous timing; that unlike in her youth she lacks the emotional resilience to deal with a critical mauling. No: better to quit with a bibliography that may be modest but is on balance respected by those who matter.

She feels a rare urge to be by herself. On the Thames, a *bateau mouche* covered with coloured dots transports art lovers between Tates. Something happened to Sherard's Damien Hirst bottle, what was it? Something absurd that got him all riled up for half a second . . .

Cynthia's sympathy is now in full retreat. '. . . Or sign up with the *Mail*. The money's good, and it's a journey that's been made before.' Taking her leave, she says *sotto voce*, 'This might be your chance.'

Daphne turns round to find herself confronted with Jez Wedderspoon, the ex-showbiz hack turned political muckraker who wrote the article about Sherard.

He's holding an unlit cigarette. ''Allo, Daphne. Got a light?'

'What are you doing here?'

'She's an ecumenical young lady, our Afua. Is that the word?' He puts the fag back in its packet.

Daphne notices clumped curls of chest hair glisten where he's left his shirt unbuttoned, as though he's recently been swimming. 'She's an absent young lady.'

'I saw you chatting to McKenna earlier. S'funny, but I don't think I could even tell you which side was he on. Seems a lifetime ago already . . .'

Wedderspoon is one of the old Street of Shame jack-of-all-trades: like Daphne, apparently, a dying breed. She hasn't forgotten his recent description of her, knowing full well she is from New Zealand, as the 'wizened of Oz'.

'As I recall, Tony sacked him for being a Brownite—'

'That's right. He came back under Brown, didn't he? DfID or something.'

'Until Gordon got it in his head he was a Blairite, and fired him.'

'I'm starting to feel sorry for him.'

'He's something of a moron, if it helps.'

His chuckle is a little dismissive: where politicians are concerned, he probably wouldn't use the term in such a discriminate fashion. 'Sherard coming this evening?'

Daphne is shocked by his breeziness. She searches, without success, for an adequate retort.

'We've got plenty of other stuff on him we could've used, y'know. I'm surprised you haven't shown a bit more gratitude.'

'Gratitude! You're lucky we didn't sue.'

Wedderspoon wears a thin-lipped smirk as he looks significantly past Daphne's shoulder. 'I wasn't talking about gratitude to *us*.'

Afua is gliding towards them in an armless black dress Daphne happens to know is Chanel. Rowan Harwood is with her, looking unbearably pleased with herself after last week's Emmy: it's absurd, in Daphne's view, that someone she once heard lamenting the assassination of Edward Kennedy should ever have been allowed to play the First Lady.

How clever of Afua to ask her guests to arrive via Black Rod's and the Lords bar, in order to reserve the longer Commons approach for her own Hollywood entrance. (Marcel is in the background, murmuring with their poet friend, the same young woman – she remembers now! – who drank Sherard's Hirst bottle.) Without quite giving the impression she has any idea who he is, Rowan gamely accepts the hand of a former Blair adviser, a man whose very presence at the party is a statement by Afua to the Brownites. She is not afraid of them. A photographer clicks away, almost stepping on Daphne's foot as he creeps backwards.

If Afua is puzzled to see Daphne with Wedderspoon, she doesn't show it. Daphne feels the smooth cheek press briefly against her own, smells its familiar limy scent.

'Looking gorgeous, Af. Can I get a few minutes with you later?'

'That depends,' she replies, linking arms with Daphne, 'if my darling Kiwi mother can spare me.'

'Oh, I expect she will. Isn't it her turn – to spare you, I mean?'

Daphne realises that, for all her fury at Wedderspoon's article on Sherard and the Arab boy, the *Mail*'s coverage was relatively muted. No clearing of the front page; not a single follow-up piece, despite Wedderspoon's claim just now that the paper knew of other compromising incidents involving her husband. As for the *Mail* hack's implication that there's one person Daphne knows with sufficient influence over the paper to intervene on Sherard's behalf: she imagines that, in return for only half-heartedly running the Sherard story, Afua will have had to promise Wedderspoon and his editor a future exclusive. Or perhaps they simply weighed up the relative benefits of, on the one hand, making a fuss about a minor indiscretion involving a political magazine proprietor cum Labour donor – neither of which is liable to make a person vastly well known outside of Westminster and North London – and, on the other, keeping onside with the rising star of British politics. Either way, the oily Wedderspoon is right: Afua has spared not only Sherard but also Daphne and Henry – the whole family – from a greater humiliation than the one they ended up facing.

Of course Daphne should be grateful – *is* grateful. But did the girl only choose to intervene because the story of Sherard's sordid little groping was slightly embarrassing for her, by association? And was Wedderspoon only invited to the party because Afua wanted Daphne to discover that these days she needs her former protégée's protection?

Daphne smiles: perhaps she is English enough, after all, to wish to show both Wedderspoon and Afua that she can be gracious in defeat. Tentatively, she places her hand over Afua's and allows herself – it's actually something of a relief – to be guided into the crowd.

32

Never complain, never explain

The good thing about Barnsbury, the location of Sherard's rented bachelor pad, is how close it is to the Holloway Road – not because he is suddenly in the market for shoddy second-hand furniture, or fume-coated fruit, or (going by the murkily-lit Latin American cantinas) wholesale cocaine suppliers, though he has a certain intrigued admiration for those who are; no, what he appreciates about this part of Islington is the plethora of drinking spots where he's certain not to bump into any of his old friends or neighbours. He chooses the pub at random, and is pleased by the discrepancy between the replica Arsenal shirts worn by most of the patrons and his own purple velvet smoking suit and Trickers brogues.

The flat-screen televisions on the walls and above the bar show a sombre Arsène Wenger, and Sherard gathers Arsenal have lost another away match.

'Who were they playing?' Sherard enquires of the group at the bar.

'The Arsenal?' says a man with impressively livid cheeks. 'Blackburn, lost 4–3. Fucking scored two own goals.'

'That sounds rather careless.'

'He's a fucking muppet, Koscielny,' says another man.

'Should never of sold Gallas to the fucking yids.'

'I said the same thing to Arsène, not quite in those terms. Perhaps I should have.'

There is a pause during which Sherard is aware of being dismissed as a fantasist. Turning his back to him, the man with the inflamed face resumes, 'What you talking about? Gallas is gash, and he's injured. We want Kompany or someone.'

Sherard has tuned out – he suddenly feels very tired – when he hears the publican's gruff *Yes, mate?*

'Do you sell any foreign lagers?'

'Right in front of you.'

He raises his eyelids a fraction. 'I accept these have foreign names; the issue is where they were brewed. If Scunthorpe were renamed "Siena" one wouldn't suddenly decide to go there on holiday.'

Sherard slips back into a semi-doze: it was possibly a mistake to finish the second bottle of Petit Mouton before leaving his little flat. Two sharp taps to the back of his wallet-holding hand alert him to the pint that's been placed in front of him. It's too dark to be any sort of lager.

'Tell you what, mate: have a fucking Spitfire. Or fuck off.'

He has finished his third Spitfire and, after a difficult conversation about the Scotch situation, moved on to bourbon, when he realises the irritatingly persistent sound of a Nokia ringtone is coming from his pocket. Sherard squints at the caller identification.

'Henry.'

'Dad, hullo. How are you?'

'All right. I assume you're married now.'

Henry stutteringly confirms this is the case. He and Fiona stayed on in Tuscany for a lovely honeymoon, bar a couple of minor issues.

'One queries the decision to visit in August,' Sherard remarks, on hearing Fiona found Florence oppressively crowded.

'Well, but she loved San Gimignano, once we arrived. I'm afraid I was a bit of a wimp about driving, and we found the local bus system somewhat confusing.'

He asks Henry if there was anything in particular he wanted to discuss.

'Only that I really am sorry about the wedding. If it was only up to me, you'd obviously have been invited.' Henry adds sheepishly he's already expressed all this in his letter.

'You have.'

'Good, well . . .'

A muffled female voice is audible in the background: Sherard has the impression they're in a car.

'Actually, I was just wondering if you were planning on coming this evening.'

'Don't know what you're talking about.'

'To Afua's drinks party? On the Commons terrace? I thought you'd been invited.'

'It appears not.'

'Oh, right . . .' Henry gives a short embarrassed laugh. 'Sorry for disturbing you, in that case: I – *we* – just thought we'd check what your plans were, because Mum's definitely coming. We thought it'd be better for everyone, in the round, as it were, if perhaps only one of you . . . I hope you understand.'

'Absolutely.'

'Well, that's great,' says Henry, sounding relieved, 'thank you, Dad. And you'll probably have a quiet evening, do you think? I started *War and Peace* in Arezzo. It's actually rather good.'

'Goodbye, Henry.'

Over his second bourbon, Sherard wonders if his son is tougher than he has previously given him credit for. There is a chance he's even weaker; that in making the telephone call he was merely doing the bidding of his wife. Does this meddling girl imagine Afua would be hosting a party at the House of Commons if it wasn't for Sherard? Come to that, does she imagine his wife would have become a famous feminist without his support – that over the years she hasn't made enthusiastic use of his contacts in the worlds of politics and publishing? It suits no one, least of all Daphne, to remember it is thanks to him she isn't Rod Depree's spiky little sister; some unloved Christchurch librarian or school-teacher who likes it to be known she has read if not deeply understood de Beauvoir.

He hardly even touched the boy. It was Daphne's return that panicked Abdul, and made him run blubbing to the aunt. If

Sherard had done that after every piano lesson with Tripp he would never have mastered the *Moonlight Sonata*; but how odd, and yet how typical, that this was the one time his wife had arrived home without announcing the fact with an almighty clatter of the front door.

Even more mysterious was the identity of whoever leaked the story to the evil little hack from Vauxhall. Not the Saudis, obviously: the family's representatives were even more mortified by the article than Sherard. Perhaps it was some shit at the tutoring agency, out for a quick quid; or a 'friend' in whom Daphne foolishly confided; or a Home Office SpAd using an MI5 briefing to try to embarrass Afua. He'd absolutely expect the security services to be keeping tabs on a Saudi royal involved with a high-profile political family, especially one with links to Labour, whom the spooks have always mistrusted.

At the bar again, a drunken Irishwoman waves her smartphone at him. The scrawny image onscreen is apparently her two-day-old grandson. Sherard frankly tells her it reminds him of a little bird sicked up by a cat. The ensuing stream of dialect leads the publican to threaten to throw them both out, and he only relents when Sherard produces a twenty-pound note, the penultimate in his wallet, and asks for two whiskeys and keep the change. He considers offering the spare whiskey to the mad Irishwoman before deciding she is already far too soaked.

Arsène has been replaced by live coverage of a La Liga match in which some hapless team appears to have conceded eight goals to Barcelona. It's such an extravagant scoreline he wonders if Sky Sports has made a mistake. No one at the bar gives him a civilised answer, however, so he takes his drinks back to his table.

He finds himself thinking about Barcelona's Barri Xinès. The reason they called it the 'Chinese quarter', he remembers, was because it was an area of turn-of-the-century immigration: most of the Chinamen who settled in the neighbourhood were in fact French writers.

The feeling of acute mental sharpness continues when it strikes him, out of nowhere but quite incontestably, that the source of the leak was Mossad. Founder of the Edward W. Said journalism prize; patron of the Labour Friends of Palestine – the Israelis have obviously been spying on him for years. What could be more satisfying than embarrassing two enemies, Sherard and the Saudis, at the same time? What more suitable outlet than the Zionist *Mail*?

He polishes off one of the whiskeys with a single satisfied gulp. Arriving at an abruptly insightful conclusion to his train of thought reminds him there was an abandoned reflection at its start. It was something dimly irksome: pretend foreign lagers . . . the Arsenal defence . . . Italian public transport . . . Ah, yes. Henry, he remembers, reaching for the spare shot. He was considering Henry. No, the boy has always nurtured a repressed loathing for him: nothing unnatural, in Sherard's experience, which is why he was never anxious to become a father in the first place. (Not that the question of offspring was ever about anything other than Daphne's grand reconciliation of motherhood and radical feminism, played out in one of the early *Liberal Review* essays that made her name.) It explains the frightful right-wing wife; the current job dreaming up policies for the Tory-led government; the one before that, on the payroll of Saudi royals. It probably even accounts for Henry's quasi-mystical belief in capital 'a' Art – or at least in grimly toiling his way through the classics – when Sherard would like to think that, no doubt for Oedipal reasons of his own, he's done his best to bring it, 'Art', into disrepute.

If Henry's patricidal impulses are conventional, this evening's attempt to bar Sherard from Afua's party at least suggests these sentiments might have shifted to a more conscious footing. He feels a stirring almost of admiration for the boy, and a conviction that this new, more self-aware Henry (self-empowered might be overdoing it, in view of Fiona's evident influence) ought to be encouraged.

He retrieves his mobile, only to replace it when he realises he doesn't know the name of the pub. Presumably the landlord has it within himself to organise a taxi to Westminster and another whiskey for the wait.

*

Sherard pauses to light a Romeo y Julieta, ignoring the glowering retinue of protection officers. The first few matches slip through his fingers. He manages to spark one and hold it to his cigar for long enough to puff the thing into life. Carefully, he makes his way along the terrace towards the bright lights of the marquee. Glowing fag ends bob in the dusk. He acknowledges with a waft of his cigar-hand the nervy, faintly ironic greetings of old faces, ministers of state when he last saw them.

Despite the fact it is an evening of early autumn, he feels a wave of heat on entering the marquee, which has a moist canvas smell he associates with interminable wedding receptions. Puffing on the cigar seems to cause the floor to lurch quite severely: he doesn't bother arguing with the bobby who blocks his path, simply surrenders the burning item and moves on.

Unless he is seeing things, the unbearable prick who wrote the story about him, Wedderspoon, is laughing with a twelve-year-old MP whose parents used to dine quite often at Canonbury Lane. The hack seems to sense his presence, and looks up to meet Sherard's gaze with a revolting grin.

Since he is now extremely keen to let the hostess know what he thinks of her guest list, it's fortunate that a *Vogue* physique isn't terribly difficult to spot in a crowd of Westminster types. He catches a glimpse of a toned brown arm towards the centre of the marquee. Sherard pushes his way through the crush of sycophants, barely stopping even when his leg is caught in the strap of a handbag someone has stupidly left on the floor, from which he disentangles himself only after hearing the ominous crunch of his foot inside the bag.

When he reaches her, Afua's lips are slightly parted and she appears on the verge of articulating some complex thought to her companion. Her face instantly assumes a look of open sociability on seeing Sherard. She's delighted he has come, she says. Sherard replies that that's fortunate, as usually he only attends parties to which he is invited.

'But Sherard, you *were* invited,' she says, with quickly marshalled charm and an unfamiliar coldness in her eyes. 'I sent you the same email as everyone else.'

'I don't read emails,' he says, accusingly.

'I was worried I was the only one. Hi, Sherard.'

Sherard turns and takes in properly the wide expectant grin, the curious 'w' etched into the bourbon-tanned forehead. 'Ah, Tony.'

Blair is waving his thumb. 'This guy . . .' he tells Afua, speaking out of the corner of his mouth in mock-confidence, but still grinning at Sherard, 'I'm not sure I ever saw Derry Irvine as worked-up as when Sherard got him on the subject of art. And, you know, speaking as one of his greatest admirers, Derry had quite a temper on him.'

'Never mind that. I want to talk to you about Mossad,' Sherard announces in his most booming voice – he wishes Wedderspoon to hear this. 'Certain stories involving me and an Arab boy were circulated in a certain Zionist publication, as you're probably aware. I'm quite sure the Israelis were the conduit. I take it you agree this is unacceptable.'

Sherard is not clear if the Special Branch officers discreetly flanking his old neighbour were there a few seconds ago. In any case, he is faintly cognisant of his unkempt state. Blair himself sounds jovially bamboozled but also tired when he says, 'Okay, I'm afraid you've lost me . . .'

'I can't see where.'

'The part where you mentioned Mossad, frankly.'

'One of course understands,' Sherard says, drawing on unknown reserves of patience, 'the Middle East is not your forte. But it's perfectly simple.'

Afua is watching someone approach behind Sherard. Her furious expression has softened into one of calm expectancy.

'*Sherard*,' says a familiar Antipodean voice behind him.

'My dear, I was just trying to explain to Tony—'

'I know what you were doing. You were making a fool of yourself.'

'I think you'll find—'

'That's enough, Sherard. Will you help my husband outside?' Daphne asks the officers. She's in a silver-sequined tunic top and black leggings: not a scrap of spare flesh on her, after all these years. 'He needs some fresh air. If he says anything too boorish I'd probably just shoot him.'

The nearest officer takes a hesitant step towards Sherard, who waves him off. 'It was not a literal instruction,' he says, gruffly. 'My wife in her inimitable fashion was addressing me.'

He feels like a conductor turning to face the audience to whom in his exertions he's been quite oblivious. For the most part the faces remain stubbornly out of focus, though he does notice Henry, looking as blanched as when once, in the days before Marta, Daphne fed him undercooked chicken nuggets.

Sherard is almost at the exit of the marquee when suddenly Devereux is in front of him. Since their brief exchange at the opening of the *Turmoil* exhibition he hasn't heard from the lawyer, except for an insultingly brief (and, worse, typed) thank-you letter plainly composed by his secretary.

The old prefectly viciousness is still there in the distinguished creases of Devereux's face. 'Wonderful performance!' the lawyer says. 'Course, one can't help thinking "never complain, never explain" would have been the more sober response to your unfortunate media attention, Zionist-inspired or otherwise, but the evening would've been *much* the duller for it. Do you know Todd Weisman?' The last three syllables are slightly drawled, as if representing a passing fad not to be taken wholly seriously. 'He's a very important educationalist, from America.'

The man, as tall and tanned as Devereux, blinks handsomely behind tortoiseshell glasses.

'I have no idea,' answers Sherard, wishing to make minimal demands of his mental faculties. 'I doubt it.'

'Pleasure to meet you,' Weisman says in a soft East Coast accent.

'I should tell you he's not always *this* much fun.'

'I really didn't mean it the way Mr Devereux was implying,' Weisman says, imprecisely but with dignity. He pushes at his glasses with an index finger – plainly a nervous habit as they haven't slipped any distance down his nose.

251

'Oh, I am sorry, Todd. I'd hate you to think I was kicking a man when he was down.'

Sherard is having the first intimations of a foul hangover. Better find some booze on his way back to Barnsbury; stave the thing off for as long as possible. 'He's already done that — down three flights of stairs. I was locked in a trunk at the time. By the way,' he continues, ignoring Weisman's confused and horrified countenance, 'it's pronounced 'Deverooks'. S'a Norman name.'

'Quite right: one doesn't bother with French pronunciation when one predates the French. Elizabeth.' He places a proprietorial palm on the lower back of an elegant young woman, who has been in a neighbouring group with Rowan Harwood and a male film director whose name Sherard can't remember. 'I see you're drinking wine, for once. Usually it's *bottles of beer*,' Devereux explains to the American. 'These young ladies are enormously modern.'

He realises the woman is Henry's friend, the one who once toasted him as she drank the Hirst bottle he'd bought at considerable expense at a UNICEF auction. She's treating him no less insolently now, watching him with a private smile that puts him in mind of Afua and, even more, the haughty Belgian. Yet despite having re-emerged glistening from some Devereux-owned oyster — he remembers her as a far plainer creature — there is a lack of conviction in this girl. Sherard detects something of Henry in her wavering eyes: a treacherous empathy, perhaps.

Outside the marquee, the terrace is now bathed in the garish orange glow of the Palace floodlights. Sherard finds the very same Marcel. He is leaning against the edge of the terrace, smoking a cigarette on his own. The usual supercilious quarter-smile is missing, and there is a grave new line down the centre of his forehead that mars his otherwise smooth Norman features. He's watching Devereux entertain the group, which Rowan and the director have now joined, with a focused hatred that startles even Sherard a little. They acknowledge each other curtly as Sherard walks past.

33

Dieu et mon droit

Buzzy watches him approach the rail and lean forward slightly, to peer at the throne. When he looks back at her his eyebrow is just perceptibly raised.

'You better not,' she says, though there's no doubt he has a princely air against the gilded canopy. 'People are worried enough about parliament being under Brussels' control. Or at least my dad is.'

She gets a glimpse of a smile before he turns to inspect a winged statuette bearing the royal coat of arms. 'I'm also a Catholic, don't forget. Come to think of it so was Pugin . . .'

'We should probably get back, actually,' she says, trying to think who Pugin was. 'Philip will be wondering where I've got to.'

Marcel had approached the pair of guards in Central Lobby. He explained he was the shadow home secretary's husband, and was hoping to show his friend the Lords chamber. His manner was a perfect balance of modesty and self-possession: he understood, Buzzy saw, that the guards needed equally to feel that they were in control of the decision and were dealing with someone accustomed to having his way. In the end they practically fell over each other to open up the chamber.

He finishes admiring the stained-glass windows, with their profusion of heraldic emblems, and concentrates on Buzzy. 'Have you spoken to Afua this evening?'

'Briefly,' she replies, peeved at his choice of topic, 'she seems to be in even more demand than usual . . .'

'She misses your friendship,' he says casually.

'If Afua wants to speak to me she can pick up the phone, like any normal person.' She sits on a red bench and rubs her chilly arms, pleased despite herself that Marcel seems not to want to leave. 'It's so much grander than the Commons chamber.' Then, trying to be less bland, 'I don't think I really approve of the principle of unelected legislators.'

'That's rich, coming from a poet,' he smiles.

'Oh yes, I forgot we were a kind of subset . . . Well, I don't especially approve of us either. Whereas I think you quite like the idea of a ruling aristocracy – *noblesse oblige* and all that.'

He joins her on the leather bench, hands in his pockets. Buzzy catches a whiff of tobacco underneath his peppery aftershave. She resents him for not confiding in her that he was smoking again.

'It's true that living with an elected representative hasn't been good for my democratic ideals. *Je parle de mon père, bien sûr*,' he quickly clarifies.

'Of course,' Buzzy says, determined not to care about this refusal to criticise Afua.

'*Être belge n'a pas aidé non plus*.'

'Belgium does seem quite *complex*, politically . . . Has anyone ever thought of just calling the whole thing off? I mean, have the French-speaking part join France and the Dutch-speaking part join the Netherlands?'

He narrows his eyes as if mulling the proposal: he deliciously understands her mode of half-seriousness, the childish pleasure she feels in revealing her ignorance. Where Henry would answer earnestly and at length, and Philip make an unchivalrous allusion to her diplomatic cluelessness, Marcel replies, 'The problem is my fellow Walloons hate the French almost as much as the Flemish, and I gather the same is true for the Flemish with the Dutch. Overall it's not an excellent example of European solidarity.'

If only it were always like this! If only Marcel didn't on other occasions go out of his way to deny her this luxuriant proximity, by behaving as though they'd just met.

'Isn't your mother French?' Buzzy ventures. 'That's one francophone alliance, at least.'

'Hardly successful.'

'It produced you!'

'In any case, my mother is from Switzerland,' Marcel continues, nobly ignoring Buzzy's blush.

'You mean you're half-Swiss? I never knew . . .' Buzzy's surprise is disproportionate, almost tipping into indignation. There's an aspect of revenge for withholding such an elemental biographical detail when she then asks him, 'Have you heard from your mother recently?'

'No.'

'Have you had any news about her at least?'

He shrugs. 'My father emailed to say she'd returned to Switzerland.'

'He didn't mention how she was doing?'

'We're not really speaking. The wedding . . .'

Marcel says this without any noticeable rancour. She murmurs how sorry she is for his ruptured relations with Anatole, leaving a degree of ambiguity as to whether she's actually apologising or expressing sympathy. 'I do think your mother has a right to know about Benjamin, at least.' She hears her own mother's voice in this sentence and wonders why she, Buzzy, is involving herself in something that's really a matter for Afua. 'I'm sorry; it's none of my business.'

He gets up and wanders over to the grand oak table between the government and opposition benches. 'It's better like this,' he says, running the tips of his fingers across the oak surface.

'Better for whom?'

'For both of us, I think.'

One of the security guards shouts from the lobby that he'll need to lock the chamber again shortly. Buzzy waits for Marcel to acknowledge this, but he's staring distractedly at the table. She follows his gaze. 'Don't they talk about "tabling" questions in parliament? I wonder if that's where the verb comes from. Is your mother very posh?'

Without looking up, Marcel smiles at the non sequitur. 'Not like my father's family. But she's rich, which is some consolation. I think you'd like her.'

'Because she's rich?'

'No, I didn't mean that. On a good day she's – I don't know the word exactly. *Pleine de vie*.'

'Oh, I see.' Buzzy, elated by the vicarious compliment, feels a superstitious need to switch subjects again. 'How did Belgium come into existence, anyway?'

'*Oof*,' says Marcel, with a bored hand-flick, as though shaking off wet fingertips. 'We had our own little version of the French Revolution, ending with *la sécession—*'

'The secession.'

'Yes, of Belgium from the Netherlands. Supposedly, it started with rioting after a night at the opera – I know,' he smiles, 'very continental. Do you remember the Wappers painting at the Musée des Beaux-Arts? With the Belgian tricolour on top of a mound of bodies?'

'No, I don't think . . . Wait – yes!' Buzzy says, excitedly. 'Was it on the ground floor of the museum, near the entrance? Like a scene out of *Les Misérables*?'

'The Hugo novel . . .?'

'Don't look at me like that.'

Marcel reprises his place next to Buzzy, close enough this time that she can feel his hip and the fleshy warmth beneath his ribcage. His arm trails over the back of the bench. '*Comme quoi?*' he asks, feigning injured innocence.

'With that little smile. I don't care what you think; it's a perfectly entertaining way to pass a couple of hours . . .'

'I hope Philip never hears of your shocking West End past.'

'He found out today, actually; I'll probably never hear the end of it.'

'What made you confess?'

'My parents gave me away when they came to Pimlico this afternoon.' Buzzy decides Marcel doesn't need to know they're right this minute watching *Phantom*. 'The whole thing was pretty painful,' she adds, trying to keep her voice light.

Marcel is looking at her with an intent expression. 'The first time you met him,' he says, 'I warned you about Philip.'

'It was none of your business!' Her excitement has spilt into irritation and a giddy feeling of loneliness. As if her judgement was that deficient! As if she'd ever have had anything to do with Philip Devereux if it weren't for Marcel. 'It still isn't,' she says bitterly.

The kiss is so sudden she actually recoils before he clasps her head still. She feels his icy fingers and nose pressing into her face, and pain in her lower lip where it's caught between sharp teeth. She struggles to free herself, to explore his lips and tongue, but the more she tries to pull away from him the more his incisors dig into her mouth.

A palace guard, watching from the chamber entrance, interrupts them by clearing his throat.

'Thank you, we're just leaving,' Marcel says, as if they were winding up a discussion on Pugin.

The guard is heavy-set, with a furtive grey-speckled beard. 'Ah,' he says comprehendingly, 'my colleagues forgot to tell me sir was a Frenchman.'

34

'I'm not in trouble, am I?' Henry asks, on being told his presence is immediately required at the Department for Education. He's sure there was no meeting in his diary, because, if so, he would have spent the weekend dreading Monday morning. Besides, he's never met either the special adviser or the departmental press officer demanding to see him, or even set foot in the ministry's Great Smith Street premises.

Tasha, his secretary of around his age – far more terrifying than his minister, a donnish Whig – says all she knows is that it has something to do with a party he attended recently. She takes a discomfiting interest in Henry as he puts his mackintosh back on, double-checks he has his security pass and heads back out onto Whitehall.

It's possible that for Tasha the idea Henry might be invited to a party is sufficiently mysterious. Recently their relations have become a little strained. It began when he got back from honeymoon and mentioned, trying to make light-hearted conversation, that her name was often in his thoughts lately on account of Natasha Rostov. Has she read *War and Peace*? Henry realised from the tone of her reply he'd said completely the wrong thing, but soon got absorbed in his work and thought no more about it. Later that day, he sent Natasha an email with a long pdf document attached so she could arrange to have it printed and bound. She never responded, despite the email sitting in his sent messages folder. He even sent the document to his own address to check if its large data size would delay its delivery (it didn't). Rather than ask her again, he waited until after she'd gone home and took the printed document to the copy department himself. Now he hides the bound document whenever she comes near his desk.

He'd been looking forward to another quiet week of party conference season, with the Liberal Democrat ministers recovering from their few days in the spotlight – less of a novelty for them, he supposes, now they are in office – and the Conservatives gearing up for their event in Manchester next week. The autumnal air is uninviting as he crosses Parliament Square towards Victoria Street, wondering why government spin doctors might want to speak with him about Afua's terrace drinks. Apart from the by now well-documented exchange between his father and the former prime minister, surely of no relevance to the DfE, there's nothing he can recall of special significance about the evening.

Although: despite his general terror of socialising, Henry would admit he found mingling easier than usual on this occasion. He'd thought about this and attributed it to a number of factors. To begin with, it was easier attending social events with Fiona. Merely having the option of standing at her side took the edge off the previous element of desperation in his behaviour at parties. As a bachelor, the more he feared being abandoned by his interlocutor (he did his best to avoid groups, since he rarely summoned the courage to make a contribution), the more forced his conversation became, until his ceaseless enquiries seemed to amount to a sort of social cruelty for all but the most committed narcissists. At some point he would relent and allow his questioning to tail off, leaving the other free, as they always did, to make their excuses. Then the only way to relieve the anxiety of standing by himself would be to go up to someone else. The problem was that the longer he deferred summoning up the courage to do this, the more pointless he seemed to himself and the less feasible or even ethical it felt to inflict his company on others.

Another obvious reason why he acquitted himself better than usual at the party was because a number of people actually sought him out. This was mostly down to his connection with Afua (even if the idea that he might exert some influence over her strikes Henry as fanciful). And of course there was his parents' notoriety

259

in those circles, some of which was inevitably passed on to him. But he was also aware that a few of Afua's guests had a moderate interest in him in his own right.

He's secretly very proud of having got the Cabinet Office job via a completely meritocratic process, beginning with passing the labyrinthine (but anonymous!) rounds of psychometric and intelligence tests. The letter he then received, inviting him to spend a day at an assessment centre in Westminster, was accompanied by a civil service brochure. In it was written: *Fair and open recruitment is fundamental to us and underlies every part of the Fast Stream Assessment Centre process. We will assess you solely on the basis of your performance in the exercises and interview.*

These two sentences greatly intensified his wish to make the cut. When the time came around Henry hardly spoke during the initial group exercise. The written policy recommendation assessment went slightly better: he found himself interested in the fictitious scenario involving various alternative energy sources for possible government investment, and enjoyed carefully evaluating the options for someone else to make a final decision. In the interview rounding off the day he was fortunate to have already prepared some thoughts on the UK implications of a Greek debt default, though his responses were couched in equivocations and he failed to make regular eye contact with either of his assessors.

A few weeks later, another official-looking letter arrived from Her Majesty's Government. It contained an offer for a job. Not in the Foreign Office, as Fiona sighingly observed, or even the Ministry of Justice, which he thought might have suited his legal background. He wasn't even exactly sure what happened in the Cabinet Office. When it transpired he would be helping with medium-term policy development across a range of departments, at one remove from the day-to-day business of government, he had a feeling this might not be the worst place to have been allocated. The quasi-academic nature of the work does indeed seem to suit him, and he's also been very fortunate in his current minister, who at briefings often sets aside time to ask what Henry is reading ('Courageous decision!' he laughed, on hearing the current choice, before recommending some of Tolstoy's short stories), and who seems entirely uninterested that his junior official is the son of Sherard Howe and Daphne Depree. This is generous, as it took Henry only a short internet search to establish that both the *Liberal Review* and his mother had been sharply critical of his boss. Most recently Daphne wrote that with his unworldly liberalism, personal wealth and strong advocacy of fiscal responsibility he 'personified the Tory Marie Antoinette tendency'.

Might Henry's unusually assured comportment at Afua's reception have led him to be indiscreet about government business? Until his conversation with Tasha he would have been positive the answer was no, despite some light-hearted prodding from the odd Labour policy adviser and Westminster think-tanker. But why then is he being summoned?

He gives his name at the DfE reception, signs himself in, and is directed to a waiting room past the security barriers. Despite the urgency of the situation as relayed to him by Tasha, minutes pass without anyone coming to collect him. He refrains from picking up the copy of *The Times* on the table in front of him, not wanting to give off a provocatively carefree impression and anyway too apprehensive to take in the words on the front page.

It's almost ten o'clock before a fresh-faced young man 'from Michael's office' sticks his head round the door. The reference to the secretary of state has made Henry's heart rate speed up so furiously that, crossing the glass-roofed atrium, he fears a full-blown panic attack coming on. Fortunately, once they're in the lift the young man (Henry didn't take in his name) talks cheerily about the amazing view from the top floor and the perils of cycling in from Camberwell, then the perils of the borough more generally. Henry is only obliged to say the odd word while working on bringing his breathing under control. By the time they step out of the lift, the other's bonhomie has gone a long way to calming Henry; he's even able to admire the vista of St James's Park beyond the open-plan workspace. The recovery goes into reverse, however, when the young official asks Henry to remind him who he has come to see, and flashes a comradely grimace when Henry gives him the two names.

'Oh, I forgot! You're the party guy . . .'

'Well, so to speak,' Henry says, reflecting that in a way this sums up everything he is not.

'Don't get up. Are you Henry Howe?'

The man clutching a Starbucks cup and jumble of documents is in his late thirties. His heavy stubble might, Henry reflects, have given him the appearance of stressed-out sleeplessness even if he'd chosen a different career. Perhaps the point is he unconsciously gravitated towards the lifestyle that fitted his appearance; except, wouldn't that imply Henry's mother was wrong and anatomy *was* destiny, after all? It's frustrating this habit of only acknowledging troublesome questions during moments of great stress, such as arriving at the town hall in Arezzo.

'That's me.' Henry has remained standing in case they are going to shake hands, and now sits down again.

The man introduces himself as Paul Harris, the DfE's deputy head of news. He wants to have a quick chat, civil servant to civil servant, before they're joined by Adam Bilimoria. Henry knows Adam to be the department's Tory-appointed special adviser for media matters. Unlike Gabriella, the policy SpAd with whom Henry is required to liaise regularly by email, he has never had any contact with Adam before.

'First off, I want to reassure you the meeting isn't part of any statutory disciplinary proceedings.'

For a phrase whose prima facie purpose was to provide reassurance, this one was not successful from Henry's point of view.

'At the moment I'm mentioning only for context Clause 4.2 of this thing' – Paul holds up a spiral-bound document which Henry recognises as the new Civil Service Management Code – 'which you should have a copy of, not least because it was drafted by the Cabinet Office. In particular,' he goes on, leafing through the pages, 'you'll note that 4.2.6 states that "*civil servants must not seek to frustrate the policies or decisions of Ministers by the use or disclosure outside the Government of any information to which they have had access as civil servants.*'" He peers at the text for a couple of beats. 'That repetition of "*civil servants*" is a bit ungainly. Anyway.'

Henry remembers enough of his aborted legal training to resist what every atom of his being is screaming for him to do: plug the silence with self-incrimination. 'I'm sorry,' he says, breathily, 'but I have no idea what this is about.'

Paul prizes the lid off his coffee and a sickly odour of cinnamon rises from the froth. 'There's a rumour at Conservative Campaign Headquarters that the mayor of London is about to give a speech, possibly later this week, calling for radical reform of the city's secondary schools.'

Thank God, Henry thinks. This can't have anything to do with him.

'Specifically, he's going to advocate the creation of a new wave of grammar schools across the capital.'

'Right,' Henry says, desperately stifling a grin.

'Of course, the secretary of state is furious; Number Ten is furious.'

'Of course . . . although, isn't this along the lines of what the government were going to propose anyway, as one of the Merton Commission's recommendations?'

Paul frowns over his cappuccino. 'Exactly.'

It is not at all evident to Henry why a Conservative mayor calling for a similar policy to that under consideration by a Conservative-led government should be a problem, or relate in any way to clause 4.2.6 of the code or indeed him.

'Right,' he says again.

Between slurps of coffee, Paul explains that since early this morning Adam Bilimoria has been trying to get hold of the relevant people at City Hall to find out, firstly, what was going to be in the mayor's speech, and then why there'd been no attempt to clear it with anyone in government. So far, Adam has established that someone in the mayor's office got wind of the as-yet-unannounced commission, with its remit vigorously to consider full academic selection for certain qualifying Free Schools, at a recent drinks event hosted by the shadow home secretary. The mayor, perhaps understandably, was furious to learn only at second hand of a radical Tory policy intended to be trialled in the capital. It was bad enough the government would keep such a thing a secret from him, unacceptable when it was at the same time the talk of opposition drinks parties, and completely unforgivable when it turned out the policy was one he thoroughly approved of. 'For our purposes,' Paul concludes, 'the relevant issues are: one, your current responsibilities in the Cabinet Office involve establishing the scope of the commission and its menu of recommendations; two, Afua Nelson is your adopted sister; and, three, we assume you attended her drinks party.'

'Not legally speaking, on point two. It's more of a de facto situation.'

'She told *Newsnight* last month that she lives in your family home in Islington.'

'Yes. No, that's perfectly true.' It seems irrelevant to mention that for a while now Afua has been talking about how the three of them, her and Marcel and Benjamin, ought to think about finding a place of their own.

'We know Alec Merton was also at the party.' Paul is building his case in increments, like a fastidious counsel. Henry wonders if the press officer is not starting to quite enjoy himself. 'But he says for quite obvious reasons he's never discussed the commission with anyone apart from his wife, who was unable to join him at the drinks event.'

In danger of missing another significant nuance, and conscious that the only other suspect has apparently just been struck off the list, Henry politely asks, 'I'm sorry, why are they obvious?'

The deputy head of news drains the last of his coffee. 'Why would Merton want to leak the commission's most sensitive recommendation before its existence has even been announced? It'd make him look like he was a Blairite patsy fronting a review he had no control over. I mean, obviously that's what he is,' Paul says, taking his empty Starbucks cup to the recycling bin, 'but obviously it's not in his interest to broadcast the fact. Maybe he doesn't even know it. At the same time he'd be burning his bridges with Labour – from all angles, it would be political hara-kiri.'

Henry sees the press officer's point.

'Are you suggesting he *did* leak this information to City Hall?'

'No, no . . . I mean, I saw him at the party, but I didn't speak to him. I certainly wouldn't claim to know whom he spoke to, or what about.'

The only person Henry noticed Merton talking with was Fiona. He hadn't been completely pleased by this, since it was his wife who told him – he felt a little insensitively, given Afua's previous employment – that Alec was rumoured to have an eye for young women. Still, there had been an element of gratitude, not exactly that Merton was shouldering a burden, but Henry was not an entertaining person and what Fiona needed above all was to be kept entertained.

'What about you? Did you discuss confidential government policy with anyone at this party?'

'I'm sure I didn't – I don't even know anyone who works for the mayor.'

'I don't just mean Boris's people. Maybe someone from the opposition, or a journalist. You must've known any leak about such a sensitive review could kill the whole thing dead, let alone the key part about academic selection.'

'But the subject never came up!' Henry says, unhappily. 'It's true I had a short chat with Edwyn Jenkins, Labour's head of press—'

'I know Edwyn.'

'But we didn't talk about my work. Or he might have asked about it, but as a joke, and then we moved on.'

Henry's heart had leapt when Edwyn pointed out a pretty girl with an older, suspiciously Tory-looking bloke. On hearing she was Elizabeth Price, the poet, Edwyn said he thought he'd recognised her from the *Standard*'s recent 'thirty under thirty' article on up-and-coming young Londoners. He then veered into a description of how Afua's prominent position in the same list (she was third) had caused something of a stir at Labour HQ. There was increasing talk, Edwyn said, of an 'Afualot' clique forming around the shadow home secretary, whose agenda was not always perceived as synchronised with the Party leadership.

'And I'd certainly never divulge policy unit work to Afua, or my parents. I hope that goes without saying.'

Adam Bilimoria sweeps into the meeting room. 'Hi – Adam.' After a short frenzy of activity, in which he whips his suit jacket off and plants his BlackBerry on the table in front of him, as though declaring an amnesty, he says, 'So I found out which City Hall bod was at the party: some Yank called Todd Weisman. Advised Clinton on charter schools, apparently.'

'I've never heard of him,' Paul says with mild indignation.

'Well, he's now the mayor's education guru. It might be some sort of unpaid secondment; I haven't got to the bottom of it yet.'

Adam stretches his arms and rocks back on his chair, landing with a thump. Henry realises both SpAd and press officer are awaiting his response.

'I've never met anyone called Todd Weisman, at Afua's party or anywhere else.'

'The latest thinking is that we're going to drop it, anyway.' Adam has retrieved his BlackBerry and is tapping out a message.

'You mean the entire commission?' asks Henry, incredulous.

'It's a lose-lose,' he says, without looking up. 'The Beeb and *Guardian* will go into meltdown over the whole grammar schools thing; and the *Mail* and the *Telegraph* will say that once again the government has left it to the mayor to set out a proper right-wing agenda.'

'The people's Tory,' Paul smiles.

'Ya. He's popular enough just with the bikes; no one's desperate to give him London's best schools as well. Though actually, my opinion is you've done us a favour,' Adam says to Henry. 'I mean, I've got nothing against selective schools, mine was great. But they're a disaster in terms of political positioning, not to mention we'd've had to concede something ridiculous to get it past the Lib Dems. Replace hereditary peers with paedophiles in the Lords.'

Henry's essential claim, he tells himself on the way back to the Cabinet Office, was that he didn't speak to anyone about confidential government business at the party. This was in answer to a question about information he might have leaked *while at the party*. Understood in narrow terms, it was at least arguable that he had spoken the truth, or at least a form of it. But the fact is he'd told two people about the possible schools reform, both of whom were at Afua's party, albeit he'd confided in them a month or so before the event itself.

He's as convinced now as he was in Italy that Marcel wouldn't have said anything: even if Henry wasn't effectively under Afua's protection, he had placed himself too obviously at the Belgian's mercy to be of any interest to him. And Paul Harris was surely right; Merton had little to gain from pre-briefing the most controversial aspects of the commission's remit at such an embryonic stage.

The unavoidable conclusion is that it was Buzzy who betrayed Henry's confidence. No, that's too strongly put. After all, he hadn't explicitly asked her not to repeat information which was at the time being withheld even from Lib Dem ministers. He'd given her no idea, in short, of the policy's political sensitivity.

Neither more generally is it Buzzy's fault if Henry's feelings for her keep getting in the way of his ability to believe himself a decent person. The loan of the Kensington mews house that didn't belong to him; his embarrassment at his wife in the presence of Buzzy and Marcel; and now his indiscretion with sensitive government policies are all stains on his character for which he alone is responsible.

Yet however blameless she is, it's hard to avoid the sense that Henry's attachment to Buzzy is holding him back at a time when he's at last making progress in other areas of his life. Three years ago, he was an eternally single law school dropout living with his parents. Today he's a married man with a mortgage and a career, at least until this morning, which he enjoys as much as he could hope to enjoy anything.

Part of the trouble has been that, not really having any other friends, it hasn't been easy to gauge to what extent his attitude towards Buzzy was developing into something abnormal. For a long while it wasn't inconceivable to Henry that other people might dream about a close acquaintance most nights, or regularly lapse into thinking about them if there's nothing else immediately to seize their attention – or at least that they might do these things if their mental space were less populated. Buzzy herself has always frequently mentioned Marcel in conversation, and her unselfconsciousness in doing so has gone a long way to licensing Henry's notion that a deep platonic friendship might influence to the point almost of dominating one party's thoughts.

Perhaps his surfeit of feelings for Buzzy has been as much about his inability to spread these among even a small group of intimates. It's not as if her qualities are, in objective terms, all that exceptional. There must be other pretty young women who hide their romanticism with dry humour, or who combine suburban insecurity with intellectual self-confidence.

But any such rationalising breaks down when Henry remembers her leaping to his defence in Arezzo, after Fiona derided the chances of his work surviving coalition *realpolitik*. (There is a certain grim irony, he concedes, in it being probably down to Buzzy that the education reform is doomed and his wife's analysis vindicated.) Or when he recalls her telling him – the New Year's Eve they spent at the Mayfair club, the same night she kissed him on the lips – that she'd like him just the same if he admitted he wasn't always happy. Even at the time he didn't fool himself the kiss had any amorous significance for her; it was more than enough as a consummation of their friendship. It seemed extraordinary that anyone, let alone someone like Buzzy, could like him unconditionally, when there were so many other more interesting people to choose from.

With Fiona, by contrast, Henry is constantly aware of his status as a work-in-progress – that she has undertaken to roll up her sleeves and make something of him. Though this is extremely generous and commendable, it's not the absolute acceptance he craves. His immediate reaction when Fiona raised the question of marriage (not a proposal so much as a brittle reference to Henry not having himself proposed) was to wonder what Buzzy would make of it. Might the notion that one girl found him marriageable be the conceptual nudge she needed to entertain such an idea herself?

Social theories on 'nudging' were then occupying his thoughts a great deal, having caught the attention of his minister; however, this was no more than a reflex delusion on Henry's part. More entrenched is his sentimental belief in youthful intimacy, and his corresponding fear that neither he nor his wife will ever really know the other in a profound sense, having met (through Charlie Wynter, a college acquaintance of Henry's) in their late twenties, an already more concealing age. Certainly in his case, Henry worries the passage of time will only mould a separate, false version of himself *qua* Fiona's husband.

Even with Afua, he doesn't for a second doubt her good intentions, but there has always been a sense of her willing him to 'come good', meaning to acquire something approaching her own levels of confidence. The implication is that his character is provisional and defective, and therefore deserving of sympathy. It's not that he's ungrateful – for a start, he'd never have survived his school years without his older semi-sister's patronage – he simply fears that her affection is based on a fantasy that he's capable of changing into someone less fearful of the world.

That he's so afraid of giving up Buzzy strikes Henry as proof enough of Afua's mistaken belief. But then he can only return, in a circular and unsatisfactory manner, to the cost of his weakness. As this morning has brought home, he's not a good person when she comes into his life, and his behaviour at these times jeopardises what he is trying to build. Whatever he decides, if he cuts Buzzy out completely or maintains their sporadic friendship, he will lose in some way.

Emerging from the shadow of the Queen Elizabeth II Conference Centre he passes behind the statue of Sir Winston Churchill, slouching magnificently on his cane. Back on Whitehall, the Red Lion pub, with its six centuries of history, where division bells still ring for voting parliamentarians and where Brown's spin doctors were said to hold bibulous Treasury briefings, is not yet open for business. The sun very faintly warms Henry's cheeks. Without warning he feels touched by something almost sublime: nature, art, the grand story of human civilisation . . . Whatever it is, it's far from Free School admissions criteria and even Buzzy. He recognises this as one of those odd moments when, after thinking intensely about her for a stretch, it's as if a mental filter in his mind becomes burnt out and he glimpses Buzzy in a sharp new light.

What if the later poems in *The Bathers* are trivially modish, if she didn't even *try* to express anything that was true and beautiful in them? What if she's displayed equal cynicism in real life, by moving in with a rich and arrogant older man? What if Fiona is right and Buzzy has become vain and snobbish? This friend of his who never gets in touch to suggest they catch up; who heard about his policy unit job from Marcel but never called to congratulate; who commiserated with him about his father's scandal only after Henry brought it up. What if it turns out he was absurd to have placed so much faith in Buzzy and the very notion of a soulmate – if this yearning for total unqualified love is the final piece of juvenilia he must put behind him?

He's relieved to be approaching the Cabinet Office: soon he'll be worrying again about work. By the time his brain is free once again to dwell on unofficial subjects, he won't find these doubts about Buzzy's character objectively implausible, in so far as he'll think of them at all. Nevertheless, they'll seem like a stranger's perspective, and as such only remotely meaningful, like the unlived wisdom of cliché.

35

On the run

Alec listens to the endless hiss of the shower and wonders if the girl is planning on leaving any hot water for him or the other five-hundred-odd hotel guests: 'Northern teachers or whatever', as a former editor of the *Telegraph* once summed up the Party faithful, in the days when he used to invite Alec to dine with him. The dismissive formulation was amusing enough at the time, or at least Alec recalled laughing along, but now he ought to be mingling with the delegates instead of wasting the penultimate morning of conference with a Warwick undergraduate.

He only arrived in Liverpool yesterday; she approached him at the drinks reception that followed the Demos debate. As a student of politics and economics, she'd found Alec's remarks on City reform extremely interesting and . . . 'Informative?' he supplied drily. Yes! So informative! Could she maybe do a quick interview with him for the student paper? He's ashamed, including of his helpless pride, not to be certain she's out of her teens.

This probably wouldn't have happened if his diary had been fuller, and he hadn't been feeling a little sorry for himself. When Alec was a Treasury minister, the annual Party conference used to be a round-the-clock marathon. Each day there were panel events or policy seminars for which he'd need to sketch out some sort of script with Tom, the SpAd who underwhelmingly (in a host of ways) succeeded Afua. Tom's other main duty was to usher Alec between endless meetings with government relations types, photo ops with fellow Humber MPs for the regional press, tours of the corporate stands, perhaps a lunchtime interview with *The World at One*. Then at the boozy evening receptions the real work would commence, in the form of furious networking with colleagues, union and private donors, wonks, bloggers and Party fixers. And that was just the Labour people. There were also the lobby correspondents, opinion-formers, editorial and sketch-writers, not to mention the broadcast media army. Whomever Alec ended up chatting with he'd need the right combination of alcohol, praise, *entre-nous* knife-thrusting and non-denial denying of his leadership ambitions.

He left last year's conference on the first day, as soon as the results of the leadership election were announced. The wrong brother won. This year Alec is unaccompanied, not being entitled to a SpAd, not needing a parliamentary researcher and not wishing to be stuck with Vernon, his constituency agent. More humbling still is that with the Demos event (where he was on a panel of five) out of the way, he has no further speaking engagements for the rest of conference. Yesterday he was so bored he even attended the Leader's speech. It was fairly depressing, with its attacks on 'corporate predators' and heckling from the floor in response to a mention of Blair.

This makes him think of Afua, at whose recent Commons drinks reception the ex-PM made a brief appearance. She hasn't responded to any of the messages Alec left on her phone yesterday. At one point in the afternoon he managed to intercept her grandly titled chief of staff, Patrick Rutherford, leaving the conference centre. Patrick assured him Afua would find some time for him as soon as she finished drafting her keynote address. Only then did Alec recall that today was her first big conference speech, raising the intriguing possibility that she's feeling a few nerves.

As if conditions in the Party weren't inhospitable enough for Alec, meanwhile, it was worrying to find out the mayor of London was today giving a speech endorsing the creation of new grammar schools in the capital. Conservative Central Office has hinted that they suspect him, Alec, of leaking to City Hall the news of the commission and its sensitive remit, deliberately to stoke tensions between the mayor and Downing Street. The Tory strategist he spoke to (Lord Glasson is another who is suddenly not taking his calls) seemed incapable of appreciating why this would be wildly adverse to his own interests. Alec has no wish to jeopardise the commission or risk poisoning his relations with the Conservatives at a time when he's increasingly isolated in his own Party, and needs to keep all his options open – though of course he couldn't admit that to the strategist.

It's rather a pity that the urgency of all this faded last night after a drink or two, but Alec needs to find Afua and let her know that he is in a slightly tight situation, while at the same time establishing – since the leaking apparently happened at her party – whether his former aide had anything to do with putting him there.

The shower has finally stopped when Rebecca calls his mobile. With the undergrad listening in from the bathroom, Alec feels slightly self-conscious speaking to his wife, who sounds frantic. Colonel is missing. He must have snuck through the sliver of a gap where their front fence meets the garden hedge, or rather meets the stone wall behind the hedge (or rather, *doesn't* quite meet the stone wall behind it). That for the last year Rebecca has been fretting about this gap, and Alec promising to cover it, is something neither of them mentions but which nonetheless hangs heavily over the conversation. Most likely, Colonel has caught the scent of a fox and made a dash for the woods behind their house; the problem, Alec doesn't need to remind his wife, is the gap in the fence leads almost immediately onto a country lane used by unsuitably large supermarket delivery lorries. Raising the lorry issue with the council is another thing Rebecca has been keen for him to cross off his to-do list.

'Let's not panic. How long ago did he escape?'

'I don't know . . . I think I must have noticed he was missing about half an hour ago, but we'd literally only just come back from our walk. He hasn't even had his breakfast!' Rebecca says, as if surprised at Colonel's failure to think this through properly.

The bathroom door opens with a heavy judder: Alec registers the girl's emergence as a blur of skinny jeans and wet curls and awkward grimace. He holds up a cautionary finger.

'. . . I'm sorry, darling,' his wife is saying, 'I know conference is madly busy but I just don't know what to do. This is so awful.'

'Don't worry, darling. Just let me think for a second.'

'I feel I should be out looking for him, but what if he comes back to the house and it's all shut up? Or should I just leave the front door open?'

'No, definitely I wouldn't do that.'

'Also, I can't remember if Colonel's collar tag has the house phone number on it or my mobile. Or was it yours?'

'It was the house phone,' he guesses, distractedly – surely they weren't stupid enough to hang their private mobile numbers around the border terrier's neck, for any stranger to see? He knows how terribly fond she is of Colonel, and that she wants Alec to drive home this instant, only he really does have to speak with Afua. It's a shame Rebecca hasn't done a better job of making friends in the village. She's become so timid in recent years Alec realises there's no one she'd feel comfortable asking to come over and help search for the missing dog. At the same time there's been a sort of flattening out of her sense of humour; they rarely seem to laugh at things as they did in the past. Rebecca's new provincialism has become a self-fulfilling prophecy: her fear of becoming boring has led, perhaps deliberately on some level, to it gradually coming true.

Alec hopes she's not intending to punish him by having a breakdown. Punish him for what? His determination to make it as a politician, he guesses, even if it meant uprooting them from Putney to Grimsby and taking a tenfold reduction in his income.

He decides to take a gamble. 'Darling, I think you should call the police.'

'The police?' she repeats, anxiously. 'I don't think you can report pets as missing, can you? They might say I was wasting police resources or something.'

'Well, possibly, I suppose. But Colonel is our property; if some-one has taken him, it's theft. Plus I *am* the MP. That should count for something.'

274

'I don't know, darling – perhaps I ought to give it an hour or two.'

Pleased to have won himself a little time, Alec agrees this sounds a very sensible idea. It's nine forty: he tells his wife if there's still no sign of Colonel by noon, she ought to give the police a call. What's more, he'll drive back from Liverpool to help look for the missing dog. Before ringing off he asks to be kept updated on any developments; he'll keep his phone switched on even if he's in the main conference hall.

'Thanks, darling,' Rebecca says. 'Sorry again to burden you with this.'

The news of the missing Colonel upsets the girl – her name is Charlotte, possibly – whose family border collie died last year after a long battle with cancer. Alec restrains himself from pointing out that the overlap between these two situations is quite modest, and tries to project vague sympathy without actually encouraging her to recount the animal's terminal stages. 'I'll probably just dash in the shower,' he interrupts, before the results of the second round of chemotherapy, 'then I really must speak with someone before I leave.'

'Oh . . . Sure, no problem,' she says, and glowers at him.

He takes his clothes into the bathroom with him to dress there. When they're both finally ready to leave, he more or less bundles Charlotte into the corridor and the path of a columnist from the *Scotsman*, who insists on stopping and chatting to Alec long enough that some kind of introduction is necessary.

'And this is Charlotte—'

'Caroline'

'—She's just interviewed me for her university rag, the *Warwick Boar*.' Alec laughs too much when the columnist asks how the last word is spelt. 'I'm not sure either spelling is a fantastic association for readers. No wonder print journalism is going to the wall.'

The columnist waves him off with a cheerful Celtic insult, Alec deciding it's not sensible for him to proceed to the hotel reception in the company of a female undergraduate with damp hair. 'Look, would you mind waiting here for a few minutes while I head off?

Maybe ten to be on the safe side . . . I'd let you go first but I've got to see a man about a dog. It's quite urgent.'

'Whatever. Good luck with your *actual* dog.'

'Oh, thanks. And, you know, sorry about Chuffy.' He wonders if he could ask her never to tell a living soul about last night, but it doesn't feel the right thing, so instead he hurries for the lifts.

Inside the convention centre, only a couple of minutes' walk from the hotel, Alec strides purposefully as if running late to address an important fringe meeting. Afua's mobile phone rang three times before going abruptly to voicemail when he tried calling just now. He needs to find someone who knows where she is and, more importantly, can get him five minutes with her.

On the conference stage, he can hear the TUC president handing over to the Party treasurer, prompting an exodus of trade union delegates from the main hall. The vibe from those who recognise Alec in the emerging crowd isn't warm. He feels a reciprocal dislike for these jowly dinosaurs, with their cheap suits and prolier-than-thou dogmatism. Not far from the hall entrance he spots a *Newsnight* producer he knows. Flat-footed and rather plain, as well as *married* married – the type of intelligent woman whose children would nevertheless be hovering at the margins of a conversation about Bank of England monetary policy, or the liberation of Benghazi – she was often the one detailed to look after Alec in the days when he was a regular guest on the programme. Now she's chatting with – yes – it's Daphne Depree. He's not precisely sure how much Daphne likes him, or even how in favour she is with her adopted daughter these days, but it seems worth at least establishing if she's prepared to be of assistance.

Alec greets her with a kiss on each cheek, finding a limp hand waiting for him when he turns to the producer. He's surprised when Daphne replies *Of course, my love* to his request for a quick word. Taking half a step back, pretending not to listen while the women conclude their chat, he's again not expecting the good humour with which Daphne bears the news she won't be appearing on tonight's conference round-up. Apparently Afua is already booked to discuss her home affairs speech and the 'feeling' among the editors is that from now on the two of them shouldn't both appear on the same edition of the programme.

Daphne jokes she'd better get used to being bumped by Afua. 'There's no doubting the girl's the future of the Labour Party – hey, Alec?' She looks at him with a twinkling expression he can't quite read, though he doesn't get the impression she's mocking her protégée-rival's rise and rise. Perhaps Daphne is even being slightly self-deprecating, by recalling her less-than-effusive tone when the two of them spoke briefly of Afua two or three years ago, at Sherard's *Turmoil* exhibition.

'Oh, absolutely. She's the real deal, and I should know.'

'Yes, I must've first come across her when she was your SpAd. How funny.'

'So I've been told,' Alec says, with a dry laugh. Neither woman joins in.

'Well, you must be very proud, Daphne. Raising the first female Labour leader feels like it would be a feminist legacy all on its own . . .'

'Wouldn't it be wonderful? I'd never need to write another word!'

After the producer has left, Daphne fixes Alec with the same ambiguous smile. 'Now, what can I do for you?'

'It's about our friend, funnily enough . . .'

'*Your* friend, maybe,' she replies, suddenly very stern, so that Alec feels his own smile die on his face, '*my* daughter.'

Back at the hotel, the smallish antechamber of Afua's suite is stuffed with fresh-faced researchers and, presumably, unpaid interns, since there must be at least twice the official staff allocation for shadow cabinet members. They briefly look up from their yapping and stapling as Alec follows Daphne into the inner sanctum. Judging by the arrogance in these kids' eyes they seem to think shadow home secretary is a shared title.

Inside the bedroom, Afua's core team is gathered round a coffee table covered by sleek Apple laptops of the sort all Tonbridge boys own, at least according to the twins. Alec recognises Patrick Rutherford, giving him a not-entirely-friendly nod, and Nicky Morris, formerly Nicholas Morris-Marsham of Erskine Chambers, widely seen as the foremost intellect among the new MP intake.

The final figure is shaven-headed Ed Tate. There was muttering in the Commons tea room when she replaced her old media adviser, a Party stalwart, with this Young Turk from a Sunday tabloid, who everyone had assumed was a Tory. Alec doesn't himself care about that, though he does find it privately entertaining that as gifted a spinner as Afua should feel it necessary to employ any comms staff at all. Noting none of the shadow ministerial team is in evidence, Alec wonders if it's wise to keep her older if more junior colleagues out of the loop; but then maybe her preparedness to make enemies is part of why Westminster is so in awe of her.

Afua seems so genuinely pleased to see Alec he half convinces himself she hasn't yet picked up his phone messages. He offers to wait next door but she insists he stay. They'll only be a couple more minutes.

'Patrick's worried,' Afua wryly observes to Daphne, so that Alec feels a stab of envy towards both chief of staff and adopted mother.

'Not at all. Section by section, I think it's brilliant.'

'But . . .?'

Patrick, who has coloured slightly, continues to stare at the script. It's obvious he's in love with her.

'The problem, I think, is the cumulative effect. We've got immigration – mistakes were made. Home Office budget – taking the hard decisions. English riots – "no excuses" narrative. And so it goes on. There's not much for conference to cheer.'

'Obviously it's too late to change anything substantive. I suppose we could tone down the phraseology,' Nicholas says. 'Excise anything too provoking.'

Ed stops tracing his stubble on his scalp. 'Fuck the delegates in the hall. I say don't change a word.'

'Hmm,' Afua says, a little stagily. (So much for the pre-speech nerves.) 'There's one opinion we haven't heard yet.'

For a second Alec is convinced she's referring to him.

'Well,' Daphne begins – *will*, it sounds like, that distinctive soft Kiwi inflection that over the years has seeped into the national consciousness, or at least the Radio Four-listening part of it. 'Ed's right. The theme of the speech, as I see it, is your personal toughness. That's the thread that connects growing up on Finsbury Estate to taking on Party orthodoxy on things like government expenditure and crime and justice policy. If you soften your language now you're going to dull that message.'

'You're right,' Afua says. 'Daph's completely right on this.'

'The point is if you want media cut-through, you actually *need* to pick a fight in the hall. But you knew that already.' Daphne turns to Ed. 'Presumably there's a follow-up plan for the press?'

'Motherhood for the *Mail*; race for the *Graun*; budget restraint for the *Torygraph* . . .'

'Can someone get Daphne a copy?' Afua says.

Alec almost feels a little sorry for the nominal chief of staff. In the authority stakes, a few years in charge of a think-tank hardly measures up against a woman whose most recent book famously resides by the bedside of the Australian prime minister.

A few minutes later they're alone. Or almost: Daphne leans against the window, looking out with arms folded at the renovated docks. Ed Tate has left for the media centre to 'give colour' on the speech to favoured journalists, while Nicholas is doing essentially the same with fellow MPs. Patrick is on the phone next door, reassuring the conference organisers loudly enough to be heard through the thin wall partition that Afua knows the make-up people are waiting for her, she's on her way over now.

Since it's clear this is going to be a brief conversation, Alec decides to jump right in and ask if she let slip to someone in the mayor's office the government's idea for fully selective Free Schools.

'Did *I* leak it?' she asks, with a puzzled smile.

'Your – brother,' he says, glancing at Daphne, 'works in the Cabinet Office. He's working on the commission's remit.'

'*Henry?*' says Daphne. 'What's he been up to?'

'And you invited someone from City Hall to your drinks party.'

'If you mean Todd Weisman, he's a professor at Columbia. We had an interesting meeting recently on crime and cultural deprivation in urban centres. Was I wrong to ask him to my reception?'

She's asking if he intends to apologise for this little misunderstanding before it hardens into an accusation. Alec feels a familiar throb of desire at her combination of physical frailty (those slender arms!) and feline aggression. It's impossible to believe she gave birth six months ago. Well, perhaps there's been a very marginal fleshing out at the hips; perhaps her jaw bones are no longer quite so violently stark, and there's a subtle new hormonal glow in her cheeks. How squalid and amateurish, how insufficient his fumbling with the Warwick student suddenly seems!

He conceals his erection by resting his ankle against his knee and laying a forearm over his groin. 'All I'm saying is: *whoever* did it, stirring things up among the Tories hasn't been helpful on this occasion. The mayor's pre-empting the government by making a speech this afternoon calling for new grammar schools in London.'

'Don't take this the wrong way, Alec, but I asked Afua to give you two minutes on the basis you weren't going to waste her time.'

'The point is it was briefed to the *Standard* last night. So whatever we're saying on education this afternoon has already been buried.'

'In London, maybe . . .'

Alec ignores Daphne, judging her remark no more than an instinctive refusal of this tactical Conservative (or at least mayoral) victory, and lacking the fortitude to make his own patronising comment about where the news agenda is set. Instead he says to Afua, 'The BBC and everyone else will obviously join in. It might even suck attention from your home affairs speech . . .'

'This Cabinet Office review,' Afua says, 'has the government asked you to chair it?'

'Yes, well, I'm not sure it's going to happen now. The leak has caused such a huge row between City Hall and Number Ten I wouldn't be surprised if the whole idea of the commission was shelved.'

'You're not saying,' Daphne says, 'that you actually *agreed* to their proposal? To front a review that's going to recommend bringing back *grammar* schools?'

'They wouldn't technically be grammar schools. It would be a case of amending the admissions criteria for certain Free Schools—'

'You silly bugger. You understand you're finished in Labour politics?' There is curiosity, maybe even vestigial concern in Daphne's question.

'I don't see it like that at all. I think I'm showing the sort of grown-up, bipartisan politics voters always say they want . . .'

'*Voters* might want it. But Labour politicians don't collaborate with the Tories, especially over something like academic selection, and then simply resume their careers afterwards. I'm amazed you thought that might be possible.'

Even if Daphne is right, Alec counters, the damage to his career is hardly irrevocable. The only Labour people who know he's been approached to chair the commission are in this room. They're also in a position to prevail on the actual leaker, Henry Howe – whom Alec accepts was acting without Afua's knowledge – to refrain from mentioning Alec's name in connection with the education review.

Afua is smiling patiently. 'I think if the PM and the mayor are fighting over the government's education policy, the public has a right to know about it.'

'No,' Alec corrects her, 'no, that wouldn't work. If we tried to hurt them over this the Tories would suspect it came from me. They'd ditch the commission, but only after counter-briefing that I'd secretly agreed to chair it.' He doesn't know how to explain it any clearer. 'Don't you see? It would be the end of me. I'd look like some sort of hapless traitor – not a good combination.'

'It's a difficult situation,' says Afua, glancing at her watch. 'The thing is, Alec, you agreed to head up the review for your own interests. You knew it would give the damaging impression of a middle-class moderate deserting Labour. Not to mention help portray the Conservatives as centre-ground reformists.'

'I don't know why I'm taking Alec's side here. But there's nothing centrist about bringing back grammar schools; the whole thing would have been a disaster for the Tories.'

'In that case they've been unnecessarily spared embarrassment!'

Witnessing this flash of impatience, Alec recalls Daphne wasn't asked for her opinion on this occasion.

Patrick sticks his head round the door. 'The Leader wants a quick word. And make-up are still waiting.'

'That's fine. I'm available now.'

'One second – *please*.' Alec swipes the air, then again until the sceptical Patrick retreats. The jutting warmth in his lap has been replaced by a rising sense of panic. He realises there's no point making a sentimental plea to Afua by reminding her he took her on when she was nothing, a blogger for Sherard's inconsequential lefty rag. 'Look, you're right to say I'm a middle-class moderate. That could be useful to you. Not now, of course, but in a few years . . .' Alec pauses, taking a little heart from what he understands to be a thoughtful silence. 'I understand economics, as you know, and *The Times* and so on would give me a fair wind. You'd have full right of veto, whatever you wanted . . .'

'Right of veto over what, exactly?'

'Well, Treasury policy.' Perhaps now would be the time to beg, but instead he says weakly, 'Youth and experience, it could really work . . .'

He takes in a ripple of lime-scented air as Afua gets to her feet. 'Alec,' she smiles, 'I've been in the shadow cabinet for nine months. Right now I have a speech to make.'

'Of course – let's talk after your speech. In the meantime, the important thing is not to speak to anyone about this.'

Afua is almost at the door. He asks Daphne, still by the window, 'You'll make sure she thinks this through very carefully?'

When Afua turns round her expression is calmly furious. 'There's really nothing to think about. You're the living embodiment of Labour's toxic relationship with the City.' He has a sense her mind has already moved on when she adds, 'I warned you some time ago not to let that happen.'

Rebecca calls as he's getting into his BMW.
'Oh, darling it's me. I have wonderful news – Colonel's back!'

36

Evening redness in the gallery

She's fascinated by him because she can't read him because she's in love with him: what a thin, paradoxical basis for living with a different man whom she detests, and dedicating herself to an art form she has no special talent for! The really depressing part of it is that this insight can't seem to prevent the lurching feeling when Buzzy is confronted with the little mole on the base of his neck. It's as if he's managed both to poison her blood and make himself the dialyser: for all her recent boredom and resentment, too long without seeing Marcel and she's sluggish, distracted, fogged-up. And even if she found some way of completely purging herself of him, Buzzy is so convinced she'd never feel that kind of passion again, that her love for him is her already passing youth, she hasn't put her heart into really trying. What if she succeeds?

She takes a listless sip of wine: Benjamin stopped crying a while ago, but the silence while she waits for Marcel to rejoin her turns out to be no less grating. It's chilly in the long gallery, and dimly lit; the last occasion Buzzy was in here she was very stoned and unwittingly depleting the art collection. Despite this, there's something comforting about the surroundings. Even though Marcel now lives at Canonbury Lane, the house, with its Aga and *Guardian* piles and neon Emin scrawl, so plainly reflects the peculiar traditions of the Howe family, and Sherard and Daphne in particular, that she's able to imagine Marcel no less of a guest himself.

Buzzy decides to play some music. Compared with Philip's massed ranks of opera, the CD collection is surprisingly modest and comprehensible; in between Cat Stevens and Simon &

Garfunkel, there's even a classical compilation album similar to the one her parents own. She opts for the Rolling Stones. For a second she thinks she's put the disc in the wrong side up and broken the sculpted sound system, but when it arrives the acoustic intro of 'Factory Girl' is strikingly clean and pure, if a little loud. As a minor revenge against Benjamin she doesn't adjust the volume, even if it'll be her loss if he wakes and Marcel is further detained.

Satisfied, Buzzy retrieves her glass of wine and tries to find a way of reclining on the little sofa, then decides it's impossible and sits forward. *Turmoil . . . (love is)*, the writing on the wall, gives out a soft blue light. She thinks of Marcel's proposal that they spend a few days (or rather nights) in Paris and wonders what to say when he returns. The practical details emerged in his usual elliptical manner: no doubt he considered it distasteful to have to spell out that Buzzy should travel by herself, stay in a separate hotel, and make herself available on the off-chance he's not working late one evening.

She'd told him, just before their discussion was interrupted by Benjamin, that the idea was far too risky. Wouldn't Philip be suspicious if it just so happened Marcel was in Paris at the same time as her? Marcel replied that he'd recently changed departments at Sullivan and Ball, so Philip would be unlikely to know of his movements. As a pretext for her going to Paris, he suggested – rather cannily, so that she wondered if he'd given this trip some thought – Buzzy make her first contribution to the *Spectator* a feature on the state of contemporary French literature.

Buzzy certainly sees the merit in convincing the magazine to cover the cost of her travel and entertainment disbursements (she imagines the research might involve taking a few authors to lunch). It seems important not to let Philip fund her unfaithfulness, even if in the scheme of things this only represents a token adjustment in the moral balance sheet, not least as she has virtually no income of her own. (The combined advance and royalties she's received from *The Bathers* is not in the same range as the wine Philip might order with his main course.)

But this is all fantasy; of course she can't go. The choice is between Paris and her dignity, not the more poetic opposition of Marcel and the void. Marcel *is* the void: not in the sense of an unknown quantity, like life without him; or simple emptiness, like Philip; but a negative space into which everything good and hopeful about her has for years now been seeping.

She feels tense almost every time he speaks, even when the conversation has settled into an intimate rhythm. The fear is always there that their intimacy is not quite special enough, as if he has very precisely measured her qualities and found they fall fractionally short (how could they not?) of what Afua can give him. She wonders if in fact Marcel's whole ambition as regards Buzzy is the systematic cancellation of any respect she has for herself. If so, it's he, the bureaucrat's offspring, who has shown up the famous Philip Devereux as no more than a gentleman amateur, lacking the imagination to grasp there's nothing as viciously painful as being understood, loved, and still found wanting. *But you consented to this*, she'll see in Marcel's dark eyes. *You wanted to be my creature.* And it's true. She did.

Cutting through Mick Jagger and the conga drums, the Howes' front door rattles shut. Daphne and Afua are at the Labour conference in Liverpool: has one of them decided to return early? What if it's Sherard, come to pick up his things or perhaps reclaim the family seat? The best she can hope for is that it's the laconic housekeeper. Buzzy gathers Marta's role has latterly evolved into being Benjamin's nursemaid; somehow it's unsurprising that the childcare arrangements in this most egalitarian of addresses are rather Edwardian.

She wonders if Marcel has heard anything from up in the bedroom. Out of an instinctive sense of propriety, she's turning off the music when someone knocks politely but firmly against the door frame and then takes a couple of heavyish steps onto the polished wood floor.

'Oh, Buzzy – hullo.'

'Hen!' She feels slightly self-conscious using the old nickname. 'You've lost weight since the summer.'

Henry grins in embarrassed delight. 'It might be this diet Fiona has me on.'

'Oh, which one?'

'I don't know if it has a name, as such. Mainly I'm just not allowed to eat a lot.'

There is a short pause.

'I didn't know anyone was going to be here, or I would've rung the doorbell or something . . .'

'Don't be silly, it's your family home.' She indicates her half-drunk wine. 'Philip's working late, as usual, so I just came over to catch up with Marcel – he's putting Benjamin to sleep.'

'Right, I see.'

'Were you hoping to see him too? Because he's the only one in residence, apart from the baby.'

'Actually, I'm after the second volume of *War and Peace* from my father's – from the study. I started reading it on my honeymoon and got really quite engrossed. That doesn't sound very romantic.'

Buzzy laughs. 'Not really, Hen, to tell the truth.'

'Have you ever got round to it – the Tolstoy?'

'I skimmed it. That and *Anna Karenina* – which I much preferred – are as far as I've got with the Russians. Marcel's read them all, obviously; sometimes I wonder if the Western canon was passed on to him in the womb.'

'Sort of pre-installed, you mean? Like a computer, except they never really do come like that, at least in my experience. Maybe it's different with Macs. Do you still have that old, what was it . . .'

'Would you like some wine? There's a bottle open in the kitchen.'

Henry demurs, saying he ought to get back to Ealing; he's going to be late for dinner as it is.

'Please stay, Hen. This isn't one of those times where you offer someone a drink because you have to or, you know, because you actually want to get rid of them.'

'Do people do that?' asks Henry, with a searching frown.

'Just for a bit – at least until Marcel's finished upstairs.'

'Well, all right. I won't drink though; Fiona and I are detoxing, on a sort of permanent basis.'

They smile at each other.

'It's not like you ever liked alcohol much, anyway,' Buzzy says.

Their knees knock for a moment when Henry sits beside her. Buzzy covers the momentary awkwardness by saying it's hard to find a comfortable position on this sofa.

'I think my father prefers people to stand in this room, for the art.'

'Does he actually like any of the stuff he collects?'

'I'm not sure that he does, really. I suppose it's not that different to ploughing through Tolstoy because one feels one ought to.'

'Except don't people do that because they believe it'll improve them in some way? Anyway, Hen, you *are* enjoying it.' She grins. 'What's funny?'

'It's rather embarrassing. I haven't told anyone about it.' Henry describes asking his secretary if she'd read *War and Peace*, and the attritional battle that his Natasha has waged against him since.

'I can see how that might have unintentionally sounded a little sarcastic on your part. But she might have read it, for all you knew.'

'To be honest, I didn't really think it through.'

'Do you get the impression she's a reader generally?'

He pauses. 'Not really, no.'

'Oh Hen,' Buzzy says. 'Is there anything else you'd care to confess, while you're at it?'

'I wrote four essays for my tort exam finals when I was only supposed to write three. I was dashing so quickly I left out a raft of key cases, and of course they never marked the last essay. I think it's why I missed out on a first overall.'

Buzzy covers her mouth with the back of her hand. 'That's not funny. I don't know why I'm . . . I don't know why . . .'

Henry has been staring fairly blankly at Buzzy. Then his fleshy lips start to twitch and his nostrils to flare as though he's about to sneeze. The laugh when it first emerges has a strangled, experimental quality, like an animal trying to sing. Buzzy is doubled-up,

288

holding Henry's shoulder for support. The heaving of her ribs has taken on an unstoppable life of its own, though after a while she finds herself capable of turning quite dispassionately to other subjects, most notably the fact that Marcel has entered the room and is now watching them.

Marcel looks soberly and immaculately handsome: hair precisely raked; face a pale blue crescent. Buzzy is furious; her urge to throw herself at his ankles is exactly the sort of thing she ought to have grown out of.

'Hello, Henry,' he says calmly, when the room is finally quiet.

She's not surprised he doesn't ask about or even acknowledge something amusing that was said in his absence. But Henry, instead of replying straightaway or getting to his feet with clumsy deference, allows the moment to stretch. Buzzy at first takes his silence for embarrassment, to find that not only is he not avoiding eye contact with Marcel but there is a new sensual confidence in his thick features. It's not, of course, lost on Marcel, who always notices everything, and who now faintly but distinctly blushes.

'I didn't hear you arrive,' Marcel says, with a new note of uncertainty. The purplish tint hasn't yet drained from his cheek.

'Henry's just picking up a book from Sherard's study. A volume of *War and Peace*.'

'I'm afraid you probably won't find it: Marta recently threw out many of your father's books.'

'She— she did what?'

'It was at the request of your mother.'

'But some of those books are valuable – I mean, they're *beautiful*! There are first editions belonging to my grandfather . . . First editions he himself published, in some cases!'

'It's possible some went to a charity shop. Unfortunately, I don't think Marta was in a position to judge which were worth more than others.'

Henry's eyes are glistening. He must be thinking that – never mind the poor housekeeper – Marcel, with all his taste and learning, was perfectly placed to rescue the most valuable books. For his part Marcel seems quite revived, having corrected to his satisfaction Henry's momentary self-assurance.

Henry makes to stand up: Buzzy, shifting to give him space, knocks over the wine glass by her feet. A neon puddle forms on the floor.

'*Houp là.* I'll get a cloth, and another bottle.' Marcel pauses at the doorway. 'By the way, I saw your education review was in the news today,' – he doesn't wait for a response.

'Yes, I think I saw something in the *Standard*. It seems like you've sparked a bit of a row, Hen,' she says, trying to jolly him. 'To be honest, I was quite relieved it's all out in the open.'

Henry is wandering round the room, turning on the side lamps. From his distracted manner – he's evidently still upset about the books – Buzzy decides he's not listening, and allows the conversation to lapse.

'Relieved?' he abruptly asks.

'Well, because I mentioned to Philip what you told us in Arezzo about the new grammar schools. I'm sorry, Hen, I didn't realise till I saw the article that even though you said it wasn't confidential it sort of *was*, wasn't it? It's just Philip likes to feel in the know about things, but I guessed he'd be too busy working to actually have time to tell anyone. Fortunately it's all out in the open now.'

Henry feels his way round the neck of a lamp near the *Turmoil . . . (love is)* piece. He blinks as the switch clicks into place: bathed in external light, the Emin centrepiece suddenly seems cheap and pointless. His voice sounds tight when he says, 'Marcel blushed.'

'Sorry?'

'He didn't realise I was here. Then when I looked at him – really *looked* at him – he blushed. He was expecting only to find you.'

'Are you all right, Hen?'

'I'm fine . . . Well, perhaps a little—' Henry swallows hard. 'It's just a shame about the library.'

'Shall we at least have a look for your *War and Peace* volume? Maybe it's still there – maybe Marta missed it.'

Henry shakes his head. 'I probably shouldn't be reading it anyway. Fiona bought me an *Economist* subscription for Christmas, which I've been rather neglecting. Then there's the bathroom – I haven't tiled it. Also, I'm late for dinner. I think I mentioned that.'

'You did, Hen. I'm sorry if I've made you late. If you felt I didn't appreciate that was important.'

'No, well. It's not a big thing.'

'But it is, Hen! It's important if it matters to you.'

'Thank you,' he says, stiffly. 'I'm touched that my appetite is uppermost in, ah—' Henry sighs and gives up the attempt at sarcasm. Buzzy finds she wants to kiss his beautiful bovine eyes. 'Let's catch up properly soon – a meal!' She follows Henry down the narrow hallway. 'Restaurant of your choice. Hi to Fiona!' she says to the rattling front door.

Marcel is pouring two large glasses of wine in the kitchen.

Buzzy draws a chair at the main family table. 'Henry's gone.'

'I heard,' replies Marcel, leaning with his back to the counter. Next to him a baby monitor flashes up a bewildering array of numbers and symbols on its LCD screen.

'You weren't very kind – telling him about his father's books.'

'Should I have lied?'

'That's not what I meant. And obviously it's not your fault if Daphne threw out a load of priceless first editions to spite Sherard.'

'I think Sherard won't care, in fact.'

'It wasn't even the *way* you said it.' Her heart is racing; she knows that, in voicing what's meant to remain unsaid, she's spoiling his game. 'It was the intent, because you felt silly standing there because we'd been laughing. You wanted to punish him.'

Marcel allows the statement to hang in the air. The crease on his forehead has been recklessly aggravated; part of Buzzy wants to say whatever soothing thing might stop him spoiling his looks like that.

'It's a funny thing. I have the impression you've always thought Henry was slightly simple – *un peu idiot*. Which of course means he couldn't be perceptive or passionate, like you,' Marcel says, levelly. 'Only maybe, it's just a guess, but maybe you've finally realised Henry has been in love with you all this time, and you never noticed. So maybe it's you who is looking for someone to punish.'

The baby monitor tinnily relays the sound of Benjamin crying in his cot.

She circles back. '*You* never showed much interest in him.'

'Why should Henry care about that?' he asks dully. 'I'm not his crazy love.'

Amour fou, Buzzy mentally replaces for Marcel's uncharacteristically inelegant translation. 'Obviously I did wonder about Henry, at one point . . .' In fact she wonders if she wasn't guilty of unconsciously deciding *not* to wonder very hard; if it didn't suit her far too much to have a dependable friend with whom she never had to make any great effort and who conveniently happened, via Afua, to be connected with Marcel. 'But then he got together with Fiona – he married her!'

'He wanted your attention . . .'

Benjamin's needy wailing is working up to an unbearable pitch.

'I don't believe Henry, or any decent person, would marry for such a cruel and destructive reason.'

Marcel's mouth flinches into a momentary smile.

'He did it to move on with his life,' she goes on, as if Marcel had disagreed, 'to grow up. That's what Henry is: a man! And I'm proud of him; I think he'll accomplish more than any of us. More importantly, he already *is* better than us. You. Me. Afua.'

'The baby is crying,' he observes.

'Oh, shut the fuck up.'

37

End of the line

Sherard wakes to find his carriage deserted. The sign on the platform says Brixton: 'Perhaps I'm dead,' he says out loud. It's a disappointment when one of the cleaning staff tells Sherard the train's now out of service and he needs to get off.

He supposes he ought to go back up the Victoria line to Oxford Circus. His original plan had been to drop in on the Groucho, see if there was anyone he might bump into, but the idea of another Tube journey feels insurmountably tedious. There's also a chance he might be sick if he doesn't get some fresh air.

Sherard is almost at the top of the escalators when he realises that classical music is being piped into the station. The idea, presumably, is to soothe the savage beasts. 'How do you explain Wagner then?' he asks the London Underground representative at the ticket barriers. 'Or what's his name – *il miglior fabbro*? My father knew him, slightly...' The stupid man isn't listening.

He hasn't been here since the summer riots, and is surprised by the number of fluorescent-jacketed police officers outside the station entrance. Not wishing to empty the contents of his stomach at their feet, even if it's only bile, Sherard starts walking up the high street as steadily as he can manage. He's only gone a few yards when he ducks into Electric Avenue to retch a few times, reassuring himself it's probably quite a familiar sight, given the awful song. After a few moments of feeling worse, his head throbbing and spinning, he decides he's ready for a drink: something clear and pure, definitely not gin, the thought of which sends his stomach churning again. Vodka will do.

Back on the high street a largish crowd spans the pavement in front of Sherard, facing gravely in his direction. Contrary to his initial impression, it's not a lynch mob but a bus stop, and they're staring past rather than at him. He's pleased to find the exception, standing subtly apart from the bus crowd, is a cork-skinned youth in a Puffa jacket. He's maybe twenty years old. A glimmer of curiosity shows beneath the boy's cultivated blank façade: he seems unable to decide if Sherard is an unwashed drunk or the sort of man who might share an actuary with the Queen. Granted, it's probably rare for him to meet someone to whom both descriptions may be said to apply, but Sherard will be pleased to expand his education. The drink can wait.

He makes his approach without any firm sense of what he's going to say or even if he's really going to go through with it, focusing rather on the boy's sunken cheeks and wide, athlete's shoulders. They're almost level already; it's too late to initiate anything. Sherard is half reconciled to a bleak search for a solitary drink when he surprises them both by stopping in his tracks. The young man's jaw tightens reflexively.

'Yes. Um. I'd like a few grams. Cocaine, obviously,' Sherard says, getting into his stride, '*sans* the baby laxative or whatever you use these days.' He takes out his wallet and removes a wad of notes, trying to get a sense of how much he's holding without having to go through the bother of counting it all out. 'I think there's about two hundred and fifty here . . .'

'Step the fuck a-*way*,' the boy says, with an impressive combination of nonchalance and aggression.

Sherard stuffs the notes into the pocket of his cashmere coat as a pair of police officers – one male, the other female – strolls past. 'As late as that?' he says loudly, and then ruins everything by peering ostentatiously at his own watch.

The police ignore him, dividing into separate paths through the unaccommodating congregation waiting for the bus. Once they're out of hearing range, Sherard says, 'Meet me round the corner in five minutes,' and without waiting for the boy to respond continues up the high street.

Beyond the traffic lights, the Ritzy is showing a film called *Melancholia*. Above the cinema entrance the director's name appears in the same bold lettering as the movie title: the mere mention of Lars von Trier doubtless had Martin, the *Liberal Review*'s long-time film critic, itching to hail the picture a masterpiece, not that Sherard has read the arts or any other section of the magazine recently.

Instead of crossing at the lights, he turns left down Coldharbour Lane. Groups of men stand outside, as if guarding them, brightly lit Caribbean restaurants and other late-opening establishments: afro hairdressers and mini-marts and a black history bookshop. Meanwhile young media types stream into Sohoish bars that blast electronic music in a desperate attempt, probably, to drown out the even ghastlier conversations about *Melancholia*.

Sherard soon tires of getting jostled. He feels a strong need to sit down for a moment or two; the narrow side-street connecting back to Electric Avenue is probably an obvious enough place for the boy to find him . . .

He's resting on the pavement when he decides to give up on this little diversion. It's one thing to have a former BBC director-general cancel dinner at the River Café; quite another to be stood up, if that's the word for a man hunched over a pile of his own stomach acid, by a low-level hustler. It may even cast doubt on whether Sherard is in a triumphant phase of life. There have been worse, he reflects. He wouldn't wish to be fourteen again, a fat little front row huffing and puffing from one ruck to the next, praying the ball would never spill loose, the tyrant Turnbull on the touchline screaming *Dive on it, Howe, you little fairy!* with Sherard's father standing only a few yards away. Another time, during an inter-house tournament, a penalty was awarded against the Drake XV. Sherard was surprised and fleetingly honoured when Prendergast handed him the rugby ball. He understood the scissors move perfectly well from practice and, having taken up position with his back to the opposition pack, tapped the ball with his boot after hearing the referee's whistle. Behind him the pack began their charge. A teammate, acting as the decoy, made an angled sprint past Sherard in the direction of the touchline. Right on cue Sherard feigned passing him the ball. He could hear the thundering stampede of testosterone bearing down on him but he knew he had time to hand the ball to the second teammate – Kendle, the fastest boy in Wellington House – running at a different angle to the decoy towards the open field of play. Sherard remembers his confusion as Kendle, just like the decoy, sailed past him without collecting the offered ball, then the howls of laughter from around the pitch ringing in his ears as eight brutes slammed into his back. On the floor, they raked him with their boot studs in search of a ball he had no intention of withholding from them.

'I thought you was hidin' from me.'

Sherard, concentrating on getting to his feet, didn't notice the boy arrive. 'Why would I do that? I specifically told you to follow me, if you remember.'

'I remember. So you wanna get high?' he asks, in a sneering tone that takes for granted rich white fiftysomethings should want something less out of life.

'That was the idea, I suppose.' Sherard adds, 'I should probably mention I'm not from the police or anything.'

'Nah they don't reek like you. Where you from, besides?'

'Oh . . . north of the river.' Because there's a silence, he adds, 'You?'

The boy kisses his teeth. 'Here, man.'

'Well, let me know if you need to mark the street or something.'

'To *mark* it? Like a *dog*?'

'You can do it now, if you want.'

'That's right.' He lets out a short husky laugh. 'I'll piss all over you.'

Sherard is about to reply that that's the spirit, when the boy asks for a cigarette. He responds he only smokes cigars.

'I'll take one of them.'

'Please, you're very welcome . . .'

Sherard doesn't make any movement beyond swaying a little. The boy yanks back the lapel of Sherard's coat and with his other hand fishes around rather roughly in Sherard's jacket pockets. He removes the cap of the Romeo y Julieta case and sniffs inside. He grins at Sherard. 'How much?'

'I don't buy them individually. A pack of twenty-five is five hundred, something like that.'

The boy tucks the cigar into the back pocket of his stone-washed jeans. He takes a step towards Sherard. 'Tell me somethin', rich man. How comes you ain't wavin' notes in my face like on the high street, in front of the fuckin' five-oh an' all that?' His aroma is sweet from mint gum and marijuana.

'To tell you the *truth*,' says Sherard, coyly, 'I think I've had too much to drink for anything you're selling.' He closes his eyes, letting the dealer's strong sugary exhalations warm his face. Time to get this over with. 'Now going back to fine cigars, one wants something full-bodied, potent, with a good draw . . .' Still with his eyes shut, his fingertips graze a powerful inner thigh, hard as a cord. 'That's what makes a chap get his wallet out . . .' He trails his hand upwards until it cups a tantalisingly warm mass. He rubs it, probing for some movement but finding only the denim seam dig into his palm.

The initial blow smashes him below the eye socket. How cartoonish, he thinks, of the stars that flash before him as his legs give way. On the pavement he opens his good eye a crack: a scurrying blur of white trainers; in the foreground, a leg swinging towards him in fast motion. Despite having seen what was coming, the force of it takes Sherard by surprise: an immediate, unlocalised explosion through his whole body. In a second or two he discerns the contraction of his already tender abdominal muscles. He's overcome with a violent need simultaneously to throw up and take air into his lungs, neither of which he manages successfully. At the next kick he feels a rib crack. The filtered sound of yelping and swearing registers dimly in his brainstem – Sherard realises the youth must have bruised or perhaps even broken a toe.

As his diaphragm starts to relax, he focuses on taking very short breaths, doing his best with each inhalation to ignore the sharp pain in his ribs. His upper cheek has already swollen enough to force shut his tearing and stinging eye. At some point soon he'll need to be sick.

He feels the dealer's hand in his coat pocket. 'Don't . . .' he begins, before running out of breath. He waits, licks his lips, and tries again. 'Don't stop now . . .'

The boy removes the wad of bills from Sherard's wallet and allows the discarded object to fall next to Sherard's face. 'Relax, faggot,' he says, 'we got time.'

38

First blush

'Oh there's Afua,' Fiona announces. 'No Marcel, I see.'

'He's probably minding Benjamin; I think Marta still has Sundays off.'

'Look, Henry, she's chatting with all the nurses. Do you think she's *electioneering*, even now?'

Henry peers up from his *Economist* for a second time. 'I think it's more likely she's finding out how Dad's doing,' he says, and returns to the magazine's editorial on the perilous state of the global economy. He's yet to make it past the second paragraph, despite the piece's pessimistic tone conforming to his new belief that reality, in the form of the euro crisis and slowing growth in China, ought to be privileged over Napoleonic battles.

'With three of them? We haven't seen that many nurses since we arrived . . .'

Henry feels vaguely implicated, via the 'we', in Fiona's unvoiced belief that Afua's special treatment from the clinical staff has less to do with her being a celebrity politician than being a fellow black woman, albeit with lighter skin and a different body shape. When Afua finally comes over, amid curious glances from the other occupants of the waiting room, she tells them Sherard will probably be discharged later this afternoon. He's on morphine for the pain, but there's not much to be done for the facial bruising and broken ribs.

Rather than answering that Daphne has already told them all this, Fiona says, after a shy glance at Afua, 'I still can't get over your father's luck. A high-crime area on a Saturday night and some actual police in the vicinity . . .'

Afua recently allied herself with a tabloid campaign opposing the rise of intelligence-led policing at the expense of traditional bobbies on the beat. She seems now not to notice Fiona's attempts to ingratiate herself, instead asking Henry how Sherard looks.

'He was sleeping when we arrived, so we only really put our heads round the door.'

'His face is a *mess*. I can't see how he's going to manage basic things for a while, like shaving or even feeding himself.'

'It must make sense for him to come home,' Afua says, 'though it's up to Daphne, of course. Is she with him now?'

'Yes, just gone in. We thought we'd let them talk for a bit.'

'Personally,' Fiona says, 'I want to know what he was *doing* there on his own, at that time of night.'

'The nurses said he was drunk.'

Henry is unsure if Afua's emphasis on the last word suggests impatience with his father's alcoholism, or Fiona for obliging her to mention it. Perhaps it's both.

'. . . Obviously all that will have to stop if Sherard moves back to Canonbury Lane; it'd only be fair to Daph.'

He wonders if his parents are to have any say in this settlement, and expresses as much.

Fiona's glare is somewhere between amazed and remonstrating. 'Henry!'

'Of course, Hen,' Afua says, so calmly and naturally he knows she's taken aback too. She gives his arm a rueful rub. 'This whole situation is upsetting, and I feel partly to blame. We shouldn't have let things get to this stage.'

'Considering he almost ruined your drinks party, I think you've actually been very patient with him. It's not as if you haven't had other things to think about . . .'

'Liverpool must have been exhausting.'

'Mm, totally,' Afua says with a sympathetic smile, as though it were Henry who'd had to survive the ordeal of conference.

'I dropped by Canonbury Lane while you and Mum were away. I don't suppose Marcel mentioned it?'

'He didn't, actually. Did you two have fun?'

'Oh . . .' Henry is always mildly alarmed by this question and the sense of a larger failure if he responds in the negative. 'Yes, I suppose so. Buzzy was there.'

'Sounds like a reunion. Mean Hen, not waiting for me!'

'It was more of a coincidence than anything; I'd only gone round to pick up a book from the study.'

'Poor Marcel,' Afua muses good-humouredly, her indignation of a second ago seemingly forgotten, 'I left him in charge of Benjamin all week, with Marta of course, and now I'm doing it again. I wonder if Daph would mind if we went in now.'

'Good idea, Henry's meant to be tiling the bathroom today.'

'I suppose Mum and Dad can chat things through later.' He gathers his overcoat and magazine. His heart is already hammering in his chest before he's taken the conscious decision to speak, but it's not the moment to wonder what this implies for the existence of the soul. 'It's funny,' Henry says, 'I think I must have taken Marcel by surprise on Wednesday.'

Afua gazes at him indulgently. 'What's that, my darling?'

'When I went home last week – to Islington, I mean – and Buzzy was there. I'm sure I did surprise him because he blushed a little when he saw me.'

'Then it's my turn to be surprised,' Afua says, after a moment's hesitation. 'Marcel never blushes.'

'*Henry* does all the time. He's doing it now, look.'

'So he is.'

A black man in a thin golf jacket approaches and asks Afua if she's 'the politician'. He's accompanied by two teenage girls, who hang behind him with appalled expressions under their braids. 'My daughter wrote about you,' he says, wagging his finger delightedly, 'for schoolwork – coursework!' Afua asks the girls which of them is studying politics, and wins exaggerated chuckles from the rest of the waiting room, now openly listening in, when she says she hopes the essay wasn't *too* rude.

The man produces a camera phone and ushers forward an older lady, presumably his mother, whom Henry hadn't noticed until now. He wants her to join her granddaughters and Afua in the photo, coaxing her until she stands beaming in the middle of the foursome, the shortest by probably a foot. 'One more!' he shouts, and for a second time the murky room is sheeted white. Others are filming Afua on their phones now, because they recognise her or want to capture her aura. She removes her thick-framed glasses and wipes her eye, saying in a flighty voice Henry doesn't recognise that it must be the flash, isn't it gloomy in here; but the grandmother doesn't respond except to repeat a slightly impatient *thank you*, as if Afua were now intruding on a private family moment.

The horror of what Henry has done is flitting at the corners of his vision. Then he thinks of Buzzy and Marcel, and his heart hardens. Right from when he first got to know Buzzy (via Afua via Marcel), towards the end of the Lent term of their freshman year, he'd assumed her relations with the Belgian, with their whiff of marijuana and *Les Fleurs du Mal*, were strictly metaphysical, so to speak. Of course he understood she was deeply impressed by him. But they can't have known each other more than a month or two before Marcel started going out with Afua, by then in her final year and one of the most pursued girls in the entire university. Terribly naively, as it turns out, Henry simply assumed that was that.

Something else Henry has been thinking of lately is George Eliot's idea that if art does not enlarge men's sympathies, it has no moral value. If it weren't for all those drawing-room scenes in Eliot and Austen, Tolstoy and James which, *pace* Abdul, Henry would never have read so assiduously if he hadn't in the first place been searching for a way to connect with Buzzy, he wouldn't have immediately understood Marcel's blush for the guilty admission it was. Had he not come across sufficiently similar situations in the classics – the same ones whose consignment to a landfill site Buzzy at the time assumed was the cause of his distress – he'd have been without the emotional intelligence (or if not, the confidence in his own judgement) to acknowledge that a most trivial event, an involuntary but commonplace physiological response, can have immeasurable significance to the person reading it.

Understanding this has, if anything, had the effect of diminishing Henry's sympathies towards Buzzy. And then what *of* Buzzy, the practising poet? *Comes still the night, starry-eyed and love struck / Cursed and kicked and out of luck*: can these words be said to have expanded her emotional repertoire in any positive sense? Hasn't being in love with Marcel made her trample on his, Henry's, generosity; deceive her parents, whom for all her teasing Henry knows she loves very much; risk destroying Afua's chance of having a real family unit of her own?

At the *Turmoil* exhibition, Buzzy agreed with Alec Merton that in fact it's as much up to the consumers – not just the thing of art itself, as Eliot had it, or its producer – to create the edifying value of the work. But by knowingly echoing the romantic errors of all those fictional heroines – naive Natasha Rostov, proud Isabel Archer – she's shown art 'does nothing' for her, morally. It's confirmed a suspicion he's until now managed to bury, that Buzzy is as contemptuous of art as his father. In some ways that's too unforgiving: his father can't be accused of trying to hide his disdain. Buzzy's hypocrisy here – her lazy reading of literature, the seemingly calculated emptiness of the later poems in her collection – is in some ways harder to accept than the actual affair with Marcel, in whatever precise form this has taken. Henry never wants to find out the details.

'I suppose there'll be a media side of things to consider, for Sherard's assault,' Fiona says as they enter the observation ward.

'Leave it with me,' Afua says, sounding her usual composed self once more.

Afua's face, in all its angular perfection, is replaced by the swollen and bandaged sight of his father, at the foot of whose bed Daphne is rather diffidently sitting and radiating (at least to Henry) repressed concern. He already knows he'll have a long time, perhaps the rest of his life, to reflect on the last few minutes and, if he wants, to try to rationalise the anger he now feels, which is shockingly deep. His initial impression is that it's directed not only at Buzzy, but his whole family.

39

Poetry and prose

'Apparently I've lost you.'

Buzzy looks up from her dim sum. She earlier called Hakkasan, careful to drop in the name of Philip Devereux, and asked to have a platter made up for two people. The lady on the other end told her whoever was picking it up should come to the restaurant's reception desk in an hour. There didn't seem much point in Buzzy going all the way to Mayfair just for the sake of it, so she had a driver from the Sullivans car service collect it on his own. Now she's half listening to Philip's account of a rival law firm's timetabling fuck-up, as he put it, as a result of which their client missed a deadline to declare their intention to make an offer for a target company. The sanction was a ban from the regulator against this prospective purchaser attempting to acquire the target's shares in the next six months, allowing Philip's client to jump in with a bid of their own.

'Not at all,' says Buzzy, who would have been thrown by this sort of talk a couple of years ago. The first time Philip mentioned the regulatory code governing mergers and acquisitions, Buzzy made him laugh by remarking that it reminded her of the courtship rules in nineteenth-century novels. 'You were saying the other firm is going to pay for that mistake, in the current climate.'

'Not the *firm* necessarily, the partner who signed off on the fuck-up. Actually, I think you met him once. Murray Dutoit.'

Buzzy frowns. 'I'm not sure I have.' She's learnt Philip will ascribe all manner of doings to her if she's not careful.

He wipes his mouth with a napkin, leaving a wintry smile. 'Well, I'm sorry I'm such a bore. I was under the impression writers were supposed to be interested in everything.'

Before she can stop herself, she asks, 'Are you saying I should compose a poem about the whateveritscalled – the takeover code?'

'No, that would be rather banal. On the other hand I wasn't aware banality per se was incompatible with your output.'

'I wasn't aware you would know.'

'Of course I've read the book,' he snaps.

'Well, that's a relief, given you never miss a chance to tell your friends it's a work of genius.'

'I can see it was terribly cruel of me to be supportive of your career, and venture to hope for the same in return.'

Buzzy is already flushed with victory. 'By the way, which is your favourite poem in *The Bathers*? The most banal, then?'

'Have you tried the scallop shumai?' Philip asks evenly, after a pause, so that Buzzy hopes she might be allowed to forget this spat – rare for its feeling – and he won't obliquely bring it up in company, weeks from now.

'They're delicious,' she says, attempting to sound conciliatory.

'And the wine – how's that?'

Buzzy stares at her glass of burgundy. 'I like it very much.'

'What about the view? Do you enjoy seeing the Thames, and the lovely wheel your parents were so excited by?'

Buzzy gives a little nod.

'I'm sorry? I didn't catch that.'

'I enjoy the view.'

'I'm so glad. There are these lovely things, and there's the take-over code. Only connect, isn't that what that Tonbridge boy said?'

Buzzy is aware that, in Philip's lexicon, Forster has just been referred to with the gravest disrespect. 'He did,' she says.

After dinner Buzzy is reading *Coming of Age as a Poet*. She admires and envies Helen Vendler's ability to read a poem with such cool impregnable authority that anyone attempting a different interpretation would seem perverse, if not actually insane.

Her mobile phone rings. Buzzy immediately wonders if it's Marcel, and then finds herself hoping it isn't. There's been a sullen silence between them since her last visit to Canonbury

Lane: any rapprochement now would be complicated by Philip listening in on their conversation. Buzzy could always leave the sitting room, but this would attract suspicion; besides, she resents Philip making her feel – in a deniably passive-aggressive, lawyerly fashion – that she's imposing on his well-being if someone calls her at eight on a Friday evening.

'Oh, 'allo, is that Elizabeth Price?' The voice is middle-aged, Orpingtonish, but unfamiliar. 'Jeremy Wedderspoon here – from the *Mail*,' the speaker adds casually, as if the last three words were barely worth mentioning.

'Yes, *hi*,' Buzzy says brightly, despite never having heard of this journalist. Philip is going through his in-tray, giving instructions to his night secretary via the digital recorder held to his lips ('Now, Georgina, I want you to make the following amendments to document number 196864/235 . . .'); pride prevents Buzzy from wanting to let on the only phone call she's received in over a week is from a complete stranger.

Wedderspoon congratulates Buzzy on her inclusion in the *Standard*'s 'thirty under thirty' feature. 'Rare for a poet to make that sort of list. Course, you're probably easier on the eye than most,' he chuckles.

This is a dubious compliment, even assuming it's well-intended, but she laughs anyway. At least *someone* has read that article and doesn't only want to talk about Afua coming in third place. 'I don't know,' she says, 'Rupert Brooke, Rimbaud . . . all my school-girl crushes are still going strong, I'm embarrassed to say.'

Philip glances at her before the recorder's red light reappears and he continues, '*Earlier-stage investors* should have a hyphen between *earlier* and *stage* – actually, Georgina, will you also draft me an email to whichever fucking useless associate is responsible for this document . . .'

'I'll 'ave a word with our arts editor; we could do a feature on sexy poets. These fellas still youngish, are they?'

'Well, yes and no.' She wonders how this man acquired her mobile number. Was she introduced to him at Afua's House of Commons reception? 'I'm sorry, but we weren't supposed to meet this evening or anything, were we? I'm worried I might have stood you up . . .'

Philip has paused his dictation and it's obvious he's listening in. Buzzy decides she's pleased with the daringly ambiguous sound of 'stood you up'.

Jeremy cackles softly. 'No need to worry about that. We've never met. You'll have to excuse me for not getting to the point; I'm the sort what gets easily distracted.'

Buzzy isn't sure if people should refer to their flaws so cheerfully, precluding any possibility of self-hatred, but neither is she convinced his jovial tone rings any truer than his suspect grammar. She forgets this when he says,

'What it is is we're running a story about you.'

'Oh, are you?' she replies, hoping to make it sound as if she's heard the same sentence, or a more elegant version of it, from half of Fleet Street. Buzzy can already hazily see the columns of text in the paper's distinctive blocky font beneath a large photo of her sitting on this very sofa, with the Vauxhall skyline in the background and the Vendler book in her lap, or perhaps on the coffee table would be better. They already take the *Mail* at home, so she wouldn't need to mention it to her parents in advance or send them a link to the article. Her mother got quite flustered and ultimately teary trying to access the *Slate* poem online; when she (or more likely Buzzy's father) at last managed to access the page, Doreen made very encouraging noises on the phone, but Buzzy could tell she didn't truly believe it was the same as being published properly, in print.

'Like a profile, do you mean?'

'I s'ppose we might do one of those, as a sort of adjunct to the main piece . . .'

'Adjunct' is an incongruously high-register word: noticing this feels a victory over the journalist, who has tried in vain to present a false version of himself, probably to lull her into feeling a sense of superiority over him. At the same time it also seems a vindication of his decision to write about her, since it's the sort of revealing detail only an artist would appreciate (or at least, remembering Marcel and indeed Helen Vendler, someone with a fine understanding of art).

Perhaps her constant doubting of her abilities has been misplaced. After all, an editor went to the trouble of revising and printing her work, whose 'fractal variations of everyday words and thoughts' were praised by an important older poet-critic. The *Spectator* wants her to apply her creativity to their magazine in some way (though increasingly she wonders if neither the job offer from the member of the editorial board, made during a slightly tipsy conversation at the magazine's summer party, nor the snippet by the diarist who overheard and wrote it up as a fait accompli, were meant to be taken literally).

If it's true she really is a poet, it follows she's wasted her potential, and Buzzy feels renewed shame at her unconfident and bad faith artistic choices. Maybe it's not too late. She could – she *will* – put aside the fragments of discourse, at once impenetrable and (in this, she knew Philip was right) banal, that make up most of the poems in *The Bathers*. She'll write a new collection that's at least truly felt, whatever its artistic merits. The sudden urge to get started immediately is not the result of any specific inspiration so much as her grasping that this kind of work can only be produced by a young poet, before her romantic spirit is contaminated by too much life and its corollary, its *adjunct*, irony. Twenty-seven is probably actually the perfect time of life, since she still has access to the unworldly convulsions of desire, but just enough ironising distance to allow her to shape them coldly on the page. Maybe this precarious state could itself be a theme of the volume, which she'll start this evening, as soon as this conversation is over.

Exactly where, if writing poetry turns out to be a process of detachment from the very thing it seeks to capture, this leaves her connection with Marcel is not a question she wants to consider.

'What's the main piece about?'

'Oh, s'about your affair with the shadow home secretary's husband. We wanted you to have a chance to give your side of the story.'

'How kind of you,' Buzzy says numbly.

308

'Now, you're upset,' he says, 'but the best thing to do in this situation – you still there?'

'Wait one second.'

Buzzy grips the phone at waist-level as she passes Philip's sofa. She's conscious her face can't be looking remotely composed. Closing the door behind her, she moves quickly through the flat, which is sizeable, the entire floor of the building. When she enters the main bedroom its oppressive Philipness makes her baulk. She backs out and for a panicky few seconds stands rooted to the spot in the corridor, unable to decide where to go and aware of how incriminating her indecision would appear if Philip has decided to follow her. In the end she locks herself in the guestroom loo, avoiding her frightened face in the mirror.

''Allo? 'Lizbeth?'

'Yes,' she croaks, not trusting her voice to hold out longer than a syllable.

'You might not want to, but the best thing to do is talk to me. Otherwise you can see how this looks, what with the baby, and you and Afua such old friends . . .'

Buzzy wonders abstractly, as though it were happening to someone else, where she might live; if she's shameless enough to crawl back to her parents after putting them through seeing their daughter disgraced in the pages of the *Mail*.

'The point is we don't *have* to go for the whole scheming-concubine-of-fat-cat-lawyers-and-Saudi-princes.' Jeremy pauses, embarrassed by his purple flourish, or perhaps making a mental note of it. 'But what we *would* need from you is a new angle; something even stronger than the icy poetess thing. Obviously Moreau's a shifty Frenchman, Belgian, whatever; but it's always the woman readers want to hate in these situations. Dunno why.'

'But this is wrong! I never went out with the Saudi – with Abdul.'

'Oh, okay . . . I just assumed 'cos you were living in one of his family's South Ken houses. Mind if I ask what your job situation was in 2008? Or maybe the folks were paying your rent back then?'

The sounds of Wedderspoon's words have the quality of an enveloping green nausea. It recalls less Baudelairean synaesthesia than a Dover–Boulogne ferry crossing she took years ago, having swallowed a lump of hash she found in her bag just before passport control. 'I don't understand. How do you know about all this?'

'Coincidence, actually,' he says jauntily. 'I kept my file from when Sherard Howe got caught being over-friendly with the prince. Nothing's wasted, as they say. Or used to. These days it's all about building your Twitter profile.'

A sudden hope arises: perhaps this is an old trick, and he's only sniffing around. It's possible he's heard a vague rumour (from where?) of something untoward between her and Marcel, and by talking as if it's an established fact, hopes to dupe her into confessing. What actual evidence can he have, after all?

On the other hand, the only thing more undignified than the situation she's currently in would be to lie about it, and then somehow be shown to be lying.

On the other hand again, she comes back to the central issue of what precisely her relations are with Marcel. They spent the night together two and a half years ago, before he was married. They kissed, briefly, last month. He proposed they go to Paris but they argued and now he's gone without her. It's irresponsible, it's inappropriate and deplorably selfish behaviour, but is it really an *affair* in the tabloid or any other sense? Isn't it conceivable that if Jeremy Wedderspoon knew these to be the full facts, he'd scoff and say it's all been a misunderstanding, there's no proper scandal here at all? For all she knows Marcel himself would laugh at the idea. Perhaps this, in fact, would be the most humiliating outcome of all: for her to acknowledge the affair and then have everyone, Marcel and Afua and the journalist, tell her she's a tragic fantasist.

'What proof do you have?'

'What's that?'

'I'd like to know what your evidence is that I've ever had a – an untoward relationship with Marcel Moreau.'

'There's a guard saw the pair of you getting intimate in the Lords chamber, for one thing. Look,' he says, 'this isn't the way to play it; I'm telling you this for your own good. Your best shot is to open up to me. Let's make it the Orpington grammar girl against the stuck-up Islington aristocracy – the arts world arseholes. Who're our readers gonna sympathise with?'

'I'm part of the arts world myself,' she says, with absurd hauteur.

'You *were*. These North London luvvies are like the Stasi, they don't forget. In twenty years' time you'll be up for Poet Laureate or something and then, whoosh, all this is dredged up and your candidacy's over. Do you see what I mean?'

The lotus granite basin, with its green-black-grey swirl and smooth inner finish, seems spitefully unsympathetic to her plight. 'I'm going to hang up now.'

'Give me something about Afua,' he says sternly, the avuncular tone gone. '*She's* the little schemer, ain't she? Getting Sherard to set her up as a blogger on his magazine. Then she stole the SpAd job – that was meant for the son, wasn't it? Henry Howe. *Then* the old boy's made some phone calls to his friends on the NEC and suddenly she's Labour candidate for Islington. She's even taken over their enormous fucking house! Don't tell me anyone should be sorry for *her*.'

The Spanish waitress at the Beaufort bar arrives with a second gin lane. Buzzy hopes, given the lack of other payment options, Philip hasn't already cancelled her American Express card. He called her when she was in the taxi to say he'd just had an interesting conversation with a journalist from the *Daily Mail*: she could return to collect her possessions, such as they were, when he was at work tomorrow. (The fact he plans to work on a Saturday is not a surprise.) There was some swearing at the end, but this was understandable considering the embarrassment she was about to cause him.

Buzzy tries calling Marcel, then Henry again. Both go straight to voicemail. Most likely Marcel is in a Parisian restaurant with clients; Hen's unavailability, however, is more puzzling. His phone wasn't switched off ten minutes ago, but rang and rang until eventually Buzzy was able to leave a message explaining something awful had happened, or rather she'd done something awful, and could he please call her back as soon as he got this.

When Afua arrives, late as usual, Buzzy watches her hand the maître d' her coat. Even without her thick glasses (spotting Buzzy immediately does nothing to diminish the sense they're an affectation), she looks glamorously severe in a dark brown head-wrap and grey business suit. If anything the drab colours accentuate Afua's beauty, especially after she's taken her seat in one of the three domed alcoves that are painted in a startling and complexion-illuminating gold leaf, looking from a distance like giant bullets lined up against the black wall. Framed by protruding Ionic columns, her semi-divinity is more unsettling than ever, since from what Buzzy remembers goddesses were not celebrated for their forgiving natures.

'I've never been here before.'

'The Savoy?'

Buzzy relaxes a little on seeing Afua's usual sardonic smile. 'No, this room. Philip's got a thing about the American Bar; it's been a haunt of his for years. Also he hates art deco.'

'It's generally quiet on weekday evenings,' Afua says, easing into her habit of not quite acknowledging Buzzy's comment.

The waitress reappears. 'We have an excellent selection of *champán*,' she proposes, after Afua has been staring at the menu for a while, looking politely unimpressed.

'Hmm, okay, I'll have a glass of the Ruinart. Thanks.'

'Makes me think of poor Sherard. How is he? I texted Hen but never heard back . . .'

'Still a little bruised, I think, but maybe in the long run it'll have been for the best – sort of creative destruction, to use an old Marx phrase.'

'First time for everything,' Buzzy hears herself say, and cringes at how it sounds out loud.

'Anyway.' Afua's stoic smile suggests this sort of backbench barracking is part of the territory. 'He's been sober over a week now, and he and Daph are getting on well, touch wood.'

'I'm glad. It must have been terrifying to be set upon like that. No offence, but most of the time it's easy to ignore politicians talking about social breakdown. It's only when something like this happens to someone you know . . .'

Afua's glass of Ruinart arrives. 'None taken. What's that you're having?'

'Gin lane, I think it's called.'

'Very Hogarthian.' She takes a sip of champagne to cover an expression of sour amusement. 'I'm not a total philistine, Buzzy.'

'Of course not! I never thought you were.'

Afua picks up the drinks menu, surprising Buzzy precisely because it's the sort of awkward move one might expect of a normal person in Afua's situation, feeling their way back into an old and complex friendship. Buzzy wonders if she hears a note of derision when Afua reads out loud, *Bombay Sapphire, bitter truth apricot, Grand Marnier, pressed lemon, almond syrup and ginger ale.*

'Do you want to try it?' Buzzy asks, knowing she won't.

Afua pouts. 'I thought you might have grown out of your gin obsession by now.'

This time there's no mistaking the hostile undertone. The waitress floats past; if Buzzy wasn't worried it might seem provocative she'd order a row of gin lanes.

'Actually, I couldn't be a "philistine".'

'How do you mean?' Buzzy asks, tentatively.

'I thought Matthew Arnold divided society between barbarians, philistines and the populace.'

'Did he? I had a vague idea he was a Victorian poet.'

'Don't be impressed: *Culture and Anarchy* is a first-year text for arch & anth students. In Arnold's view, the philistines were the middle classes.'

'Who were the barbarians?'

'The ruling elite, if I remember.'

Does Afua exclude herself from the philistines because she considers herself ruler or populace? 'It does sound like quite a cynical view of civilisation,' Buzzy says, from a helpless

313

competitive need, even now, to belittle a well-known argument she's never heard of.

'But it wasn't, really. He thought it didn't matter what class you were born into because you could transcend your background, by learning, and the pursuit of culture. It's more or less your credo, isn't it?'

'I don't know about *that* . . .' Buzzy says, and witnesses Afua inhale the foolishness of refuting a proposition that wasn't sincere in the first place. Fortified by the burn of Afua's sarcasm and the last gulp of her cocktail, she says, 'I called because there's something important I need to tell you. A *Daily Mail* journalist contacted me earlier. He says he's writing a story about me having some kind of affair with Marcel.' She bites her cheek. 'Obviously I thought you should know.'

Afua's tone is impatient, unpitying. 'Of course I *know*.'

'I don't understand . . . How can you? I haven't spoken to Henry or— I haven't spoken to anyone.'

'Did you think you were so famous and important,' Afua says, acidly, 'that Jez Wedderspoon was following you around at my party just on the off-chance?'

'No! I mean, I don't know what I thought. The whole conversation was a blur.' Buzzy has a disorientated feeling from finding herself suddenly out of her depth with someone so familiar. '*Was* he following me around?'

Afua sighs portentously. 'I spoke to Henry the other day. After that I made my own investigations.'

'Did you give the *Mail* my mobile phone number?'

'I've used Jez before,' Afua says, as though discussing a hairdresser. 'He knows how to handle this sort of story.'

Buzzy never contemplated Afua would use the same methods against her that she deployed with such success at Westminster. More than that, she's shocked Henry could feel so sure of what he'd read in Marcel's blush. It was so *bold* of him! How little she's understood him; how he must hate her for that, too!

She can't think about poor Hen now. 'I know this is the way you do things, and I deserve whatever's coming. But what about my parents?' Buzzy pleads. 'What about *your* family – Benjamin!'

Afua's fingers are trembling a little when she takes another, more determined sip of champagne. 'It's kind of funny – that you'd fuck my husband, and then lecture me on protecting my family.'

The American couple at the next alcove look across in disapproval. They didn't come to London, let alone the Savoy, for this coarseness.

Buzzy lowers her head in penitence. 'I'm so sorry.'

'What's hard to understand, actually, is I gave you your chance with Marcel years ago, when I let you go to Brussels for his father's wedding. If you didn't take it then—'

Buzzy focuses on the sharp rise and fall of Afua's sternum.

'Ah. You did. I didn't realise that.' Afua takes a moment to gather herself. 'The great mistress of literature!'

Buzzy forces herself to look up. Afua's face appears subtly but repellently distorted: despite her considerable skill, she hasn't managed to reabsorb her rage without it leaving an ugly vestigial trace on her even features. For Buzzy it's a Pyrrhic victory, since her bitter pleasure is also the end of any hope she's not a wicked person. In this context there seems little point telling Afua there was never much to her relations with Marcel, carnally speaking, beyond Brussels and the stupid second's kiss in the House of Lords.

'I hope you're not going to decide you're bored of him, now he's given up everything for you.' Afua arches her eyebrows. 'Even *you* must get that he's finished at Sullivans, and the chances are no one else is going to hire him if it means crossing Philip.'

'I don't know – I suppose I haven't thought about it . . .'

Afua makes a signing gesture for the bill. 'Isn't this normally your cue to leave?' she asks icily, without taking her eyes from the approaching waitress.

Buzzy understands a response is not required.

A photographer is waiting outside the main hotel entrance. *Elizabeth! That's it, over 'ere*, he shouts, as a bowler-hatted doorman guides her into a taxi. She has the impression the latter is only feigning his disapproval of the paparazzo for her benefit; that, since Buzzy isn't famous enough for him to recognise her, she must be pleased with the attention.

She thanks the doorman profusely while climbing into the cab, wishing she had cash for a tip.

'Where to, love?' the driver asks.

The meter is already running. She wonders what to say.

40

Shadow home secretary splits from cheating husband

Daily Mail, *8 October 2011*

EXCLUSIVE: Rising Labour star Afua Nelson shocked Westminster last night by announcing she has split from her husband, lawyer Marcel Moreau.

The 28-year-old MP telephoned Mr Moreau in Paris, where he is currently staying on business, to inform him their two-year marriage was over after learning he cheated on her with her best friend. The couple have a 7-month-old son, Benjamin.

Steamy embrace

Parliamentary staff discovered Belgian Mr Moreau, 26, in the House of Lords chamber on a Saturday evening 'locked in a steamy embrace' with 27-year-old poetess Elizabeth Price. At the time his wife was hosting a reception on the Commons terrace attended by Tony Blair among others.

A spokesman for the sergeant-at-arms said: 'The peers' chamber is reserved for the scrutiny of legislation and certain ceremonial functions, such as the opening of parliament by Her Majesty the Queen. If true, this is highly inappropriate behaviour.'

It is understood Ms Price has been a close friend of both Mr Moreau and Ms Nelson since the three of them met as students at Cambridge university.

Ms Price's current partner, veteran City solicitor Philip Devereux, 56, with whom she shares a penthouse apartment in Pimlico, was last night unavailable for comment.

Prior to meeting Mr Devereux, Ms Price was romantically linked with the then 19-year-old Abdul-Latif Al Saud, a member of the Saudi royal family. Her debut poetry collection, published earlier this year, features an erotic poem about 'half-caste lust'.

Britain's first black prime minister?

Until now the MP for Islington South has enjoyed a stellar political career.

Just six months after entering parliament Ms Nelson, daughter of a Ghanaian mother and white English father, now deceased, was appointed shadow equalities minister.

In January's reshuffle a then heavily pregnant Ms Nelson was promoted a second time to shadow home secretary. The move raised a few eyebrows in Westminster, not least among her older and less telegenic colleagues.

The 28-year-old has since proved one of Labour's most assured front bench performers. Most recently she earned plaudits for her robust response to the August riots, in which she risked angering some on the left by condemning rioters as 'senseless hooligans'.

Despite her Islington social circle Ms Nelson's allies are clear she aims to make Labour the natural party of law and order.

A friend said: 'Afua grew up on a tough council estate and she's seen at first hand the blight of gangs and anti-social behaviour on working-class communities. When it comes to the hoodie bully boys, this lady's not for hugging.'

Speculation Ms Nelson might one day be Britain's first black prime minister has increased in recent weeks, with commentators comparing her media-friendly interventions with those of Tony Blair when he held the home affairs brief in the early nineties. The appearance of Labour's three-time election winner at Ms Nelson's Commons drinks party last month was seen by some as a tacit endorsement of the Islington MP.

Power couple

The shadow home secretary and her husband are regarded as one of Westminster's power couples.

Mr Moreau, son of the senior EU official and former Belgian interior minister Anatole Moreau, was educated at the elite European School of Brussels. He went on to study law at Cambridge, graduating with a starred first.

In 2007 he joined Sullivan and Ball, the blue-chip City law firm where Mr Devereux is a senior partner. Last night the firm declined to confirm whether Mr Moreau remains in their employment.

A shadow cabinet source said: 'If Afua can handle a setback like this, she'll have shown she's tough enough to deal with anything – certainly whatever Westminster can throw at her.'

Her adopted parents, Sherard Howe and Daphne Depree, themselves prominent figures in left-wing circles, are also showing their support. The feminist author told the *Mail*: 'Afua can stay with my husband and me for whatever time she needs to get back on her feet. Knowing Afua as I do, I'm sure that won't be long.'

SEE ALSO: **Elizabeth 'Buzzy' Price**: portrait of a home-wrecker, pp. 4&5.

41

Marcel (2)

The presiding theme of Geneva airport, established by innumerable backlit advertising boards, makes for a depressing introduction to Switzerland. Wherever Buzzy turns as she follows the signs from the arrivals concourse to the adjoining train station, she's plagued by visions of luxury timepieces and the acerbic thought that Philip very much does not consider himself a humble custodian of his Swiss watch for the next generation, as the slogan everywhere insists.

She can feel an artery pulse in her cheek when she approaches the Swiss Rail window. Mumbling her way through asking for a single ticket to Les Diablerets, she nods uncomprehendingly when the male ticket vendor fixes her with piercing blue eyes and says something about Aigle, which is where she knows she needs to change to take the uphill mountain train. Only after the American Express transaction has gone through does Buzzy gather herself, and enquire which platform her train will be leaving from.

Despite being exotically double-decked the intercity to Brig, stopping at Aigle, is packed. What's more, the stream of people boarding the train is such that before she's had the chance to leave her luggage in the racks, Buzzy is swept into the lower-floor carriage. Unable to turn back, she drags her suitcase down the aisle, Smythson travel bag over one shoulder and Prada handbag over the other, repeating *pardon* every time she ruffles a newspaper or jostles an elbow.

The family in front of Buzzy swoops on an unoccupied table. Every place in the carriage, whether in the rows of two-seaters or the four-seaters with tables, now appears taken. She's so preoccupied with accepting her fate that she nearly doesn't notice the couple has only one child, a voluble toddler clutching a dinosaur by its tail as if it were a lizard he had personally just clubbed to death. All Buzzy has to do is grab the last free seat before the grey-stubbled fellow approaching from the other direction can get there. He isn't dressed in business clothes, like almost everyone else on the train, but faded jeans and water-proof winter jacket. Perhaps he's retired. But he's a long way from *elderly*, she reassures herself; probably no one in this country works after fifty.

Buzzy can hear the couple is English, and hopes that will count for something if it comes down to a dead-heat between her and the rather grizzled Swiss. 'Hi!' she says in a quasi-familiar tone. 'Do you mind if I . . .?'

The wife has sharp, elfin features. 'We do, actually.'

'Oh – you mean it's taken?'

Buzzy notices, among the phones and tablets and crime paper-backs splayed across the table, a folded-up copy of today's *Telegraph*.

'No, it's free. But we mind if *you* sit here.'

Along with the already-seated passengers and queue of new boarders drilling a hole in her back, Buzzy's rival, the middle-aged Swiss, is listening to this exchange. From his triumphant expression he's clearly grasped at least the essence of the situation, that Buzzy will under no circumstances be taking up the seat.

She turns instinctively to the husband, looking not, as it appears, to appeal his wife's decision – Buzzy would rather throw herself from the train than sit there now – but for any glimmer of sympathy.

'We noticed you on the flight,' he says, as if there were no more decently to be said on the matter.

Her cheeks burn as she silently indicates to the Swiss gentle-man that she'll need to get past. Still without resorting to speech, they agree this will be easiest achieved if he first settles into the vacant spot, and she ends up standing in range of the antiseptic

321

funk of the loo until the train reaches Aigle an hour and a half later.

This being her first time in the Alps, she's no more surprised to discover the mountains are still green in mid-October than if the gabled roofs of the high street had been crowned by a foot of snow. The air is a shock, however: its purity causes her throat to tingle if she inhales sharply.

The directions to the chalet are suspiciously simple. Assuming Marcel has elided several dull-but-crucial elements, she's prepared for an hour or two of dragging her suitcase around the village, and is half disappointed to find the chalet after only ten minutes or so. At least if she'd got lost she'd have had some time to settle her nerves. The thought occurs to her to pretend she hasn't realised this is the correct address, only by now Buzzy is in plain sight of the chalet and she worries that walking straight past might give the impression she is either cowardly or dim.

'And I hear you're a poet? Is it poet, or poetess?'

'Either is fine.' Buzzy says, before reconsidering. 'Actually, I prefer "poet".'

'I *adore* poetry. There are words which move me so much! Sometimes only the sound of them. *Hiroshima mon amour*, for example: really it's a boring story, but the title is so beautiful it makes me want to cry. Do you find this?'

'Absolutely; it's so interesting how sounds can have aesthetic qualities that are completely independent of the words they constitute. Like the English word 'bucolic', which is so ugly I can never really believe it's invoking a rural idyll. I suppose it's the association with the 'bubonic', as in 'bubonic plague' . . . Les Diablerets is certainly bucolic; in a good way, of course . . .'

Sylviane's response ('*Hein*') doesn't seem to be reaching for any phonological or semantic heights. Instead of wittering nervously, Buzzy wishes she'd simply tried to look a little moved by the *Hiroshima* title.

322

She wonders when Marcel will return from hiking on the massif with the mysterious Alain. Sylviane has referred to this person several times with a meaningful air that's made Buzzy feel that asking who he is would be somehow owning up to a personal failing.

'When does the ski season start?'

'Ah, *non*, we must be patient there,' Sylviane says, as if Buzzy were already clutching a pair of salopettes. 'The snow arrives later. December . . .'

Buzzy says it must be a beautiful place to come to ski.

'Of course.'

'Which side of the valley do you prefer?'

'The view on this side is more impressive – you can see Mont Blanc from the top – but Meilleret is a bigger ski area. Then there's the glacier, though I believe the pistes are not interesting.'

'You've never skied up there?'

'Me?' Sylviane asks, with a superior smile. 'You'll think I'm old-fashioned, but for me skiing is something for men. I love their excitement first thing in the morning; their happy tiredness when they return; most of all, the peace and quiet in the day.'

'No, I can see that. I can't think of anything more civilised than sitting next to this fire, reading books all day.'

Sylviane's smile has stiffened somewhat. It belatedly occurs to Buzzy she's been trying too hard to go with the grain of Marcel's mother's remarks, and the thing to do was act a little more shocked by them.

'We used to come here every winter when Marcel was younger, just for a week or so. Sometimes I'd take the *télécabine* to meet him for lunch. If I arrived too early, I would look for the boy making the most graceful turns.' She makes her own rather stylish snaking motion with her hand. She reminds Buzzy of an ageing French New Wave film star who hasn't lost her essential glamour or bone structure or hint of madness. 'It was always him.'

Before they leave for a walk round the village, Marcel's mother asks if Buzzy would like to unpack first. She declines, judging her hostess enthused by the prospect of the outing and eager to leave straightaway. She apologises for having brought so much luggage with her: 'I had to leave another suitcase in storage at Luton airport.'

The awkwardness of this remark, with its reminder of the shameful context of her visit, is compounded when Sylviane suggests that Buzzy take her things upstairs. She wonders if her hostess is being mischievous in giving no indication of whether Buzzy is to share with Marcel, or take one of the two or three (depending on Alain's status) unoccupied bedrooms. She's not even completely sure, for that matter, where Marcel would prefer her to stay.

'Upstairs . . . *Thank* you, yes . . .'

'Tell me,' Sylviane says, leaning forward in her chair, 'is his father very angry with him about this . . . scandal?'

'They're not speaking, as far as I know.' She senses it might be better to remain vague as to when exactly Marcel and his father fell out.

'I see. And Anatole has met you?'

Buzzy confirms he has.

'Does he hate you *very* much?'

'I think . . .' she begins, biting her lip and gazing melodramatically into the distance. 'I think yes, he does.'

Sylviane sits back, eyes glazed with delight. 'Marcel's room is the last on the left, opposite mine. There is plenty of space for your things.'

When Marcel returns from hiking, his cheeks streaked with red, the teapot is cooling and several rather leaden Swiss scones are missing from the plate, though the trail of crumbs leads in only one direction. (Sylviane touchingly but slightly obsessively spent much of the walk repeating the importance of getting home in time for *le thé du five o'clock*. Having at no point mentioned lunch, she seemed to think Buzzy would lapse into catatonia without high tea.) He removes his woollen ski hat, revealing glistening and dishevelled hair, followed by the swishing fluorescent jacket that acquired improbable dignity around his shoulders.

Buzzy is as timid as she's ever felt in his presence. It doesn't help that the last time they saw each other, at Canonbury Lane, she'd sworn at him and stormed off. When he asked her, in the course of a short and stilted phone conversation on Saturday, if she'd like to join him at this Swiss mountain retreat, she wasn't sure if it was to discuss how to handle the press attention, or because he felt sorry for her, or because this was the inevitable start of their future life together. She knew only that she couldn't bear to spend another second in the depressing Holiday Inn near Oxford Circus.

She's not ready to know the reason for her invitation yet, and is relieved that, under the scrutiny of Marcel's mother, their greetings are confined to discussing the weather.

'Listen to you two,' Sylviane says. 'So British! But where is Alain?'

Marcel is unwinding the laces of his walking boots with a slow even rhythm. '*Il arrive.*'

When Alain enters Buzzy sees he is lean and fit, with a humourless moustache. '*Enchanté,*' he says, giving her hand a grim pump.

Sylviane asks if they saw chamois along the pass between Meitreille and Arpille, Marcel replying they saw several. It's hard to tell if this is a familiar exchange between them. Ignoring the taciturn men (unlike Buzzy, who is annoyed they've made Sylviane's delight about the chamois seem rather foolish), she clasps her palms together and announces Alain is cooking tartiflette this evening.

'Oh, wonderful!' Buzzy gushes, 'That's just what I was hoping you'd say.'

Marcel, heaving off the first boot, makes expressionless eye contact with Buzzy. After his attention has returned to the other boot, there's a chance his mouth twitchingly acknowledges that, for all Buzzy knows, tartiflette might be a sort of shellfish. For some reason this gives her hope everything might turn out all right.

Despite feeling heavy from the scones, in the end Buzzy has to restrain herself from falling on the tartiflette. Even the potatoes and bacon, by no means objectionable, seem superfluous to the magnificence of the melted roblochon.

'This is *amazing*,' she tells Alain, 'I'll never eat anything else.'

Alain explains why confining herself to tartiflette would be inadvisable.

'You would be thick as a mountain cow!' Sylviane summarises.

'I meant to ask,' Buzzy says, more interested after the roblochon and a third glass of wine, 'when we were walking around this afternoon I kept seeing the image of a boy with horns. He was dancing and playing a flute. Is he a symbol of the village?'

'In French, Les Diablerets means "little devils",' Alain says. 'We have many folkloric stories. Remember that in the nineteenth century, before the tourism arrived, this was a remote community: farmers and *bergers* . . .'

Marcel interrupts his chain-smoking. 'Shepherds.'

'This *diableret* with the flute lives in the massif – the Col de Cheville, near the glacier.'

'I believe it's the Creux de Champs.'

'You are both wrong.' Sylviane finishes off the red, earning a scowl from Alain. 'The boy is not a little devil from the massif, he is *the* devil. One night he came to a dance in the village and waltzed with a beautiful elf. Of course, she fell in love with him.'

'What happened to the girl – the elf?'

'Oh the usual, I imagine . . .'

'Moved to Brussels,' Marcel says, ashing his cigarette.

Sylviane grabs Buzzy's arm, an apologetic gesture more alarming than the initial shriek. Suddenly serious, she continues, '*De toute façon*, the devil is not only a shepherd's fairytale. I've seen him.' She looks defiantly round the table. 'Of course. Many times.'

Buzzy clears her throat. 'Do you mean in the village – with a flute?'

Once again Sylviane dissolves into cackles. 'Look at Alain's face! He thinks I'm crazy,' she says, winking at Buzzy. '*Complètement folle.*'

326

Marcel holds the empty bottle of red up to the light. His manner suggests Alain's disapproving glower is about as concerning as horned flute-players. 'I'll get another,' he says to no one in particular.

After dinner, Sylviane suggests they play a game. 'What about *Jass*? You loved that when you were younger.'

'Buzzy hates card games.'

'That's not true! Maybe I'll enjoy this one. Is it very complicated?'

'Not at all.'

'*Assez compliqué, quand même . . .*' Alain mutters, glancing at Buzzy.

'No, let's play it. Marcel can help me.'

Marcel is not persuadable.

'What about party games?' Buzzy suggests.

'Yes, yes!'

Having proposed the game (if it has a name she doesn't know it), Buzzy feels she's assumed responsibility for everyone's enjoyment of the evening from here on in.

'Right, is everyone ready?' she asks, her cheeriness inversely proportionate to her belief this isn't going to be a disaster. 'Alain, why don't you start?'

Alain touches the square of paper crudely sellotaped to his forehead. Written on it in Buzzy's block capitals are the words WILLIAM TELL.

'Don't read it!' Sylviane cries.

'I thought it was going to fall.'

'Ha, like the apple!'

Alain narrows his eyes. 'Am I Guillaume Tell?'

'Well done.'

'It seems a very fast game,' Sylviane says with a frown.

'Shall we move on to Marcel?' Buzzy squints at the word Sylviane has chosen. 'I'm not sure that's really . . . Let's make this a sort of trial round.'

*

'I'm not a man or a woman. I'm not dead or alive.'

'We should give him a clue,' Alain says, smugly.

'Good idea. You're more a concept. A noun.'

'Pah! *De quoi tu parles*, "concept"? You are a *feeling*. Here,' Marcel's mother says, pressing her breast.

Marcel blows out his cheeks.

'Like this—'

'That's enough help,' Alain says.

Using her palm over Alain's mouth as leverage, Sylviane gets to her feet and makes her way to where Marcel is sitting. Bending down she seizes her son firmly by the shoulders and, almost toppling into him, smothers his cheek in kisses.

'*Ça suffit, maman*,' Marcel protests.

Sylviane grins and presses her lips to the note still attached to his forehead. '*L'amour*,' she says, rejoining Alain's sofa. '*Tu es l'amour*.'

A doubles tennis game is being played down on the village's flood-lit clay courts. During their walk Sylviane mentioned how after December these are converted into an ice hockey pitch. Teenage shouts bounce around the valley, making a homely contrast with the inky-black mountains.

Buzzy wonders if she should unpack, if only to busy herself with something. She decides it might seem presumptuous. What if Sylviane asks her to leave tomorrow? What if Marcel does?

'I hope it didn't seem rude, retiring so early . . .'

Marcel takes his cigarettes out onto the balcony. He closes the door behind him.

Thump thump thump. Alain is like an interminable metronome: that this is somehow unsurprising to Buzzy doesn't make hearing him any less disturbing. She's fairly certain he's Sylviane's paid carer, but perhaps her readiness to imagine such an unconventional professional arrangement only shows how European Buzzy herself is becoming.

Marcel slips out of bed. Buzzy hears the balcony door open, and then nothing until the click of his lighter. She holds out as long as she can before opening her eyes.

He's leaning against the door frame, looking up. Watching him, she knows he is familiar with the major planets and constellations, that he'd never point them out unprompted, but if asked would do so patiently.

Buzzy throws off the warm duvet: dressed in only her nightie, she's already starting to shiver by the time she reaches the open balcony door. She resists pressing herself against him.

'What are you going to do?' Marcel finally asks.

He flinches when she raises her hand above his chest, past his mouth and eyes until the tip of her index finger touches his forehead, just beneath his hairline. She traces her finger up and down his cool brow until, slowly, carefully, she's finished spelling *L'amour*.

'I thought I'd live in the mountains, with you.' The suggestion is punctuated by a louder and hopefully concluding thump. 'We might need to get our own place.'

Hours later, in the warmth of the bed, Marcel asks again what Buzzy is going to do. Maybe she'll start work on a new collection of poetry? Or (sounding more encouraging) teach English, like when she was in Buenos Aires?

'I don't really want to do anything at all.' She's very tired; it must be getting on for six a.m. 'Doing things', she says with a yawn, 'was such an unsatisfying you-substitute.'

Buzzy slides a foot down his bristly shin, hoping to stop him from falling asleep. At one point she clenches and feels her toenails dig in to him but he doesn't say anything or move his leg. 'I didn't tell you that when I got on the train at Geneva there was one spare seat in the carriage, next to this English family. The wife wouldn't let me sit next to them; she'd read an article about me – well, both of us – in the *Telegraph*. It was so humiliating,' she says drowsily, 'I wanted to die.'

At first Marcel doesn't respond, because of her hyperbole, Buzzy assumes, which she was too tired to filter from her speech, or he's drifted off. Then she hears him exhale and say, '*C'est comme ça*,' though before she's had any chance to think about these words she's fallen asleep.

'*Bonjour les enfants*,' Sylviane trills. 'Alain is making you scrambled eggs and bacon.'

Buzzy thanks her gratefully. 'Aren't you having any?'

'Ah, *non*.' She gestures to the contents of a small tray beside her, a glass of water and a plate containing a selection of pills.

Buzzy watches her take a mouthful of water, tilt back her head and push the first couple of capsules into her mouth. The swallowing sound is embarrassingly indelicate and Buzzy is careful to avoid looking at Marcel. She hears him announce in French he's going to help Alain in the kitchen.

'My son hates seeing this,' Sylviane says as he's leaving.

Wondering why, in that case, she has waited for him to appear before taking her medication, Buzzy says, 'I'm sure it's not easy for either of you.'

Sylviane takes the next pair of tablets dry, like a teenager necking M&Ms at the Bromley Empire. 'Before it was easier; they gave me Valium for everything.' She scoops the last two tablets off the plate. 'The problem was it seemed to do nothing for me. Eventually my doctor confessed two milligrams was not so strong; maybe I could take four pills instead of two. Well, if a doctor says four it means you can take eight. So I took eight and it was the same: nothing. What else could I do? I went back to the doctor. This time, he agreed if after another week Valium still wasn't working he'd give me something else.' She tosses back the last of the tablets and freezes in position, eyes bulging at the ceiling. 'There was a reception at the Palais de la Justice – very grand, you know. Anatole insisted I go with him. Me, I was the same as usual, crying crying, bla bla bla, so I decided just to take the whole bottle. Twenty pills.

'Of course this is excessive, but I'd been drinking and my judgement at the time was *une catastrophe*. Besides, the whole problem was I could take eight with no effect at all.' Sylviane rakes her hair, which is black like Marcel's, except for odd glints of silver in the morning sunlight. 'Well, this time I felt something. Faint at first, then vomiting; I couldn't go to the dinner. Anatole was furious.'

'He left without you?'

'It was Marcel who called the ambulance. I didn't understand why he looked so worried. I told him it was probably just my nerves, or the wine.'

'Were you wrong – *was* it the Valium?' Buzzy asks.

Sylviane smiles. 'It was aspirin. Since the beginning Marcel was making a switch, *tu m'entends*? He was selling the Valium at school.'

'What did his father say?'

'He never found out. What was the use of telling him? Marcel didn't know I would drink too much and take twenty pills at once. *Enfin*, maybe the drink wasn't a surprise. I was a horrible mother, you can't imagine.'

On their balcony, zipped up in a ski jacket, Buzzy can feel the sun on her face. Marcel looks up from *Le Temps retrouvé*, a pristine copy he perhaps bought in Paris before his sudden departure. 'I have to go on an errand tomorrow; it'll require a bit of a trip.'

'Okay. Anywhere exciting?'

'Not in the least.' He returns to his book. A moment or two later he closes it, leaving his thumb carefully on his current page. 'I wondered if you wanted to come with me.'

'Of course I do. Though if I'm going looking like the Michelin woman' – Buzzy tugs on her voluminous ski jacket – 'I'll need to know exactly where we're going.' She means she's keen to avoid contact with other Brits, possibly for ever.

'Brussels. There's still time to change your mind.'

He smiles quizzically at her approach. Buzzy takes his face in her hands and stares deeply into his eyes. 'I will follow you into the jaws of Belgium.'

*

'Did you keep your promise?'

'I don't know if I should be offended. Is it because of what I said about only eating tartiflette?'

'*Réponds-moi.* This is serious,' Marcel says, though his countenance suggests otherwise.

'I hereby swear I had one coffee, and not a bite to eat – even though you're late.'

They start wandering from their meeting point, the steps of the Musée des Beaux-Arts.

'I'm sorry for that. Lawyers are terrible timekeepers; or rather, timeliness is not a priority when they're charging by the hour.'

Marcel's continued membership of the profession goes unaddressed. Buzzy does however bring up one matter that has been puzzling her. 'It's none of my business,' she begins, 'but since you mentioned this meeting was about your finances, I wondered if it was something like a trust fund situation? My unfailingly unpleasant conversations about money have always been with a bank manager, not a lawyer.'

'One could call it a trust situation, more or less.'

She'd like to know if he'd find it harder to introduce this constant teasing ambiguity in his own language, without the non-native-speaker's opportunities for idiosyncratic speech.

'It's just Philip once told me trusts don't really exist in continental legal systems.' If Buzzy feels slightly devious, she's confident Marcel enjoys this sort of gamesmanship. Lacking the instincts of a true Machiavellian, however, she rambles on, 'They originate in England from the Crusades, apparently – oh, are we here?'

Until now Buzzy hasn't properly taken in the black wrought-iron building Marcel has stopped in front of. It's undoubtedly a very interesting example of art nouveau, with its eccentric turret and glass dome, beneath which the words OLD ENGLAND are inaptly emblazoned in gold lettering. Nevertheless, she's slightly disappointed this is the surprise Marcel promised her, at least until they step inside. 'The Musical Instruments Museum,' she smiles.

'There's a reasonable view from the rooftop restaurant.'

'I remember you saying.' She feared it might be vulgar or sentimental to allude to their previous time together in Brussels, and has more than once stopped herself from doing so since they arrived this morning.

In the glass cage of the lift Buzzy fights a gloomy sense that the tenor of her behaviour has not been correct since Jeremy Wedderspoon's article, or articles – the profile, of course, was by far the most wounding – appeared in the *Mail*. Her guilt and shame have been interspersed with a perfidious happiness that comes from being with Marcel uninterruptedly, from the moment she wakes in the morning to lying next to him at night. (She's at least had the decency not to be sleeping well.) Even the reassuring constant nausea is, she fears, more to do with Marcel's plans for the future, whether there is to be a 'we' beyond these initial few days, than the merely figuratively sickening consequences of her behaviour for little Benjamin, Afua, Henry, her parents, even Philip.

It's not even true to say her emotions oscillate between appropriate guilt and her happiness, which, though thoroughly improper, is at least prompted by a powerful irrational force to which more admirable people than Buzzy have succumbed. (And it *is* love; she's abandoned the idea – real enough on occasions, but prone to fade without conscious nurturing – that her feelings towards Marcel were curdling into indifference or even hatred.) Since Saturday she's more than once caught herself lost in some quite ordinary thought or other, and worries this failure to be weighed down at all times by her situation – a wicked temptress in the eyes of complete strangers, without proper employment or home or network of friends – is above all one of imagination, when that's the only thing she's supposed to have going for her.

All the tables on the rooftop terrace are already occupied by diners making the most of the October sunshine. Marcel guides her round the perimeter, his fingers a faint and possibly imagined presence at the base of her spine, pointing out landmarks by their

333

distinctive peaks: the spire of the Hôtel de Ville rising above the Grand Place; in the distance behind it, not far from the drab *banlieue* tenements, the green copper dome of the Basilica of the Sacred Heart. Nearer by, he draws Buzzy's attention to the neoclassical church in Place Royale, with its incongruous (it seems to Marcel) wooden bell-tower; and the gilded nipple-like (it seems to Buzzy) cupola of the Palais de Justice. She searches his face at the mention of the last, asking when it was built and if it was perhaps modelled on the law courts in Paris. In response she detects only vague puzzlement at her interest; certainly there's no sign of the building stirring painful memories in him.

'You were talking about the Crusades,' Marcel says, after they've taken a table by the window and ordered light food, quiche for her and goats' cheese salad for him.

Buzzy has resolved not to refer to Philip again, but worries Marcel can hear his former boss's mordant sing-song in her account of knights returning from years of slaughtering infidels in the Holy Land, only to find their land and assets appropriated by the very friend who'd been entrusted to look after them. 'Basically I think the king, or someone, came up with the idea of a trustee as a legal owner of property purely for the benefit of someone else – he couldn't enjoy the assets himself, or sell them for personal gain.'

'It's the origin of the doctrine of equity,' Marcel says, when he's sure she's finished. 'As you mentioned, it's particular to common-law jurisdictions; there's no direct equivalent in the Napoleonic codes. You can admit it.'

'What?'

He grins provokingly.

'You think I'm interested in the *law*?'

'Part of legal practice is paying close attention to language. Perhaps a poet would take pleasure in that. According to Daphne,' Marcel says, with only the faintest sense of listener-beware, 'Flaubert attended law school. So did Henry James.'

Rarely has Marcel made such a weak or easily refutable point. 'And they both hated it! I can't even bring myself to read my shopping receipts, let alone a contract, let alone *write* one. It's a ridiculous thought,' she huffs. 'Maybe you've got altitude sickness.'

'*C'est compris*,' he says, emolliently. 'You'd be a disastrous lawyer.'

First teacher-training college, now law school: where does he fit into this depressingly practical careers advice? She's too riled to keep her self-imposed ban on mentioning Philip. 'Talking of Henry James,' she says, 'that time in Arezzo you used the phrase "remarkably well-seasoned" to describe Philip: I remembered where it comes from. It's Gilbert Osmond. The old monster is describing how he and Isabel Archer complement each other. She's . . . what is she?'

'"*Remarkably fresh*", I think.'

'Well, anyway. It was an insensitive thing to say.'

'It's normal,' Marcel says, or it might have been *C'est normale*. Either way the phrase seems a Gallic acceptance of man's ineluctable cruelty. 'I was trying to hurt you.'

Buzzy wills an angry tear back down its duct. What is she supposed to do with this casual admission? She has a bleak feeling that, for reasons she can't grasp, Marcel is trying to make it as hard as possible for her to broach with any dignity the question of their joint future.

'Have you heard from Henry?' Marcel asks.

'No; I don't think I will.' Buzzy doesn't add that, for Henry's sake, she's glad he's so angry with her – glad that it was him who, by raising Afua's suspicions, brought about her and Marcel's punishment. 'What about Afua?'

'Just briefly.'

'How was it?'

He shrugs. 'Quite cordial, more or less.'

'You know,' Buzzy says, 'what really depressed me about your *Portrait* line wasn't so much the truth of it – about Philip's unsuitability, I mean – but the fact that, even though I wrote my dissertation on that book, it was you who'd really absorbed it.'

'It was a phrase I happened to remember. I find certain English sentences stay in my head more easily than French ones, I don't know why. You shouldn't read too much into it.'

'Isn't "reading into things" precisely what literature is supposed to teach us to do? What I read into this is that I'm a failure as a reader, never mind a poet. That's a given.'

'Now it's you who's being ridiculous, talking as if one's appreciation of literature is measured by one's power of recall.'

'No, it's also about noticing everything, as James tells us. You have that ability to see through every person, every situation. It's what I've most admired in you.'

'*Putain de merde!*' Marcel says. 'Is that what you think?'

Buzzy is taken aback. 'It's hardly a slur.'

'A good reader has sympathy: you have that, towards Henry, for example. The other thing is courage.'

'You know,' she says, quietly, 'I mean *precisely*, what everyone in a room is feeling. Don't you see it would only require the tiniest step, to turn that knowledge into sympathy?'

He throws up his palms. 'Always me!' And then, calmer: 'Let's not talk about me. It's so dull.'

The food arrives, and is still untouched when the waiter returns to ask, with mild concern, if everything is to their satisfaction.

'You went to see your mother,' Buzzy says, undeterred. 'That was a brave, a *good* gesture.'

'I needed her signature,' he says, with a hint of satisfaction. 'It couldn't really have been more cowardly.'

'I don't believe you.'

Marcel observes she hasn't touched her food. Is she unwell, he wants to know? Buzzy understands that he's drawing a line under the previous discussion, and that it's very important not to allow him to do this. Purely to dispense with the topic, she lies and says she has a slight headache, that's all.

This turns out to be a mistake. Instead of probing why a minor headache should have affected her appetite, Marcel summons the waiter and asks if it might be possible to find his friend some sort of analgesic; Buzzy hears the word *aspirine* mentioned. The waiter replies with a stern *Bien sûr*, his forehead crinkling up when Buzzy interrupts in resolute franglais that she's grateful but really she doesn't need anything at all. He looks from Buzzy to

Marcel as though this were part of a test: '*Vous voulez ou pas?*' Marcel's response is infuriatingly measured and impenetrable, so she interrupts to reiterate in what might qualify as a shout that she's already said she doesn't want anything. The waiter makes a no doubt rancorous departure but Buzzy is already facing away from the men, pretending to study the Brussels skyline.

For a long time they sit in silence.

'I think I'll go to the train station.'

'Your luggage is at the hotel,' Marcel points out, as if expecting this.

'It doesn't matter,' Buzzy says, clearing her cheeks. 'I don't need any of it. I just want to go home.'

'*Comme tu veux.*'

As she gets up to leave his indifference seems to fall away and his eyes are wide and frightened as she's never seen before, but the moment passes. He retrieves his cigarettes from his jacket pocket and heads towards the terrace.

Buzzy walks past the statue of the knight on horseback in the Place Royale in a state of numb calm. She'd failed to spot it on passing through the square earlier, which must have been around the time she was bringing up the Crusades. Likewise, until this morning she hadn't fully appreciated Brussels' grandeur, albeit of an eccentric kind. She only partly attributes this to the miserable weather on her previous visit, or Marcel taking her to a drug-dealer's flat and the Congolese quarter instead of the Grand Place and the picturesque narrow streets of Sablon, where she'd had coffee this morning. She just isn't very good at noticing things.

Once, at a college dinner in her first year, she found herself sitting next to a professor of French. She was still daunted by the formality of such occasions – the gongs, the Latin grace, the gown-wearing – and very drunk from getting through an entire bottle of wine in someone's Old Court rooms before the meal. The conversation inevitably turned to French literature. Although Buzzy had by then read a handful of works in translation, *Madame Bovary* and *The Human Beast* and *The Mandarins*, the only one she could at that moment remember was *The Outsider*. This was unfortunate, as she knew all the professor's freshmen would all have read Camus's novella, and because the freshmen probably hadn't read it in a hash-haze, they could probably recall the plot and muster one or two passably interesting comments about French colonialism, for example, or why Camus's reputation as a philosopher has aged less well than Sartre's.

In her desperation all Buzzy could summon to mind was a line on the first page of the book, in which the narrator, Meursault, refers to the sun and the oppressive heat of the day, which was also the day of his mother's funeral. Accordingly she slurred something about the physical world being a key trope of the novel, and felt like kissing the professor, a lanky and not unkind Irishman, when he politely agreed this was indeed so, hadn't the narrator scandalised society by ascribing his crime to the presence of the sun. It was clear that if Buzzy had shown no evidence of original thought, neither had she proved herself embarrassingly unworthy of her surroundings. (Later she checked and saw that she'd slightly misremembered: there was no mention of the sun on the first page, only the heat, and wondered if the professor had charitably decided not to correct her.)

Buzzy aspires now to Meursault's congenital emptiness: to feel nothing except the sun against her face, to lightly *exist* rather than heavily *be*. Ascending the smart street leading to Porte de Namur metro station she passes a Laura Ashley shop. *I like that dress in the window*, she thinks to herself, and is pleased. She tries again: *Soon I'll be at Porte de Namur, where I'll take the metro to Gare du Midi*. And again: *At the train station I'll purchase a Eurostar ticket*. This is quite doable, really; all she needs is to keep it up for the next four decades.

In the immediate term she has a decision to make about the train ticket. Somehow it would feel more than usually unconscionable to fund her journey home with Philip's AmEx card, assuming that was still possible. Perhaps she'll get to the Gare du Midi and review her options. It's hard to believe Eurostar, or the

British consulate, would leave a respectable-looking young woman with a story about a purse missing from her Prada handbag stranded in Belgium.

Abruptly she halts by a bin, fishes out the credit card and snaps it in two, indifferent to the bemused glance from a passing *madame*. There will be no stories about stolen purses. If the truth doesn't work, and they won't accept her promise to pay for the ticket once she's back in England, she'll raise the money by selling her handbag to the African street-sellers outside the station. Even if they don't believe it's real Prada, the wholesale price of a fake might cover the cost of a one-way ticket to St Pancras. Anyway, she'll think of something.

The end of the street is in sight now, but confining her thoughts to simple and mostly factual observations, let alone preserving the immaculate mental vacuum of an existential anti-hero, is increasingly a challenge. Buzzy tries to focus on immediate sensory stimuli: the boy ahead of her clutching a cardboard poster tube; the faint smell of praline wafting from the open door of the Neuhaus chocolatier; a siren wail in the distance—

It strikes her she never pushed him on the trust fund issue. If trusts don't exist in Belgium, what did he need Sylviane's signature for? From there, she finds herself wondering if it was likely that Marcel's pride could tolerate asking his mother for money, even if it legally belonged to him; or whether, assuming for a moment he really had asked her, Sylviane would have had the restraint not to allude to this in Buzzy's presence.

And then the more she thinks of Sylviane's mental instability the more questionable the whole Valium story seems. Even a messed-up adolescent Marcel wouldn't do something as tawdry as flogging his mother's prescription drugs for personal profit. Besides, Buzzy has seen for herself that Sylviane is a woman with a mischievous and even vindictive streak: revelling in Marcel's 'scandal', so long as it angered Anatole; that embarrassing love-making display with Alain . . . Perhaps Sylviane found the idea of her son being happy with Buzzy intolerable, and made the whole thing up to poison Buzzy's feelings for him.

A nearing police siren drowns out her argument as it's reaching its climax; still, Buzzy feels her walking pace start to slacken. *The point is*, she prompts herself. *The point is . . .*

She is only twenty-seven years old. A normal life, secure and happy and, yes, banal, is not beyond her reach.

The point is: what if Marcel visited the lawyer to put his affairs in order? What if he were encouraging her to think the worst of him in order to provide perverse validation for the terribly selfish thing he was about to do?

The police car has raced past her down towards the Place Royale, joined by a second siren wail, this time more staccato.

She's been wrong to conflate Marcel's great attentiveness to human frailty with 'seeing everything'. But if she understands this now, it's both thanks to him and at his cost. Forcing Buzzy to see that the thing she worshipped him for was a gift he never possessed suggests in itself – given his considerable vanity, a frailty of which she's well aware – an element of the sympathy and courage he claims he lacks.

Despite dragging her feet, she's reached the end of the Rue de Namur. The metro station is on the other side of a wide avenue which reminds her vaguely of the Nueve de Julio in Buenos Aires. The second siren, a flashing yellow ambulance, snakes between busy lanes of cars.

The pedestrian light flashes green: if she crosses, she'll be at the metro station. If she gets on the train she'll be at Orpington in a few hours.

Perhaps it's some sort of test. If she chooses to believe that Sylviane was lying, and that Marcel not only allowed the lie to stand (didn't he hear his mother begin recounting the story to Buzzy as he left the room? Is the stealing claim one he has heard before?), but went on to suggest lies of his own – that his only reason for visiting his mother was so she could sign over money to him; that he didn't care if Buzzy walked out of the restaurant – all to try to ensure Buzzy couldn't *not* hate him; if she chooses to believe that he did all this for what he perceived to be Buzzy's own good, because she's better off thinking he's worthless, she'll have shown him she can be a brave reader. That she has faith in him, no matter what.

And if she doesn't go back to him, if she fails the test, is there a sanction? Who pays it? She thinks of Marcel leaning over the rail of the rooftop, finishing the cigarette.

She turns and runs.

Acknowledgements

I am vastly indebted to Karolina Sutton and Mark Richards. Thank you also to Anna Davis, Jonny Geller, Stephanie Glencross, Sharif Hamadeh, Quentin Liger, Sharmaine Lovegrove, Norah Perkins, Christopher Wakling, Caroline Westmore, my fellow CBC alumni and, most of all, my parents, Richard and Valerie.

From Byron, Austen and Darwin

to some of the most acclaimed and original contemporary writing, John Murray takes pride in bringing you powerful, prizewinning, absorbing and provocative books that will entertain you today and become the classics of tomorrow.

We put a lot of time and passion into what we publish and how we publish it, and we'd like to hear what you think.

Be part of John Murray – share your views with us at:

www.johnmurray.co.uk

 johnmurraybooks

 @johnmurrays

 johnmurraybooks